“Quiet,” Rowan breathed into my ear. “Someone is at the window.”

“I know,” I whispered back as he pulled the door flush against us.

A rustle of the drapes had me tensing, but before I could do anything, Rowan suddenly twisted around, pinning me against the wall with his body. For a few seconds, we were pressed together from knees to chest, and I was extremely aware that I was a woman, and he was a man...

“Oh,” I breathed softly, unable to keep from taking a deep breath so that my breasts smooshed happily against his chest.

I swear his eyes got darker at that, and he hesitated for about two seconds before he murmured, “To hell with the job.” His breath burned on mine, and then his mouth was moving over my lips.

With one hand, I clutched him, pulling him even closer so that he caught my moan in his mouth. His tongue twined against mine, stroking fires inside me that I hadn’t known existed.

RAVE REVIEWS
FOR KATIE MACALISTER

Dragon Fall

"Katie MacAlister has funny characters and always makes me laugh... Aoife's story will have you charmed."

—*USA Today*'s "Happily Ever After" blog

"Wacky situations and offbeat humor run rampant through this book, making it an instant classic!"

—RT Book Reviews

"A great mix of romance, humor, and a great story line. I highly recommend this new series, even if you have not read the other series."

—BookedandLoaded.com

"There is a huge amount of fun in this story, which I *completely* enjoyed. Aoife has a sharp sense of humor, deep compassion, and equally deep strength. And a number of unusual made-up swear words that caused snorts and giggles... A surprisingly strong new entry into Urban Fantasy—one that guarantees that I will be checking out other books by Katie MacAlister."

—SoIReadThisBookToday.com

Dragon Storm

"MacAlister packs oodles of humor into her stories."

—RT Book Reviews

DRAGON SOUL

Also by Katie MacAlister

Dragon Fall
Dragon Storm

DRAGON SOUL

KATIE
MacALISTER

FOREVER

NEW YORK BOSTON

Forever
Hachette Book Group
1290 Avenue of the Americas
New York, NY 10104

www.HachetteBookGroup.com

Printed in the United States of America

First Edition: March 2016
10 9 8 7 6 5 4 3 2 1

OPM

Forever is an imprint of Grand Central Publishing.
The Forever name and logo are trademarks of Hachette Book Group, Inc.

This book is dedicated to all of the furry kid moms and dads out there. Hug those furry little beasties for me!

Acknowledgments

Once again, the Katie Mac Street Team has kicked serious booty! I'd like to shower blessings on everyone who participated, and who helped move the dragons toward total global domination! A huge thank you to the following Street Teamers:

Chantal Clem
Mary McCormick
Dawn Henry
Veronica Godinez-Woltman
Shawna Szabo
Rebecca Taylor
Stacey S. Lewis
Barbara Bass
Erin Havey
Dawn Addleman
Kayla Lindberg
Julie Atagi
Susanna Jolicoeur
Theresa McFarland
Dawn Addleman

Mandy Johnson
Katie Fortenbacher
Misty Snell
Amy Hallmark
Kala Bartic
Leona Merrow
Stacia Ahlfeld
LaJean Rodewald
Lisa Partridge
Christine Brooks
Tracy Goll
Heather W. Mottel
Nicole Harris
Cheryl Ann Moore
Lynne Smith-Kinniburgh
Carrie Parker

DRAGON SOUL

One

"I'm sorry for waking you. Would this happen to be your vibrating butterfly?"

The man I was crouched next to squinted at me even though the lighting on the plane had been turned down so as to be conducive to sleep. His face scrunched up even more when I gingerly held up a bright pink object wrapped in a crinkly plastic package, and his voice, when he spoke, was thick with sleep. "What? Who are you?"

"I'm so sorry I woke you," I apologized again, shifting a little when my calf muscle began to complain about the fact that I had spent the last twenty minutes squatting my way up the first-class aisle on the flight from Los Angeles to Munich. "My friend—really, she's more my charge than my friend—appears to have mysteriously acquired this object from someone on this side of the plane, and I wondered if it was you."

His eyes focused on the sex toy. "The hell? Do you think I'd use something like that? I'm a man!"

"Oh! That's mine, George," his seatmate said with a little giggle. She flashed him an embarrassed little smile, and said in a rush, "I thought we could try it out once we got to the hotel. Second honeymoon and all."

I assumed the last part was aimed at me, and I duly dropped the toy into her outstretched hand with a murmured apology and plastic rustle that seemed overly loud in the hushed cabin.

"Although I don't know how it fell out of my luggage..." She glanced upward at the overhead bin as if expecting to see her belongings hanging out of the opened door.

I gave her a wan smile and stood, gratefully stretching my cramped muscles. "My client must have mistaken your bag for hers. Sorry to disturb you both."

The husband grumbled in a low tone to his wife, but I didn't wait around to hear how she was going to explain her plans for their stay in Germany—I had an elderly lady to watch, and as the last few hours of the flight had shown, I had to watch her like a hawk.

I hurried to the galley area between the first-class section and coach, and slipped in with a couple of flight attendants busy with beverages for the few folks who were still awake. Next to them, seated on a small pull-down emergency seat, sat a tiny old woman, her hair a mass of white curls and her brown face bearing a myriad of wrinkles and crisscrossed lines. She bore an air of fragility and profound age that made one think she was crumpling in on herself, but I hadn't been with her for half an hour before I realized just how false that impression was. "Here I am, back again. Have you enjoyed your visit with the flight attendants?"

The old lady, clutching a can of Coke and gleefully stuffing crackers into her mouth, shot me a look out of eyes the color of sun-bleached jeans. "I told them you took away my pretty pink shiny, but that I forgave you because you're taking me to my beau."

I smiled the smile of a martyr—even if my martyrdom was short-lived, I already felt very much at home with it—and said gently, "That sexual device was not yours, even if it was a nice shade of pink. I'm glad you've forgiven me for giving it back to its rightful owner, although I didn't know you were meeting a gentleman friend in Cairo. Your grandson...er...drat, I've forgotten his name. All he said was that you were going on a cruise."

"I have been kept from him for a very long time," she said, confusingly scattering pronouns along with a few cracker crumbs. "But you will take me to him. And you will find me more shinies."

I spread my smile to the nearest attendant, who earlier had taken pity on me and offered to babysit while I returned the pilfered object. It was the second item I'd had to return since I picked up my charge at an L.A. hotel—the first had been a watch that I had seen Mrs. P pluck from some unwary traveler's bag. "Thanks so much for your help."

"Oh, it was no problem, Sophea," Adrienne the flight attendant said in a chirpy voice that perfectly suited her manner. "We enjoyed having Mrs. Papadom...Mrs. Papadonal..."

"Mrs. Papadopolous," I offered. "She likes to be called Mrs. P, though."

"Yes! Such a difficult name." A look of horror flashed over her face when she realized what she'd said, and she hastily added, "But an interesting one! Very interesting. I like names like that."

"It's not my name," Mrs. P said, letting me assist her to her feet. "It never *was* my name. He gave me the name. He thought it was amusing."

"I'm sure Mr. Papadopolous had an excellent sense of humor," I said soothingly, giving Adrienne a little knowing look. She'd been on my side ever since I explained how Mrs. P had used my visit to the toilet to blithely rifle through the bags of fellow sleeping passengers. I herded my charge toward the last row of seats, saying softly, "Now, would you like to watch another movie, or do you want to have a little rest? I think a nap is an excellent idea. We still have another five hours before we land in Germany, and you don't want to be tired when we get there, do you?"

Mrs. P turned her pale blue eyes to me. "I like gold. You must like gold, too. Isn't it pretty when it glistens in the sunlight?"

"Uh... pardon?"

She gave me a beatific smile. "I knew your husband when he was a youngling dragon, still learning to control his fire."

"Dragon?" I gawked at her, not sure I heard the word correctly.

"Yes. He has much better manners than you. He would never treat me as if I have no wits left to call my own."

I stared at her for a few seconds, unsure of how to take that. "I didn't... I apologize if I seemed rude, Mrs. P, but my husband was most definitely not a dragon. And for the record, I'm a widow."

She said nothing, just pursed her lips a little, then slid me a gently disappointed look.

"As in, my husband died almost three years ago. And yes, he had lovely manners, but he's not around anymore, and in fact, when I met him, it was the first time he'd been to the U.S. He spent most of his time in Asia running a family business. Let's get you back into your seat. Hello again, Claudia."

The last sentence was spoken when we approached the woman across the aisle from our seats, a pleasant woman in her mid-forties who was on her way to visit family in Germany. She had been very chatty during the earlier part of the trip, taking an interest in my plight when I hurriedly explained to her that Mrs. P was an elderly lady in need of watching. When we stopped at our row, she was holding a book on her lap.

"Ah, you have found the owner of the pink sex toy?" she asked in a voice that was very slightly German. She tipped her head in question while I got Mrs. P settled in her chair.

"Yes, thankfully. It was owned by a lady on the other side." Wise to the ways of Mrs. P, I made sure to buckle her in before relaxing my guard.

"I will watch a movie," Mrs. P graciously allowed. I got her headphones plugged in, and flipped through her movie choices, stopping when she said, "That one. No, the one with the male dancer. Did I tell you that I was a president's hoochie-coo girl?"

"Yes, you mentioned that when I picked you up at your hotel."

"I was quite the dancer in those days, you know. I received many shinies for my dancing, many pretties that I kept hidden. Men used to ogle me when I danced, and afterward, they gave me things." She cackled quietly to herself. "It was a long time ago, a very long time ago, but I remember it well. I remember each of the shinies given to me, although I don't remember all of the men. A few I do remember, but they were the ones who gave me the best pretty things. I won't tell you the president's name, because I never was one to kiss and tell, but one time, he wanted me to pretend that he was a walrus—he had a very big mustache—and that I was a little native girl, and so we got naked while he took a tub of lard—"

"I'm sure you were an awesome dancer," I interrupted, trying to expunge the sudden mental image she had generated, "but as I think I mentioned in L.A., for you to have been that particular president's . . . uh . . . companion would mean that you were a very old lady indeed."

Still chortling at her reminiscences, she patted my knee with a gnarled hand. "Appearances can be deceiving. You remember that, and you'll survive just fine."

Survive? I didn't realize that was in question. I gave her another suspicious glance, but she was settled back happily watching her movie. Mrs. P had a way of inserting an unexpected word into a sentence that made me feel uncomfortable. And then there was her mention of knowing my late husband . . .

"She is quite the character, isn't she?" our rowmate said with a benign smile directed past me toward Mrs. P.

"Hmm? Oh, yes, she surely is that."

"And you said you are going to Egypt together?"

"Cairo," I agreed. "My husband's cousin . . . uh . . . man, I really can't think of his name . . . he asked me if I'd escort Mrs. P to her Nile river cruise since he couldn't take her, and she's a bit frail and could use a helping hand."

"Oh, that sounds so very exotic," Claudia said with a little sigh. "I can only imagine how wonderful a cruise up the Nile would be."

"Down it, actually." I made an apologetic gesture. "The Nile flows north, so the ship sails downriver."

"How fascinating," she said politely, then added, "Will your husband be joining you there?"

I leaned forward and pulled my own book from the bag under my seat, using the time to put a placid expression on my face. "My husband passed away a few years ago."

"Oh, I'm so sorry," she said, her expression contrite. "I really put my foot in it, did I not? Please forgive me."

"There's nothing to forgive. Jian... my husband... we weren't married very long." Her face was filled with sympathy, so I did something I seldom did: I unburdened. "In fact, he died less than an hour after we were married. We didn't even get a wedding night together. It was... it was so horrible."

"You poor thing. How terribly tragic." She leaned across the aisle to give my arm a sympathetic pat. "Do you mind if I ask what happened? If you do not wish to talk about it—"

I glanced over to make sure Mrs. P was still settled, and was relieved to see her eyes closed. "I don't mind at all, but there's not too much to it. I met him while I was working as a tour guide in Chinatown. The one in San Francisco."

"How very interesting. I don't think I've ever met a tour guide."

"I'm not one anymore. I really got the job because I look Asian—well, I suppose I *am* Asian, or at least partly so, according to the orphanage where I was left as a baby—and the owner of the tour company said tourists liked authenticity." I shrugged, but I wasn't certain if I was dismissing the eight months I spent showing tourists around or the fact that I didn't know my own parents' ethnicities. "One day, I bumped into a handsome man on the sidewalk in front of one of the shops we take the tourists to, and four days later, we were getting married at the courthouse.

Unfortunately, there was a drunk driver outside, and as we were crossing the street to the parking lot..." I swallowed back the harsh memories. "Jian knocked me out of the way so I wasn't hurt, but he...he wasn't so lucky."

"How very tragic," she repeated. "I'm so sorry for your loss."

"Thank you," I said, swamped with remembered guilt. "If he hadn't taken the time to push me out of the way..."

Her hand moved again, as if she wanted to give me another reassuring pat, but stopped herself this time. "You can't think like that. What ifs will always plague you if you let them. I'm sure your husband did what he thought was best."

"Yes," I agreed sadly, struggling with the secret fact that although I'd fallen hard for Jian, we had been together such a short time, I wasn't sure anymore if I was grieving for his loss or for losing our potential life together. "It's been a hard couple of years. He wasn't American, you see, and I had no idea who his family were in China, and no way to contact them. I tried to go through the Chinese embassy, but they just said they had no record of him. I even hired a private detective, but he drew a blank as well, saying that Jian must have come into the country illegally."

"Oh, my. That doesn't sound..." She bit off the rest of her comment, no doubt aware it was less than polite.

"No, it wasn't good. There I was, newly widowed to a man I barely knew, with no idea of who his family was or how to find them. I had quit my job to marry him, and the owner of the tour company was so pissed, he refused to take me back. Then things just kind of went to hell in a handbasket when the police were asking who Jian was, and why I had married him so quickly, and on and on."

"You really have been through it," Claudia said, stretching out and giving me another sympathetic arm-pat.

I shook off the old but familiar memories. "I have, but I feel like it's time to put that behind me. I'm taking this job as an omen that things are going to turn around for me." I gave her what I thought of as my brave smile. "And even if I don't get to actually go on the Nile cruise, I will get to see Cairo. I'll have a day there before I have to fly back home."

To what? A little voice in my head asked. *Back to the couch that your best friend lets you sleep on because you don't have a job, or money, or any sort of a life?*

I ignored the voice. I'd had long experience doing so after Jian's death.

"I'm sure that will be a lot of fun," Claudia agreed, and picked up her book.

I stared at mine for a while, not really seeing the words, but too tired to care. Memories of the events of the last ten hours flitted through my brain. Meeting Mrs. P at the hotel. Realizing right away that she had more character in her little pinky than most people have in their entire bodies, which was quickly followed by the awareness that her pinky—as well as her other nine fingers—were extremely sticky. And then there were the tales of her wild youth, with which she regaled me during the ride to the airport, and which I had a feeling were told in an attempt to shock me.

The drone of the engines and white noise of the air circulating through the planed lulled me into a half sleep. I must have dozed off because one moment I was mentally wandering in a bleak landscape made up of a pointless life, and the next, I realized that Claudia was gone and a strange man was leaning across me with one hand stretched out toward the sleeping Mrs. P.

"Hey!" I said on a gasp, instinctively jerking backward against my seat. "What are you doing?"

The man's head turned, his dark eyes narrowing on me. There was something about his face that wasn't... right. It was his eyes, I think. The pupils in them were elongated, like a cat's. That and there was a sense of doom about him that had part of my mind screaming warnings.

"You have caused us enough trouble," the man hissed, his voice pitched so low that only I could hear it. "Do not interfere again."

That's when I saw a glint of metal in his hand. I didn't pause to think about how the man had managed to get a knife on board the plane, I simply reacted to a threat to a relatively nice—if somewhat confused—old lady who was in my charge.

"Terrorist!" I squawked, simultaneously pulling up my knees and using them along with my hands to shove the man into the seat in front of us. "Help! Air marshal! Someone help!"

He hissed again, not a normal sucking in of air, but an animalistic hiss, and jerked away. At least that's what I thought he did, but I realized there was a second man beyond him, one who had evidently grabbed Hissy Narrow Pupils by the back of his jacket and pulled him off us.

I checked Mrs. P quickly to make sure she hadn't been harmed, but her eyes were closed, her mouth opened a smidgen as she gently snored, and one earbud dangled free of her ear. Anger roared to life in me, sending me lurching to my feet to where the two men were standing.

"That man tried to stab my old lady!" I snarled, jabbing a finger toward the hissing man. He stood with his back to the dividing curtain, his head down as if he was about to charge, but the other man had a fistful of his jacket. "Are you an air marshal? I hope you arrest him, because he was clearly about to attack an innocent passenger."

The second man turned his head slightly, just enough that he could look at me. He was a few inches taller than me, had short, curly, dark auburn hair, and gray-green eyes framed with the blackest eyelashes I've ever seen. It was like someone had dipped them in kohl. "I don't think that's very likely, do you?"

"What do you mean it's not likely? I saw it!"

The green-eyed stranger considered the other man for a moment before turning back to me. "Why would he wait to kill her on a plane when he could have done so at any time?"

"What is going on here?" Adrienne pushed aside the curtain, accompanied by two male flight attendants. "Who was yelling? Is something that matter with Mrs. P?"

"No, but only because I woke up in time to catch this man trying to stab her. And then the air marshal here heard me and grabbed him."

"Stab?" Adrienne asked. One of the other flight attendants said, "Air marshal?"

"Yeah, him." I nodded toward my green-eyed savior. "And yes, stabbed. As in, with a knife. You can see it in his hand." I gestured to where a bit of metal glinted in the man's hand. He lifted his head at that, and shot me a look with so much malevolence, I swear there was a faint red glow to his dark irises.

Handsome Green Eyes released his hold on the jacket and took a step back, shaking his head a little. "I'm afraid the lady is confused. I'm not an air marshal."

"No, he's not. He's a passenger," Adrienne said with a little frown.

"Well, whoever you are, you stopped that man from stabbing my little old lady," I told him before adding to Adrienne, "I hope you guys have some restraints on the plane for nutballs."

"I have no knife," Mr. Hissy said, holding out his hand.

I stared in confusion at the curved metal bracelet that sat on his palm. The silver crescent glittered even in the dim lighting of the plane, designed to resemble a twisted braid. It was very pretty, but not in the least bit deadly.

"Wait... that's not what you had in your hand... I could have sworn it was a knife..." I frowned, trying to make sense of it all. Had I seen a knife, or did I just assume the man was attacking Mrs. P?

Adrienne turned to the green-eyed man. "Did you see a weapon, sir?"

"No." His gaze flickered toward me for a moment, then away again. "I heard the lady complain about this man assaulting her, and was about to ask if I could be of assistance when he retreated."

"I thought it was a knife—" I stopped myself and made a wry face. "I guess I just saw a bit of metal and assumed that's what it was. I apologize for accusing you of trying to attack Mrs. P. Although... why were you trying to put a bracelet on her?"

"The lady dropped it, and I was simply returning it to her," Mr. Hissy said smoothly, then handed me the bracelet before he made a little bow to the flight attendants. "Since you are acting as the lady's guardian, I will give it to you to return to her. Now, if I may return to my seat...?"

"I do apologize for the confusion and any inconvenience you may have suffered..." Adrienne's subdued voice drifted off as she and one of the flight attendants escorted the man back to his seat, located several rows forward.

"He looked like he was attacking her," I explained to the remaining flight attendant and the handsome man. "He was leaning across me to get to her. What would you have thought if that had been you?"

"I would have asked the gentleman," the flight attendant said gently, then with a little purse of his lips she returned to the coach section of the plane.

I turned to the remaining man, about to thank him for the assistance that it turned out I didn't need, but simply watched in silent amazement when he plucked the bracelet from my hand, saying with an unreadable look, "I'll take that. I'm sure there's some sort of nasty binding spell on it, and we wouldn't want any accidents, would we?"

He walked away without another word, leaving me staring in disbelief. Binding spell? I opened and closed my mouth a couple of times, tempted to accost him, but decided I'd better not. Perhaps I'd misheard him, or perhaps he was not quite all there... either way, since I didn't have the slightest belief in the strange narrow-pupiled man's story that he was returning Mrs. P's bracelet—one that she hadn't been wearing—I decided that I'd just let it go and forget about the whole episode.

I didn't, of course, and when Claudia returned from her visit to the toilet, I told her in a near whisper of the happenings. She agreed that it was most startling to be woken up in such a manner, but didn't seem to think anything odd was going on.

"You said you were certain the bracelet didn't belong to Mrs. Papadopolous, so does it matter if the other man took it? Perhaps it was his to begin with, and the other man was mistaken in attributing it to your employer."

"But then why didn't he say that? And what was that business with a binding spell?"

"You must have misheard him." She pulled out her book again. "Perhaps he was trying to save you from any further embarrassment."

That shut me up on the subject, and pretty much for the rest of the trip. I sat vigilant the remaining hours of the flight, too embarrassed about raising a fuss over nothing to relax, and yet at the same time, oddly suspicious. What was that man doing leaning over me? Why had Mr. Handsome walked off with the bracelet without so much as a "do you mind?" And was it just paranoia to wonder if Claudia had disappeared into the bathroom at the ideal moment for an attempted attack on Mrs. P?

Too far, my mental sage warned. *You'll start seeing conspiracies everywhere if you go down that path.*

Fortunately for my peace of mind—what was left of it—Mrs. P slept the rest of the way to Munich.

You just have to get her through a change of planes, and then onto a ship in Cairo, my sage pointed out. *How hard could that be? Do that one little thing, and you'll pocket a cool two grand, which will give you a start to fighting your way out of a dreary future, frustrating talks with the unemployment office, and an all-around loveless existence.*

Unbidden, my gaze traveled along the rows of seats until it settled on the head crowned with short auburn curls.

My so-called savior was dressed casually in clothing that wasn't in the least bit flashy, but still gave that off that subtle whiff of money. A navy blue blazer covered up a shirt in a lighter shade of blue, which was tucked into a pair of black chinos. Sharply creased chinos. This was a man who exuded quiet self-confidence, and absolute comfort in his own skin.

Even the fact that he wore lace-up dark gray, somewhat scarred boots rather than shoes didn't ruin that impression. I was musing on what sort of man he was that he was so with it and together, yet marched around an airport wearing a pair of boots that would be more comfortable striding across a moor, when he must have felt my unabashed scrutiny, because his head turned and he glanced back at me.

Our gazes met in a way that left me breathless. My first impression of him had been one of chilly disinterest, but as I held his gaze, something kindled in the depths of those stormy green eyes, a brief flash of amusement that had me feeling strangely warm. One side of his mouth twitched, and he tipped his head a fraction of an inch in acknowledgment of... what? Awareness that I was clearly staring at him? Or perhaps it had something to do with our interaction with the nasty hissy man?

He turned back to the book he held, leaving me feeling oddly bereft.

The blush I had been working on faded as I stared at the back of his head, admitting that it was just too bad I wasn't going to see Mr. Bracelet Thief again. Those cool gray-green eyes combined with an air of mystery left my mind wandering down all sorts of paths, and not all of them were rated PG.

Two

There were red dragons everywhere.

"Just what I need—competition," Rowan said under his breath.

His gaze moved along the two lines of people queued up to go through passport control, counting no fewer than three red dragons, including the woman named Sophea.

Not red dragons, he mentally corrected himself. They were red dragon–demon hybrids. His sister, Bee, informed him that there were only a handful of non-demonic red dragons left alive, of whom Sophea was clearly one. His gaze paused on her as she assisted her elderly charge into sitting down on a walking stick that converted into a tri-legged seat. If he didn't know why Sophea was helping the old lady, he'd have been fooled into thinking she was exactly what she appeared: a thoughtful, helpful caretaker assisting a woman in need.

She looked every bit her part—of mixed Asian descent,

she had shoulder-length glossy black hair, cut in wispy layers that seemed to catch every light breeze. The long strands would occasionally caress the soft pink of her cheeks, making his fingers itch with the need to brush the hair back where it belonged. It looked smooth as silk, that hair, and he wondered what it would feel like trailing across his bare chest.

He frowned at the sudden erotic image. Where had that come from? Certainly it was true that Sophea was a pretty woman—with warm brown eyes that made him think of the dark, hidden depths in a pond; a heart-shaped face; and curves that would drive a saint mad with desire—who would no doubt attract admiration wherever she went, and yet, that did not mean he had to watch her so diligently.

Another strand of her hair flicked in the air, disturbed by a custom officer passing by Sophea. Rowan desperately wanted to brush his fingers across the soft curve of her cheek.

Stop it, he told himself. *You're acting like a randy stallion. Focus on what's important, and remember that she's a dragon, and thus the enemy.*

Still, there was the episode on the plane with the demon-dragon who had made a bold attempt on the old woman. That was puzzling until he realized that Sophea clearly wasn't working with her demon kin...or perhaps she had been, but changed her mind and decided to keep the old lady to herself.

The line shuffled forward a few feet at the same time that his phone burbled a notice that someone had texted him.

Did you find the ring yet? the text from his sister Bee read. *We can't do anything until you have broken it.*

How do you expect me to get this all-important ring

when eight hours ago I didn't know it existed? he texted back, tiredly rubbing his eyes. *For what it's worth, you were right and the old woman was on the flight to Munich. I'm watching her now.*

Two minutes later Bee texted back an answer. *For all that's good in this world, steal the ring from her!*

I'm not a thief, he answered somewhat angrily. *I don't relish stealing things from a nice old lady. If you wanted the ring so badly, why didn't you get it yourself?*

It had to be the exhaustion making him so snappish, he thought absently as he waited for Bee's response. It came almost immediately.

She's not a nice old lady—she stole that ring from Bael. She's got to be some sort of badass who-knows-what to do that. And we'd get it if we could, but we're working on locating the sword Bael has hidden somewhere in Russia. Besides, you owe the dragons. GET THE RING ASAP!

Rowan rolled his eyes and put his phone in his pocket before he was tempted to text back something rude. He noticed that Sophea and the old lady—who was going by some impossibly long name—were nearing the front of the customs line. It was just his luck that he had picked the slower line. At least the other two red dragon–demons were three people behind his target.

Ten minutes later, he was free of customs and hurrying through the crowds at the airport, his eyes scanning for the figures of the two women. They had a head start on him, but given how slowly the old lady was moving and the fact that they'd have to get their luggage, he had hope of catching up to them.

Rowan paused for a moment when faced with a sign pointing out the various transportation options. It wasn't likely the elderly woman would take the train or bus into town. "Taxi," he said, making a snap decision and praying that he was correct. He turned to the left and bolted for the section of the airport that served as a taxi stand.

Cries of people greeting arriving family members filled the air, along with the growl of traffic, the squeals of excited children, and voices babbling in at least a dozen different languages. The scent of diesel hit him as cars inched alongside the drop-off area. He jogged along the pavement, the rucksack slung across his back banging painfully against his kidneys, dodging people emerging from cars and taxis, avoiding mounds of suitcases and the chaotic streams flowing into and out of the airport in the usual manner of humanity until he found a line of taxis. Quickly he scanned the crowd, but didn't see the bent old woman and Sophea. He stopped in frustration next to a stack of luggage almost as tall as he was, his hands on his hips as he panted, spinning first one way, then the next in a desperate attempt to spot his prey.

Dammit, Bee would have his guts for garters if he lost them. His backpack bumped into something, and he automatically mumbled an apology.

"Sorry, I don't speak German... oh, hi again."

He almost stumbled, so quickly did he turn around to see the woman who spoke. Hidden behind the mountain of luggage belonging to another traveler was Sophea, her charge at her side, sitting on the little camp stool.

"Fancy seeing you here," Sophea said with a wide smile that reeked of innocence.

He narrowed his eyes, moving slightly to the side when a man who bore the livery of a chauffeur began to pull the bags next to him into a limousine, absently wondering what game Sophea was playing. Did she believe she could fool him into thinking she was not abducting the old woman? Perhaps she didn't realize that he was on to her. If that was the case, then it would behoove him to feign ignorance. "Hello. Yes, it's quite a coincidence, isn't it? Are you staying in Munich?"

"Who's that?" the old woman asked, peering around Sophea. "Who do you have there, gel?"

"I don't *have* anyone, Mrs. P," Sophea protested.

"Think I don't recognize it when a man ogles his woman? Did I tell you I was a hoochie-coo dancer for a president?"

"Yes, you did tell me," Sophea said, with an apologetic glance toward him. "But he's not mine. He's the man from the plane. He's the one who stopped—oh, you slept through it. Never mind."

Rowan moved a couple of feet to the left and made a little bow to them both, handing Sophea one of his business cards. "My name is Rowan."

"I'm Sophea Long. This is Mrs. Papadopolous, although everyone calls her Mrs. P." Sophea tucked his card away without looking at it.

The older woman looked oddly pleased. "Your man has manners," she said with a little nod of approval. "The bow was well performed, not the silly parody you see these days. And most men don't carry calling cards these days—very right and proper. And he's nice looking. Long legs. Torso is a bit short, but he has a broad chest. Good lung capacity. He'll give you strong children."

To his amusement, Sophea's cheeks turned a dusky pink as she babbled something about not even knowing the man, let alone planning on having children with him.

"Are you staying in Munich?" he asked, wondering how far Sophea would take her innocent act. Judging by the ease and familiarity with which the old woman spoke, he assumed that she was clueless as to who Sophea really was. The question was, did that make his job of stealing the ring she'd taken from the demon lord easier or more difficult?

"Just for the night," Sophea answered, not meeting his gaze. She gestured toward the taxis. "A car is supposed to meet us, but I don't see it."

"The driver should have met you at baggage," he pointed out. "Did you not see anyone with your name on a sign?"

"No." She bit her lower lip and looked worried. He had to remind himself that it was all an act to make him think she wasn't after the same thing he was. "I'm not sure if there's someone we should call or if I should just get us a taxi."

"What hotel are you staying at?"

She glanced at a small notecard. "The Hotel Ocelot. Wait, that can't be right. Ocelot? Is that even a German word?"

"It is my favorite hotel in Munich," Mrs. P said with a little curl of her lips. "I used to go there with one of my most inventive lovers. You've heard of strudel, yes? Well, he used to take a generous piece—"

"Yes, well, I think we can do without that image right now," Sophea said hastily before flashing him an apologetic smile. "I'm sure Mr. Dakar has important places to go and people to see."

"As it happens," he said with a show of genial concern, "I'm staying at the Hotel Ocelot as well. Why don't you share my taxi?"

"Well... we wouldn't want to impose—" Sophea started to say, but the old lady, with a little grunt, got to her feet and gave him a nod as she held out her hand for him.

"I'll grow roots if I sit here any longer, gel. Rowan, did you say your name was? What do you do?"

"I'm a sociologist," he said, somewhat taken aback as he held out his arm for the woman. She clutched it tightly, walking with a slow but dignified gait toward the waiting taxis. "I work with tribes in Brazil."

"No, no, what do you *do*?" she asked again, putting emphasis on the last word.

He had no difficulty understanding what she meant, but he had absolutely no intention of telling her about his other job, or the reason he was standing there at that moment in time, helping her into a cab. He eased her inside, aware that she was watching him closely. He gave her a bland smile. "I help indigenous peoples come to terms with modern society while retaining their traditions and lifestyles. Is this all the luggage you have?"

"Yes, just those two. Mrs. P travels light," Sophea said, grabbing one of the two wheeled suitcases and hauling it around to the back of the cab, where the driver was waiting.

"And your luggage?"

"Got everything I need right here," she said, patting the messenger bag slung over her chest.

He set his rucksack into the trunk and waited until Sophea slid in next to the old woman before taking the jump seat. "I, too, believe in traveling light. Is this your first time in Munich?"

They maintained polite chat during the time it took to drive into the city and to the dingy white building that sat on a corner with cars lining the streets on each side. The hotel's entrance was at the intersection, and Rowan couldn't help glancing up at a sign that hung drunkenly, little Tibetan peace flags fluttering dismally in the misty rain of the early afternoon.

It looked more like a questionable hostel than a desirable place for a romantic rendezvous, but perhaps it was nicer inside.

He escorted the ladies inside, helping Sophea with the luggage.

"Go ahead," Sophea told him when they reached a battered reservation desk that bore a half-dead fern, an old-style registration book, and a small orange cat sleeping on a pillow. Behind the cat, a young man wearing an eye patch with a skull and crossbones embroidered on it glanced up from a book.

"Ladies first."

She flashed him a smile that seemed to brighten the room by several degrees, then gave the waiting male desk clerk Mrs. P's name.

"Papadopolous, did you say?" The young man, who had bright orange hair and matching eyebrows, got to his feet and swung the book around to face him. He flipped up the eye patch, and consulted the page. "Ah, yes, you have the Oriental Suite. Passports?"

The ladies handed over their passports and Sophea signed them in.

"I don't know you," Mrs. P suddenly said, her gaze on the young man. "Where is Karl Amsterdam?"

"Karl Amsterdam?" The clerk's face scrunched up. "The man who started the hotel? He died back in the 1920s."

"Ah." Mrs. P looked sad for a moment. "I didn't even get to say good-bye. Who are you?"

"Hansel Franz. Karl Amsterdam was my great-great-grandfather."

"And are you going to pump us up?" Sophea asked with a little giggle.

Hansel, Mrs. P, and Rowan all stared at her.

Her giggle faded. "You know, 'Ve are going to pump *you* up!' Hans and Franz!"

Silence filled the room for the count of five.

"Oh, sure, I'm the only one who watches *Saturday Night Live*," she grumbled, her cheeks pinkening ever so slightly.

For some reason, that blush charmed Rowan as nothing else could. A woman who could feel embarrassment over something so trivial could not be all bad, could she?

"Your room is one flight up. I will take your luggage as soon as I am finished with him," Hansel said, handing Sophea the key. He flipped his eye patch down and considered Rowan. "Do you have a reservation, too?"

Rowan was very much aware of the near presence of Sophea as she gathered up Mrs. P and one of the suitcases before herding the former to a tiny old-fashioned elevator with twin wrought metal doors. "Er... yes. Of course. Rowan Dakar."

Hansel flipped his eye patch up before consulting the register again. "I don't see you listed here."

Sophea and Mrs. P entered the little elevator. Rowan raised his voice slightly over the sound of the doors that Sophea swung shut, making sure she heard him. "I made the reservation some time ago. Look again."

"I don't need to look again," Hansel said, pointing to the book. On the right side of one page was a listing of names and dates of the travelers' stays. "You aren't there."

The elevator's gears ground as it lurched its way upward. Rowan waited until Sophea and Mrs. P's feet disappeared from sight before turning back to the clerk. He slid a twenty euro note across. "My mistake. What will it cost me to get a room here? Preferably one near my... friends."

Hansel looked at the twenty euros and replaced his eye patch, an inscrutable look in the visible eye as the twenty euros slowly disappeared off the edge of the desk. "My mistake. You are listed. There are only two rooms per floor, and the other on the second floor is taken."

"Do the rooms have balconies?" Rowan asked, a dashing picture forming in his mind of himself being very James Bond by climbing down to the balcony below his and slipping into Sophea's room while she was sleeping.

"Yours doesn't. Mrs. Papadopolous's does."

Rowan instantly replaced the James Bond vision with one of him handily picking a lock and slipping into the darkened room that way. He ignored the fact that he wouldn't recognize a lock pick if it bit him on the ass. "I'll take it."

Ten minutes later he was seated on a black-and-white-checked chair in a tiny room furnished with equally eclectic furniture, none of which matched, all of which had the air of being cast off from a previous century. He glanced at his watch, not particularly because he wanted to know the time, but because he had propped up his phone and was engaged in a video conversation with his sister Bee. "It's almost six, and I've been awake for more than twenty-four hours. Do you think I could get a little sleep before you have me committing felonies?"

Bee's lips thinned in irritation. "I can't believe you're whining about a little lack of sleep when the world is facing a massive catastrophe. No, not massive—world-breaking. Don't you understand? Bael is trying to collect three tools that he'll use to rule not just the Otherworld, but all those millions of innocent mortals out there. Do you want that, Rowan? Do you want the mortals killed and maimed because you were sleepy and wanted a nap? Because I'll tell you right here and now that we don't."

A head came into view behind that of Bee. It was a man with shoulder-length brownish-blond hair who Rowan assumed was the dragon to whom Bee had bound herself. "Is this the Dragon Breaker?" the man asked.

Rowan flinched at the title. It had been a long time since he'd heard it, but it didn't make it hurt any less.

"He doesn't resemble you at all." Bee's dragon looked suspicious.

"That's because I look like my mom, and Rowan is kind of a mix of Mom and Dad. Rowan, this is Constantine." Bee smiled over her shoulder at the blond-haired man, and seemed to be distracted for a few seconds until Rowan cleared his throat.

"Is the Dragon Breaker refusing to help us?" Constantine asked Bee, frowning at the camera in Bee's laptop. "He is obligated to do so. Every dragon knows that—the First Dragon himself said he had to assist dragonkin without protest until his debt had been paid."

"My *name* is Rowan, and I'm here, aren't I?" Rowan said somewhat acidly. "And you don't need to go into old history. We all know who I am."

"You are the Dragon Breaker," Constantine insisted. "You killed four dragons with your magic."

"I'm an *alchemist*—I break magic, I don't make it. And I didn't kill those dragons—they interfered during the process of breaking down a catalyst, and were destroyed because of it." Rowan felt as if he'd been on the earth at least three hundred years. Had that horrible night really been twenty years ago? He shook his head to himself. If only he'd had the wisdom to stop the process before it had gone too far, before the dragons, in their lust for gold, had interfered... and paid the ultimate price for that interference.

"The First Dragon wouldn't have bound danegeld on you if you weren't at fault," Constantine replied with irritating complacence.

"Look, I am not guilty—"

"Enough, Rowan. You too, Constantine. This is not the time or place to debate what's happened in the past. Let's have bygones be bygones, and focus on what's important. Rowan said he'd get Bael's ring—"

"I said I'd *try* to get the ring, but I'm not a thief or James Bond. My window doesn't even have a balcony."

Bee's forehead wrinkled. "What does that have to do with the price of tea in China?"

"Do you know what a lock pick looks like?" Rowan demanded to know, suddenly so tired that all inhibitions were long gone. So, evidently, was the filter between his brain and mouth. "Because I don't, and I object to you sending me tersely worded texts asking me where the ring is when I am probably the least qualified person in the world to steal it. I'm a sociologist, Bee. I can explain to even the most isolated tribe who the white people are and why they are cutting down the forests, but I am *not* a thief."

"You just admitted that you are an alchemist," Constantine said, leaning his head in front of Bee's. She whapped him on it and forced him to move. He resolved the situation by pulling her onto his lap, so they could both face the camera. "That ring is a magic item. You break magic down to its essential parts, and we want the ring unmade so Bael can't use it. It's just that simple."

Rowan rubbed his face again. He eyed the bed with the lime green duvet dotted with what looked like ladybugs, and thought seriously about going to sleep for at least a week. "Nothing is ever simple where dragons are concerned. Speaking of which, you didn't tell me there was a red dragon with the old lady."

"I told you the red dragon demon guys were sure to be tracking her down," Bee said pointedly. "Bael evidently went ballistic when the Papadopolous woman broke into his house in San Francisco and stole it, and I have no doubt that he's got every demon and demon-dragon hybrid that he controls out looking for it. I'm not surprised if you saw some of them sniffing around her."

"There were two of them, but that's not what I'm talking about. The companion, the woman who has possession of the old lady—she is also a red dragon."

Bee's shoulders slumped as she gave Constantine a worried look. "Then it's all over. Bael must have the ring back, and we'll never find it now."

Constantine swore. "The gods alone know what sort of security he'll wrap around it..."

"No, that's not what I said." Rowan rubbed his eyes and stifled a yawn. "I'm sorry if I'm not making a lot of sense, but as I said, it's been over twenty-four hours with no sleep. The old woman's caregiver or companion, or whatever you want to call her, is the red dragon—and not a demon type, just a plain old red dragon—and she doesn't seem to want to have anything to do with the two dragons who are tracking them. At least, she damn near screamed down the plane when one of the dragons tried to put a bracelet on the old lady."

"A what?"

"Bracelet." Rowan held out his hand, gesturing toward his wrist, avoiding looking at the bed again. He didn't think he'd be able to refuse its sirenlike call. "You know, the thing you put on your arm. It's in my bag now, where it can do no harm."

"What on earth are you babbling about?" Bee glared at him. "Why would someone want to put a bracelet on her?"

"I assume because they imbued a binding spell on it." He rallied the strength to give a shrug. "I'm just reporting the facts, such as they are."

"It doesn't seem to me like you're doing anything—" Bee complained, but before Rowan could try to gather enough ire to take umbrage at that accusation, Constantine said something to her about being too harsh on him even if he was the infamous Dragon Breaker.

"He's my little brother," Bee told her dragon. "I'm allowed to be blunt."

"In this case, more understanding is in order. I wish for him to get started as well, but he is mortal and is clearly exhausted. He can't perform adequately if he is likely to fall asleep at any moment."

"How thoughtful of you to worry about me," Rowan said with a slight tinge of sarcasm.

"Do not thank me, Dragon Breaker. I merely wish for you to be able to do your job properly. It was *my* kin you killed with your magic."

"By the gods, *I don't make magic*!"

"Knock it off, both of you." Bee took a deep breath, then made a face at Rowan. "Constantine is right. I'm being overly harsh, for which I apologize, but I just don't think you understand how important this is to us. All of us, not just the dragons, but everyone."

"I understand," he said, lifting a hand, and with resignation, he looked again at his watch. "And for that reason, I'll do everything I can to get into the old woman's room and go through her belongings. But right now it's too early, not to mention the fact that I can barely function. I'll get a little sleep, wait until the small hours of the night, and then sneak into her room and try to find the ring, all right?"

"All right," Bee said reluctantly, then softened the words by giving him a warm smile. "Don't get hurt, okay? I mean, we want that ring—we have to have that ring so you can break it down—but you won't do anyone good if you're dead."

"Thanks for caring," he said wryly.

She made a face at him. "I almost forgot to tell you that May and Gabriel should be joining you soon. They were headed to Cairo, but said they'd stop by Munich when I told them that the thief was spending the night there. I'll tell them where your hotel is, so keep your eyes peeled for a silver dragon and his mate."

Great. More dragons. Just what he needed. "They are welcome to take over—" he started to say, but Bee interrupted him.

"I told you that the dragons are limited in what they can do. The First Dragon made it very clear that the person who could help us was mortal."

"Mortal born," Constantine corrected.

"Same difference. That's why we're having to rely on you to do the hard work, Rowan. But Constantine said that this silver dragon feels he can help support you somehow, and frankly, I figured you would welcome the help."

From a dragon? Just how much help was he likely to receive? Not much, given the dragonkin's view of him.

"I very much do welcome any and all help." He stifled a yawn. "Is there anything else?"

"Not right now. Just get that ring!"

"Do my best."

"I know you will. Love you, kiddo."

"Love you, too. I'll let you know what I find."

He ended the video call, and sat numbly while his brain tossed around the new bit of information that Bee had kept from him.

The First Dragon was involved, even if peripherally. The demigod progenitor of all dragonkin was not a person whom you soon forgot, and Rowan had painfully sharp memories of the times he'd met the First Dragon, especially the last contact.

Worse yet, fate had driven Rowan from his comfortable hiding spot just at the time when the First Dragon would be calling in the debt of danegeld, and Rowan had absolutely no way to pay it.

Until now.

"This had better do the job," he told himself. "Because if saving the world from destruction doesn't pay off the debt, there won't be anything of me left to worry about."

On that less-than-cheerful thought, he managed to set an alarm on his phone and remove his shoes before falling onto the bed in an exhausted heap.

He had a very bad feeling about his upcoming burglary, and fell asleep practicing a not-very-believable explanation of just what he was doing if he should be caught.

Three

"Is your man going to take us to dinner?"

I sighed and watched as Mrs. P cleaned out a small basket of seashell-shaped soaps, dropping them into her suitcase alongside the tiny shampoo samples, two washcloths, and a stack of notepaper from the zebra-striped desk that dominated the Oriental Suite. "Rowan isn't my man, and no, so far as I know, he won't be joining us for dinner."

"I like him." She gave a complacent nod, then patted her suitcase. "He will serve us both well, I think."

I waited until she padded into the bathroom in search of more things to take before removing the towels from her suitcase. "Serve us well? You mean in helping us get taxis and things? Just because we're at the same hotel doesn't mean we can count on him for help getting to the airport tomorrow."

"Serve us well helping us get me to my beau, of course," she answered with a placidness that was disarming. She looked like she could have been anyone's grandmother, and yet there she was trying to stuff a rubber shower mat into her suitcase.

"I think perhaps you're a little confused about a couple of things," I said as gently as I could. "You remember that we're on our way out to Egypt where you're going to take a trip down the Nile, right?"

"You are going to help me across the Duat to find my beau. You and your man," she answered, nodding before glancing around the room for anything else that looked likely. She eyed a lampshade, then gave a little shake of her head.

"I just don't... what exactly is a Duat... boy, I wish I hadn't left behind that piece of paper with your grandson's phone number on it. What *was* his name? I think he needs to know that you're a bit... confused."

"I am not confused," she answered, straightening her back and giving me a look that made me feel like a big meanie for picking on a little old lady. "I know more about what's going on than you do if you don't think your young man will help us."

I gave up trying to reason with her and decided that it was probably better to humor her than point out the obvious. So I nodded, and made a conciliatory gesture. "Are you hungry, or would you like to have a little nap? Or perhaps take a little stroll around the neighborhood?"

She let her eyelids drop halfway. "I had a nap on the plane."

"I suppose we could have dinner early—"

"No." Mrs. P eyed me, her lips pursing at what she saw. "You need to be lithe to cross the Duat."

"Hey, no judgments," I said, tugging down my t-shirt.

"I am entirely comfortable with myself and don't allow people to body shame me. Yes, I could lose a few pounds, and yes, I stopped swimming because there was an outbreak of chlamydia at my local pool, but that's no reason to look at me as if I was Sophea the Hippopotamus."

Mrs. P stared at me in surprise.

I made an irritated gesture. "Okay, it wasn't chlamydia—that's some venereal disease that koalas get, but it was something that started with a C. Crypto-something. Whatever the reason, I stopped going to the Y every day for a swim, but that doesn't give you the right to judge me. *Viva la difference*, that's what I say! Everyone is beautiful in their own way, especially those women who refuse to conform to society's stupid unrealistic standards of beauty!"

I took a deep breath to continue my tirade, but Mrs. P stopped me by gesturing to my feet. I'd worn the only slip-ons I owned through the airport, which were my sole pair of heels. "Your shoes, gel, your shoes. You can't be lithe in those things. You'd likely wrench your ankle if you had to run more than a few blocks."

"Oh." I looked down at my shoes. "Oh, I thought you meant—never mind. Sorry I jumped to that conclusion. It's just that body shaming is so prevalent these days."

She took the towels that I had removed from her suitcase, and tucked them back into her luggage. "Why should you feel any shame about your body? You are round and fleshy where women are round and fleshy. Your man must enjoy that. My beau always took much pleasure in my breasts and hips. He often said that my hips could talk him into anything."

I couldn't help but note her wizened figure, with nonexistent breasts, and no sign of curved hips at all, and then was instantly ashamed of myself. I was doing the very same thing I objected to in others. "You go, girlfriend," I told her, and as penance for my slipshod ways, allowed her to keep the two towels. "Well, then, I guess we could take a stroll around the block. You know, just to get a bit of fresh air and to see the neighborhood."

"No."

I sighed to myself. It was going to be a very long night if she continued to be so obstinate. "Would you like to see a movie? I'm not sure where we could find one in English, but—"

"I wish to attend a séance."

"You what?" I sat down on the striped couch, and wondered if the jet lag had caused me to hear incorrectly. "A séance? For whom? Or rather, what?"

"Spirits, of course." She toddled into the bathroom and returned with a roll of toilet paper.

"Of course. How silly of me. Whatever was I thinking?" I took a couple of seconds to stifle the urge to giggle somewhat hysterically, and said, "I wouldn't know how to even begin to find someone who could conduct a séance for us—"

"Across the street," she interrupted, moving to the mirror to examine herself. She patted her fluffy white hair and brushed off an imaginary speck of dirt from her sleeve. "The tearoom. They have séances every afternoon. Quickly, gel, or we won't get my favorite table."

I thought of pointing out that I hadn't remembered seeing a tearoom across the street from the hotel—assuming they had tearooms in Munich (it sounded like an awfully British establishment)—and that even if one existed, just because they had them in the past, when Mrs. P was last in Munich, it didn't follow that they continued to have such a thing in this day and age of relative enlightenment. All of that went through my head in a very short space of time, but I decided it was too convoluted to speak aloud, and instead duly rose.

"Change your shoes," Mrs. P said helpfully as she opened the door to the hall.

"The only other pair I brought with me are my tennis shoes, in case I have the chance to walk through one of the Cairo museums before I fly home, and they aren't at all fashionable," I pointed out. "Certainly not something one would wear to a tea shop."

"I just hope you don't hurt yourself running," she said in the manner of one imparting a dire warning, and sailed through the door.

"I'll take that chance," I said with a little roll of my eyes and followed her out of the room.

"You going out?" Hansel asked when the odd little elevator grumbled and lurched its way down to the ground floor with us in its steely clutches. I had to admit that I rather enjoyed the two wrought iron doors that you had to close before punching a button and pulling a crank to get the elevator to move, but the noises that emanated while it did so made me wonder when the last elevator safety examination had been held.

"Yes, we thought we'd take a look around outside," I said, following Mrs. P when she headed toward the front door.

"You must leave your key here," Hansel said, his hand outstretched. "It is the policy of the hotel."

"But we're just going—oh, whatever." I trotted over to the desk and laid the big black key on his hand, pausing long enough to add, "You do know that those keys are pretty old, and not that secure, right?"

He pursed his lips. "What are you saying? You don't like the key?"

"Not at all, they're very art nouveau, but that's probably because they're at least a hundred years old, which means your door locks are the same age. I took a course in lock picking a year ago," I said by way of explanation. "The instructor had a passion for old padlocks, and he said that a lot of locks shared keys. I was just pointing out that your keys might fall under that description."

He lifted his eye patch to give me a long, pointed look, then lowered it again, and picked up his book. "The patrons at the Hotel Ocelot do not sleep in fear."

Which was an odd sort of thing to say, when you think about it. And I did, for about as long as it took me to escort Mrs. P outside, and across the street, where we found a small ethnic grocery store, a brightly lit electronics store that blared Middle-Eastern music . . . and a tea shop.

"I'll be damned," I said, staring at the front of the small shop with faded curtains shading the lower half of the windows, no doubt to screen the customers sitting there.

"I hope not. Not in those shoes, anyway," Mrs. P said with another derisive glance at my feet.

"Ponyhof?" I asked, reading the sign that said *Das Leben ist kein Ponyhof.* "That's something to do with a pony, isn't it?

"It means 'life isn't a place for riding ponies.' You will take your shoes off to enter."

"Really, what is your obsession with my choice of footwear—oh." I read the small sign that lurked at knee level, and stated in three different languages that shoes were to be deposited at the entrance.

We entcred, and immediately it felt as if I'd been swept

back a hundred years. The room was lit by small shaded lamps perched in the center of tiny round tables, each of which was covered by a colorful paisley shawl. The lamps dripped with jet beads, while the room was dotted with large potted plants. The whole ambiance of the place reeked late Victorian/early Edwardian, and was oddly comforting.

That is, until I bent down to pluck off one of my shoes (and admittedly looked forward to it since even the most comfortable pair of heels has limits) when I caught sight of the two men sitting at the table half screened by a large potted palm.

One of them was a stranger, but the second was the man from the plane—the one who had tried to knife Mrs. P.

Except the handsome Rowan had said that it wasn't a knife.

"My favorite table," Mrs. P said, bustling forward barefoot and plopping herself down in a chair at a table that was already occupied by a man and woman, both of whom watched her in surprise.

I stopped frowning at the man from the plane, removed my shoes, and hurried after my charge.

"Er…hello," the woman said to Mrs. P. She had a short black bob, the sort that flappers used to have in the 1920s, while her companion had dreadlocks pulled back into a ponytail, latte-colored skin, and the most brilliant gray eyes I'd ever seen.

"I'm so sorry for disturbing you," I said hurriedly, tapping Mrs. P on the arm while simultaneously trying to pull back her chair.

She clung to the table with a ferocity that I hadn't expected, but the presence of the man who had tried to attack her made me very nervous, and I decided that the best thing was for us to skedaddle. "My...companion...is a bit enthusiastic. We'll take ourselves away."

"No. This is my favorite table. It has the best view of the spirits," Mrs. P insisted, and gave a loud squawk when I tried to pull her chair back from the table.

"These nice people were already here," I said in a reasonable tone that faded away to nothing when I realized that everyone in the tearoom—which was about three-quarters full—was watching us with horrified expressions.

"I don't want to go back to the hotel!" Mrs. P said indignantly.

I slid a glance toward the plane man. He was tapping his fingers on the table and glaring at me.

"I really think we should be leaving," I said, trying to gently heft Mrs. P from her chair without looking like an abusive caretaker who ran roughshod over her client's wishes.

"The séance hasn't started. We can't leave until it is completed," Mrs. P insisted, clutching the edge of the table. "Why aren't you listening to me, gel?"

"I *am* listening to you, but I don't think you're safe here."

"Nonsense. You there, tell Sophea that we can't leave until the séance is over."

The bobbed-hair woman smiled at Mrs. P. "Absolutely you must stay for the entertainment. We heard it wasn't to be missed, so you really shouldn't leave on our account... oh." The last word was spoken when the woman had glanced at me. Her eyes rounded for a few seconds before she slid her companion an odd look.

He too was staring at me, his eyes at first narrowed and calculating, but then suddenly, the shadow that I hadn't realized was there had cleared, and he smiled, revealing dimples on either cheek. He stood and pulled out a chair for me. "Of course you and your protector must remain, madam...?"

"This is Mrs. Papadopolous," I answered.

"That's not my name," Mrs. P said, shaking her head and looking very pleased with herself.

"I'm Sophea Long, and that's really sweet of you to offer to let us sit with you, but—"

"Sit down, gel. They can't start the séance until you do."

I cast a worried glance over to the man from the plane, but wearily gave in and allowed myself to sink into the chair.

"Gabriel Tauhou," the man said, gesturing toward the woman. He had an Australian accent that was oddly lyrical. "This is my mate, May. I must admit, we are surprised to see you. We hadn't heard that any of your kind survived untainted."

"*Survived*?" I asked, my voice rising an octave. "Untainted? Untainted by what?"

"Shush," Mrs. P said, whapping me lightly on the arm as one of the tea servers, who was dressed in what I thought of as Renaissance Faire gypsy, took the center of the room, and began speaking in German.

"I'm sorry," I whispered, leaning across the table toward the man named Gabriel. "But what did you mean that you were surprised that I survived?"

"The curse," he said, nodding just as if that meant something. "I can think of only two red dragons who escaped the fate Abaddon held for them, and since then, both have been killed. But no mates survived. In fact, I was not aware that Jian had claimed a mate."

I stared at him for a minute, the jet lag making my

brain react more slowly than normal, but at last his words filtered through my mental fog, and I sat back, my stomach tight with worry and unnamed fear. Was everyone around me mad? First Mrs. P, and now this man? And just how did he know about Jian?

I was unsure of what to do—should I ignore Mrs. P's objections, remove her from the tea shop, and hustle her back to the hotel? I couldn't just walk away and leave her, not when she was so vulnerable, especially with the man from the plane watching our every move.

Time drifted past as I sat there waffling back and forth—to leave, or to just tough it out until the end of the séance, that was the question. Meanwhile, the woman hosting the séance continued in German, before switching to French, and then finally English.

"We will conduct a gathering of spirits, what is commonly called a séance, although here, you are the mediums. The spirits may speak through you, or speak to you—that is personal for each of you. Are we ready to begin?"

I slumped back, not paying the woman or her patter much attention, one eye on Mrs. P (clapping happily before telling the flapper named May that she was hoping the spirit of one of her lovers would present himself so they could catch up). The rest of my attention was split between the man from the plane and the silver-eyed man across from us who apparently had a few screws loose.

"Sophea."

I hadn't dozed off, but I must have slipped into a reverie, because I caught the echo of my name before it was repeated.

"Sophea!"

I looked up from where I'd been staring at the table,

glancing first at Mrs. P, then at our tablemates. All three were looking at the table next to us, where a small, round woman with a mound of fat blond curls was staring at me, urgency written into her body language. "Sophea," she repeated a third time.

"Yes?" I said, confused. Had I met her before? Was she someone who'd been on the plane?

"Let go of the guilt," the woman said in a heavy German accent.

I frowned. "Um... okay. What guilt would that be?"

The woman frowned as well. "You were my mate, even if only for a few minutes. It was only right that I should give my life for yours."

"Uh..." I stared at the woman in growing confusion. "Who..."

"It is me, Sophea. Jian. I take this opportunity to tell you to release the guilt you feel at my death."

A little sob gathered in my throat. "I don't..." I shook my head, blinking back unexpected tears. "I don't... Jian?"

The woman's voice softened and warmed. "It was only ever my desire for you to be happy. Know that, and carry it with you."

Disbelief warred with a horrible suspicion that I was being taken for a fool, but how could this woman, this stranger know about Jian? How could she know about the guilt I carried so deep inside that I had survived when he hadn't? How could anyone know these things? "Are you..." I was at a loss for words to ask what I wanted to know, blurting out, "Are you happy?"

"I am at peace. Now it is time for you to let go of the past and embrace what you have before you."

I looked askance at the two people sitting in front of

me. They wore identical speculative expressions. "Are you speaking metaphysically, or literally?" I asked.

The woman chuckled. "It was your humor that first attracted me, and your spirit that captured mine. But now it is time for me to release you from our bond. You have great things in store. Be brave, my heart. Be strong. Do not doubt."

The tears rose again at the gentleness in the words. I blinked furiously, not wanting to bawl in front of everyone, but not entirely believing what was happening, either. "I'm glad you're at peace. I do miss you."

"And I you. But it is time for you to find your feet again. Look to the dragons. They will guide you."

My gaze flickered to Mrs. P. Dragons again. Was this German woman working in cahoots with Mrs. P? Even as the thought crossed my mind, I rejected it. It had to be Jian speaking to me—no one else would know the things he said. "I don't think I know—"

"You have great things in store," the woman repeated before slumping dramatically onto the table.

I sank back into my chair, not aware I'd been tense and holding my breath until the woman had stopped speaking, and the séance hostess moved on to someone else.

"Did you know that woman?" I asked Mrs. P quietly, taking from her the salt shaker she was in the act of stealing.

"No." She pouted a little, nodding at the silver object in my hand. "They have many others. I like it. It's shiny."

"She mentioned dragons," I whispered.

"Of course. Your husband was one." Her eyes focused on me with a clarity that I found startling. "He came a long way to release you from your bond to him. That bodes well for your man."

"You think that's what he was doing?" I bit my lip

in thought, allowing her to take the salt shaker from my hand. "I haven't really dated much since he died. I tried once or twice, going out for coffee or that sort of thing, but it always seemed... wrong. Like I was betraying him."

She added the pepper shaker to its mate in the depths of her purse before shifting her attention to the person across the room who was arguing with a spirit about who was responsible for a broken lamp. "He had not released you then. He has done so now."

I mused on that for a few minutes, wondering if the strange visitation was truly Jian, or if I'd been so desperate for it to be that I was willing to believe a handful of generic comments meant more than they did.

It was your humor that first attracted me, and your spirit that captured mine. I smiled a sad little smile. That was pure Jian—he had said the very first day we met that he loved my sense of humor and the bright shininess of my spirit. I hadn't known then what he meant, but we were alone when he spoke those words, and I'd never mentioned his comment to anyone.

"Good-bye, Jian," I whispered, and blinked back a few more tears that made my eyes sting.

Surreptitiously, I sniffed and brushed away an errant tear that escaped. Something caused me to turn my head, and I realized that the man from the plane was standing behind us, a long, pliable object dangling between his hands. Instantly, every movie I'd ever seen where someone was garroted from behind rose in my mind, causing me to knock my chair over backward as I leaped to my feet. "What the hell?" I shrieked, lunging between the man and Mrs. P, providing a barrier to her that would keep her safe. "Get away from her, you murderous freak!"

The man snarled something rude under his breath, but didn't move...until a swirl of wind ruffled my hair, followed by a dark shadow falling across us.

"Is there a problem?" a familiar voice asked, and with a sigh of relief, I turned to smile at the newcomer.

"Hello again, Rowan." I could have cried I was so happy to see him. "You seem to be making a habit of rescuing us from this bastard. Sorry, Mrs. P. I shouldn't have said the word *bastard* in front of you."

"It doesn't bother me," she said with a little shrug. "My favorite epithet has always been murderous whoreson, but if bastard rings your chimes, then you go with it."

Rowan, whose curls were all over the place and whose face bore a pillow crease on one cheek, rubbed his jaw as he looked from the murderous whoreson to me. "I'm happy to be of help, naturally, although I'm unsure of what the issue is this time."

I ignored the slight emphasis on the last two words. "He was going to garrote Mrs. P. Look, he's even got the garroting thing right there out in the open where anyone can see it."

The plane man smiled and held up his hands. Between them dangled a silver chain. "This is a simple gift to express my apology for having unwittingly disturbed the lady earlier today."

I snorted, disregarding the fact that such actions are never feminine, let alone charming. "Oh, pull the other one, it has bells all over it. You were going to strangle sweet little old Mrs. P, and there's nothing you can say to convince me otherwise."

"You seem to believe the worst about this individual," Rowan said. "Almost as if you knew each other and are suspicious about his motives."

I felt like he was poking around trying to get at something, but I wasn't sure what he was after or why. "I don't know him," I said slowly, my joy at seeing Rowan fading somewhat. "I don't even know his name."

"Mauritius Kim," the man said, bowing. I blinked a couple of times at that—I mean, what were the odds of meeting two men who bowed like that? And was I expected to respond in kind? Maybe curtsey? My jet lag had me giggling again at the thought of even trying to pull off such a move, which resulted in the plane man—Mr. Kim—giving me a mean look.

"Sorry," I said, passing my hand over my mouth as if that would hold in the giggles. "I'm seriously jet lagged. I don't know what your deal is with Mrs. P, but she doesn't want any of it."

Mrs. P looked the man over. I half expected her to come out with a risqué comment, or at least a mention of how she used to be a hoochie-coo dancer, but she just gave a little sniff, and said, "No."

"See? It's not just me being paranoid."

"No, of course she doesn't." Rowan reached out and, before Mr. Kim knew what was happening, snatched the necklace from the latter's hands.

"What do you think you're doing?" Mr. Kim snarled, his face flushed with anger. Something about him set off all my warning alarms, and I decided right then and there to get Mrs. P out of the tea shop no matter what.

I put my arm around Mrs. P and hefted her to her feet, much to her surprise.

Rowan examined the necklace closely for a moment, then raised an eyebrow at Mr. Kim. "I believe what I'm doing is obvious."

"That's the second time you've taken my property," Mr. Kim snarled, and took a step forward as if he was about to throw a punch.

I kept my arm around Mrs. P, with my other hand on her free arm as I turned us and started toward the door. "And now I think we'll just take ourselves off and get some dinner."

"And you mean to do something about it?" Rowan shook his head, and gestured with the necklace toward the rest of the room, which was continuing on with their séance just as if we were not there. "With so many witnesses to the action you were about to make? Witnesses who, I might add, apparently include the silver wyvern and his mate."

Gabriel smiled and slowly got to his feet. Despite the dimples, it wasn't a pleasant smile, focused as it was on Mr. Kim. I sent up a little prayer that thanked whatever deities were around that the smile wasn't directed at me. "It is as the Dragon Breaker says."

Dragon Breaker? What on earth was that about? I shook my head at the question; it didn't matter what sort of game these people were playing. "We need to get out of here before there's any trouble," I said softly, and stopped at the row of shoes, quickly picking out our pairs.

Mr. Kim choked on whatever it was he was going to say, then shot me the most malevolent look I'd ever received, one so potent it sent shivers down my back and made my stomach feel like it had just been spun upside-down.

Mrs. P crossed her arms over her sunken chest when I tried to hand her the shoes she'd worn in.

"Please," I whispered to her, glancing over her shoulder. The air felt downright static-filled. I wanted us out of there pronto.

"No," she said. "I wish to speak with one of my former lovers."

"Had a change of heart, have you?" Rowan continued to verbally prod the other man, which earned him extra bravery points. "Perhaps this would be a good time for you to leave. And by leave, I mean vacate yourself from Mrs. Papadopolous's presence. You won't get what you want, and you're just going to annoy a great many people."

Aware that reasoning with her wasn't going to work, I bent down to try to slip one of her flats onto her feet. She responded by curling her toes into the Turkish carpet lining that section of the shop.

Mr. Kim's hands tightened into fists, and his lips twitched as he sneered, "As if I care for the opinions of mortals. Not even dragons disturb me, and they certainly don't bother my master."

And we were suddenly back to fantasy world, the one made up of seemingly normal people who went nuts.

"You're leaving?" May asked me, rising and giving her husband an odd look. I'd almost forgotten about her, so caught up was I with protecting Mrs. P from Mauritius Kim's clearly nefarious intent. "You don't have to leave, you know. Do you fear the Dragon Breaker? If so, you needn't. You're quite safe with us."

There wasn't a whole lot I could say to that. It certainly wouldn't do for me to point out that her husband was talking about dragons and other magical things as if they were real. So instead of arguing, I simply said, "It's getting to be dinnertime, and I think we're both tired from the long flight."

"You are quite safe in my presence," Rowan said to us, his voice level, but the way he was looking at Mr. Kim was an open invitation to dispute the statement. "You may stay if you wish."

I looked helplessly at Rowan—the way he had stood up to Mr. Kim told me that he saw the latter as a threat just as I did, but how he could suggest we stay was beyond my understanding. I didn't feel in the least bit secure, not so far as the vulnerable Mrs. P was concerned. "Thanks, I think we'll just leave now."

"If you wish to do this the difficult way, so be it," Mr. Kim said, gesturing toward his friend, who rose and moved to his side. "My master does not care about witnesses. They are easily disposed of."

I stepped back, feeling like someone had punched me in the gut. Mr. Kim alone was bad enough, but with his buddy standing next to him... I shivered and said quietly, "Put your shoes on."

Mrs. P pursed her lips, but still refused to comply with my urging.

"Do you know what a bane is, mate?" Mr. Kim called to me, lifting his voice to be heard over the sound of the séance. "In the case of the one that Elton is about to cast upon you and the thief, it will make you our slaves, your wills totally subjugated to ours. Banes aren't easy to cast, of course, and require the blood of an innocent to cast, but luckily..." He smiled over my shoulder. "Luckily, that is easy enough to come by."

Air swirled behind me as the door was opened, but before I could turn to see who had entered, Rowan was suddenly at my side, his gray-green eyes no longer sleepy. In fact, I figured they were about as close to spitting out laser beams as they could be. Before I could say anything, his left arm shot out, followed by a squeal of pain.

Still on my knees before Mrs. P in an attempt to either cajole her into putting on her shoes or force them on myself, I looked into the tearoom to see if no one else was curious about the craziness going on at the front. No one was even looking our way. I wondered if this was part of the floor show, but decided I didn't want to stay to find out.

Gabriel and May hurriedly moved around the table toward us just as Mr. Kim instructed his companion to begin. His friend closed his eyes, started drawing symbols in the air while chanting unintelligible words.

"Right," I said, standing up and grabbing Mrs. P's arm. I spun her around, lifting her over the man who rolled on the floor in the doorway, evidently disabled by Rowan. "We are so out of here."

"My shoes," Mrs. P wailed when I hustled her barefoot across the street, holding up an apologetic hand at the drivers who had to slam on their brakes to avoid mowing us down.

"I'll go back and get them in a bit," I promised, and mouthed apologies to the drivers while pushing Mrs. P forward until I got her back into the lobby of the Hotel Ocelot. There I released her and peered through the window to see if anyone from the tearoom was following us.

No one emerged from the door, but while I was watching, a man's body was slammed up against the window, causing some plants in pots sitting on the interior windowsill to fall. All I could see was the back of the man, so I couldn't tell who it was, but after a few seconds, the man slid slowly down the glass, leaving a smear of blood behind.

"And with that, we go upstairs and lock the door, and don't open it for anyone," I told Mrs. P, who was telling

Hansel about how I had forcibly parted her from her shoes across the street. "I just hope it was the nasty Mr. Kim and not Rowan. Come on, Mrs. P. Let's go barricade ourselves in. I have a feeling this is going to be a much longer night than I originally imagined it would be."

Four

"You *are* the silver wyvern, I assume?" Rowan flexed his shoulder, winced, and wondered if he might not have cracked his collarbone in the fight that ensued as soon as Sophea had removed Mrs. P from the tea shop.

The man next to him nodded, and examined his knuckles. They were covered with blood, and cut in several spots. "I am Gabriel Tauhou, yes. This is May Northcott, my mate. And you are the Dragon Breaker."

Rowan was expecting that, so didn't feel the little zip of pain that usually accompanied such statements. He glanced at Gabriel's hand, but could muster little sympathy when it was he, and not Gabriel, who had dealt with the demon who had come in the door behind Sophea, as well as Mauritius Kim. The silver wyvern and his mate only took down the demonic dragon casting the bane.

"I've heard of you from Gabriel," the woman, May,

said, eyeing Rowan thoughtfully. "You killed some dragons a while ago."

He was silent for a moment, his shoulder hurting, his brain still a bit muzzy from less than an hour's sleep, and his soul crying for solace. "If I told you that I didn't kill them, that their deaths were due to their own actions, would you believe me?"

"Possibly," she said without hesitation. "But that's not what the dragonkin say about you."

"No, it is not," Gabriel said, a chilly look in his eyes. "All dragons know of the Dragon Breaker and how the First Dragon punished you. We know he charged you to aid us whenever we needed, but you seemed to disappear immediately after that pronouncement. How is it you avoided detection?"

Rowan gave a jaded smile. "Perseverance and dedication to being lost to the world."

"And yet you are here now."

It was a statement not a question, but Rowan was an intelligent man. "My sister asked for help. As soon as I knew it was to aid dragons, I felt obligated to do what I could."

"A noble intention, given your past with us," May said with a little nod. "And now I suggest that since we have to work together, we let the events of the past go."

Gabriel stayed silent for a moment, his eyes seeming to sear through to Rowan's soul.

"Let it go," May said, nudging her mate. "He says the story that we know isn't the truth, and it may well be that's so. Regardless of what happened twenty years ago, we need his help now. He's the only mortal-born alchemist around."

Gabriel sighed and nodded, his gaze warming up

slightly. "You are right, as usual, little bird. Very well, Dragon Breaker—"

"My name is Rowan."

Gabriel made a little face, then his lips twitched in a smile. "I will trust my mate's judgment on this, Rowan. We will work together in amity."

Well, that was something, Rowan supposed. It might not be an outright declaration of his innocence, but at least one dragon had been persuaded to give up that horrible name for him.

"Did you know that they would be here?" Rowan asked, tilting his head toward the tea shop, where the three now-unconscious beings were stacked tidily in a corner. He paused, waiting for a break in traffic before jaywalking across the street to the entrance of the hotel.

"Not them specifically, no," Gabriel said.

"We knew it was likely that Bael would send someone, though," May said. "And Bee—she's your sister, yes?—said that you would be here and that you'd seen a whole gaggle of red dragon–demon hybrids, so we thought we'd keep an eye on the hotel."

"I don't suppose it was luck that brought the thief to the tea shop while they were there waiting," Gabriel said, rubbing his chin.

Rowan would have liked to do the same thing, since his face was itchy with the drying blood of Kim, but that would mean lifting a hand, and at the moment, his left shoulder refused to consider that movement, while his right hand was throbbing and swollen from the fight. He'd get a bucket of ice, check to make sure that Sophea and the old lady were safely locked into their rooms, and then try to recapture the sleep that he'd been rudely woken from when his sister called to say the silver wyvern had arrived and was waiting for him across the street from the hotel. "Hmm? Oh, probably not. It's not like fate to make anything easy for me, and that includes dealing with the old woman."

They stopped outside the door to the hotel. The street was busy with evening traffic, whose noise helped keep their conversation relatively private. "You don't mean to say that the thief is working with the demons, do you?" May asked, looking confused.

"No, I didn't mean that. Sorry, I'm a bit rummy from lack of sleep. Bee called me about half an hour after I'd gone to sleep, so my brain is a bit less than it should be. I simply meant that from what I know of the old woman, it's just like her to end up being right where trouble is."

"And what of the mate guarding her?" Gabriel asked.

"Mate? You mean Sophea? She's a dragon, isn't she?"

"No. She is a wyvern's mate. Jian, the wyvern of the now-extinct red sept, must have claimed her before he was killed."

"I could have sworn she was a dragon..."

"To outsiders, a claimed mate is all but indistinguishable from other dragons. That is why you were confused."

"Regardless of that fact, I don't think that Sophea is guarding Mrs. P." Rowan frowned a little, but that made his eye hurt, so he contented himself with lowering one eyebrow instead. "At least, not in the sense that I think you mean it. She is a captor, perhaps, but the only reason she's keeping Mrs. P alive is so she can take the ring herself."

Gabriel's eyes narrowed on him. "Are you sure about that?"

Rowan didn't dare risk a shrug with the pain in his shoulder. "It makes sense. She's a red dragon. Or rather, a red dragon's mate."

"Yes, but Jian had not been tainted by the demon strain. He died right before that happened. And to be honest, his mate didn't seem to be the sort of woman to do as you are suggesting. Far from it—she was definitely protecting the thief from harm."

"For her own purposes," Rowan argued.

"Perhaps." Gabriel managed to shrug.

Rowan damned him and decided a cocktail of ice and painkillers would be in order for the evening.

"I think we should talk to her," May said, leaning into her wyvern. "She seems nice, if a bit... not standoffish, exactly. But more keeping us at arm's length. Untrusting, I guess."

"You're welcome to talk to her until the cows come home. Right now, I'm going to get some ice and sleep, in that order."

"We'll remain in the area in case our friends back there decide to make another attempt on her," Gabriel said, gesturing to the tea shop.

"I wouldn't turn down your help, but you do realize that now that the demons know you, they will be wary of letting you see them."

Gabriel and May shared a smile. "They won't see us," May said complacently. "Gabriel and I can both access the Beyond. The demons will never see us there."

Rowan gave them a little nod and made his way into the hotel, fetched his key, and headed to the elevator, too tired to take the stairs. He wondered what it was like to be in the Beyond, that part of the Otherworld that was more or less a shadow world, one where spirits of many types resided... but was definitely not a habitat for him.

"My place is a small tent in a muggy bend of the Amazon where the mosquitoes eat you alive, and a bad conversation with one of the indigenous tribes could result in a poisoned dart poking out your back. Ah, bed, blissful bed."

He didn't even bother with the ice, just collapsed on the bed, took a couple of painkillers, and was thinking about summoning up the energy to change his alarm so that he could get an extra hour's sleep before he had to creep into the thief's rooms, but just as he reached for his phone, it rang.

The number was not one he recognized, but he answered it nonetheless.

"Hi! It's Sophea and Mrs. P. We were wondering if you'd like to have dinner with us? As kind of a thank you for coming to our rescue twice in just a few hours. We're going to eat here in the hotel, since that little episode in the tea shop has made me swear off stepping foot outside the building until it's time to leave for the airport, but you're more than welcome to join us if you're hungry. Our treat."

He thought longingly of the bed, of just sinking into the depths of the mattress, and sleeping for a good three or four days. Then he remembered his sister and the fact that a demon lord was running rampant and about to strike out at the mortal world as well as the Otherworld, and he told himself that sleep was underrated.

"Hello? Uh...this is Rowan, isn't it? I can hear you breathing, so I know you're there, but...did I get the wrong number? I could have sworn I punched in the one on the card..."

"Sorry, yes, it's me. I was just thinking, which is not normally such a slow process, but it's been a very long twenty-some hours. I'd be happy to join you for supper, although there's no need to provide it for me. Quite the opposite, it would be my pleasure to take you two ladies."

A slight pause followed that statement. "Um...to dinner,

I assume you mean. Because otherwise, you just propositioned both of us, and as charming as Mrs. P thinks you are, I don't think even you have the stamina for her." Sophea's voice dropped to a whisper. "She may look frail as hell, but man, that old lady is a goer! She's worn me out with her demands I learn how to hoochie-coo. Did you know that was an actual dance? I thought it was kind of a made-up word, but holy hells, she made me try it."

Rowan couldn't keep from laughing. He tried to remind himself that Sophea was the enemy, and that she was clearly putting on an act in order to lull him into believing she was not after the very same thing he was, but at the same time, he found her funny and charming, and actually quite enjoyable.

"Must be my lack of filters," he said to himself.

"Hmm?"

"Nothing, just talking to myself. Why don't you tell me about how one hoochie-coos over dinner? Shall we say in half an hour?"

"I was kind of hoping you'd be ready to go sooner than that. Mrs. P is—hold on a sec..." Sophea clearly put her hand over the mouthpiece of the phone, because her demand that Mrs. P stop trying to unhook the drapes was muffled. "Sorry, just a little issue going on here. And on. And on, but we won't go into that now. How about five minutes?"

He looked at himself in the mirror that was mounted on the wall opposite the bed. He looked like he'd been dragged through a thornbush backward two or three times. "Twenty minutes."

"Fifteen, and we reserve the right to be nibbling on bread when you show up. I'm famished, and it'll give Mrs. P something to do with her hands that isn't illegal. And I didn't mean that to be a sexual innuendo. Mrs. P has to be ninety if she's a day."

He laughed again. "Very well. Fifteen minutes."

As he hung up, he could hear Sophea saying in a plaintive tone, "No, Mrs. P, I don't think you can fit that pillow in your bag..."

Rowan set down his phone, wondered what he had done in life to deserve such punishment, then remembered exactly what it was.

The First Dragon had sworn to never let Rowan rest until he'd paid off his danegeld, and clearly, Sophea was the latest in a long line of torments he had to bear. With a sigh, he stumbled into the tiny bathroom, managed to get a fast shower before scraping from his face the worst of its whiskers. He was only two minutes late when he strolled into the hotel restaurant, which occupied the basement level of the hotel.

The room had a close air that was common to all subterranean areas, but the five tables that dotted the room each bore a candle that gave off a warm, golden flicker. Three of the tables were occupied by other patrons, while the fourth was being used by Sophea and Mrs. P. True to her word, Sophea was eating a piece of bread, while shoving a bowl of butter spheres at the old woman.

"How do you know you don't like it when you haven't even tried it?" Sophea asked as he approached the table.

"The butter they use in this century is inferior to what I'm used to," Mrs. P complained, then brightened when her pale eyes turned to him. "Ah, there is your young man. He looks tired. You should take better care of him. I always took exceptional care of my lovers. I made sure their mental states were positive, that they had eaten properly, and had suitable rest so that they were fit for our sexual congresses."

Sophea cast a glance at him that was half frustration and half amusement. "Sorry I'm taking such poor care of you, Rowan. I'll be sure to bring you a granola bar and tell you a joke or two tonight when I tuck you into bed."

"No chocolate?" he asked, joining in with her bantering tone. "I much prefer chocolate over granola bars. Chocolate has aphrodisiac properties, you know."

Sophea's cheeks warmed, the bantering tone gone when she fussed with the basket of bread rolls, finally offering him one, but not meeting his eyes. "Ha ha, yes, that's right. I'd forgotten that. Chocolate for sure."

He sat down next to her, marveling that a woman who appeared so sophisticated could be so easily rattled by a little flirtatious talk. Not that he had much experience in that area, but still, he liked to think that he could hold up his end of a flirty conversation.

Sophea cleared her throat and made an obvious change of subject. "So, did you see the special of the day is some sort of sausage? It comes with potatoes, and looks really good. I do love me some sausage..."

A horrified look crawled over her face, her cheeks turning pink when she gazed at him.

Rowan had to stifle a laugh at her embarrassment.

"Oh, balls," she exclaimed, then slapped a hand over her mouth, her face scrunching up and turning even redder.

He just stared at her, trying hard to hold his laughter, since for some bizarre reason that he had yet to fathom, he didn't want to hurt her feelings. But as he watched her, her shoulders heaved, and tears leaked out of the corners of her eyes. Finally she could stand it no longer and removed her hand to say in a voice choked with laughter, "Tell me I didn't just announce how much I loved sausage."

"You did, you know." He chuckled, relieved to see that she had a good sense of humor and the ability to laugh at her own innuendo. "Not that I can blame you for it—I like a good bit of sausage myself. Gods, now I'm doing it."

"I do not understand what you are finding so funny, gel," Mrs. P said in a voice slightly tinged with annoyance. "One minute you were discussing your man's testicles, which I assume are pleasant to behold because he is a handsome man, although one doesn't necessarily follow the other. I had a lover once who was quite comely in the face and figure, and yet he had the most repulsive stones I'd ever seen on a man. Imagine, if you will, a withered plum that has sat on the edge of a frog pond—"

"No, Mrs. P," Sophea interrupted, shoving a roll at the old lady. "We are not going to hear about your poor boyfriend's testicles. It's not pertinent, and I'm sure they were perfectly horrible. Did you look at the menu? You need to eat so you can take the pills your grandson gave me."

"I don't have a child, so I don't see how I could have a grandchild," Mrs. P told her.

Sophea pointed to her menu.

"Very well," the old woman said with a sniff. "But I hope you are not this bossy in the bedroom. Men find such things demoralizing, and it makes it difficult for them to raise the sun."

She buried herself behind the menu while Sophea's face scrunched up in a delightful manner. "Raise the sun...?"

"Erection, I believe. I could be mistaken, but that's what I assumed she implied." He picked up his own menu, and cast a quick glance over it. "I say with all innocence and not the least bit of innuendo that I agree the sausage special sounds like the best choice."

She snorted a little, but managed to keep from either blushing again or bursting into laughter. She did lean over to help the old woman go over the dinner choices. Rowan watched her as she read the small print, explaining what the various dishes were. The more he was around Sophea, the more she puzzled him. Dragons and their mates could be deceitful just like anyone else, but he wasn't catching the least whiff of that with her. Instead, she was treating the thief just as if she were a perfectly normal old lady, and Sophea was her caregiver.

He shook his head to himself. He needed to stop being so sympathetic and remember why he was there.

"I think you would enjoy the pasta, but I refuse to ask where they got their olive oil from. I'm sure it's perfectly fine even if it wasn't imported from Greece."

"That shows what you know," Mrs. P said with a knowing smile. "Take a word from me, gel, and never say that in front of Zeus. He's always been adamant that the cradle of western civilization is Athens."

Rowan signaled the sole waiter that they were ready.

"Zeus is a mythical god," Sophea argued. "So he's hardly likely to be upset if I say that good olive oil comes from places other than Greece."

"Where did you get that idea?" Mrs. P asked her, rearranging her silverware into first one arrangement, and then another.

Rowan absently noted that his silverware was missing.

"About the olive oil?"

"No, that Zeus isn't real."

"I don't know, maybe…reality?" Sophea said, pulling

Mrs. P's handbag from the floor, and deftly extracting Rowan's silverware from it. She hesitated a moment, shot the old woman a telling look, and pulled from the bag a small vase containing a single rosebud. The water was still in the vase.

"You know her better than I do," Mrs. P said, addressing him. "Is she refusing to admit the truth, or is she just ignorant?"

"Hey!" Sophea said, pausing in the act of buttering another roll. "Let's keep the name calling to a minimum. And just for the record, Rowan does not know me. We just met on the plane, remember?"

Rowan studied Sophea. He liked her face. It was what people referred to as heart-shaped, but softened, so her chin didn't look pointy. Her eyes were deep set, but with a little tilt that belied her mixed ancestry. Her hair was a rich shade of brown that reminded him of the chocolate they'd just been mentioning—it hung to her shoulders, a rippling curtain of silk that drew him like no other woman's hair had.

For a moment, the idea of her straddling him, her hair teasing his naked flesh, flashed through his head, but he quickly stifled such inappropriate thoughts and tried to remember what the conversation was about.

"Er...do I have something on my face?" Sophea asked, becoming aware of his scrutiny.

"Eh? Ah, no. My apologies for staring. I was considering what I knew of you and why you would try to make us think that Zeus wasn't a real person."

She gawked at him, and it was so genuine, he had a niggle of suspicion that she wasn't faking her reaction. "Oh, come on, now. You're not going to start with that weird stuff that the others are doing, are you?"

"What weird stuff?"

She nodded toward Mrs. P. "She told me she knew who my husband was despite the fact that Jian had only come to the U.S. once, and then he was killed. And she said some pretty odd things about him. She said he was a dragon." She gave a short laugh. "A dragon! Have you ever heard anything that crazy? It's right up there with insisting that a mythical Greek god is alive."

"The Greek pantheon are demigods, not full gods, I believe," Rowan answered, wondering what she had to gain by refusing to admit the obvious. She must know that he wasn't fooled. Perhaps if he made it absolutely clear that he knew just who and what she was, she'd drop the pretense. He had a feeling he'd like her a whole lot more if she stopped pretending.

She snorted. "Right, of course they are. Because why wouldn't they be?"

"Just as you are a dragon's mate. A red dragon's mate, one whom the silver wyvern says was not tainted by demons." He met her gaze squarely, hoping she could read the sincerity in his eyes. "I understand what you are doing, but you should know that the act isn't necessary. I have no fight with the dragonkin... quite the opposite, actually, since I've been engaged to help them, not to mention my history with the First Dragon."

She stared at him for the count of eight, then gave a little shake of her head. "And you look so very sane. Sadly, you're just as cracked as the rest. Well, fine, be that way. If you guys want to insist that the unreal is real, you go right ahead. But I'm just going to ignore it."

"Why are you..." He stopped, and looked at Mrs. P.

She shrugged. "She is as she is. I cannot change it."

"Are you saying she's telling the truth?"

"Hey!" Sophea said, indignation causing her lips to thin. "I'm sitting right here, you know."

"Possibly," Mrs. P said, just as if Sophea had not spoken. "It's difficult to tell, and really, I don't see that it matters."

"I have the horrible feeling that one of you is calling me a liar," Sophea said through apparently gritted teeth.

"If she *is* telling the truth..." Rowan fully considered this previous suspicion. If that was the case, then it changed everything. Or did it?

"Yoo hoo!" Mrs. P, obviously tired of the conversation, dipped her knobby fingers into her water glass, and flicked the water at a middle-aged man sitting by himself at the table next to them. "You there, in the blue. Yes, you. Do you like older women?"

"You're about to get a swift kick to the shin, buster," Sophea told Rowan. "How dare you imply I'd lie? I never lie! It's a personal policy of mine, one that I started when I was a little girl at the orphanage and had to be nice to people who might want to adopt me. Do you have any idea the sorts of people who want to adopt plump half-Asian girls? Let me tell you, they aren't the cream of the crop."

Mrs. P leaned out of her chair at a perilous angle, the better to speak to the now-startled man at the next table. "You look like you have lots of energy. Limber, too."

"Er..." the man said, glancing around as if for help, but the other few people in the dining room were focused on their own affairs.

"Everyone lies at some point or other," Rowan told Sophea. He wasn't sure what to believe about her now. Either she was a very good actress or she was as innocent as she professed. But even if she was the latter, would she stay that way for very long once she knew the truth about what Mrs. P had in her possession?

"I don't," Sophea insisted.

"Not even a white lie to keep from hurting someone's feelings?"

"Not even then. I'd find some other way to get around being hurtful."

Mrs. P leaned so far out of her chair that Sophea had to grab her to keep her from toppling to the floor. "What's your name, handsome?"

"Edvard," the man said in a pronounced Scandinavian accent. He scooted his chair a little farther away from Mrs. P and tried to focus on his meal.

"So you're telling me in all honesty—because you never prevaricate—that you are not a red dragon?" Rowan asked, the twisting conversation making him feel like he was a dog chasing its own tail.

"Edvard is a nice name. I bet a handsome, limber fellow like you would like to make a crisp, new American dollar, hmm?"

"Of course I'm not—" Mrs. P's words must have registered with Sophea because she suddenly stopped speaking and gave an outraged, "Mrs. P! You are not to solicit others. I thought we had that clear earlier at the L.A. airport when you tried to sit on that young man's lap."

"My beau does not mind, if that is what you are thinking," Mrs. P said, and pulled a dollar bill from her pocket, which she waggled at the unfortunate Edvard. "He only cares about his world, not this one. I will be faithful to him there, but here, anything goes."

Rowan couldn't help but admire the old woman's

moxie as she waggled two tufted white cotton ball eyebrows at the unwary diner.

"Please, behave yourself," Sophea said, pulling Mrs. P's chair a bit closer to her. "If you harass that poor man, we'll have to have dinner in our room. It's much nicer to have it here with Rowan, even if he did call me a big fat liar."

"I said nothing of the sort," Rowan protested. "I did not call you a big fat anything—for the record, I happen to like women with curves, and in fact, think you are quite attractive—and I didn't call you a liar. I simply asked Mrs. P if she thought you were . . . er . . ."

"Telling the truth," Sophea finished triumphantly. "Which is another way of saying a liar. Well, I'm not, as I said. So you can just move on, and Mrs. P, so help me, if I catch you trying to seduce anyone else, I will march straight upstairs and take everything out of your luggage and give the stuff back to their rightful owners."

Mrs. P stopped blowing kisses to Edvard and gave Sophea a sour look. "You have no sense of fun. I hope your man takes care of your needs so that you aren't so cranky all the time."

Sophea gaped at her for a few seconds before transferring her astounded expression to Rowan.

He gave her a smile, and without realizing it, said, "Let me know if you need cheering up."

"I . . . you . . ." Her eyes narrowed. "Did you just proposition me?"

He rubbed a hand over his eyes. "Apparently I did. Or rather, my mouth did. Wholly without permission, I should add. I'm desperately tired, you see, and I think I'm at that stage where my brain has given up the ghost and is allowing me to say whatever I want without consideration of whether it's appropriate or not. I humbly apologize, and hope you will forgive a sleep-deprived man for a careless thought."

Sophea, to his surprise, did not continue glaring at him, nor did she read him the riot act that he deserved. Instead, a curious expression crossed her face, part amusement and part a wistful something that suddenly made him want to be heroic. "Apology accepted. I'm a bit jet-laggy, myself, and I know how it can be when your mouth runs off with you. And actually, you didn't say anything offensive. At least, that part wasn't offensive. The whole thing about me lying is another point."

"You really don't know that you're a dragon's mate?" he couldn't help but ask.

"How can I be a dragon's mate when my husband wasn't a dragon?" Sophea asked with another little shake of her head. She gestured toward herself. "He was perfectly human-shaped. As am I. I know I'm not any great shakes so far as looks go—thank you for the compliment, by the way—but do I look like a giant scaly she-beast?"

He was silent for a moment, trying to prod his almost-numb brain into working. If she was telling the truth, and she didn't know... He reached across the table and took her hand in his. "There is a test."

"A test to see if I'm a scaly beast or not?" she asked, looking skeptical.

"Yes." He took up the paper check that would allow them to sign for the meal, and dipped one corner of it into the candle in the center of the table.

"Really?" Sophea eyed the burning paper with evident worry. "It's not going to be a Spanish Inquisition sort of—aiiieee!"

She screamed when he dropped the paper onto the palm of the hand he held, prepared to dash water over her hand if he was wrong.

The second the burning sheet hit her hand, there was a flash of red in her eyes, and instantly, the flames were extinguished.

"Great Caesar's ghost!" Sophea said with an audible gasp.

Rowan released her hand and watched with tired satisfaction as she examined first the paper, then her hand, rubbing her thumb over her palm before looking up to him. "What just happened?"

"You are a dragon's mate. That more or less makes you a dragon. Think of it as dragon lite. One of your abilities is to control fire. If you were not who you are, the fire might have burned your hand, although I did have my glass of water at the ready."

"I can't be a dragon," she said, still rubbing her palm. "Or... what do you call it... a dragon's mate."

"Why not?" he asked.

"Because..." She glanced over at Mrs. P, who had succeeded in making a paper airplane out of a dollar bill, which she sailed over to Edvard, and was currently engaged in making two more. "Because they don't exist."

"Says who? Mortal beings? They do not know about dragonkin. And before you point out that you have neither scales nor a dragon body, let me inform you that dragons these days prefer human forms. In fact, you seldom see one as anything but a human. I gather it makes it easier to do things like drive a car and play a video game, not to mention keeps down the number of curious scientists and their vivisection kits. You, Sophea Long, were married to a dragon who looked just like any other man, but he wasn't. And that means you aren't what you appear. You are immortal, can control fire, and are quite possibly the only one of your kind left, since I understand all the red dragons were destroyed or demonized into new forms."

Sophea sat with her mouth open while he gave his little speech, finally snapping her jaw shut to say in a voice filled with wonder, "I'm a dragon's mate? Jian was a dragon? A real dragon?"

"He was, and you are."

She evidently thought that over for a few seconds, her expression running a gamut of emotions, from disbelief to curiosity to acceptance. "Jian had a special quality about him that I thought meant he was my soul mate, but I suppose... goddess, I was a dragon's wife. I'm a dragonette. Why am I not freaking out at this?"

"Because you're also a smart woman who knows that you aren't just a mere mortal," Rowan said, suddenly feeling each of his thirty-six years. When had his life become so complicated? Had it been the night when he was sixteen, and he had inadvertently killed four innocent dragons? Or had it been the following day, when the demigod originator of all dragons who ever were, and who ever would be, had called him before him to pay for his crime?

"I thought I was perfectly normal, but I'm not. I'm a she-dragon," Sophea repeated, clearly having a bit of trouble wrapping her brain around that fact. "It's really true. I squashed that burning bit of paper with my mind. Jeezum-crow! This is amazing! I'm a dragon in human skin!"

"Human form is, I believe, the preferred nomenclature," he told her, wondering what he was going to do. If she wasn't with Mrs. P because she, too, sought Bael's ring of power, then it had to be the most colossal bit of irony that the two women found each other. And what stance would Sophea take when she found out just how desired the ring was? Would she use it to further her own interests? Or would she understand that it had to be destroyed?

"I'm a dragon. Mrs. P, I'm a dragonista," she told the old woman. "You were right! Jian was a dragon dude."

"Anyone could see that," Mrs. P told her dismissively. "Do you have any dollar bills?"

"I have like a thousand questions," Sophea said a few minutes later, after their meals were deposited in front of them. "But I'll start with the most important one. Are you a dragon, too?"

"No," Rowan told her, looking up from his plate. "I'm a sociologist. I believe I mentioned that."

"Now your man is lying," Mrs. P said, making kissy sounds at Edvard as he hurried past them out of the dining room. "Tell the gel the truth."

"Yes, Rowan," Sophea said with a biting asperity, "tell me the truth."

"I'm not a dragon—that is the truth," he insisted. "And that's what is important right now."

"Hrrmph." Sophea didn't look convinced, but she let the subject drop in favor of peppering him with other questions. "How did you know I was dragon lite? Boy, oh boy, I can't believe that I'm saying that without having a major mental breakdown. But that fire thing was pretty convincing. Except...I don't feel any different."

"You aren't any different," Rowan answered around a mouthful of sausage and sauerkraut. "You are exactly the same person you were five minutes ago when you hadn't the least idea of your heritage. And I knew what you were because you looked to me like a dragon, although I've since been corrected as to your real status. I'm told that mates appear as dragons to the rest of the world."

"Really?" She touched her hair as if it was signaling him. "How? Do I have *dragon babe* stamped on my forehead that only people in the know can see? Do I look different from other people? Do I smell different? Oh, I hope it's not that, because I'll be paranoid for life that I stink or smell weird or something like that."

He managed a rusty chuckle. "You don't smell of anything but—" He closed his eyes for a moment and took a deep breath. "I'd like to say something pleasant like wildflowers or honey, but all I can smell at the moment is dinner, and I don't think telling you that you smell like sauerkraut is going to flatter you."

"You don't have to flatter me," she said with another of those fleeting smiles to which he was beginning to look forward. "So you just look at me and . . . know?"

"Basically, yes," he said, pushing around a bit of boiled potato. "Also, I am a sociologist. I'm trained to study people in order to better understand them."

"Do I have wings?" Sophea asked, absently toying with her food. "Do I breathe fire and hoard treasure and chase hobbits?"

"Not that I can see, you can, that's a question only you can answer, and has one been pestering you lately?"

Her smile turned into a full-fledged giggle. "Not really, no. But I'm still coming to grips with the fact that I was the wife to a mythical creature, and am now a quasi-one myself."

"Not so mythical, and not so different from anyone else. You simply have the ability to handle fire, and possibly have a deep love of gold."

"Gold," she said on a long sigh. "Oh, I do love jewelry. I had to sell everything I had after Jian died, but I fought long and hard to keep my gold wedding ring. It was the last to go."

"I'm sorry," Rowan said, hit again with another one of those urges to be heroic. He frowned at the very idea of him making a grand gesture to impress Sophea—he knew full well the sorts of tragedy that could result from such experiences, and he wanted nothing to do with any such idea.

"For the fact that I'm a widow or that I had to sell my wedding ring?"

"Both. Perhaps the latter more than the former, if I'm being truthful, although naturally, I am saddened by your loss."

"It's all right," she said, her gaze on her plate as she pushed the sausage through the mound of sauerkraut. "We were only married for a few minutes before he got run down. It was horrible, but not..."

"World changing?" he suggested.

"Oh, it changed my world all right—I'd quit my job to go live in L.A. with Jian, but then he got run down as we were leaving city hall, and there I was, suddenly alone. I didn't know who his family was, and the embassy didn't help. My boss was furious because I'd left, and refused to give me back my old job. I had the money in Jian's wallet—once the police gave that to me—but it was barely enough to cover burying him. It was surreal, to be honest. I'd met a man, fallen in love with him, and married him all in a few days, and then he was gone and I had no idea who he was. No one ever came forward who knew him. I left word with the Chinese embassy, but when I last inquired, no one had even asked about him. It was as if he never existed."

Rowan fought the need to protect her from the sorrow she clearly grappled with. It wasn't his place, he told himself, and then was immediately ashamed. What was wrong with offering sympathy to a woman who grieved her dead husband? What was wrong with showing basic human kindness? He placed his hand on hers, giving her hand a sympathetic squeeze, wishing he could take her in his arms and make her forget her sadness. "It must have been a horrible time. But you lived through it."

She nodded, her eyes tinged with sadness. "It was horrible. But you know what's the worst?" She looked embarrassed for a moment. "I can't believe I'm telling you this. But after the séance... well, it kind of feels good to talk about it. Cathartic."

"He has released you," Mrs. P said with a nod, and filched the wine list. "It is time you speak of it and let go of the guilt."

"Guilt?" Rowan asked, still struggling with his urges. Sexual interest, he understood. Hell, it wasn't just awareness that Sophea stirred in him but downright lust, and he had his own sense of guilt about feeling lust for a widow. "What do you have to feel guilty about?"

"Surviving," she said simply. "That and not grieving the way I should have. You see, I'd only just met Jian a few days before he died. We had a whirlwind romance, so I didn't really have much of a chance to get to know him as a person. As bad as I felt that he had been so tragically killed, I spent most of my time after his death worrying about what I was going to do. I see now that I wasn't mourning the man so much as I was the future we were going to have together.

And that's why I feel guilty. Felt guilty." She gave a little smile. "I guess it's time I accept that part of my life is in the past, and move forward."

He gave her hand another squeeze, then released it when he realized he'd much prefer to continue holding it. "If you don't think it's too presumptuous of me to say so, you're making a good start by being here."

"In Egypt, you mean?" she asked, *tsk*ing at Mrs. P and replacing the bread plate on the table.

"Yes. How is it you two found each other?"

"Oh, that was Jian's cousin." Sophea's brow wrinkled.

"His cousin? I thought you said you couldn't find any of his friends or family?"

"I couldn't." Her frowned deepened. "Now that's odd. I never really thought about it, but you're right—no one ever responded to the obituary notice I had placed in a bunch of California papers. How did the cousin—man, I wish I could remember his name—find me? And why didn't he come forward before?"

"He didn't think of it," Mrs. P said enigmatically.

Rowan glanced at her, feeling she wasn't nearly as scatty as she led people to believe.

Sophea was clearly going through the events of the last few days. "He called me up two days ago... no three, and said he was Jian's cousin, and that he was in the area only briefly, and could I escort his grandmother to Egypt. I don't—honestly, I don't know why I didn't see it was so very odd, but I do now. How did he find me? Why didn't he ever come forward when Jian died? And what was his name? Gah!"

"I do not have any children," Mrs. P said with blithe indifference. "Thus, no grandchildren, named or otherwise."

Sophea made a little face at Rowan. "As you can see, she needs someone to help make things go smoothly. Although that really is weird about Jian's cousin. I can't even picture him in my mind. He's just kind of a vague memory."

"So you don't know anything about the ring?" The words were out of his mouth before he realized it. Immediately, he damned his lack of sleep for allowing him to be so obvious.

"What ring?" Sophea asked, just as he knew she would.

"It doesn't matter. Forget I said it."

"Oh, like that isn't going to make me wonder all the more. Wait, this wouldn't happen to be a magic ring that lets its wearer turn invisible, would it? Because if so, we're back to *The Hobbit*."

"I am finished," Mrs. P announced, pushing away her plate. "If you are going to sit there talking rather than eating, we can leave."

"Rudeness does not become you," Sophea told her.

The old woman straightened her bent shoulders and gave a haughty look. "I am priestess of Heka, a vessel of Isis, and a hoochie-coo dancer extraordinaire. I am not rude!"

"Priestess of what, now?" Sophea asked.

With an effort, the old woman got to her feet. "I fear for the success of our journey if you refuse to acknowledge the truth. Your man will accompany me to my room if you desire to eat."

"I will?" Rowan asked, setting down his fork. The look he received had him on his feet without thinking. He held out his arm for Mrs. P, who took it with a little nod. "I guess I will."

"I'm done," Sophea announced, sliding her plate away

as she rose. "I'll go up to the room with you so Rowan can finish his dinner."

But they were already moving, heading slowly toward the rickety elevator. "Would you mind signing the check for me?" Rowan asked over his shoulder.

Sophea stopped following them, and turned back to the table to scribble on the half-burned check.

"You might take it a little easier on her since it's apparent she really did have no idea who she is," Rowan said softly to the old woman.

She allowed him to open the doors to the elevator before entering it. "If I did so, she would never accept the truth. And we will never make it across the Duat if she is not prepared."

He looked at her, wondering just what it was she was up to. "How did you steal a ring from someone so powerful as Bael?" he asked before he could stop himself.

"Ha!" She gave a short bark of laughter and poked him in the chest with a knobby finger. "That was the easy part. What is to come is the challenge."

"Did you know this cousin of her late husband who she seems to be unable to remember well?"

"He must have used a glamour," Mrs. P said thoughtfully. "One intended to make him unremarkable in her memory. That was smart, don't you think? That would keep her from asking questions."

"Who are you talking about? You do know the man, then?"

Mrs. P lifted a package of mints from his pocket, popping one in her mouth before tucking the rest away in her purse. "I've met her husband, but not any of his kin. The red dragons always kept themselves to themselves."

Sophea joined them at that point, and Rowan said no more. He wanted badly to think about the things that the thief had told him—as well as consider Sophea, his feelings about her, and the ramifications of her new self-awareness (not to mention how the last item would affect his job)—but his brain seemed to stop altogether, and refuse to do anything more.

"Nightcap?" Sophea offered when he walked them to the door of their room.

"No, thank you." He gave her a wan smile. "I'm a bit tired and sore."

"Oh, yeah." Her gaze wandered around his face, no doubt taking in the cuts and abrasions from the fight with the demonic dragons. "I wanted to ask you about that, but I guess it can wait until tomorrow. We will see you again, won't we?"

His gaze slipped over her shoulder to where Mrs. P was taking the pillowcase off of a pillow and stuffing it into a side pocket of her suitcase. "You can count on that. You can definitely count on that."

Five

Rowan's lips were hot, but mine were hotter.

"Oh, yes," I moaned when he took one aching nipple into his mouth, swirling his tongue in a manner that had me floating off the bed, my body curling around his.

"I want to make love to you, Sophea."

"That sounds perfectly wonderful." I breathed the words, my toes curling when his mouth moved lower, to caress my belly.

He looked up at me, his eyes changed. No longer the grayish-green, now they were brown, with bright gold and red flecks, just like a pretty stone.

Thunk.

"Tell me you want me, too," he said, his voice rubbing against my flesh like the finest velvet.

I pulled him up to where my body floated, rubbing my hand up his thigh to take hold of his penis. It was erect, silken flesh over hot steel. "I've never wanted anyone more than you, Rowan."

Thunk.

"Take me," I cooed, twining my leg around his, snaking my foot down his calf, and arching my back so that my breasts were thrust up at him. "Take me now. Make a dragon out of me."

His eyes glittered in the darkness, the passion in them making them glow.

THUNK.

My eyes shot open even before I was awake. I lay in the hazy dark, my entire body tingling with the highly charged erotic dream I'd been having, wisps of it clinging to my brain and making it hard for me to distinguish reality from the dream world.

The dark room was lightened somewhat by the glow around an almost-shut bathroom door. I listened with my breath held.

Had I heard a noise from out in the main room? Or was it a remnant from the dream?

Part of my brain boggled that I had fallen asleep at all, given the events of the day and amazing revelations of the evening. The other part instantly wanted to return to Rowan with his strange eyes, delicious tongue, and tempting body.

Tinkle, tinkle, tinkle.

"Right, that is definitely a noise," I whispered to myself, and slid out of bed as silently as possible. I'm not normally a heroic person, but the idea of Mauritius Kim and his unwholesome buddy trying to harm Mrs. P had me snatching up the lamp nearest the door and whipping the cord out of the wall. As quietly as possible I slid open the door and peered out into the living room section of the suite.

It was dark and silent. Just as I was telling myself that I must have imagined it, I heard a faint whisper of a sound, almost so quiet it didn't even register, the merest swish that wasn't what one expected to hear from the room of a sleeping elderly lady.

"Mrs. P? Are you okay in there?" I asked, opening the door to her room, my lamp held high.

The room was just as dark as the outer one, and just as empty.

"Mrs. P?" I flipped on the light next to the door and frowned at the unoccupied bed. The sheets hadn't even been rumpled. "Mrs. P, are you okay? Did your dinner disagree with you?" I tapped on the closed bathroom door, but after a moment of listening at it, I opened it and found that the bathroom, too, was *sans* one old lady.

"Well, hell, she's given me the slip," I said, going back into the bedroom, the lamp cord trailing behind me. That's when I noticed that something was not right. Instead of sitting on the luggage rack, where I'd left it, Mrs. P's suitcase was on the floor. "What the—" I started toward the suitcase, but at that moment, there was a sibilant *hoosh* from behind the curtain, and I knew without a doubt that someone had just opened the window from the outside. Quickly I glanced around, trying to find a hiding spot. Under the bed? Not enough room. The bathroom? Too obvious. The armchair wasn't big enough to hide me, but next to the room door was a large wardrobe, its doors spread wide to either side like a giant wooden moth. Perhaps I could hide behind one if its doors long enough to ascertain who was breaking into the room.

The thought flitted through my head that a lamp wasn't much protection against an intruder as I ran to the farthest wing of the wardrobe, but that evaporated into nothing when I scurried behind the door...only to find the space was already occupied.

Rowan must have heard the intake of my breath preparatory to screaming, because his hand was over my mouth before I realized what had happened.

"Quiet," he breathed into my ear, his breath warm against my head in a way that had little shivers spreading across my back. "Someone is at the window."

"I know," I whispered back as he pulled the door flush against us. Unfortunately, the lampshade was too big to let it fit behind the door with us, which left my hand sticking out with the lamp gripped firmly in it. "It's okay, though. I have a lamp."

The light behind the opened wardrobe door wasn't very bright, but it was enough to see the odd look he gave me.

A rustle of the drapes had me tensing, but before I could do anything, Rowan suddenly twisted around, pinning me against the wall with his body. For a few seconds, we were pressed together from knees to chest, and I was extremely aware that I was a woman and he was a man, and it had been way too many years since I'd entertained the carnal activities that had been uppermost in my mind right before I'd been awakened.

"Oh," I breathed softly, unable to keep from taking a deep breath so that my breasts smooshed happily against his chest.

I swear his eyes got darker at that, and he hesitated for about two seconds before he murmured, "To hell with the job." His breath burned on mine, and then his mouth was moving over my lips.

With one hand, I clutched him, pulling him even closer so that he caught my moan in his mouth. His tongue twined against mine, stroking fires inside me that I hadn't known existed. I was about to let the lamp fall so I could slide my other hand into his hair when suddenly he was gone. He moved out past me, out from the cover of the wardrobe door. I stood there for another handful of seconds just reliving the kiss before my brain pointed out that Rowan had gone out unarmed to face whomever had broken into the room.

With a bravery I hadn't known I possessed, I flung back the door and, swinging my lamp forward, yelled, "Ha!" in the very best martial arts manner. The cord snapped out like a whip, slashing through the air and striking the man directly in its path who luckily wasn't Rowan. No, Rowan was standing with his arms crossed, and his back against the door leading to the living room.

Mauritius Kim swore and leaped to the side, one hand to his face where the metal plug had cut his cheek.

"We meet again!" I said, suddenly full of bravado. I had no idea where it had come from, but dammit, if I was truly the wife of a not-so-mythical creature, and thus someone who could control fire, then by god, I wasn't going to be afraid of some loser like Mr. Kim! "And this time, I have the advantage!"

Mr. Kim stared in disbelief at the lamp in my hand, as did his buddy Elton, who emerged from the drapes. "Are you insane?" he asked, giving me a scathing look. "Or just stupid? That's not a weapon, it's a lamp."

"Tell your cheek that," I said, swaggering forward a couple of steps. To my annoyance, he didn't back up. Perhaps a little more threatening was in order. I shook the lamp at him and said, "In case you don't know, you're not just dealing with a normal person."

"Oh, lord," Rowan said under his breath, before adding a bit louder, "Sophea, I don't think you want—"

"No sir, you're dealing with a dragon's mate. That's right, I'm a bona fide dragon. Of sorts. Kind of. So Rowan says, and

I have no reason to doubt him because he did the test. I can control fire, and likely do all sorts of other dragony things, so you had just better take your scummy little friend there and get the hell out of Dodge while the getting is good." I grasped the cord with my hand, snapping it toward Mr. Kim.

He actually took a step back.

"Sophea, you really do not know—"

"It's okay, Rowan," I interrupted, giving him a decisive nod. "I got this."

"No, I don't think you do."

"That's right," I said, pointing the plug at Mr. Kim. His friend was now next to him, the pair of them watching me with absolutely no expression on their respective faces. Perhaps they were as stunned as I'd been to find out just how awesome I was. "You heard me. I'm dragon. A *crimson* dragon!"

"Red," Rowan corrected.

"*Red* dragon. Rawr!" I said, making a little claw gesture with my hand. "You may now leave before I unleash my unholy dragon stuff upon you!"

Rowan sighed and rubbed his face like he couldn't face watching the ass-whooping that was about to be unleashed on Mr. Kim and Company.

"Well?" Mr. Kim said.

"Well what?" I asked, suspicious. I gestured with the lamp. "Well, as in, Rowan is blocking the door and you can't leave?"

"Well as in let's see you unleash your mighty mate's powers on us."

I blinked and glanced over at Rowan. He was now standing with one hand covering his mouth, as if he was trying to keep from speaking. "You're better at this than I am. Will you tell these guys just how badass dragons are?"

He lowered his hand and gave me a wry smile. "They know."

"Then why aren't they running away?" I shook my lamp at them. "I'm a fire wielder. Or whatever they call it. Maybe I can turn into a giant scaly beast!"

"Go on, then," Mr. Kim's friend said. "Let's see you."

"I don't want to," I said, tilting my head so I was looking down my nose at him. "I have to be in the mood to be a giant scaly dragon, and I'm not right now. But I can do the fire thing just as I am, so you'd better vamoose before I call down a rain of fire that will singe the hair right off the tops of your heads And you know how bad burnt hair smells!"

"Sophea," Rowan said tiredly, and stopped.

"What?" I asked him, keeping my eyes on the two men in front of me.

He gestured vaguely, then shook his head. "Never mind. Proceed."

"Show us your rain of fire," Mr. Kim said in a snotty tone.

"Don't think I can do it, do you?" I said, wondering wildly what my stupid bravado had gotten me into. I didn't dare ask Rowan how to make it rain fire, which meant I either had to do something to distract the men or put my money where my mouth was. What was a rain of fire? It was little blobs of fire dumping onto someone. The question was, how did I get the fire going? I looked around the room, spied Mrs. P's handbag, and said, "Fine. Give me just a sec."

All three men watched with interest as I dug through her bag, finally pulling out a silver lighter, the old-fashioned kind that people in black-and-white movies used. With the lamp tucked under one arm, I screwed up a room service menu and lit one end on fire.

"Fire," I told Rowan, nodding toward the two hoodlums. "Now I'll make it rain on them."

"I look forward to seeing that," he said politely.

I eyed him for a few seconds wondering if he was being sarcastic, but he just looked tired, so I figured he was being supportive in a non-obvious way. I turned to face the two men, held out the burning menu, and tried to force the fire onto them.

It just burned down the paper.

"Well, crapballs." I gnawed my lower lip as I watched the fire, strangely captivated by it.

"Allow us to show you *our* rain of fire," Mr. Kim said.

"Maybe I'm doing something wrong with it...wait, what? *Your* rain of fire?"

Mr. Kim smiled, and out of nowhere, little balls of fire began to fall from the ceiling onto me. I shrieked and dropped my lamp to slap the fireballs when they hit me, feeling both relieved when they didn't burn me and confused as hell.

"You're a dragon, too?" I asked Mr. Kim, picking up my lamp with the fire stopped falling.

"We are demons, servants of Lord Bael, the premier prince of Abaddon. We have dragon blood in our veins, but we are demons first and foremost, and now you will give to us the ring that the thief stole from our master, or we will kill you right here and now." As if to prove he meant it, both men pulled long, wickedly sharp daggers from sheaths strapped to their thighs.

I looked over at Rowan. "Are they telling the truth?"

"Unfortunately, yes," he said, strolling over to stand next to me.

"They're demons."

"Demon-dragon hybrids, to be exact."

Quickly, I ran through my options. I didn't like the way that Mr. Kim was lovingly caressing the blade of that dagger, and I had little hope that there were such things as good demons around. Which meant I had to do something to save Rowan and me.

"We tire of your games," Mr. Kim, said, gesturing to his friend. "Elton, slit the mortal's throat. I'll take great pleasure in separating this mate from her head, and then we will search the room for the ring."

"I don't like them," I told Rowan. "I don't think they play nicely with others."

One corner of his mouth quirked up, and I had the worst desire to kiss it. That shocked me out of my sense of befuddlement, which is why no one, least of all Mr. Kim and Elton, were expecting me to rush forward, lamp held forward with one hand, and my burning menu in the other. To my surprise, just as I thrust the menu forward, a ball of fire shot from it and hit the two men, sending them staggering backward to the window.

"Scarlet dragons to the rescue!" I yelled, and whacked Mr. Kim over the head with the base of the lamp. It shattered into a bazillion pieces of ceramic, but I didn't wait to see how he handled that: I whipped around, and with a kick that I had no idea I could do, planted my foot squarely on Elton the demon's chest, and sent him tumbling through the window.

Mr. Kim roared in fury and lunged at me with his dagger in hand, blood pouring out of a jagged cut on his forehead, but before I could try to coax another fireball from my almost-burned menu, Rowan was there in front of me, knocking the knife out of Mr. Kim's hand and kicking his knee, causing him to crumple. Rowan grabbed Mr. Kim by his shirt collar and, twisting it viciously, dragged him over to the window. "I've had about all I'm going to take from you. The next time you bother us will be your last."

Mr. Kim tried to spit out an oath, but Rowan's stranglehold was effective enough to keep him from doing anything but making garbled noises. Rowan heaved the upper half of the man out of the window, and added, "Tell your master the ring is lost," before shoving the man's legs out with the rest of them.

"Tell me that we didn't just murder two people," I panted, dropping the menu when the flame finally hit my hand. I stamped it out and sidled toward the window, both shocked that I could kill a person so easily and thrilled that I was as badass as I had hoped.

"Demons are immortal," he replied, and stuck his head out of the window. I edged up behind him, not wanting to see the result of a fall from a third-story window, but reminding myself that the men had planned on killing us. To my surprise, there were no bodies on the sidewalk, only black smudges.

"They're gone? Did they walk away?" I asked, prepared to be amazed.

"No. You can destroy a demon's form, but it will simply return to Abaddon to get a new one."

"Abaddon?"

He closed the window and surveyed the room. "It's what mortals think of as hell. It's where the demon lords and their minions reside. Do you know where the ring is?"

"What ring? You keep talking about one, but I have no clue what you're going on about."

"Mrs. P has a ring. It is very valuable."

"I don't doubt that she does, since she obviously has a

ton of money." I zipped closed the suitcase and got to my feet. There were shards of a broken drinking glass on the desk that I swept into the tiny waste bin before gesturing toward the door and following him out to the main room. I frowned as a thought struck me. "What are you doing here?"

"I'm on my way to Cairo, just like you."

"No, what are you doing *here*. In this room."

His gaze dropped to my mouth.

Instantly, I wanted to kiss him again. And more...

"You're not some sort of a jewel thief, are you?" I couldn't help but ask once I wrestled my mind out of its smutty meanderings.

A flash of amusement passed over his face. "Not in the least. I'm just... interested... in unique items, and I heard that Mrs. P has one."

"Good, because if you think you can buddy up to me in hopes that I'll help you steal from Mrs. P, you're sorely mistaken. Stealing is one of those things I don't do. I may not have a ton going for me—although now I'm a super kick-ass dragonette who can push demons out of windows and play with fireballs—but I don't steal. Or lie. I was going to add murder to that list, but I think I just killed a demon, so sadly, I'm not as righteous as I'd like to be."

"You needn't be worried that the destruction of a demon's physical form will stain your soul," he said with a pained twist of his lips. "It won't."

"You speak like you have experience in this matter. How many demons have you offed?"

"None before tonight." He hesitated, then added slowly, "Why aren't you worried about Mrs. P's whereabouts?"

"That was a really excellent change of subject."

"Thank you." He made another of those little bows that looked incredibly sexy, rather than silly as I'd expected.

"I'm not worried because I fully expect to find her in the embrace of Edvard. Or at least trying to seduce him. She's quite the character. I'll Google demons to see if what you said is true, you know."

"I'm sure you will. Do I need to apologize?"

"To Mrs. P for rifling through her things and breaking a hotel glass? Probably not. I'll put things back the way she had them, and she doubtless won't even notice. I'm forever taking the things she lifts from her bag anyway."

"No, I meant for that kiss. I didn't intend to do it. I just—you're so—and we were there. Together."

I smiled. Slowly. "I enjoyed it, actually. You're quite the kisser."

"So are you." His voice seemed to have roughened. He cleared it and made an embarrassed gesture. "I enjoyed it as well. Perhaps another time we could do it again."

"That sounds like a lovely plan," I said, just as if he'd casually mentioned getting together for coffee. I don't know what possessed me then. I can only attribute the fact that I walked over to him and planted my lips on his to the fact that I'd been woken up out of the most erotic dream of my life, coupled with the adrenaline rush of having dealt with murderous demons.

If anyone was due a little distraction, I figured it was me. Especially now that Jian had given me his blessing to move beyond what we had together. I smiled at Rowan, feeling that it was somehow right we should be together at that moment.

It was as if fate had brought us together...and I was never one to take fate for granted.

Six

"Sophea..." Rowan cupped my behind, and pulled me against his hips, groaning into my mouth when I parted my lips for him. "We really shouldn't."

"Why not? We're both adults. I assume you're not involved with anyone and I know I'm not, and great Caesar's gizzard, do I want to see if you live up to the dream. Besides, Jian said at the séance that he wants me to move on, and I assume that includes finally being with another man."

"Dream?" he asked, peeling off the t-shirt that I slept in. "Finally? You haven't...erm..."

"No. Not since Jian." Cool air hit my naked flesh, making me shiver...until his hands cupped my breasts, instantly making them feel like they were on fire.

"I'll do my best to live up to such an honor," he murmured, his hands and mouth making me wild.

"I have no doubt you'll do just that. I think...oh yes, do the other, please...I think we'd better go into my room just in case Mrs. P comes back early. I wouldn't want to shock her."

He murmured an agreement into my chest, still kissing and nibbling and licking as I backed us up into my room, nudging the door closed behind us.

I bit the tendon on his neck, licking the spot afterward as I unbuttoned his shirt, peeling it off to expose his chest.

Goddess above, it was a gorgeous chest. He had lovely soft chest hair that emphasized the swells of muscle, and a long line that led down into the waistband of his pants. I stroked one pectoral, the memories of the dream mingling with reality until I couldn't differentiate between the two.

"You're on fire," he said, sucking my earlobe at the same time he slid off my cotton shorts.

"Only for you," I answered, working on his belt.

"I meant that literally," he said, pulling back to give me a smile filled with pure heat.

I looked down. Around my feet, a ring of fire had formed. "Eek. Um. Should I be worried?"

"No. It can't hurt you."

I tamped out a bit of fire that was meandering toward Rowan. "I can make fire?"

He tipped me backward, his cheeks rubbing against my breasts, the sensation making my toes curl in ecstasy. "Dragons can, yes. I guess this means their mates have that ability, as well. From what I understand, it's a reaction to strong emotions. Are you feeling strong emotions, Sophea?"

"That's an understatement," I said, whimpering when he molested first one breast, then the other. My hands were still working on his belt, and finally got it free from the buckle, and the button on his waistband undone.

"Tell me what you want," he said, cupping my breast.

"You?" I said, hoping he wasn't going to make me catalog my every desire, because at that moment, I had a metric butt-ton of them.

That must have been the answer he was looking for, because he scooped me up and carried me to the bed. "That's ironic, because I happen to want you very badly. Impossibly so, as a matter of fact."

"Did you have a dream, too?" I asked, trying to arrange myself on the bed so I looked like a goddess about to receive her lover rather than a rumpled tourist with unsexy underwear and jet lag.

He paused as he was about to undo his zipper. "Why do you keep mentioning a dream?"

"Ignore my mouth. It says unimportant things," I said, donning a come-hither pose.

He dropped his pants, then quickly removed his underwear and crawled across the bed toward me.

"You changed out of your boots," I said by way of conversation, suddenly feeling shy. What did I know about Rowan, really, other than the fact that I wanted him more than anything I could think of?

He paused as he loomed over me, glancing toward the floor where he'd slipped out of a pair of brogues. "Yes, I did. Sophea?"

"Hmm?"

His eyes were guarded. "Did I misread your signals? Do you not wish for me to be here?"

"Not in the least. I really do want to be with you, Rowan. I want to make love to you. I want you to make love to me. I'm just...it's been a long time since I was with a man, and the first few minutes are always kind of awkward, don't you think? I mean, in the dream, you were just there, naked, kissing my breasts and touching me, and holy hells, your penis was Mr. Hello, I'll Be Your Penis for the Night. Oh, goddess, I'm babbling, aren't I?"

He laughed and pulled me up to him, one hand moving down to my thigh at the same time he leaned forward and kissed me. The dull heat inside me roared to life at the touch of his hand and mouth. "I like it when you babble. It's been some time for me, as well, but I don't see anything embarrassing here. All I see is a seductive woman who makes me insane with desire, one who has silky skin, glorious hair, and breasts that could make a sinner repent. Would you mind if I continued what we started in the other room?"

"You have my fullest cooperation," I said with a little giggle that turned into a gasp when he pulled off my underwear and bent over my personal bits, a wicked grin lighting up his eyes.

They weren't gold, though. They were a cloudy green.

"I'll hold you to that. Now, let's see if you like this."

His head dipped down and I damn near came off the bed.

"Yes!" I shrieked. "Yes, I like that. A whole lot. Do it again, please."

He did it again, and when I came close to going over the edge into an orgasm, he stopped.

"You are . . . that was . . . mmrowr," I purred, wanting to crawl up his body, and touch and taste him, all the while having him do the same things to me.

He smiled. "I'm glad you enjoyed it. You are very responsive."

"If that's your polite code for quick off the mark, you're absolutely right," I said, my entire body tight and humming and wanting so much more. I bit his shoulder, and gently pushed. With a raised eyebrow, he obligingly rolled onto his back.

"Not that this is a time to mention past experience, but dear heaven, Rowan, you really do know your way around lady parts. Do you mind if I reciprocate? And touch you? All of you?"

He tried to chuckle but it came out tight. "Be my guest."

My entire body was humming with anticipation, various and sundry parts of me demanding that I stop playing around and get down to business, but I've never been one to forgo some romping in the form of foreplay. I stroked a hand up his leg, thrilling in the sensation. "Mrs. P was right… you have really nice legs. I especially like your thighs."

"I object," he said, looking down his body at me as I spread his legs and knelt between them. "I didn't get to inventory you. If that's your intention, then I want equal time. I—"

He made an inarticulate noise and went stiff when I wrapped a hand around the base of his penis, giving it a friendly squeeze, not hard, just enough to let him know I was there.

"Such an odd piece of the body," I said, leaning forward to touch my tongue on what I figured was a sensitive spot. "And yet so very fascinating, too."

"Very," he gasped, his hips bucking at my touch. "Sophea, you must stop doing that or I won't be able to finish what I started."

I gave his sensitive spot one last swirl of my tongue, then enjoyed crawling up his body, kissing and nibbling my way up past that glorious chest. "I don't suppose you have a condom?" I asked when I reached his mouth.

He was writhing beneath me by then, but he stopped thrashing long enough to think. "No, I don't. I'm sorry, I didn't know I was going to meet you. I'd have brought an entire box if I had."

"It'll be okay this time," I said, gently biting his lower lip. His hands closed around my hips, trying to position me where he wanted me. "I get a shot that takes care of birth control, but if we do this again, we should probably have a little talk."

"I'll talk anytime you want," he promised, his hands moving around to my breasts. His thumbs made gentle little sweeps across my nipples that drove the inferno in me out of control, and without a thought of whether or not what I was doing was smart, I positioned him in the appropriate spot, and slowly sank down.

He groaned and closed his eyes with pleasure.

I gasped and said in a voice about an octave higher than normal, "Goddess, you're a lot beefier than you look. That's just... I know it's been a while, but still... criminy, there's *more* of you?"

All my intimate muscles rejoiced at the visitor and greeted him with a welcome embrace. And just when I was wondering if I'd ever come to the end of him, he started moving beneath me, and it was my erotic dream all over again.

Heat and desire and the incredible sensation of having him move within me drove me into a spiral of pleasure that absorbed every iota of my being until, with a particularly vigorous thrust upward, he sent me falling over the edge into an orgasm to end all orgasms.

I was dimly aware of Rowan's hoarse cry when he joined me, but I did notice, a few minutes later when my brain managed to kick-start itself, that he was breathing just as raggedly as I was. I looked up from where I'd collapsed on his chest to bite him on the chin.

"Ow," he said without opening his eyes. "What was that for?"

"I was checking to see if you were conscious. Great Caesar's ghost, Rowan, that was a hell of an experience. Beyond hell of an experience…it was…would earth-shattering be too much, do you think?"

Both corners of his mouth curled up, but his eyes remained closed. "That description works for me. And I can't take all of the credit. You did some of the work. A minuscule amount, granted, because my part was clearly the most important, but I don't want to be mean with regards to your contribution."

I wiggled around on him, doing a little Kegel to remind him that he was still inside of me. His eyes shot open. "Your part may have been the star of the show, but let's have a word of praise for my girly muscles. Those babies really worked overtime on you."

He grinned and kneaded my behind. "They did, indeed."

I rolled off him and glanced at the clock with a sigh. "Dammit. I should go check on Mrs. P, when all I want to do is snuggle and watch you fall asleep because you're a man, and pillow talk bores you."

"How do you know?" he asked, cocking an eyebrow at me. "Perhaps I am the pillow-talkiest man who ever lived."

He had me there. I realized in the post-coital glow that I really had done it this time—I'd thrown myself at a man whom I knew very little about.

"Sophea?" He propped himself up on an elbow, his expression concerned. "Did I say something wrong?"

"No." I sighed, and sat up. "You merely pointed out that I've gone and done it again."

"Done what again? Had sex? You weren't a virgin, were you? I'm not an expert, but you seemed to know what you were doing—"

"No, not that." I tried to explain, but couldn't find the words. "It's just... I'm sorry."

"I have a horrible feeling that this is the part of the evening where you say the words, 'It's not you, it's me,' and I will end up returning to my room to sit by myself and wonder what the hell happened."

I looked at him, really looked at him sitting there with his adorable mussed-up curls, and his chin that I just wanted to bite again, and that glorious naked chest, and I wondered what on earth I'd done. It wasn't like me to meet a man and suddenly fall under his spell... except that's just what had happened with Jian.

It wasn't like me to want to touch a man I'd just met, and enjoy being with him, and think long, lengthy thoughts about his mouth, and what I'd like to do it, and what I'd like it to do to me.

Except with Jian. I'd wanted to kiss him the first day I met him, too.

I was an independent woman, one who didn't need a man in her life to be happy. Just because I started to squirrel away thoughts with the intention of sharing them with Rowan didn't mean I was smitten with him. Women didn't become emotionally attached to men after just a day.

And yet, that's exactly how long it had taken me to want to be with Jian forever.

Oh, dear heaven, I was doing it again—I was falling in love with a man who was going to sweep me off my feet (in this case, literally)—and then after a mad whirl of a courtship, he'd leave me alone and grieving and empty inside again.

"Ack!" I leaped from the bed, and gathering up my pants and shirt, made a dash for the bathroom.

A minute later there was a polite tap at the door. "I'm

going to guess I've made a huge error by assuming you were as into this as I was, and will take myself away so you don't have to hide in the bathroom to avoid looking at me."

I opened the door, grabbed his head, and kissed him with everything I had in me.

"Or not," he said when I released him. He looked as confused as I felt. "Would you like to tell me what's going on?"

"If you die in the next day, I'm never going to forgive you," I told him.

He looked like he was thinking about that for a few seconds, then gave me another of those sexy bows. "Very well. I accept your terms."

I smiled. I just couldn't help myself. "You do make me happy. I'm just . . . I don't have the best luck with men who make me happy. They tend to get run down in the street."

"I promise I'll look both ways. Do you want me to help you find Mrs. P?"

"No, I'm pretty sure I know where she is."

He nodded and turned to leave. I followed him to the door to the hallway. "Rowan?"

"Yes?" He glanced back at me.

Dammit, I wanted to kiss the quirky corner of his mouth again. And the rest of it, come to think of it. "Thank you for helping with Mr. Kim and his buddy. As seriously awesome as my dragon's mate self is, I'm not sure I could have handled both of them."

He smiled and started to turn away, then suddenly pulled me up against his chest, bent me backward, and kissed the breath from my lungs. His tongue did a sinuous dance that had my legs melting from underneath me. By the time he was done, I was just a giant puddle of desire. He propped me up against the door, and said, “I think you’re much more awesome than you give yourself credit for. Just don’t underestimate Kim and his ilk. They are more dangerous than you know.”

I watched him walk to the doorway that led to the stairs before sliding down the door to the floor, fanning myself for a minute. “Hoo, boy. I think you’re the one I ought to be worried about.”

I ran Mrs. P to earth twenty minutes later, after I had a quick wash and bribed the desk clerk to give me Edvard’s room number.

“I want to talk to you in the morning,” I told her when I forcibly removed her from his room, where she was currently doing what she called the Dance of the Seven Towels. “We have a few things to chat about, not the least of which is why people have such an interest in your jewelry.”

“You’re too serious,” she told me, humming to herself as she entered her room. “Why isn’t your man here? He should be taking care of you, not leaving you to fend for yourself.”

I smiled a secret smile to myself, wondering if there was any chance in the world that I’d have a future with Rowan, or if our budding relationship was doomed from the beginning.

“Now that smile is much more hopeful,” she said, closing the door in my face.

I returned to my bed with the memory of Rowan’s body beneath mine, and erotic thoughts fighting with a good dozen or so questions for active brain time.

It didn’t occur to me until hours later that he never answered my question about what he was doing in Mrs. P’s room.

Seven

Stepping out of the Cairo airport was like going from a madhouse to a madhouse located in an oven.

I clutched Mrs. P's arm and said under my breath, "Thank god for Akbar One. I couldn't cope with this on my own."

The man in question must have heard me despite the din of taxis, people, and what seemed like a bazillion cars all crammed into an extremely small strip of road. "Yes, yes, I take good care of you," Akbar said with a flash of very white teeth. He was a young man of probably early twenties, and introduced us when we arrived in Cairo by explaining that we'd see a lot of Akbars around (and we did—there were at least three others holding up signs reading Akbar followed by a number), but that he was the best. "You follow me, I take care of you. Very nice car will drive you to your hotel. I show you pyramids, yes? You want to see pyramids?"

"Right now what I want most is a cold shower," I answered, plucking my shirt from where it was stuck to my sweaty self.

"Hotel first, yes, then pyramids," Akbar agreed with an amiable smile, and continued to force his way through the great herds of people that swarmed the taxi and pickup zone.

"I wouldn't mind a good stiff drink," a voice said behind me.

I made a face at the owner of the voice. "This is a Muslim country, Rowan."

"That doesn't mean one can't find alcohol," he answered and gestured me before him.

I took a firmer grip on Mrs. P's suitcase handle and plowed forward, keeping her close to me so she couldn't escape on another one of her "adventures."

Akbar led us through the throngs, noise, and general sense of chaos to a medium-sized sedan.

"I shall sit up front with the comely young man," Mrs. P said when I tried to help her into the back of the car. She slipped out of my grip, and before I could do anything, she scurried into the front seat where she sat with a defiant glint in her eye.

"I don't think that's really wise—" I started to say, but was interrupted when a somewhat breathless woman arrived and said, "Oh good, you got a car. We didn't have time to book one, what with trying to take out the remainder of demons in Munich before we had to fly out here."

May, the same small, dark-haired woman who was in the tea shop, brushed past me and entered the car, followed by Gabriel, the latter giving me a brief smile before he plopped himself down on the backseat.

I looked first at Rowan, who was busy typing something on his phone, then into the car. "Uh... hello again. I hate to be rude, but I don't think there's enough room for all of us. Mrs. P and I invited Rowan to ride with us to the Hotel Cleopatra, and this isn't a very big car..." I let the sentence trail off in obvious significance.

"Oh, that's all right," May said, lurching forward awkwardly. "I'll sit on Gabriel. He doesn't mind."

"Far from it," he said with a look that I felt was intended for her eyes only.

"But..." I glanced back at Rowan, not wanting to be outright rude in throwing out these interlopers, but at the same time, I had been looking forward to spending some time with him since we hadn't been able to talk at all during the flight from Munich to Cairo.

Rowan finished his text and tucked his phone into his pocket, looking at me expectantly.

I rolled my eyes toward the car in an attempt to get him to notice the occupants and, hopefully, have some advice about how to deal with them. Perhaps we could take a separate taxi? A glance down the taxi row left that idea dead at the start. Swarms of tourists were four deep on the sidewalk, all fighting over the available vehicles.

"Go ahead," he said, gesturing toward the car.

Akbar hovered behind me, adding, "Yes, yes, there is much room, plenty of room for all. Your friends wish to see the pyramids, too? I shall take you to them and you will have a most excellent experience."

Resigned, I sighed and slid into the backseat. Rowan followed, giving May and Gabriel a little nod before smooshing himself in next to me.

I had to admit that I didn't mind being pressed up against him, especially since his hand was resting casually on my thigh, but after a few moments of enjoying that, I had to remind myself that even if I was now technically a merry widow, it didn't mean I had to make obvious the fact that I wanted to jump Rowan's bones right that very second.

Dignity would be my watchword, I decided, covertly sliding my hand up Rowan's thigh. Dignity and circumspection.

"I understand you had a visit from our friends at the tea shop," Gabriel said as Akbar pulled into traffic and immediately slammed on the brakes to avoid hitting a car that cut him off. He muttered under his breath, shot a look to the side where Mrs. P sat, and we started forward again.

"Yes, we did. They were more obnoxious than ever, but we took care of the matter," Rowan answered in a distracted tone.

I stopped wondering how I could cop a quick grope of Rowan without the other two (unwanted) occupants seeing and leaned forward to say in a low tone, "I will ask Akbar to pull over if you continue such shenanigans, Mrs. P."

She shot me an injured look that melted into a high-pitched cackle. "Your man wouldn't like that at all."

"This isn't about Rowan. It's about you behaving yourself when we are in a moving vehicle capable of killing us or others. No shenanigans, please."

"Shenanigans," she repeated, rolling the word around in her mouth. "I like that. Would you care to engage in some shenanigans later, young man?"

Akbar, luckily, was too focused on the hellish nightmare that was traffic streaming from the airport into Cairo proper and didn't answer.

"Hands to yourself," I reminded her and sat back in my seat, smooshing myself against Rowan. I tried to tell myself it was silly to get so worked up over a little innocent contact, but the girly part of my mind was squealing softly to itself, and wondering if it was too soon to ask him to spend the night in my hotel room.

"There were three others who arrived in the small hours of the morning, but we handled them, as well," Gabriel said, pulling my attention from the pleasant (if smutty) thoughts about Rowan.

"Three other who?" I asked, throwing grammar to the wind. "Or should I say what?"

Gabriel glanced toward the driver, but as Akbar was now providing a running commentary to Mrs. P on the various buildings we were passing, Gabriel evidently felt it was safe to speak. "Our friends from Bael are more what than who, but as they were once our kin, I shall refrain from saying more."

Rowan's hand brushed my leg again, causing heat to pool low inside of me. Just how long was this cab ride going to take? I began to speculate how much time it would take to get Mrs. P settled before I could pounce on Rowan.

"We should be safe enough for a few hours," Gabriel continued.

That pulled my attention from my plan to seduce Rowan. "Really? Rowan said that the...uh...guys who attacked us weren't really...you know...but that they just had to re-form, so to speak."

"He's correct," Gabriel said with a little nod.

Rowan felt nice and solid next to me. He turned his head to face Gabriel, which meant his breath teased my hair when he spoke. I might have leaned a bit into him.

"I've heard that the re-forming takes time," he said, "unless the being in question is summoned to a new form. Is that true?"

"Absolutely," May answered. "Which should give us

just enough time to transact our business once we get to the hotel before the baddies get themselves back here."

"Business?" I asked somewhat suspiciously. I was getting a bit tired of being so paranoid as to suspect everyone I met, but given the experiences that Mrs. P and I had had during the last twenty-four hours, I figured it was allowed. "What sort of business?"

Gabriel's silver gaze flickered toward the driver, but he said nothing. Apropos of nothing, I decided that I liked Rowan's eyes better. Rather than just one color, there was depth to the greenish gray of Rowan's. One moment they were downright verdant, and the next they looked like clear water over a mossy rock. Mind you, I liked the dream version best of all, but that was just a fantasy, and I was more than happy to settle for reality.

"Wait a minute." A thought intruded on my contemplation of Rowan's eyes. "*Our* kin? You're talking about..." I made claw hands and said softly, "Rawr?"

Gabriel looked startled for a moment.

"Gabriel is the wyvern of the silver sept," May said, giving him a look that beamed with pride.

"Are you indeed. How nice." I wondered what the hell a wyvern was, not to mention a silver sept, and made a mental note to Google both once we were at the Cairo hotel.

"Yes. Although he doesn't get very...rawry...often."

"Only when there is room for a proper chase," he said with a solemnity that was ruined by a glint in his eyes that had May leaning in to whisper something in his ear.

I glanced at Rowan to see how he was taking this banter and whether he might like to do a little whispering of his own, but he was leaning back in the seat with his eyes closed. I "accidentally" jostled him with my arm, causing him to jerk and open his eyes.

"Hmm?" he said.

"Didn't you get any sleep?" I asked, concerned for his welfare, and not just because I had plans for him that night.

"Not really, no."

"But it wasn't even midnight when I fetched Mrs. P back from her assignation with the unwilling Edvard."

"He had nice thighs," Mrs. P piped up from the front seat. "Horseman's thighs. Like your man's. Too bad you interrupted us before Edvard had time to demonstrate his riding abilities."

"Mrs. P!" I said, scandalized at her innuendo.

She cackled to herself and edged closer to Akbar.

"I'm going to be so glad to hand her over to whoever is here to pick her up," I told Rowan *sotto voce*. "And speaking of that, I know we had a heck of an evening, but the rest of last night was pretty quiet."

"Yes. But I didn't know it was going to be so uneventful, or I would have gone back to my room and gotten some sleep."

I twisted around to look him full in the face, noticing the darkness under his eyes and the little lines of strain around his mouth. He also had a light stubble that made my fingers itch to touch it. "What do you mean? You didn't sleep at all?"

"No." He leaned back and closed his eyes again. "I watched your room all night in case others came to disturb you."

Something inside me warmed at his words. "That... I had no idea... oh, Rowan, I wish you'd told me. I would have sat up with you."

The corner of his mouth that I liked so much quirked

upward for a few seconds. "That would have been counterproductive. My goal was to ensure you two rested uninterrupted, and if you had been with me... well, I doubt if you'd have gotten rest."

I cleared my throat in a meaningful manner and slid a look toward May and Gabriel. They were conversing softly and didn't appear to be listening, but you never knew. With a neutral voice, I said, "At the cost of your own sleep. Well, at least you'll be able to sleep well tonight. Mrs. P is due to get on a river cruise this evening, so you can relax and not worry about her being pestered by those guys again."

"Mmmhmm." His face softened and I had the worst urge to snuggle into him and keep watch while he took some much-needed rest.

But before he drifted off completely, I leaned into him and whispered very softly, "What's a wyvern?"

"Dragon leader," he mumbled, and wiggled his shoulders to get more comfortable against the seat, his head turning toward the window.

I fought the urge to brush back a strand of hair that had fallen down over his eyebrow and told myself that despite our assignation the night before, he was not my man to fuss over. We had just gotten together to scratch a couple of mutual itches. Despite my propensity for falling for men without waiting to know them well, I couldn't count on him feeling the same way about me as I felt about him. Men just didn't dive into emotions like that.

Besides, there was the Jian factor to be thought of. What if I was cursed? What if Rowan risked his life to be with me? Four days was all it had taken before Jian and I marched down the steps of city hall, and already I'd known Rowan for two days. What if he left tomorrow to go back to his Amazonian rain forest, leaving me to return to L.A. alone?

A familiar sense of loneliness swept over me, one that had beset me ever since Jian was killed.

To stop myself from dwelling on the many ways my life was messed up, I turned to Gabriel and May, and with a quick check of Akbar (now telling Mrs. P about how he was happy to escort her through a Cairo museum to better understand the exhibits), I asked quietly, "So you're both dragons?"

An odd look crossed May's face. "Gabriel is, of course, although to be strictly accurate, I wasn't born a dragon. First I was his mate, and then due to an interaction with the First Dragon, I became . . . more."

"The who now?" I asked.

"The First Dragon is the progenitor of all dragonkin," Gabriel answered. "All dragons who ever were and ever will be are descended from him."

"And he made you one, too?" I asked May, feeling a whole lot less special, which was stupid because I was a dragon's mate, too. I was almost a mythical being, and how many people could say that?

"I guess he did," she said after a few seconds of significant looks exchanged with Gabriel. "Although I never thought about it in that light. It's not like he just bopped me on the head and made me that way, though. I'm not sure he can do that, to be honest."

"He can do anything he desires," Gabriel said drily.

"Including damning innocent men for acts beyond their control," Rowan said, his voice muffled since his chin was wedged into his shoulder.

Gabriel was silent for the count of five. "I don't know

about that, but I do know that we owe our existence to the First Dragon. And he was good to May, which I will be thankful for to the end of my time."

"He can't be that good of a dad to you guys if he has children like Mr. Kim running around," I said, remembering the glint of the knife Mr. Kim had used to threaten us.

"Ah, but that is not the First Dragon's fault. That is the doing of Bael."

"Sure it is," I agreed, wondering if I should go to the trouble of nudging Rowan and asking him who Bael was or if I should just let it go.

Just get Mrs. P to the hotel, I told myself. *Then you can hand her over to the cruise people and go home, where life is normal, and there are no dragons and demons and people trying to steal other people's possessions, and no heartbreakingly handsome men with gray-green eyes to lust after, and worry about, and wonder if he'll last longer than four days.*

A tiny little voice told me how sad it would be to live a normal life without Rowan to spice it up, but I ignored it.

I fell silent at that point, paying little attention to the discussion that May and Gabriel held about whether or not more demonic dragons would show up in Cairo or if they'd give up the attempt now that they knew the dragons were protecting Mrs. P.

The Hotel Cleopatra wasn't at all what I was expecting, but then, what had been on this trip? "Well, that's... interesting," I said as we got out of the car. A giant bust of Cleopatra loomed over the entrance, much like a figurehead sat on the prow of a ship. On each side of her were twin half-naked Nubian slaves, each with a palm in hand that jutted out over the entrance, providing shade from the merciless Egyptian sun. "It kind of reminds me of Disney."

Rowan glanced up at Cleopatra, his eyes widening when he took in her impressive bust barely encased by what surely was a teenage boy's idea of historic costume appropriate to Cleopatra's era.

"Unusual, to be sure," Rowan said before taking his rucksack from Akbar.

"Especially in a mostly Muslim country. Oh well, we won't see her from inside," I said, grabbing Mrs. P as she started after Akbar. "Come on, let's get checked in for the few hours it'll be before we have to get you to your cruise."

"You are checking into the hotel just for a few hours?" May asked.

"Mrs. P will be here just for a few hours, yes. I figured we can do a little sightseeing if she's up to it, and if she's not, she can rest. Then she'll go on to the cruise and I'll spend the night here and leave in the morning." A little pang of sadness hit me at my words.

"Bye bye, sweet cheeks," Mrs. P told Akbar, blowing him a kiss. "I'll tell my beau how knowledgeable about his life you are. He will be appreciative to know his time is remembered so well."

"We're going to see him in a couple of hours if you're up to the tour of the pyramids, so you needn't make a dramatic farewell scene yet. And what on earth was all that about?" I asked her as we entered the hotel. "All I heard Akbar talking about was Egyptian myths and what life was like back then and stuff like that."

"He is a nice lad. As polite as your man, but not so stuffy. Probably has more stamina in bed, though. Stamina is such a waste on the young. I want some tea."

"All righty. Let me just get us checked in, and I'll get

us a late lunch, okay? Hello. I'm Sophea Long, and this is Mrs. Papadopolous. We have reservations."

We finished checking in and I scooted to the side while Rowan acquired a room of his own (he didn't book ahead) before asking him, "We're going to have some lunch in a short bit. Did you want to join us? It'll be our treat for you sitting up all night making sure we were safe."

He looked like he was going to say no, but just then his stomach growled audibly, and he gave an apologetic little laugh. "I believe that is answer enough."

May and Gabriel were now at the reception desk, obviously getting a room. I knew I should extend the offer of lunch to them, since they clearly had some role in keeping the demon dragons at bay, but a wave of selfishness had me steering Mrs. P toward the elevator with one hand while grasping Rowan's arm with the other. "Tell you what, I'll order room service so you won't have to face sitting in a restaurant surrounded by tourists. Then you can go have a nap."

He turned when we reached the elevator and nodded toward May and Gabriel. "What about them?"

"They can find their own lunch, I'm sure." I immediately felt guilty at the flash of surprise in his eyes. "I'm sorry. That's catty of me. If you would like them to join us, I'll ask them."

A little frown pulled his eyebrows together. "I get the feeling that you don't care for Gabriel and May."

"I don't. Rather, I don't trust them."

"Why not? They are your own kind, after all."

"They don't *look* like dragons," I said, glancing past him at the people in question.

"Neither do you."

"No, but I clearly *am* dragonish," I said with a complacence that I realized was fully at odds with the fact that less than a day before, I refused to accept the fact that there even were such things as dragons in human form, let alone that Jian was one of them. "Did you see the way I kicked Elton out of the window? That was a serious dragon move going on there."

He gave a little chuckle and escorted us into the empty elevator when the doors opened. "It was indeed, but I believe you're judging Gabriel unfairly because he wasn't there to help us fight the demons. I have no doubt he's capable of equally impressive dragon moves, as you call them."

I kept the door from closing and nodded toward the reception desk. "Maybe. Do you want me to invite them or not?"

Rowan shrugged. "I'm sure you're right and they can find their own lunch. I just thought you'd like someone relatable that you could talk to."

"Another time, perhaps," I said, knowing full well that I'd be on a plane heading back home the following day.

By myself.

Without Rowan.

And worse, without the likelihood of ever seeing him again.

I grew morose at that thought, a feeling that stayed with me while I bustled Mrs. P into the room we would share for a few hours until she went off to her cruise and made her a cup of tea while trying to keep her from confiscating everything she could see.

Finally, I got her to relax on the bed with her feet up for a little bit. "I told Rowan to meet us here in half an hour, which gives me to time to call the tour company in Cairo and make sure everything is copacetic for your trip. No, you can't take that. The Gideon people put it there for others to use...oh, what the hell. Knock yourself out. You might want to read up on the bit about thou shalt not steal, though."

It took a good fifteen minutes, but at last I worked my way through to someone at the cruise company who spoke English. "Hello. I'm confirming the arrival of Mrs. Papadopolous for the Duat River Cruise leaving tonight at eight p.m. Am I correct in the assumption that she'll need to be to the ship an hour before sailing?"

"Yes, that is very correct," answered a man in lyrical English. "Let me check the records. Papadopolous, you say? I do not have anyone by that name."

Panic hit me. I hadn't even thought about what I'd do if something was munged up with Mrs. P's reservation. "Uh...are you sure? Her grandson told me he booked her reservation himself. Maybe you could look again?"

"Does Madame have another name? I do not see Papadopolous."

Unreasonably, I felt the urge to burst into tears. We'd come such a long way and been through so much in the last twenty-four hours. "She doesn't have another name, no."

"I do," Mrs. P said, looking up from the TV where she'd put on a channel of Middle Eastern music videos. "I am known by many names."

"I doubt very much if your grandson would have booked you under your hoochie-coo dancer name," I told her, my hand over the mouthpiece. "Did he book it under your maiden name or something?"

"I have never been married," she said with a sniff, and turned up the music video. "My beau gives me much leeway in this world, but he wouldn't allow me to bind myself to another."

"What is your maiden name?" I asked, more than a little desperate now.

"My name when I was a maiden?" She smiled. Oddly, it made her faded eyes look brighter. "Aset."

"Asset?" I asked, confusion now adding to my frustration. "Like something a company has?"

"No, Aset." She spelled it for me, putting the stress on the first letter of the word. "It is my child-name."

That sounded like a maiden name to me. "Would you have a reservation for a Mrs. Aset?" I asked, uncovering the mouthpiece.

"Madame Aset? But of course." The man sounded so matter-of-fact it confused me even more. "We have the reservation for Madame Aset and companion in Grand Suite B. It is our finest accommodation, you understand."

"Awesome. I'll have her to the ship by seven . . . wait, did you say Mrs. Aset and companion? What companion?"

"We were not informed of the individual's name. Our understanding was that information would be provided upon boarding. Is there anything else I can help with?"

"No, thank you, that will be all." I hung up and looked at Mrs. P, who was now eying a woven cotton wall covering with a speculative eye. "Who is going on the cruise with you?"

She gave me a pitying look. "Has the prospect of lunch with your man caused you to lose your wits? You are my guide."

"I'm not a guide," I said, startled. "I'm a . . . well, helper is as good a description as anything. I'm just here to get you to your ship. I'm not going with you on it."

Her eyes narrowed on me. "You must help me across the Duat to my beau. You agreed to do so. You cannot back out now—I can't face the challenges by myself. I am a priestess of Heka, not Isis herself."

I sighed, suddenly wishing like the dickens that I'd never answered the door to Jian's cousin. What *was* his name?

"Mrs. P," I said gently but firmly. "I realize that you have a really splendid imagination, and that you were absolutely right about Jian being a dragon, but just because you were right about that doesn't mean that everything you think is real is actually so. You're just a little confused. Duat is the name of the cruise line—it's not a real place."

She shook her head sadly at me.

"And Isis is . . . was . . . an Egyptian goddess. I think. I'm not very hip on Egyptian myths and lore. So while I agree that you are not Isis, I'm not sure where this idea came from that I'm your guide."

A knock sounded at the door. I got up to answer it.

"You must guide me," she insisted. "You are a dragon's mate. Only your kind can defeat the challenges that will face us."

"Hi," I said to Rowan when he stepped into the room. I was sorry to see that he'd not only combed his hair but also shaved. So much for that tempting stubble. "I hope you're hungry. I'm famished, and I think Mrs. P could use a little food in her stomach. I suspect her blood sugar is low and it's making her a bit . . . scattered."

He raised his eyebrows and took the chair I gestured at, while I went to fetch the room service menus. "The trip from Munich seemed fairly uneventful."

"Oh, it was, and Mrs. P dozed most of the way, but now she's insisting that I'm supposed to go on the cruise with her, and I'm having a hard time making her understand that I'm just a helper monkey, and not a tour guide.

Now, Mrs. P, do you feel like something light or a more substantial meal? I'm sure there will be snackies on the boat when you get there, but since that's a good four hours away, I'd suggest getting a full meal now. It looks like they have chicken thighs stuffed with rice and pine nuts, or a tenderloin with grilled veggies that you might like. And some lamb dishes, but I personally won't eat a wee little baby lamb. Not that it matters to you, but still."

"Tell the gel she must come with me," Mrs. P demanded of Rowan. "I cannot make the trip alone. It is too dangerous. Too many people want my offering."

Rowan looked startled.

I asked, "Your what now?"

"My offering." She gestured toward her chest. "It is for my beau. Without it, we can't be together. And I can't give it to him without a guide taking me to him."

"Mrs. P…" I sat silent for a moment, helpless against her fantasies. Clearly some sort of dementia was beginning to grip her, despite the fact that she'd been unusually prescient about my true origins. But this was just beyond me. "I don't know what to say."

"She can't go with you," Rowan said quickly, and gave a little embarrassed cough. "That is, I got the last available cabin. There won't be any more available. And I would be more than happy to guide you."

I looked at him with wonder and a wee bit of suspicion. Why was he being so helpful all of a sudden? And did he just try to get me out of the picture?

Hurt pierced deep and hot, but I pushed that aside to try to think rationally about the situation. Did Rowan's sudden offer have something to do with this ring he was so interested in? Surely he couldn't have nefarious plans for it, not after we'd spent such a wonderful time together. And he seemed as much into me as I was in him…

Slowly, my gaze dropped, a sick feeling in my stomach.

Had he used me just to get in a position where he could rob Mrs. P?

Eight

Rowan was panicked, good and simple. Here he thought he'd been one step ahead of Sophea by booking the last available cabin on the ship, and now Mrs. P was demanding that Sophea be included in the trip.

Dammit, he had had a hard enough time sneaking into Mrs. P's room without having to contend with a watchful Sophea, not to mention one who, if she learned the truth about the ring, might very well take it for her own purposes.

His brain came to a screeching halt at that idea. As if Sophea—warm, wonderful, giving Sophea—would do something so heinous. He might have had suspicions of her at first, but not now, not when he knew just what a wonderful woman she was.

One who made him hard just thinking about her.

He crossed his legs and thought strenuously for a few minutes about the plight of the Incas under the rule of the conquistadors.

"Oh, that doesn't matter," Sophea said, and for a moment, Rowan had forgotten the direction of the conversation. Sophea's voice sounded choked.

It was on his lips to ask her what was wrong when she continued.

"Mrs. P evidently has some super fancy suite, and I'm sure that means it has more than one bed. But the fact is that I was hired to bring her here, not take the cruise with her. And certainly not guide her. I don't know the first thing about the Egyptian sites." She glanced at a clock on the nightstand. "Although Akbar is due to pick us up in an hour for a trip to the pyramids, so I suppose I'll learn something there."

"I'm sure you'd much rather be home where the weather isn't into triple digits during the day and the company is more congenial than a bunch of elderly tourists," he said, feeling his powers of persuasion lacking. "I know I would much rather be at home where I could continue my research rather than be here."

"Oh?" She seemed to be avoiding catching his eye. For some reason, she was hurt by that, wondering if he'd inadvertently slighted her. Her nose wrinkled in a way that he found utterly adorable. "Then why are you going on the cruise if you'd rather be elsewhere?"

"It's part of a job I have to do," he said after several awkward seconds of silence. "Not one I want to conduct but unfortunately, necessary."

"Huh," she said, studying her hands.

Rowan felt like a heel lying to her in that manner, but he didn't want to ask her what was wrong when she had her hands full with Mrs. P.

Later, he promised himself, his body reacting to the idea of spending the night with her. Later he would get the source of her suddenly unhappy mien. Except...later he would be on a ship, and she would be going back home.

And that thought filled him with the morose satisfaction that everything that could go wrong was going wrong.

Except Sophea. She was the one bright, shining delight in the hellish nightmare his life had become, a delight he wasn't going to allow to be harmed. "If you're worried about Mrs. P's safety, I can assure you that I'll keep a very close eye on her," he reassured her.

"But you are not a dragon," Mrs. P said fretfully.

"No, but I can keep you safe."

"I must have a dragon. Only a dragon can face the challenges and keep my shiny safe." Mrs. P fretted with the material of her blouse.

"Well..." Sophea bit her lower lip in thought, and Rowan was aware of yet another surge of blood to his nether regions. Quickly, he thought of various methods of medieval torture. Once he had his desires under control, he chided himself for having such an instant reaction to Sophea.

He'd have to be a saint not to be affected by her, he told himself by way of excuse for what appeared to be a permanent erection. He casually picked up a throw pillow and laid it on his lap.

Dammit, it wasn't his fault if she was a temptress, a silken-skinned, desirable temptress. Perhaps it was her innocence that appealed to him or the fact that she needed a mentor, one who could teach her what world she had been born into. Or the need to shelter her, to protect her from the harshness of the world that she'd had all too much experience with. Then again, it might be the purity that wrapped around her like a cloak. She wasn't tainted by tragedy, as he was. She was wholesome and intriguing, and very, very feminine. And he very much wished he was buried in her right at that moment.

"To be honest, I don't really have to go home to anything. I mean, I'm not working, and I have to admit, a cruise does sound heavenly. But I'd have to clear it with Jian's cousin first. For all I know, he might have someone arranged to join Mrs. P here, and just didn't mention it to me."

"Jian's cousin?" he asked.

"Jian was my husband," Sophea explained, still not meeting his eye. "His cousin is the one who called me up and asked me to get Mrs. P to the boat. I found his number this morning, but haven't had time to check in with him. I suppose I should give him a quick call now."

She rose and took the phone with her into bathroom, obviously to make her call in private.

Rowan looked at the old woman on the bed as she perused the menu. "Why do you want Sophea with you so badly?"

"She must accompany me. There are monsters in Duat and many challenges. Only a dragon can triumph over them."

"Is that why you stole the ring? Is it your offering?"

She peered over the top of the menu at him. "I have changed my mind. You must come, too."

He stared for a moment, startled. "You know that I want the ring, do you not?"

"Everyone wants it." She returned to her examination of the menu. "None but my beau shall have it, though."

"Do you know why I want it?"

She said one word, but it damned near pierced his heart. "Danegeld."

"What do you know about that?" he asked, pulling the

menu from her hands. He was exhausted and worn down by what seemed to be endless worry. "Who exactly are you?"

She straightened her shoulders. "I am Aset. Who are you?"

"You know who I am," he said, slowly sitting down on the bed next to the old lady's.

"You say you are nothing but a mere mortal, but you are not." She plucked the menu from his hands and opened it. "It is clear to me that you must come on the journey as well. Your debt is due to be called in. You must pay for your sins. You must pay for the deaths of those dragons."

His stomach tightened painfully, and his voice, when he spoke, was hoarse. "What do you know about that?"

She gave a one-shouldered shrug. "Where do thoughts come from? My knowledge is my own, but it is accurate. If you do not make this journey across the Duat with us, you will forfeit your life."

"I'm going to lose it anyway if the dragons tell their ancestor that I'm here." Rowan rubbed his face. "I've been living on borrowed time for the last twenty years."

"The First Dragon was merciful," she said, looking once again at him over the top of the menu. Her eyes were substantially brighter than they had been a few minutes before. "He gave you time to repay the debt, but you did not."

"I couldn't," he said, shaking his head. "I had to go into hiding. If the dragons knew where I was, they'd demand that I do nothing but practice my art for their benefit, and who knows where that would end. Possibly in more deaths."

"You are such a bad alchemist, then?"

"I am an unlearned one, and that equates to being bad, yes. I haven't broken any magic since that horrible night."

"The First Dragon will not be pleased," she said, still shaking her head.

"I doubt he ever was pleased when it concerned me," Rowan said tiredly. He tried to organize his thoughts into sensible clumps. "I wish you'd tell me how you know about my past. It's not something that people outside of the dragon circles know about. In fact, the only people I told about my first experience in alchemy were my parents, and they are both dead."

"The First Dragon knows," she said coyly, and slowly raised the menu so that it blocked his view. "Do not discourage Sophea. You will need her, just as I will need you both."

"I must have that ring," he said, a sense of almost unbearable tiredness settling firmly around him. "I don't wish to take it from you by force, but I will if I have to. The fate of the mortal world rests on it."

"The fate of my happiness rests on it as well, and I have been too long without my beau," Mrs. P countered without even flicking the menu at him. "Without my offering, all will be lost."

"You can say that again. Look—I can get you something else of value to offer your boyfriend. Gold, if you like. Precious jewels. Hell, even stacks of money if that's what you want. All I ask for is that you give the ring to me, and I'll make sure you have something of tremendous value to use as your offering."

"You owe danegeld to the First Dragon for the deaths of his descendants," she said with what sounded like a righteous sniff. "You cannot even pay that, and yet you offer me the world?"

"I'll deal with the danegeld later," he said somewhat snappishly. He moderated his voice, feeling like a brute who would yell at a little old lady. "It's not like the First Dragon is going to join us on the cruise and demand I pay it right then and there."

"Ha!" She tossed the menu aside as Sophea emerged from the bathroom.

He wanted to ask Mrs. P what she'd meant by that, but Sophea, with a couple of lines between her brows, said slowly, "I can't reach him. I get some weird answering service that makes reference to the owner of that voice mailbox being permanently unavailable. Why do you have voice mail if you are not ever going to get it? And why, oh why, didn't I write down his name? I can't even look him up online to find another phone number for him."

He didn't answer, and Sophea cast him a questioning look. "Are you okay? You look pale."

"I'm fine," he croaked, and cleared his throat. "I'm just a bit…frustrated." He gave her a potent glance, hoping she would pick up on his meaning, but she simply went over to sit on the end of Mrs. P's bed. "I think we'd all feel better with a little food. Did you pick out what you want for lunch, Rowan?"

He was tempted to answer, "You," but caught himself in time. He wished Sophea would sit next to him, as she had in the car, where he could breathe in the sweet scent of her, one that reminded him of orange blossom honey.

She tasted just as sweet, and once again, he had to adjust the pillow in his lap to keep his thoughts from being obvious. Part of his mind was irritated that she held such power over him, while the other part was cataloging all the things about her he liked, everything from that sleek, glossy black hair to the tilt of her enticing eyes, and the way she seemed to exude warmth.

He wanted her to exude on him, again. He wanted her making shy little touches to his thigh, and pressing into him until he just wanted to take her in his arms. He wanted her mind, her unique mind thinking about him. He wanted to hear her brag how badass she was, and to make sure that nothing dinged that newfound confidence in herself.

He had no idea why he'd become so fascinated by her, but he wasn't going to fight the attraction.

Except, of course, that he had to get her out of there. She wasn't safe on the trip into Duat, and he wasn't sure if he had the power to keep her from harm. Just the thought of something happening to her while they were in the Egyptian underworld left him feeling cold and clammy inside.

He had to keep her away from potential trouble. Once he had the ring, once the demons weren't trying to get it, then he would return to her and beg her to take pity on him.

The problem was...he shook his head to himself. Sophea had warned him she wouldn't help get the ring, not that she knew the importance of it, but instinctively, he knew that even if she had been aware of it, she'd be loath to do anything to harm Mrs. P.

Dragons were fiercely loyal beings, and even though she wasn't a full-fledged member of that species, clearly Sophea had given Mrs. P her loyalty and would move heaven and earth to protect her. No, he said to his warring bodily desires. She had to be kept safe. And the only way to do that was to get her to go back home.

"Rowan?"

"Eh?"

She waggled the menu at him. "Lunch?"

"Ah." He cleared his throat a second time, and said only slightly hoarsely, "The steak will do nicely for me."

"Meat eater, eh?" She flashed him an irrepressible smile that almost immediately faded to nothing. "I try to stick to a vegetarian diet, but then I cave to temptation, like last night."

He was tired, that was all. Overly tired, and stressed, and unhappy over being involved in this unpleasant job, and that's the reason why the time he'd spent with Sophea the night before had blown up in his mind to an event the likes of which he'd never experienced.

"Those sausages were something, weren't they?"

And now you're lying to yourself, his quiet inner voice said with a disappointed *tsk. Just admit it—she has a body that fits you perfectly, a naiveté that makes you want to protect her from the evils of the world, and a quirky mind that exactly suits your own warped sense of humor. You fancy her, mate, pure and simple. So tell her, already, and be happy for a change.*

"Oh, shut up," he muttered, but evidently not softly enough, because Sophea tossed a startled look his way.

"Pardon?"

"Sorry, it was nothing. Just me talking to myself."

Her nose scrunched in that delightful manner she had. "I thought you were referring to my sausage double entendre. Do you often tell yourself to shut up?"

"I do when my mind is being obnoxious. If you'll excuse me a moment, I'll go wash my hands before we eat."

He used the few minutes of privacy in the bathroom to get his errant mind (and related body parts) under control. The face that stared out of the mirror at him bore obvious signs of strain—there were silver threads starting to show up in his hair, his cheeks had a gaunt look that he hadn't noticed before, and lines that he hadn't remembered had suddenly sprouted at the edges of both eyes.

"You look like hell," he told his reflection. "No woman in her right mind would consider you as a viable sexual partner, let alone someone to spend any length of time with. Get the job done and go back to Sao Pedro where the only thing you have to worry about is interfering tourists."

His inner voice had some things to say about that, but he ignored them, instead focusing his intentions on talking Sophea out of taking the cruise. He had a horrible feeling she was misinterpreting his desire to keep her safe, but he would simply straighten that out later, once he knew she was removed from any danger.

"—well and fine, but don't know what I'm going to do about clothes. I mean, this cruise is for a week, and I only packed two days' worth of clothes," Sophea was saying when he exited the bathroom. "And I don't have much money to buy more."

"Cruises always call for lots of clothing," Rowan said, nodding sagely just as if he knew what he was talking about. Which he didn't—he'd never been on a cruise in his life. "Far better to save your money for other things, don't you think?"

"I'm a pretty thrifty person, so I tend to agree," Sophea said slowly. "But... the thought of a free cruise is awfully hard to turn down."

"There's the souk," Mrs. P said, stuffing some pens and hotel paper into her bag. "Clothing can be had there for a few coppers."

"The bazaar?" Sophea pursed her lips in thought. It just made him want to kiss her. "I doubt if things are that cheap, although I did read that people here expect you to bargain for things. I wonder..."

"I wouldn't risk it," he said, nodding toward the clock.

"You wouldn't have time to get to the bazaar district, shop, and get back for the sailing."

"Yeah, that's true," she said, biting her lower lip. "We're all supposed to go see the pyramids anyway. Although I suppose we could souk it up after that, if there's time."

He had to look away, lest a lascivious expression give away his memories about nibbling on that delicious pink lip.

"My beau will reward you once I am returned to him," Mrs. P said, tucking the cordless phone into her sizeable purse, along with an ashtray and the mints from Sophea's pillow. "Stop blathering and get me some tea."

"Well..." Sophea looked him full in the eyes. "What do you think I should do?"

Go home, he ordered his mouth to say. The words were on the tip of his tongue when he opened his mouth, but somehow what came out ended up being, "Take the cruise, of course. Mrs. P says she needs you."

"You're right," she said with an oddly unsure look at him. "It would be stupid to look a gift horse in the mouth, right? Sorry, Mrs. P, I didn't mean to call you a horse. But you're both right—I'd kick myself for the rest of my life if I didn't take this opportunity. Stop waffling and take the bull by the balls, the matron at the orphanage used to say, and that's just what I'm going to do. If we don't have time to go to the bazaar after the pyramid tour, then I'll just buy some clothes at the villages we're sure to stop by. Well! This is exciting, isn't it? Rather than being sad because I'm going to be leaving you, we're all setting off on an exciting adventure. *Together*."

She put an emphasis on the word that baffled him—was she implying she was looking forward to more rendezvous as they had the night before, or was she hinting at something else? And if it was the former, why did she have a glum air about her?

Sophea rose at the sound of a knock and waited silently while a waiter delivered their food.

He stared dumbly at the plate set before him, his mind alternating between berating himself and fighting the desire to grab Sophea and kiss her like he'd had the night before. What had he been thinking, telling her to join them?

Well, he'd just have to work doubly hard to make sure that she was not put in harm's way if the demons should return—and despite Gabriel's optimistic outlook, he had little doubt that they'd not seen the last of them.

In the end, he ate his food, letting Sophea run the conversation, answering only when she asked him a direct question.

"You look tired," she said as they finished the meal. "Why don't you go take a nap for a couple of hours rather than go with Akbar to see the pyramids? Unless you really want to see them, that is."

He looked first at her, then at Mrs. P, who was busily rolling up a small rattan mat and sliding it into her suitcase. "I think that's an excellent idea. I'll rest while you're out. Away from the hotel. Er... seeing the sights."

Sophea exclaimed at the time. "Criminy, how did it get to be this late? Akbar will be waiting for us in ten minutes. I'll just take a fast shower before we go, Mrs. P, all right? Be sure to drink all that tea—we don't need you getting dehydrated while we're out seeing the pyramids!"

The room seemed strangely empty when she hurried into the bathroom with her bag in hand.

Silence reigned for a few minutes before Mrs. P, sipping noisily at her cup of tea, set it down and observed, "Her exuberance for life is endearing, is it not?"

He got to his feet slowly, feeling as if he were at least two hundred years old, and moved casually toward the door. Sitting on a small table next to it were two key cards. "Did you tell her the truth when you said you knew who her father was?"

Mrs. P cocked her head, and to his surprise, winked. "Perhaps I did, and perhaps I wanted to waken the gcl to the truth. Go, now. You cannot be my champion if you are likely to drop from exhaustion. We have many trials ahead of us before I will reach my beau."

He paused at the door, opened it, and turned back to face Mrs. P, using his body to shield the fact that he was taking one of the key cards. As a distraction in case she noticed the movement of his arm, he asked, "I take it your boyfriend is in the Underworld?"

The wrinkles in her face rearranged themselves into a smile. "Of course. Who else but a denizen of that realm could summon me to him?"

Rowan slid the card into his back pocket and racked his mind through the dusty corridors of past history classes. "Set was the lord of the Egyptian underworld, wasn't he? No, I lie—it was Osiris. Is that who you think you're going to meet?"

She wrapped her scrawny arms carefully around her hunched torso. "He has called me home at last. Somehow, he acquired the means, and we will be reunited again. And with my offering, he will be made whole, and will at last take his rightful place in the world."

Rowan tried to get his tired brain to process that, but it refused. It just outright refused. Instead, he nodded and quietly closed the door, returning to his room where he collapsed on the bed.

But not before setting an alarm for an hour. By that time, Mrs. P's room should be empty, and he would be able at last to search her things...and Sophea's. Just in case Mrs. P got clever with hiding places.

Exactly an hour and ten minutes later, he tapped on their door, heard nothing, and quietly opened it.

The room had been torn apart, everything from the bedding to the clothes, even to the cushions on the chairs torn to literal shreds. Little particles of furniture stuffing floated gently in the air, stirred by the quiet rush of coolness from the air conditioner. He surveyed the damage. Even the luggage itself had been destroyed, leaving no doubt that if something had been hidden in a bag lining, or false bottom, it had been discovered.

Rowan closed the door and returned to his room. If he had any hope of getting out of taking a cruise down the Nile, his chances had just dwindled to nothing. Assuming, of course, that whoever had destroyed the room had not found the ring...and suddenly, he was quite confident that it hadn't been found.

"The old biddy has it on her person," he said aloud and called down to the front desk to lodge a complaint about the disturbance he heard in Mrs. P's room. The room clerk promised to send someone up to investigate, after which Rowan, without even taking off his shoes, lay down on the bed and fell asleep in less than five minutes.

Nine

"Hold on, don't leave yet! We're coming, we're coming. We just got held up—oh, thank you. Would you mind helping Mrs. P, please? The dock is a bit uneven. I'll grab our bags. We were robbed, our stuff totally destroyed. It was horrible! Ack. Sorry, yes, I have money. I'm not trying to run off without paying you." I dug out a few bills from a pocket where I'd stuffed some money I'd exchanged for Mrs. P and paid off the taxi driver, who had followed yammering about me trying to rob him, when I shoved Mrs. P from the car and made a dash for the boat that was about to pull out from a rickety little dock extending twelve feet into the Nile.

I grabbed the plastic bag with basic accessories that I'd had to fetch from the hotel's shop—toothbrushes, soap, shampoo, and assorted other necessities—and with a note from the hotel giving me information about the police officer in charge of our case clutched in my sweaty hand, trotted after the crew member who was helping Mrs. P get onto the ship.

"It was a nightmare, a total and complete nightmare. Everything was destroyed. They even squeezed out our toothpaste, and of course, we didn't find out our things had been violated until we got back from seeing the pyramids, which was half an hour before we were supposed to come here. What? Oh, yes, tickets. Hold this, would you?" I shoved my bag of items at the man in a spotless white captain's hat and rummaged around in my pockets. "One of them got torn in half, but the people at the reception desk taped it back together. Here we go."

The captain eyed my less than pristine self (dusty, sweaty, and wrinkled from our trip to the pyramids), pursed his lips, and considered the tickets. He was very Omar Sharif with dark eyes, an impressive mustache, sparkling white naval suit complete with glistening gold braid, and a general air of being the suavest man at the party. He also intimidated the crap out of me, an unreasonable feeling at best, but there was just something about him that seemed almost ruthless.

He looked up from the tickets, taking me in again. If he was the top of the barrel, sartorially speaking, then I was wallowing in the dregs at the bottom. "I see. Welcome to the *Wepwawet*, Madame. I am Captain Kherty. There was no need for you to rush—Mr. Dakar told us you were delayed and would be along shortly."

"Oh, he did, did he?" I walked up the brief gangway onto the ship, my mind simultaneously processing the traces of adrenaline resulting from the mad dash to the ship, the thrilled sensation of being on an actual river cruise about to set sail down the exotic Nile, and the on-again, off-again suspicion that Rowan had first used me to get to Mrs. P and then had torn apart our room and belongings.

My initial response on seeing the destruction had been

to blame it on Mr. Kim and cohort, but a memory of how interested Rowan had been about Mrs. P's jewelry rose to usurp that. Just until I realized what I was doing, at which point I banished the thought, because I couldn't truly suspect Rowan of doing something so heinous, could I?

No. I could not.

Except... damn. If only he hadn't talked about Mrs. P's jewelry. And just how did he know we'd be late to the ship? There hadn't been time to call him for help—no, it had to be his guilty conscience at work.

That thought depressed me like nothing else could.

The captain handed us over to a stewardess, a tall African woman with the looks and demeanor of a supermodel. She hustled us into our stateroom suite with softly intoned comments that assured us of our welcome and that we would have a safe, enjoyable trip. Considering I hadn't seen any of the armed guards on board the ship that I had at other locations around Cairo, I wondered about that, but eventually decided that I wasn't going to let anything spoil the trip.

Not even the destruction of my clothing and assorted sundries. The thought that Rowan had used me might do it, though... but no. "He just couldn't have. He is not that sort of a man. I may not be the wisest woman in the world, but he couldn't have deceived me that way. At least... oh, goddess, I hope he didn't."

"Pardon?" The stewardess gave me an odd look.

"I couldn't call him," I told her. "I mean, I could have, but some part of me was suspicious despite the fact that he seems so nice... I just couldn't call him."

"I see," she said, pursing her lips slightly.

"Sorry. I'm mostly talking to myself, trying to untangle my feelings. Just ignore me."

She handed over two door keys and wished us a happy journey.

"Well, this is pretty darned nice," I said after she left us. The suite consisted of two bedrooms, each with its own minuscule bathroom, and a shared sitting room that ran the width of the bow of the ship. Windows on the shore side looked out at the hustle and bustle of vendors running to and fro trying to sell wares, while on the other side, the Nile itself glistened and glimmered in the setting sun.

Golden-orange rays smudged across both the darkening sky and the river, the latter giving the impression of a living being the way the light undulated across it.

"Okay," I said, reveling in the beauty of the scene. "This doesn't make up for having our stuff trashed, but it's pretty damned gorgeous nonetheless."

"What is? Oh, the river." Mrs. P emerged from the bathroom, a hand towel stuck in her purse.

I removed it and returned it to her bathroom, reminding her that we'd need our towels. "And besides, this is a super nice cabin, and I'm a bit afraid of Captain Kherty. He looks like the sort of man who'd throw a towel thief overboard without a moment's hesitation."

"Pfft," she said, and took a seat in an Egyptian-motif settee done in shades of turquoise and gold. "He is a ferryman, nothing more. Where is your man? Why did he not meet us?"

"I don't know, and I don't know, but trust me—I have a lot to say to him," I answered grimly. "Even if I don't think he did break into our room—and I'm sure he couldn't have, because he's just not that sort of man—I don't like the fact that he knew about it. And is he using me? Man, I hate feeling like this! I know he's not, but at the same time, I worry."

Mrs. P frowned at me. "You are speaking too many words."

"I know," I said miserably. "I'm babbling. I blame Rowan. He's turned me all inside out and I don't know what to think anymore."

"He's a man," she said, considering a painting of an ibis. "That is what they do."

"Right, well, I'm done with all this angsting. I'll talk to him later and find out whether my instinct is right or if he's a rat bastard. But first, let's see if this ship runs a shop, and if they have something we can wear."

"This is a very nice pillow," Mrs. P said, giving it a long look.

I opened the door to find two women in their sixties wearing identical one-piece bathing suits swathed with gauze wraps.

"Oh, goodness!" said the shorter of the two. She had washed-out reddish-blond hair, and was, like myself, on the fluffy side. Her companion had short dark curls shot through with gray, and a long, lean figure that boded of a metabolism of the gods. "What a fright you gave me! Barbs, did you see me jump? I must have cleared at least a foot."

"Hullo," the tall one said. She tried to peer past me into the room, but I didn't need anyone seeing Mrs. P trying to appropriate a throw pillow, so I blocked their view and quickly closed the door. "Going out to see the ship, are you? We're on the way to the pool."

"Hello," I said politely, and shook both women's hands when they were offered.

"We're Ken and Barbie," the shorter woman said with a little apologetic laugh. "I know, right? It's actually Kendra and Barbara, but all our friends call us Ken and Barbie, and it's become second nature by now. You're Sophea, aren't you? I heard the captain talking about you. You're American? We're from Ireland, although you wouldn't know it the way Barbs speaks. She's veddy, veddy BBC neutral."

Barbie was in the process of giving me a good visual once-over. She nodded as her companion spoke, but other than saying, "Pleased to meet you," didn't offer much to the conversation.

"Yes, I'm Sophea. I was just on my way to find a steward or ship person to see if there is a shop on board. I wasn't sure if there was because it's so small, but I am praying there is because otherwise everyone is going to get tired of seeing my employer and me in the same clothes."

"Your employer?" Barbie asked at the same time Ken made a face and said, "Dear me, dear me. Lost your luggage, did you?"

"Something like that."

"You must have a generous employer to take you on this trip," Barbie said.

With the memory of the scene Mrs. P had made in the tea shop uppermost in mind, I gave them both a bland smile and declined to comment on the eccentric old lady who was probably even now stripping the cabin bare of all she could stuff into her luggage. "Very generous."

"There is a shop," Ken said excitedly, waving her hand toward her midsection. "We got our suits and these darling wraps there! I didn't know there was going to be a pool on board. Honestly, the thought of swimming in a pool sailing on a ship just seems like the height of decadence, doesn't it? And at night! But it's so warm out, it's like swimming during the day."

"It certainly does seem decadent. Where is the shop located?"

"On the lowest deck. That's two below us. It's right next to the first aid. You can't miss it."

"Awesome, thank you. I'll head right down there."

"Have fun!" Ken said chirpily. "We'll let you know how the pool is. Honestly, a late-night swim in a pool while sailing down a river... it's just so crazy, isn't it, Barbums?"

Her voice drifted off as they headed upstairs to the pool.

I poked my head back into the cabin. "There's a shop where we can buy clothing. Are you ready?"

"For many things," Mrs. P replied, coming forward, making a good attempt to hide a scarf that had been draped decoratively along an end table. "What did you have in mind? Will I be required to dance? I have a scarf, if so."

"No dancing, and you're going to put that and anything else you've pilfered back later," I told her sternly, taking her arm and escorting her down the passageway.

It took us a bit to get there, since the ship, a small river cruising variety, was not one of those behemoths that roam the ocean and didn't have elevators, but at last we made it to the lowest level of the ship, where the shop was tucked away. Inside the shop was a tiny desk holding a variety of travel-size items like aspirin, shampoo, and razors. A couple of t-shirts bedecked the wall, as well as a stand containing a variety of the same navy blue one-piece swimsuit as I'd just seen on the two Irish women. There were also a couple of men's trunks in pale salmon and a box displaying sunscreen.

But no everyday clothing.

"Hello," I said to the woman who was on her knees setting out some sort of anti-viral hand sanitizer. "I was told that you had some clothing available for purchase. Do you have anything more than swimsuits and t-shirts?"

"I want a swimsuit," Mrs. P said, and plucked one from the wall, holding it up to herself. "I shall bathe my soul with my sisters in the light of the morning sun."

"Bound to be chilly then," I pointed out. "But if you really want one, that's fine with me."

"All our costumes are behind the screen," the shop woman said in heavily accented English, nodding toward a fabric screen that had been angled to hide the back part of the room.

Costumes? I shook my head as I scooted around the screen, assuming it must have been an odd phrasing.

I stared at the collection of sparky, bespangled, and billowing tulle offerings that hung from a variety of hooks and available coat hangers.

"No, she meant costumes," I said, my heart falling.

"What sort of costumes—oooh!" Mrs. P pushed past me into the secluded area, and perused the offerings with a delight. "Fancy dress! This trip will be more fun than I thought. I like this one."

I eyed the skimpy Cleopatra-esque outfit, and didn't say a single thing.

At least, not about that.

"Hello again," I said, popping my head around the screen. "I'm sorry to bother you, but these appear to be all costume party outfits. Do you have anything normal? That is, not meant for a costume contest?"

The woman didn't even look up from her bottle arranging. "This is not that sort of a shop. We provide costumes for the patrons who did not bring one for the final evening costume party."

"Great. Just...great." I turned back to where Mrs. P

was struggling to get her gauze tunic off so she could try on what appeared to be a harem girl outfit. "I assume we'll stop somewhere tomorrow where we can get some clothes. I guess we can just wear what we have—Mrs. P, no!"

I was too late. She'd already shucked her clothes and had donned the blue marabou and sequin harem top. The floofy chiffon pants followed, and she admired herself in the mirror with little noises of satisfaction.

"Yes, that is quite nice. It's a very . . . striking . . . outfit," I agreed when she asked what I thought. I noticed a glint of gold in her wrinkled belly skin and figured that was just so Mrs. P to get her belly button pierced at her advanced age.

"I shall wear it tonight to the champagne reception," she said, wrapping a matching blue marabou boa around her waist, hiding the wrinkles, and making the outfit a little less risqué. "Everyone will admire it."

"That they will." I refrained from pointing out that the ensemble was not quite suited to someone of her advanced years, since it wasn't my place to make judgments. Besides, if she was comfortable wearing the costume and she liked it, then who was I to ruin her fun?

There remained the subject of my own less than sterling appearance. I brushed a hand down my badly wrinkled and grubby pants, and tried not to think of how much fun it was going to be to hand-wash my undies each night.

"I really would like to get something else to wear . . ." I bit my lower lip, trying to decide if I should spend some of my precious money to get a costume or just tough it out and keep wearing what I had on.

The idea of seeing Rowan, the ever cool and collected, while I looked like something that had been dragged around the desert, drove me into action.

"Right. Let me find something that isn't too obnoxious."

Mrs. P held up a sexy nurse outfit.

"Not in a million years. Is there something here less revealing?" I poked through the offerings, finding fault with all of them. "No to Cleopatra rig, hell no to the naughty housemaid, the female vampire might have possibilities if it were not for the plunging neckline and thigh slits on either side of the slinky skirt. What's that? Oh. No, definitely not a catsuit."

Mrs. P pulled a dark brown leather costume out from behind a pink marabou baby doll and gave it a jaded look. "This covers most of your bosom."

I looked over at where she was pointing. She was holding what I thought of as a Xena, Warrior Princess outfit, with a leather corset top embellished with decorative swirls of metal around the boobs, the bodice of which did, indeed, cover everything in the torso. Accompanying it was a knee-length skirt made of strips of studded leather, a sword and back scabbard, and a pair of lace-up sandals.

I held the corset top up to myself and examined my reflection. "I'm not sure... a sword? Strapped to my back? Really? That'll just get in the way."

"It'll be helpful," Mrs. P told me, snagging a pair of stretch fabric slippers with curly toes. "You'll need a weapon to guard me. There are slave bracelets, too."

I looked at the arm bracelets she held out, along with a pair of gauntlets. "I don't think they call them that anymore. But I do admit they might cover any untoward upper arm pudginess." I eyed my reflection again and decided to the throw caution to the wind. It might be a silly costume, but at least it wasn't overly revealing, no more so than a knee-length sleeveless dress would be.

Mrs. P took the chakram, a circular weapon that accompanied the outfit, and plopped it on her head with satisfaction, tipping it at a rakish angle, and tying it in place with yet another feather boa. "I'll take the hat."

"I'm not sure that's a... never mind. You can wear it as a weird sort of hat if it makes you happy."

Twenty minutes later, the passengers on the upper deck of the *Wepwawet* ceased their pleasant chattering, gossiping, laughing, and in one case, singing along to the tinny song emerging from an aging boom box. All of the passengers, as well as the crew members present, turned to watch with silent amazement as Mrs. P and I stepped out onto the deck.

The captain, a drink frozen halfway to his mouth, stared with unblinking eyes.

"Good evening," I greeted everyone with what I hoped appeared to be good humor and not a desperate attempt to pretend nothing out of the ordinary was happening. "I'm sorry we're late. Mrs. P was having some trouble with one of her curled slippers not fitting right."

The eyes of the twenty or so tourists moved from me to Mrs. P's feet, then returned.

"You are aware," Captain Kherty said in a deep voice, "that the costume party is the *final* night of the cruise."

It was a statement, but I waved such concern away with leather-braceleted arm. "Yes, and I'm sure we'll be able to pick up something a little less showy when we stop at a town, but until then, we're forced by circumstances beyond our control into these little ensembles."

"My sisters!" Mrs. P squealed with delight, and hurried over to the far end of the ship where a group of six women was laughing and chatting and clinking glasses with one another. They greeted the newcomer with cries of happiness.

"She has sisters?" I asked aloud, noting that all the women were apparently in their twenties, and probably all had jobs as underwear models.

"That is very interesting," the captain said, and with a dark look cast at the group of women, murmured something and toddled off.

"There you are. What a very unique ensemble," said a familiar voice. A small clutch of about four people nearest me parted, and May came through with a smile, Gabriel following her. "We heard about what happened at your hotel. I'd offer you some of my clothes, but I'm afraid they wouldn't fit you. Perhaps Mrs. P, though... where is she?"

"Chatting with some friends, evidently."

By now the other people on the deck had gotten over their shock from our costumes and continued their previous activities.

"I'm sorry," I said, aware my confusion was showing. "Why are you here? Are you stalking us?" After the events of the evening, I wasn't about to trust anyone, not even people who seemed like they had our best interests in mind.

"Stalking?" May's eyebrows rose a good inch. "Not in the least. We're here to help you."

"By following us?" I asked suspiciously. "Look, I know that you're Rowan's friends, but that doesn't mean—"

"Friends?" Gabriel looked appalled at that thought. "With the Dragon Breaker?"

"We said we were going to put that behind us while we had to work together," May pointed out.

"That does not mean that we need think of Rowan as a friend."

"Did I hear my name being invoked?" Rowan suddenly appeared at my side, wearing an unrumpled linen shirt, brown khakis, and a pair of sunglasses pushed up into his hair. He looked like the personification of a wealthy, sophisticated man on his yacht, as coolly collected and in control as anyone could be.

A familiar faint lemony smell teased my nose, instantly making me want to romp all over him.

No, I told my libido. *Not until we get a few things straight, like whether he had anything to do with the room or if he misled me into thinking he was interested in me.*

His lips curled into a little smile at me, sending a hot wave of emotion that no doubt manifested itself in pink cheeks. I couldn't tell if I was angry, aroused, or annoyed. Possibly all three. *Definitely* all three.

He examined me from head to lace-up sandals. "Interesting choice of cruise wear. I didn't know you were a fan of Xena."

"Isn't every woman? She was a warrior princess," I said as nonchalantly as I could. With a move I had practiced in the bathroom while changing, I pulled the sword from my back and made a couple of movements with it. "All the better to protect my employer from nefarious brigands who would do her harm."

Rowan glanced around. "Where is our light-fingered friend?"

"Gel," Mrs. P said, right on cue, leading her herd of models to us. "My sisters are here."

"Er..." I said, eyeing them. "Sisters?"

"We are all priestesses of Heka," one of the models said, a brunette with a flawless complexion. "As is our sister Aset."

"Pleasure to meet you, but... sisters?"

"Sisters," Mrs. P insisted. "The one next to you is Ahset—she has an H in her name, whereas I do not—then there's Ipy, Khenut, Henit, Dedyet, Bunefer, and the tipsy one is Gilukhipa."

"I love champagne, don't you?" Gilukhipa said with a happy little hiccup.

"Wow. That's... that's some sisterhood you have there." I tried not to look like someone who needed to lose twenty pounds. "And how lucky for you that they're on the same cruise."

"We came to help our sister," the one named Ipy said. She seemed to be the ringleader, since the other ladies just murmured in response. "We knew she would have need of us to guard her secret from those who would discover it, and thus we are here."

"My sisters will let no harm come to me while you are handling the challenges," Mrs. P said to me.

"No, we will not, although I think we should get Gilly to our room," Ipy said, giving her priestess sister a gimlet eye. "Lest she succumb to the lure of more champagne."

"Give her our room key, gel," Mrs. P told me.

"Huh?"

"The sisters are staying with us, naturally."

"But..." I glanced at Rowan, who looked as surprised as I felt. "But don't you have your own rooms?"

Ipy shrugged. "We cannot guard our sister if we do not sleep at her side. Come, we shall make the accommodations ready for our dearest one while the champion is guarding her."

I didn't see any way out of it. Mrs. P was paying for the trip, and I had no right to keep her friends from our cabin if that's what she wanted. Reluctantly, I handed Ipy the key, and the ladies all took off.

Except Mrs. P, who told Rowan, "The shop has men's costumes. Tiny ones. You might want to perk up your romantic life with one."

"I don't need to wear a costume, tiny or otherwise, thank you," Rowan said stiffly as she cackled and snagged another glass of champagne before sitting down in a chair next to where May and Gabriel were now talking in low voices.

I gave Rowan a look that told him he should know better. "If you are implying that we're doing this for the hell of it, we aren't. We literally have nothing else to wear. And speaking of that, how is it you knew about our room being trashed? You wouldn't happen to have been there, would you?"

"Yes, I was there," he answered, taking me completely off guard. "That's why I called the hotel's front desk—so that they'd send someone up to find out what happened before you returned to see it."

I took a step closer to him, and immediately was aware once again of the scent of him, part citrus and part something that made me think of leather-bound chairs in a private library. "And just why were you there?" I asked in a soft tone, making sure to meet his gaze. His eyes, now more gray than green, were wary, but as I took another step closer, the interest in them turned molten. "You wouldn't be trying to steal Mrs. P's jewels, would you?"

"As a matter of fact, I was, but someone beat me to the job."

The words pierced me as if they had been arrows. It took me a minute to be able to answer him, but I was proud that when I did so, my voice was steady. "You're a thief? You really do want to steal from Mrs. P? That's... that's... that's just infuriating, Rowan!"

"There's a reason for what I'm doing—"

"On the contrary, there's no reason. Not a valid one. Not for theft." I took a deep breath. "Well, at least you're honest about the way you've been using me."

"What? No!" He took me by the arms, his eyes clouded now. "Sophea, what we had last night is nothing to do with this—with the ring. What we did was about us, no one else, and I'm more sorry than I can say if I gave you the impression that you were a stepping stone on the way to Mrs. P. I would never use you like that."

"But you just admitted that you want to steal from Mrs. P."

His lips thinned. "Not for my own gain. Not for money, or satisfaction, or hell, even by my own free will. There's a situation, and I'm more or less obligated to help fix it."

"Obligated like being blackmailed?" I asked.

Pain flashed in his eyes for a few seconds. "You could say that."

I searched his face for signs he was lying, but there was nothing in it but sincerity. And something heated that left me feeling restless and needy. Although I didn't condone his plan to steal from Mrs. P, it made much more sense that he was being forced into doing so. I wondered idly what he'd done that was so bad it could be used to force him into his present acts, but decided that was a discussion for another time. "Now I feel like I should apologize," I said, my emotions tangled into a giant ball of confusion.

"Don't. You have nothing to apologize for." He rubbed a hand over his face. "I seem to have messed things up without being aware of it. What can I do to make it right with you?"

"Well, the biggest thing is to stop trying to steal Mrs. P's jewelry." I touched the side of his face. He still looked tired, but there was something in his eyes, a layer of pain that I knew I had a part in, that made me forgive him. "I am sorry for thinking you were the sort of man who'd use me. I should have known better."

"It was entirely reasonable to think so," he said, pulling my hand up to kiss my knuckles. "If I promise you that I won't take anything from Mrs. P without her permission, will that return your faith in me?"

I felt as if a heavy weight had been lifted from me and realized with a start the true depth of emotions that were tied in with Rowan. This wasn't just a case of me needing to have a good time with a man...it was something more profound. And while it was true my emotions were tangled together, they were emotions that had lain dormant for the last few years, emotions I was happy to feel again.

Trust you to fall for the first pretty face you've seen since Jian died, I said to myself, the name of my deceased husband generally dousing any feelings of attraction for another man, but for the first time since his death, it didn't leave me feeling as if I'd had a bucket of water dumped on me. "Yes, it would help if you stopped being a cat burglar. For one, I don't think it's very honorable, and for another, it's bound to end badly, and I don't want to see you end badly. I want you to end good. Er... well."

"Thank you," he said with another one of those little bows that thrilled me to my toes.

"And as for not telling us about our room... I don't know whether to scream at you, hit you over the head with something heavy, or ask the captain to throw you overboard. Why didn't you tell me that someone destroyed our things?"

"I had no way to contact you. I did what I could by ensuring someone from the hotel would find out what happened before you got back, and left it at that."

"But you would have stolen Mrs. P's jewelry if her things hadn't obviously already been gone through?" I pointed out, then shook my head. "Never mind, it's a moot point now. Not only have you just sworn not to steal anything from her, whatever she had is gone."

His eyes glittered with humor. "For the record, it was just one item, and it wasn't hers to begin with. She has done exactly what I tried to do—taken it from someone else."

"Oh, is that the story now?"

"It's the truth." He slid a look at Gabriel, who was chatting with May and Mrs. P, then suddenly grasped my wrist and left the deck, taking me with him.

"Hey!" I protested, digging in my heels when we got to the top of the stairs that led to lower decks. "What do you think you're doing?"

"We need to have a talk. A private talk. My cabin is on the floor below us."

"I can't leave Mrs. P alone. The underwear models—not that I even know if I can trust them—they're down in the cabin, and she's all alone. Someone will try to hurt her. Or steal her jewelry." I put a lot of emphasis on the last sentence, but he seemed to ignore it.

"Gabriel and May will stick with her."

"That's just what I'm worried about," I said, snatching my hand out of his. "Someone trashed our room, and who's to say it wasn't them?"

"I highly doubt if it was."

"But you don't know for certain."

"No," he said slowly. "But I trust them. They may not seem like people who have our own interest at heart, but I don't believe they will betray our trust."

The implication was obvious—he had trust where I had none.

"Are they the ones who are blackmailing you?" I asked, wanting to comfort him, and seduce him, and yell at him, all at the same time.

"No. Not them directly. It's really all of the dragons collectively who are forcing my hand."

He looked miserable, utterly miserable, and my heart begged me to wrap my arms around him and keep the world from him.

"Isn't there any other way around whatever's going on?" I asked, fighting my need to fling myself onto him. "Some way that doesn't involve stealing?"

"Trust me when I say that if there was any way on this earth I could avoid the situation, I would do so. But my hands are tied. And I've been assured that it's a necessary act, one needed to save not just dragonkin, but mortals, as well."

My reservations crumbled under the stark anguish in his face and voice. I threw caution to the wind, knowing I might be making the biggest mistake of my life, but believing every word Rowan spoke despite it all. I threw myself against him, kissing every bit of his face that I could reach. "I'm sorry. I'm so sorry. I blamed you when you're just a victim of—"

He stopped me talking then, but only because his tongue was busy persuading mine to go visiting in his mouth. It obliged, and we remained locked in a steamy kiss until a passing waiter coughed discreetly before edging past us.

"Wow," I said, gazing up at him, my mind trying desperately to get a grip on itself.

His eyes widened, then a little smile flirted with his lips. "You're on fire."

"I know I am. I told you that you're a heck of a kisser."

"No, I meant literally."

I looked down at where he pointed. A small ring of fire encircled my feet. "Eek! Where did that come from?"

"You." He gave me a heated look that made me want to rip off all his clothes and cover him in something lickable, like chocolate. "You are a mate, remember?"

"Kick-ass mate," I corrected automatically, wondering how much chocolate the ship had on board.

"That goes without saying."

"I still can't get over this whole making fire thing." I gazed up at him, and wondered how I could broach the subject of sexy times in the near future.

Rowan made a face, then admitted, "I don't think I'm going to be able to last until later." His voice was husky in a way that made me shiver with desire just hearing it. "I don't suppose you would like to—"

"Yes," I said, taking his hand and starting down the stairs. "Right now. Sooner, in fact."

He chuckled as he trotted behind me. "I'm glad to know you are just as impatient as I am. I haven't been able to stop thinking about you—*oomph*."

He bumped into me when a sudden, horrible thought made me stop midway down the stairs. I turned to face him, a horrible suspicion in mind. "Just one minute. You may trust May and Gabriel, but I don't, and I'm the one who was hired to help out Mrs. P. Although she may be a bit scatty and frustrating as sin sometimes, she's still a pretty nice old lady, and she did let me come on this cruise when she didn't have to, so I'm going to do my job the very best I can."

"She's told you more than once that she expects you—*us*—to protect her. I wouldn't be assigning to her quite so many altruistic motives as you seem to be wont."

"You're trying to distract me—"

He lifted his hand as if he was taking an oath. "I have no ulterior motives in getting you into my bed other than licking every square inch of you. Twice."

Goose bumps rippled down my back at both the look in his eyes and mental image of his words. But I had to think of Mrs. P, so I pushed aside my own need. I brushed past him retracing my steps to the top deck. "That doesn't mean I trust those two stalkers up there."

"They aren't stalkers. Gabriel and May are here to protect Mrs. P," Rowan argued.

"So they say, but do you know for certain?"

"I know they are not trying to harm anyone, yes." I reached the top of the stairs and turned to go out on the open part of the deck when Rowan scooped an arm behind me, and hefted me over his shoulder, one hand holding onto my legs as he descended to the floor below.

"What the hell?" I squawked, and slapped him on the back a couple of times before I realized that my boobs were perilously close to falling out of the Xena bodice. "Eek! Put me down! This costume wasn't meant to defy gravity in this manner."

"We're almost there. You'll be fine," he said, and when

I struggled to push myself off him, grabbed my legs with his free hand.

It was as is if I'd been touched by fire. Warmth swept up my legs, pooling in secretive parts of me, parts that wanted Rowan to revisit their depths. My breasts, nearly bursting free from their upside-down confines, were sensitized and heavy, the nipples rubbing on the soft interior of the corset cups making little shivers flicker down my arms. When the thought of Rowan's hands and mouth on my breasts flashed into my mind, it was all I could do to keep from whimpering.

Mrs. P, I desperately told myself in an attempt to keep from ravishing Rowan the second he released me. I had to remain focused on her.

But when his hand slid up higher, under my leather skirt, and his fingers dove into the very parts that were pleading for him, I just about came unglued.

"Put me down!" I shrieked, kicking my legs wildly.

To my surprise, he did just that.

"Goddess above, man, you can't do that to me," I said, stuffing my breasts down into my Xena corset. "At least, not out in public where someone could see us. And just what do you think you're doing by abducting me in that manner?"

"I'm arranging for us to have a private talk. It's only fair you know what's going on, since you have taken up the role of Mrs. P's protector," he said, opening his cabin door and tugging me inside.

"Oh, no sir," I said, clinging to the door frame. I glanced over his shoulder, noticed the bed sitting smack-dab in the center of the cabin, and immediately my smutty thoughts went into overtime. "I know what's going to happen. I won't be able to resist you, and then May and

Gabriel will run amok all over poor Mrs. P, after which you'll propose to me, get me to agree to marry you, and then die, leaving me alone again. Well, I won't have it, do you understand? I simply will not have it!"

Rowan paused as he entered the cabin, giving me the oddest look I'd ever received. "Did you…I'm not sure… did you just *propose* to me?"

"Don't you dare be adorably confused at me!" I said, shaking a finger at him. I wanted to pounce on him, and yet, I needed to protect Mrs. P from the predatory dragons on the deck above us. "I refuse to fall for your charms! The steamy, mind-blowingly fabulous sex will have to wait."

"Sophea," he called after me as I spun around and marched up the stairs. "Wait a minute. I'll explain."

"I don't want an explanation. Aha!" I stopped at the sight of the two dragons with Mrs. P between them. I pointed dramatically at them. "I knew it! You're trying to steal Mrs. P's valuables!"

"My shinies," the old woman said, clutching at her marabou-lined harem top.

"Unhand that woman this instant!" I demanded.

"Unhand her?" May looked faintly amused. "I don't think I've ever heard anyone say that before."

I pulled my sword from the scabbard and waved it about in a manner that I hoped was suitably impressive. "You are not going to steal anything from her, do you understand? Mrs. P, come over here where I can protect you."

"I'm tired," she said and with a little sniff walked past me to the stairs. She took Rowan's arm—he had arrived at the top of the stairs and was watching the scene—and demanded that he escort her back to our suite.

"Stay!" I told May and Gabriel, waggling the sword at them.

Gabriel turned to May with an indescribable expression on his face. "Did she just give us a command as if we were dogs?"

"She did," May said, nodding. "I think she's upset with us."

"You have *no* idea," I snapped, then sheathed my sword and trotted after Mrs. P and Rowan.

Ten

"And to think," I said when I caught up to Rowan and Mrs. P, "if I had let you seduce me as you planned, even now Mrs. P would be in the clutches of your nefarious friends."

Rowan stood back as Mrs. P and I entered our suite, following after us. "I'm not sure what I can do to reassure you that May and Gabriel are not going to take anything from Mrs. P, so you'll just have to trust my judgment about that point. And yes, I'm aware of the irony of that statement."

"Dammit. You pulled the trust issue. Not fair, dude, not fair at all given what I was thinking earlier." The leather straps that made up my skirt swung out in an arc when I spun around and gawked at the room. It was filled with luggage, and from Mrs. P's room came a babble of conversation. I trailed her into the bedroom. "Wow, it's like a can of sardines in here."

There were models everywhere...lying on the bed,

lounging on the two available chairs and the window seat beneath a porthole, and seated cross-legged on the floor.

"The room is safe for you, my sister," one of the models called out. Ahset, I think it was. "Ipy is verifying that the shower contains no scorpions or asps."

"Good news! We are asp free, ladies," Ipy said, emerging from the bathroom. "You may bathe at will. I see the mortal is here." Ipy nodded toward me.

"She is a dragon's mate," Mrs. P said corrected.

"Ah. We would welcome you to the sisterhood, but we do not have time for the initiations. Know that you have our gratitude, however."

"Er… thanks. It's all in a day's work." I sidled over to where Mrs. P was admiring one of the ladies' necklace. "I take it you don't need me to help you get settled?"

"No, go off and be with your man," she said, putting the necklace around her neck and easing herself onto the bed. "If he can't make you happy, I don't know what will. He has quite an admirable set of buttocks."

"He does, doesn't he?" Ipy said. "You are to be congratulated on your choice in men."

"Thanks. I'm not… uh… never mind."

Ipy frowned. "You do not think your man has a fine set of buttocks?"

"No. I mean, he does. His behind is awesome, not that I stare at it, but what I saw of it last night was pretty damned spectacular."

"A man with a good pair of buttocks is a man worth keeping," she said sagely.

I couldn't help but do a little bragging. "His hands are nice, too. And his chest. Oh, that chest! I swear, his chest would make a nun weep. With joy, obviously. And lust.

Lots and lots of lust, just touching it and petting it, and maybe even licking the little round nipple nubs. I love his nubs. I wonder if he's a nipple man. Hmm."

Mrs. P snorted from where she sat on the bed.

I pulled my thoughts back from the land of Rowan. "Sorry, what was that?"

"I snorted at you."

"Ah." I glanced around. "You're sure you're going to be okay with this many people in the room?"

"Our dormitory was much smaller and not nearly so grand," one of the ladies (Bunefer?) said on her way into the bathroom with a big towel.

"It'll be like a slumber party," Ipy said, nodding. "You may rest easy that we will guard our sister well so that you may do your job."

"Awesome. Well, good night, I guess."

"Keep your sword handy," Mrs. P said, removing her circle hat. "We may need it before morn."

"I will. Be sure to lock up after me, and yell if you need anything, okay?"

"Enjoy molesting your man's superb buttocks," Ipy called as I opened the door to leave.

Rowan stood right outside.

I frowned at him. "Hey, were you eavesdropping?"

"Yes." He had an odd expression, a combination of pleased and exasperated. "Do you really want to lick my nipple nubs?"

My cheeks, as per usual in these situations, heated up instantly. But I've learned not to give in to the fact that I blush at the drop of a hat and I met his gaze. "As a matter of fact, I do. Does that bother you? Are you repulsed by the idea? Are you sickened and disgusted and outraged that I, a mere woman, should lust after your chest, reversing the normal roles of men and women and sexual attraction?"

"I like that you're wordy," he said, his head tipping to the side a little. "Some women never tell you what they're really thinking. With you, I don't have to guess."

"That had better not have been an insult."

"It wasn't, I assure you. I'm quite sincere in that I like the way you speak your mind."

"Good. Answer my questions," I said, prodding him on the arm.

"No, no, and no, assuming that was a total of three questions. I couldn't tell for sure since there were many parts to that last bit, plus, I'm now imagining what your mouth on my nubs would be like."

"Damn good," I said with confidence.

"I'm sure it will be. And in fact, so long as we're discussing plans for nipples, I'd like to put in a request for time with your breasts. They have been uppermost in my mind all day."

"Really?" I looked down at where Xena cups presented my breasts for Rowan's viewing pleasure. At least, that's how they viewed the situation. "They're just boobs. They hang off me, and get in the way sometimes, and because they're a bit on the fluffy side, like the rest of me, they are a pain in the patootie to take jogging. Not that I jog much. I prefer swimming. Am I babbling? I feel like I'm babbling."

"You are not babbling, but you are speaking unfairly of your breasts. I really want to make love to you, but before we indulge ourselves in mutual exploration of nubs and their related parts, I'd like to make something clear."

"Mutual exploration sounds good, assuming you were propositioning me this time. Were you?"

"Yes. Although I prefer to think of it as wooing with my manly attractions. Sophea." He took both of my hands in his.

"Hmm?"

"I really do need to talk to you."

"About what?" I fluttered my fingers in his when his thumbs stroked identical patterns on the backs of my hands. I swear, my whole body went up in flames.

"Myself. My past. Why I'm here with you now."

"You're here because I'm in a sexy Xena outfit, and you can't resist the lure of a kick-butt dragon with a sword strapped to her back," I suggested.

He laughed and kissed the back of each of my hands, pulling me over to a love seat that sat under two portholes. "I didn't realize it before this moment, but you are absolutely correct. Tell me, did you notice that May and Gabriel referred to me as the Dragon Breaker?"

"Yes. I figured that was your rock star name. Or something. Why, does it have any importance?"

"Only to the extent of my life and probable upcoming death." His lips twisted in a wry manner that pierced the haze of sexual interest that had gripped me.

"In what way?" I asked, guarded lest he be teasing me. I was very well aware that I knew nothing about this man… well, practically nothing. I knew he had a protective streak a mile wide—no one else would have come to our rescue as many times as he had if he hadn't been one of those people who naturally come to the aid of others—but other than that, and the fact that he had a glint of humor in his eyes that I found incredibly appealing, I wasn't very conversant with his history.

He sat on the love seat, waiting for me to take a seat

beside him before he answered, "When I said I was a sociologist, I wasn't being exactly accurate."

I frowned, my lust dying a swift death. If there was anything I disliked, it was men who lied. "Oh, really?"

He flinched. "That was downright frosty, but I guess I deserve it. I *am* a sociologist, and I do work with emerging tribes in eastern Brazil. But in addition to that I... well, I'm an alchemist."

I let some of my iciness melt. "I heard someone say that. I thought I must have misheard and the word was really pharmacist. What's an alchemist when he's at home?"

"Someone who is highly sought after by just about every being in the Otherworld." He took a deep breath, his gaze looking beyond me. "You know what magic is, don't you?"

"The stuff magicians do? Sure."

"No, not that. At least, not what you see mortal magicians do. Magic is real, just as real as dragons are, and it's entirely possible to imbue objects with it. Magic, that is, not dragons."

"You know, my mind is having a bit of a hard time accepting the idea of real magic, but given that I'm a dragon lite, I'm going to tell it to get with the program. Okay. Magic exists, and you can stick it on things. What things?"

He made a vague gesture. "Pretty much whatever you want. That magic usually makes the object much more powerful, kind of like it enhances the quality of the item."

"So if I magicked up my Xena sword, it would become a super Xena sword?" I asked, trying to wrap my brain around that idea.

"Yes."

"Okay. Considering I'm almost a mythical creature

that I had no idea existed a few days ago, then I'll buy the whole magic thing."

"Alchemists break magic. That is, we take it from whatever it's imbued and re-form it into its essential components, rendering the object magically impotent."

"And you do this?"

"I have. Once before."

The way he said the words raised all sorts of warning bells in my head. "And?"

He was silent for a moment, his gaze slipping away from mine. "And the first time I tried it, some people interfered with the process. I should have stopped them, but I was only sixteen at the time, and cocksure. Not to mention the fact that the people in question—dragons, to be exact—weren't inclined to take no as a suggestion. They paid the ultimate price for their interference—the breaking went wrong, and instead of turning a relic of a demon lord into a harmless object, it exploded with dark power. I was thrown back by the blast, but the four dragons who were with me... they took the brunt of it."

"Oh, how horrible," I said, scooting closer to him. I wanted to wrap my arms around him to comfort him, but I had an idea he had a little more soul-baring to do... not to mention I wasn't sure if he'd welcome the gesture.

"It was. More than horrible, it was devastating, especially considering I'd tried to get the dragons to leave while I attempted the breaking. Once I recovered from my injuries, I was visited by a being who claimed he was the progenitor of all dragonkin."

"I have a feeling he wasn't there to chitchat," I said, risking a little squeeze to his arm.

He slumped back, his face filled with remembered

pain, and suddenly it was too much for me. I clutched him by both arms, pulling him to me so I could hold him and ease the anguish.

"He wasn't," he said, his face pressed into my bosom. His voice was muffled, his breath hot on my skin. I ignored that sensation, though. It wasn't at all right to get turned on while trying to offer solace. "Would you mind if I asked what you're doing?"

"Comforting you," I said, stroking his back.

"Ah. I suspected it was something along those lines."

"Do you not like to be comforted?" I stopped rubbing his back and peered down at the top of his head.

"I'm quite enjoying it, as a matter of fact," he said against my breasts. "But I fear if we remain in this position for much longer, I may be forced to take action."

"Action? What sort of action?"

His tongue snaked out into the valley between my two Xena'd breasts. "We have been discussing nipples, after all."

I shivered, my body alternating with flashes of heat and waves of desire. "Great galloping ghosts, hurry up and get off your chest whatever it is you want off, so we can go into my room and go wild on each other."

I'd released him by then, and he pulled himself upright, giving me the wickedest grin I'd ever received, a grin that ignited flames of passion.

Literally. I stubbed out the flames burning merrily about my feet. "Dammit. Go on."

He was silent for a moment, his gaze losing a lot of its heat. "Your connection to the dragons is why I felt it important to tell you my history. The dragonkin know me as a murderer of their own kind. I wouldn't want you to think the stories they tell about me were true."

I tugged up my breastpiece, which had shifted a smidgen during the comforting process. "What did this dragon daddy guy want?"

"Revenge. Well...of a sort. He bound a danegeld to me. Do you know what that is?"

"I do, as a matter of fact. My roomie is a huge historical fiction fan, and she's always forcing books on me. It's a tribute people had to pay their overlord."

He nodded. "The First Dragon demanded that I pay for the deaths I'd caused." He made air quotes around the last word. "He gave me five years to pay back the cost of each life. He said that I didn't have the payment by the time the entire period was up, I would forfeit my own life."

"Well, that's just bullshit," I said, outraged on Rowan's behalf. "How dare this high and mighty guy lay down the law on you. You're innocent until proven guilty, and if everyone is ignoring the fact that you weren't responsible, then that's not your problem."

"Unfortunately, it is." He fell silent, but absently, as if he didn't realize he was doing it, he took my hand and rested it on his thigh, his finger stroking across the top of my hand.

Another fire broke out at my feet. I stubbed it out with the toe of my sandals before Rowan could see it.

"It's one of the reasons I was in Brazil—if the dragons had known where I was, they would have demanded much of me. The danegeld bound to me meant I couldn't refuse a legitimate request if it was made of me, so I made sure they wouldn't find me."

"How much do you have to pay the dragon guy?" I asked, thinking of the two thousand dollars I'd received from Mrs. P's nephew.

I hated to lose my seed money, but Rowan clearly had a greater need than me.

His eyes closed for a minute. "I took four lives from the dragonkin. Technically, the danegeld is to replace those lives, but how I'm supposed to do that, I have no idea."

He looked so sad, my heart gave a little squeeze.

"I don't think you're to blame at all for the deaths," I said in an attempt to make him feel better. "And since I'm kind of a dragon, I'd be happy to talk to this guy if you want. Would you like me to comfort you some more, or do you want to be left alone?"

The corner of his mouth twitched. "I'd have to be dead to say I didn't want more of your particular brand of comforting, but that isn't why I wanted to talk to you."

"You wanted to tell me that those dragon people think you're a murderer. But I'm not them, Rowan. I'm a pretty good judge of people, and I can tell you're not the sort of man who would let people be hurt if you could prevent it."

"We're a pair, aren't we?" he said with another quirk of his mouth. "Here's me trying to save the world, and you trying to keep one old lady safe. Oh, what the hell. I'm due a little comforting."

He slid an arm around my waist and pulled me close, his head tipping down toward mine. Instantly, my body demanded that I press every part of it against every part of him, but just as I was tipping back my head to accept the kiss that he was surely going to press upon me, his words sunk in.

I slid my hand up to stop him, and ended up with his mouth pressed against my palm. "What do you mean you're trying to save the world? Save it from what? Surely not Mrs. P—she might be a bit odd, but she's no threat to anyone except men who she fancies, and even then, she's not violent."

He gently bit the tip of one of my fingers. "Remember that ring I mentioned yesterday? It's an important object. Very important. It belongs to a demon lord, who quite badly wants it back. The dragons want it as well, but only so they can destroy it—or rather, have me break its magic."

"A ring?" I frowned in thought. "But Mrs. P doesn't have one. At least, not one she wears."

"No she isn't wearing it, and I assume by her comments that she didn't keep it in her luggage, which means she must have it on her person. Probably on a chain around her neck."

"I don't think so," I said slowly, mentally going over the scene in the ship's shop. Mrs. P had removed her clothing in front of me without batting a single eyelash. "I've seen her in her underwear, and she didn't have on a necklace of any sort."

"Well, she has to have it somewhere upon her person, because she intends to use it as some sort of offering to Osiris."

I leaned back so I could get a better look at him. "She *what*?"

He nodded. "I take it she's been waiting a long time to return to him. There's more of a story there than she's telling, but the important point is that she has the ring, and we need it."

"We?" I asked pointedly. "I don't see where the *we* comes into it."

"If the demon lord gets the ring, he will use it to unleash boundless evils upon the world, both immortal and mortal. That's one of the reasons why the dragonkin want the magic in the ring broken."

I stood up, the fire inside of me dying down to nothing. "I think you'd better leave."

He looked confused. "I thought we were going to indulge in nipple exploration, among other things?"

"I'm sorry about what you went through in the past," I said after sorting through my emotions. "But I have a feeling you told this to me in order to get me on your side, so I'll help you take Mrs. P's ring. No." I held up a hand when he protested. "I know you said you weren't going to take it from her without permission, and I appreciate that. But now you're trying to get me on your side so I'll help you browbeat her into handing it over, and I'm not going to do that."

"There's no side to be taken," Rowan said, slowly getting to his feet. His eyes were filled with sadness. "It's a matter of simply weighing the need of one person against those of the rest of the world."

I went to the door and opened it, waiting silently for him to leave. He did with a sigh, his shoulders slumped as if the weight of world was upon him. And it sounded like much of it was, if the dragons really had cornered him at last and forced him into this scenario.

That didn't make my heart any less pained. It mourned the loss of Rowan with a sadness I didn't think I could overcome.

Eleven

Ten minutes passed while I paced the main room of the suite, alternating between wanting to go find Rowan, tell him I was sorry, then seduce him like he'd never been seduced before, or standing guard at Mrs. P's door to make sure that no one tried to get to her. Not that I thought that the priestesses would let anyone in, but I felt obligated to do what I could to protect her.

Just as I was at the end of my wits with the thoughts that kept squirreling around and around, there was a tap at the cabin door.

"Rowan," I said hopefully, my heart singing a happy little song about nipples and manly chests and other masculine parts.

"Hi! It's us, Ken and Barbie," Ken said, now dressed in a mauve linen pantsuit. Barbie stood behind her, holding a small overnight bag. "We heard all about what happened at your hotel. I can't believe someone shredded all your clothes! That was just spiteful, if you ask me."

"Spiteful," Barbie agreed, shoving the overnight bag at me. "We brought you and your employer some clothing."

"We just couldn't live with ourselves knowing that you and your boss were here without anything to wear but those ghastly costumes." Ken smiled sympathetically at me. I eyed first her rotund shape, then Barbie's slim, tall form, and decided not to point out that neither Mrs. P nor I had body types similar to theirs.

"Thank you, that's very thoughtful of you. Um. How is it you found out about the attack on our things?"

"The captain, of course. He was most interested in your experience," Barbie said, trying to nonchalantly peer over my shoulder into the cabin.

I could hear faint noises of chatter coming from Mrs. P's room, but figured it was better to let go the explanation of why there were seven women stuffed into a single bedroom. I had a horrible feeling the captain wouldn't allow it. I shifted slightly to the side to block the view of Mrs. P's door, and said in a carefully neutral tone, "That's awfully sweet of you to think of us."

"Sweet is what we do best," Ken said, beaming at me. "Isn't it, Barbs? It comes with the territory."

Barbie looked less than thrilled, but summoned up a weak smile.

"Territory?"

"Yes, you know." Ken waved a hand in a vague gesture.

"No, I'm afraid I don't know," I said, more confused than ever.

Her eyes opened wide in surprise. "Oh, didn't we tell you? Barbs, can you believe it? We didn't tell Sophea who we are when we met her earlier."

"Who are you?" I asked, suddenly worried.

"We're cherubs. From the Court of Divine Blood, you know? And so of course we're here to help you and your employer. We know all about her and what you're both doing here."

If I hadn't been startled by the news that the two older women standing before me were cherubs, I was by what Ken was hinting. "The court of what, now?"

Ken giggled while Barbie *tsk*ed, and said, "The Court is what mortals think of as heaven. It's not, of course, but it's what they based the idea on centuries ago."

"And you're the little winged fat babies who float around ceiling decorations in cathedrals and rococo buildings?" I asked, my skepticism obviously showing, because Ken laughed.

"No, of course not. That's the mortal conception of us. We are as we appear, of course," Barbie said gruffly.

I had the feeling I'd insulted her, but I was still trying to cope with the idea that these ladies thought they were cherubs. "I'm...to be honest, I'm not quite sure what to say to that. I guess I'll just go with thank you for your concern. I'll show Mrs. P what you brought us, and if there's anything we can't use, we'll send it back." I edged the door closed a few inches.

"If you need any help, any help at all, feel free to call on us," Ken said with a glance over my shoulder. "We will be happy to do whatever you need. Isn't that right, Barbie?"

"Whatever you need," Barbie agreed.

Ken beamed at me and patted me on the arm braced against the door. "Any time of night or day. We don't mind being disturbed at all."

"Gotcha. Thank you," I said simply.

"Even something minor, like taking your friend to lunch for a bit so you can be with your boyfriend. Oh yes, we know about him, too!" Ken giggled. "He's so very rugged and handsome, isn't he? You're a lucky girl. I just wish I had a man half so attractive."

"He is handsome, isn't—"

"I haven't had a partner in ever so long," Ken interrupted me, a wistful expression wiping out her sunny smile.

I shot a startled look at Barbie, wondering what their status was.

"Oh, Barbs and I aren't partners," Ken said, rightly interpreting that look. "I mean, we are, but Barbie is—I would never consider myself—"

Barbie grabbed Ken's arm and gave her a none-too-gentle shove. "Let us know if you need our help," Barbie said in what I was coming to think of as her usual terse method of speaking.

"Will do, and thank you again."

I closed the door on the sound of Ken apologizing to Barbie. "That's an unhealthy relationship if I ever saw one," I said to myself. I set down the overnight bag, and with a speculative glance at Mrs. P's bedroom door, made up my mind. I knocked on it.

"Enter," she commanded loudly over the babble of the models.

I frowned as I opened her door. "You were supposed to lock it."

Mrs. P sat on the bed, one of the priestess models painting Mrs. P's toenails. I could hear the shower running in the bathroom, and sitting in a circle on the floor playing cards were the remaining ladies. "I have the sisters," she said with a shrug.

I did a double take at Mrs. P, not because of the situation, but due to her appearance. "Did you do—did you put on some makeup or something?"

"Why would I do that? Do you think I should get a bikini wax? Khenut says that a landing strip is the in thing."

"Totes the in thing," one of the card-playing models said.

"Or perhaps a Brazilian would be better? I read in a magazine that those are also popular." Mrs. P's face scrunched up, and I couldn't help noticing that not only was she gaining color to her skin, there seemed to be a lot less of it on her neck and face. Excess skin, that is. "I have always loved Brazilians."

"I... you..." I stammered, staring in disbelief.

She gave a dream sigh, and gave a catlike stretch. "The men are so masculine. Very dominating, but passionate. And can they dance!"

"I love a man who can dance," said Bunefer, who was capping the bottle of nail polish. "It's so romantic, isn't it?"

"Okay, first, that's not the kind of Brazilian that the magazine means," I said, scooting around the models on the floor in order to sit on the end of Mrs. P's bed. "And second, I don't want to tell you what to do with your own body, but I'm not sure you really have a pressing reason to... er... prune down there."

Bunefer giggled, and slid off the bed, saying, "Bath free? I so need a bubbly soak," when Ipy emerged from the bathroom with her head wrapped in a towel.

"Ah. Champion. You're back?" she asked when she saw me.

"Yes." I glanced at the other ladies. "I wanted to ask Mrs. P a few questions."

Ipy took possession of the window seat and began to

towel dry her hair. "Please yourself. Deal me in to the next round, girls. The latest alimony check is burning a hole in my pocket, and mama needs a new Gucci bracelet."

"Mrs. P," I said in a low voice, then *tsk*ed and plucked the magazine from her hands. "I want to ask you a couple of questions, and I would appreciate it if you'd tell me the truth."

"I have done so since we met," she pointed out, taking back the magazine. "Don't smear my toenails. I want to look nice when I see my beau."

I moved my hand away from her foot. "Okay, here goes: do you have a magical ring that can save the world from some bad guy demon lord?"

"I have a shiny, yes. It is my offering to my beau."

Well, crap. There went my very faint suspicion that Rowan hadn't been telling me the absolute truth about his interest in Mrs. P. Which just made me feel all the worse for even suspecting such a thing. "And you stole it from this demon lord fellow who is evidently bad news?"

"Bael." She gave a sniff. "It was not his to begin with, so I don't see what all the fuss is about."

"I think the fuss is because this ring is a lifesaver. Literally, if Rowan is to be believed, and I don't see why I shouldn't believe him. Mrs. P, I told him I wasn't going to do this, but I've changed my mind—you have to give the ring to him."

"I do not." She hummed softly to herself as she eyed an article on how to use erotic novels to spice up your love life.

"Let me restate that: you *should* give it to Rowan. I know you want to give it to your boyfriend—I'm still a bit confused about all that, but we'll tackle that one another time—but you have to see that the fate of the world is more important."

She looked up and pinned me back with a stare that should have scared the dickens out of me. Her eyes were brighter than they had been, the soft lighting of the cabin doing much to diminish the wrinkles that beset her face and neck. "If I do not give the shiny to my beau, we will not be able to be together. Nor will he resume his rightful place in the world. We have been separated too long, gel, far too long. I was cast out of the Underworld by Isis, who was jealous of me, and who swore we should never be together. My shiny will defeat her."

My mouth had dropped open a smidgen as she spoke. When I realized what I was doing, I closed it, trying to process everything she'd said. "Your boyfriend has a *wife*?"

She shrugged. "Osiris is the lord of the Underworld, and Isis is his wife, although that has not stopped his eye from wandering. She has ever been jealous of me, but she shall not keep me from my true love. He is mine, now. Or he will be when I take him this shiny."

"There's nothing else you can give him?" I asked, torn between demanding she hand over the ring (which I had no right to do), and begging her for it, which I didn't feel qualified to do since I had a tenuous grasp at best on the whole story, not to mention the fact that I should be thinking of what was in her best interest rather than my own.

"No. This shiny has the power he needs to escape this domain. No other will suffice."

I stood up and silently opened the door, turning the lock in the knob as I did so. "I want you ladies to lock the bolt at the top after me, all right?"

"Why? No one will be able to get past us to our sister." Ipy didn't take her eyes off her cards.

"Right, but I took on the job of protecting Mrs. P, and I mean to keep on doing that."

Ipy shrugged. "You will be right next door."

"Not right away. I have to go apologize to Rowan. And that might take a bit of time because... er..."

"Because he has sublime buttocks," she said, nodding. "If it will make you feel better, we will set the bolt so that you may enjoy yourself with your man without worrying that someone has defeated all six of us."

"Thank you. Yell if you need me, Mrs. P," I told her as I left.

She waved a languid hand toward me and inquired if there was going to be a round of Truth or Dare.

I took the precaution of locking the suite door, tucking the key into my cleavage since I wasn't taking my purse with me. While I made my way up to Rowan's deck, I glanced out to see the ship had pulled up to a small pier. Beyond it, I could barely make out the flat shapes of a small village. There wasn't anyone on the pier, so I imagined we must have stopped to fix something in the engine or perhaps take on some supplies.

Voices drifted down to me from the upper deck, along with the sound of light music. Evidently our fellow passengers were enjoying the balmy night and romantic moon. "Whereas I have to apologize for being such an ass," I said softly under my breath before knocking on Rowan's door.

He opened it, making the apology on my tongue dry up into nothing.

"Chest," I squeaked, my eyes eating up the sight of his naked chest. And arms. And legs. The only things covered were his naughty bits, and even those were noticeably bulgy in a pair of tight red bikini briefs.

"Yes," he answered, his gaze on my Xena boobs. "Very much so."

"I've come to apologize," I said, dragging my mind back to what was most important.

He stepped back and gestured me into the room. I sat primly on the bed, hands folded on my lap, making no objection when he stood before me, although I had to admit that with his crotch close to eye level, my gaze might have strayed there once or twice. "I want to apologize for what I said earlier. Or rather, for throwing you out of the cabin."

"I wasn't aware I'd been thrown out."

"Dude, I'm a dragonette. I kicked a demon out of the window. Do you think I couldn't throw someone out of a room?"

One side of his mouth quirked. Goddess, I loved that quirk. "Quite possibly you could, although I am not without my own abilities."

"Oh, I'm well aware you're Mr. Martial Arts. You took care of the other demon quite handily. I'm just saying that I'm not a doormat or anything."

"No," he said, putting his hands on his hips. "That you aren't."

"I talked to Mrs. P. She confirmed what you said. I'm not sure I understand the whole bit about her going to see her boyfriend, who is some Underworld lord, but she refused when I asked her point blank to hand over the ring. She said it's the only thing that will let them be together."

"She said much the same thing to me."

"So I was thinking—if she won't accept anything else to substitute for it, then maybe the dragon people would. To save the world, I mean."

"It doesn't work that way. The ring has to be destroyed

in order to safeguard the world from it ever being used by Bael."

"That's the demon head honcho?"

"Yes." Rowan made an odd little face. "Evidently one of my sisters inadvertently released him from where he had been confined. It seems my family has a habit of doing things like that."

"You have a sister?" I asked, somewhat surprised by that. I don't know why I was, but I relished hearing something personal about Rowan.

"I have two, one older and one younger. Ironically, both are mated to dragons."

"So you're just surrounded by dragonettes, then, huh?"

He smiled and instantly, a little pool of fire formed at my feet. I absently tapped it out while changing my posture to be less forthright and more "let me see your nipple nubs."

"I certainly know which dragonette I'd like surrounding me. Are you, by any chance, here just to apologize, or are you interested in continuing the activities we started last night?"

"Does a dragon breathe fire?" I asked, then thought for a moment. "Wait, they do, don't they?"

He laughed and knelt at my feet, his hands warm on my bare knees. "I'm told they do, although I haven't seen it for myself. Sophea, you understand the situation I'm in. I must get that ring."

"I understand. And although I won't steal it from Mrs. P or help you steal it, I will do my best to help persuade her that we really need it. Perhaps there's some other way around the situation that we just haven't thought of. We can brainstorm the issue tomorrow, okay?"

"Well..." His hands slid up my thighs, sending waves of anticipation rippling upward. "I suppose we deserve an evening off the clock, so to speak. How do you feel about oral sex?"

"I am so go for it right now," I said, sucking in my breath when his fingers reached ground zero.

"Good. Because I've been wondering what you taste like everywhere."

I shivered at the heat in his eyes and the sensations his fingers made as they danced across my underwear.

"Why don't we get you out of all this leather, and then I'll indulge myself, hmm?"

"All right, but I think we should get your undies off as well." I slid off the bed onto my knees when he stood to shuck his briefs, the material strained to its limits. "Here, let me do it."

He frowned. "You said you wished for me to pleasure you first."

"And you will. But I get to do this. Because I'm the dragon chick, remember?"

"Rawr," he said, mimicking my claw gesture.

"You learn quick." I caressed the bulging front of his underwear. "Glorioski, that's... you're... were you this big before?"

"Sophea," he said in a strained tone. "Stop tormenting me with your heated looks, and teasing fingers, and for the love of the saints, don't stroke me! You have no idea how close I am to disappointing you."

"You could never do that," I said, but stopped stroking my fingers lovingly across his bulges. "Now, if I ease your undies down just a bit, just enough to give you some breathing room—"

Something stopped me just as I was about to slide his underwear down his hips. I felt something move behind me, but when I glanced over my shoulder, there was nothing to be seen but the other side of Rowan's cabin.

He stiffened, and stared past me.

"What...did you see something?" I asked him, releasing the waistband of his underwear.

He frowned, his eyes narrowing as he stared at... nothing.

I turned to look, but didn't see what held his attention... until a movement in the air caught my peripheral vision. Over by the porthole, the air began to shimmer. That's the best way to describe what happened—it was as if the air was collecting itself, twisting and twirling upon itself, tiny little motes of nothing collecting to form something.

The little motes grew brighter until they gave a little shake, and a man emerged.

Only he wasn't a man. Oh, he looked like one—he looked perfectly normal, but there was something about him that wasn't human. It was his eyes, I think. He stepped forward, his eyebrows rising as he took in the sight of me kneeling before Rowan, the color in his eyes seeming to shift and change subtly. And his pupils weren't round... they were elongated, just like Mr. Kim's had been.

"Um..." I said, glancing up at Rowan. His face was absolutely without emotion, a circumstance that scared the crap out of me. Hurriedly, I got to my feet to face the intruder. "Er...excuse me, this is a private room. The kind you shouldn't materialize in without first asking permission."

The man looked surprised at my words, and I realized that any being who could just appear in a room the way he did probably shouldn't be addressed in that manner.

"That is," I said quickly, clearing my throat a little, "it's polite to knock before you enter a room where other people are staying."

"Ah," the man said, after eyeing me curiously for a few seconds. "You are the red mate. But my red children are no more." His gaze flickered over to Rowan, who visibly flinched. "As you well know, Rowan Dragon Breaker."

Oh, no. A horrible suspicion began to form and I took a step closer to Rowan so that I was pressed against his side. This had to be Mr. Big. "Are you the dragon daddy guy?" I asked, glancing at Rowan.

His expression was still blank, but I saw dread in his eyes, and that pierced my heart like nothing else could. I wanted to hold him, to make love to him, to make him forget that dread. I wanted to bring him light and happiness and lots and lots of sex. I moved forward a step, as if to protect him, but his hand pulled me back against his side.

"The dragonkin are all my children," the man acknowledged with a little tilt of his head. I remembered that the others had referred to him as the First Dragon, a nomenclature that was evidently his name as well as a description. He looked back at Rowan. "Payment is now due for the lives that were lost."

Rowan's arm tightened around me. "I don't know how to give you back the dragons who died. I told you that when you bound the danegeld to me, and I say it again. If I could, I would bring them back to life. I would stop them from interfering with magic they knew nothing about, but I can't change time. I can't repair the past."

"The penalty is the loss of your own life."

It was all happening again, just as it had with Jian. I met a man with whom I had an instant chemistry, started building thoughts of a life together, and then he was taken from me.

"Not this time," I said aloud, and stepped forward in front of Rowan. "Listen here, Mr. First Dragon. My husband died horribly, and I don't see you blaming the drunk driver who took him down. What Rowan did was just as much an accident as that, so you have no right to blame him."

Rowan gave a martyred sigh and pulled me back at his side. "Love, I appreciate you standing up for me, but it's not necessary, and might well get you killed, too."

I turned to gawk at him. "Did you just call me *love*?"

His eyes flickered toward the First Dragon. "I don't really think a discussion about my choice of words is in order at this time."

"But you did say it."

He made an exasperated noise. "Yes, I said it. We're sleeping together—I felt it appropriate to use such terms of endearment in that situation."

"All right. I'm willing to accept that. But I want to have a pet name for you, too." I smiled at him, and for a moment, forgot about the person watching us.

He didn't forget us. "What makes you think the death of your mate was an accident?"

I stared at the First Dragon. "What do you mean? Jian was run down by a drunk driver."

"So the mortal police told you. In fact, he was killed by demons because he could not be turned to their lord's purpose." His eyes, those uncanny, ever-shifting eyes, glowed with a gold light for a second. "That demon is no more."

I glanced at Rowan. "Okay, he's more badass than we are. We could only break their forms."

Rowan's expression grew serious. "You have no idea."

"And now the time has come for you to pay for the loss of the four dragons who were taken," the First Dragon said, raising his arm as if he was going to just smite Rowan where he stood.

I flung myself in front of Rowan again, my arms spread wide to deflect any such attack. "Wait!" I yelled. "There has to be another way around this. You want four dragons to replace the ones you had? What about me? I'm a red dragon now, aren't I? I count as one."

"You're a wyvern's mate," the First Dragon, lowering his hand.

Rowan, for a third time, wrapped his arm around my waist and pulled me back. This time, however, he kissed my cheek and murmured his appreciation for my attempt to save him from the First Dragon.

"But that's like a dragon lite, right? Rowan said so."

I swear the First Dragon's mouth twitched. "Do you know Ysolde?" he asked suddenly.

"No," I said, confused. "I don't know anyone of that name."

"You will. Shortly, too, unless I am mistaken. She will enjoy you greatly. Very well." He addressed Rowan again. "I accept this wyvern's mate as payment for one dragon. There are three others for which you must make amends."

Rowan shook his head. "I don't know any other dragons who aren't already in the weyr, other than a couple of the demon hybrids who have been attacking us."

"Those are *not* dragonkin," the First Dragon said with another golden flash of his eyes.

"There has to be something we can do to find others," I said, more than a hint of a begging tone to my voice. "You can't just kill Rowan for something he didn't do. Or rather, something he did but that wasn't his fault. If your kids hadn't been so pushy, they wouldn't have died, you know. I think you should take some of the responsibility for having such headstrong and frankly stupid descendants."

The First Dragon seemed to consider that. "There is a point in what you say. I won't agree that it is an encompassing one, but it does bear some truth. Very well, I will allow you payment for a second life in acknowledgment that my children are not always as circumspect as they should be. And for the other two lives?"

Rowan looked helplessly at him. "I have nothing. I'm sorry, I just have nothing."

"Is it possible to make someone a dragon?" I whispered to him. "Like with your magic powers?"

"No. You need to be mated to be considered part of the dragonkin," he answered. "The only other way is to be born into it."

"Ah," the First Dragon said, eyeing me speculatively, then glancing briefly at Rowan's red underwear. "Your solution has merit. I will accept that as payment."

"Accept what—" Rowan started to say, but at that moment, the First Dragon lifted his hands, and the air was suddenly filled with a golden light so bright, it seemed to pierce every bit of me, filling me with joy and love and happiness so intense, I wanted to shout in exultation.

Then just as suddenly, it was gone, and Rowan was on his knees before the First Dragon.

"Your firstborn will fulfill the danegeld. I will grant you an extension of time due to the circumstances." The First Dragon placed a couple of broken bits of glass in Rowan's hands. "The shard that was broken when the red sept was destroyed is now yours. Guard my children well, wyvern. Make the world safe for them, and you will carry with you my blessing."

And then he was gone. He just disappeared, without even so much as a blink. One moment there, the next gone. Rowan staggered to his feet, looking absolutely gob-smacked.

"What... what just happened?" I asked, clutching him when he lurched to the side. "What on earth was that light? Are you okay? You look... odd."

Rowan held out his arm. Before our eyes, his hand holding the bit of pale pink glass changed, morphed into long red fingers tipped with gold claws.

We both stared in complete, absolute disbelief.

"I think the First Dragon just decided I'd pay for the debt after all." He looked up and met my gaze. His eyes were now brown, with tiny gold and red flecks. "I think I'm a dragon."

Twelve

"This...you...how?" Sophea seemed to be having as much trouble understanding what had just happened as Rowan himself.

He flexed his red-scaled fingers and willed them back to normal. It took a couple of tries, but at last his fingers returned to a more familiar shape and color. He glanced at the bits of broken shard that the First Dragon gave him and tucked them away in a pocket.

"How did he do it?" Sophea asked. "How did he make you a dragon?"

"He's a demigod. He started the dragonkin." Rowan gave a one-shouldered shrug. "He obviously has the power to increase the tribe. Weyr. Whatever a collective of dragons is."

"Rawr. It's a rawr of dragons," Sophea said absently. She eyed Rowan with speculation. "Your eyes changed. They're just like they were in my dream."

He touched the edge of an eye as if it would feel any different. "Are they freaky now?"

"No. Just brown, with really pretty flecks of gold and scarlet in them. How do you feel? Do you hurt?"

"Not really, no. I feel..." He did a brief survey of all his limbs. "I feel different. More..."

"More what?" she prompted when he didn't finish.

"More... *more*, I guess. More powerful. Like the world is mine, and all I have to do is reach out and take it. It feels—"

The door was flung open at that moment and several people rushed into the room.

Instantly, Rowan was swamped with emotions—anger, lust, a fierce protective sense that warned him that his mate was in danger, and lastly, irritation. He snarled and pulled Sophea behind him, the better to protect her from the potential threats.

"What happened?" Gabriel asked as he crossed the threshold. May quickly followed with, "We felt something amazing—it was like sunshine streaming through us. It was the First Dragon, wasn't it? He was here?"

"Yes, he was here," Sophea answered, moving alongside Rowan with an annoyed look cast his way. "He put on a hell of a show, too. I don't like him, I have to say. He's awfully high-handed."

Another woman entered, saying, "Welcome to the club." She had long silvery blond hair and was accompanied by a male dragon.

Rowan narrowed his eyes at the man, waiting for him to take even so much as one little move toward Sophea.

"What's going on?" another woman called from behind the two strangers. She pushed forward, stopping to stare in surprise at Rowan and Sophea. "Sorry we're late. Drake insisted on checking the boat for demons before he let me aboard, which is silly because I could have told him that there weren't any here."

"Hello, standin' right next to you," a large black dog said, plopping his butt down next to the latest newcomer. The dog tipped his head to consider Rowan. "Wow. New dragon. And a mate, huh? Did I miss any hot mate-claiming action?"

"What on the good green earth is that?" Sophea asked in a near shriek, pointing toward the cluster of people.

Rowan was having a hard enough time trying to keep all the wyverns under his intense scrutiny without having to explain to Sophea that some demons choose to pick nonhuman forms, as the dog clearly had.

As it turned out, it wasn't the dog she questioned.

"Hi, everyone, we're here! Connie and Bee will be right along. Did we miss any of the good explanations of what happened? Jim! Long time no see, buddy. Excuse me, Mr. Drake. Miss Aisling, would you mind scooting just a smidgen to the left? Connie got me this fabulous new set of solar-powered wheels and what with the cup holder and solar array, it has a bigger footprint." A disembodied head sitting on a radio-controlled jeep rolled forward, the joystick control within easy reach of the head's mouth.

Sophea stared at it as it stopped in front of the crowd, her eyes doing a remarkable approximation of bugging out in horror. "What. Is. It?" she asked in little panting gasps.

Rowan took the chance that the wyverns were not going to try to steal her from him and glanced down. "It's a head."

Sophea pinched his arm. "I can see it's a head, silly."

"Then what was the purpose in you questioning me?"

he couldn't help but ask. "Can't you see I'm busy trying to keep all those wyverns from jumping on you?"

She turned to face him. "I asked because it's not a sight you see every day, now is it? I mean, I can count on one hand the number of times I've seen a disembodied head riding around in a toy jeep. No, I lie, I can count on one finger!"

Rowan was confused by the ire in her voice. He frowned at her to let her know that he didn't appreciate her distracting him when he was doing the important job of keeping her from being stolen by all the wyverns present.

"And furthermore—wait, what? Who's going to jump me?" She stopped looking annoyed and switched to confused. "Is that why you're being 'Mr. I'm Going to Stand in Front of You'? Because if it is, you can just knock it off. I'm not a weakling who needs to be protected. I'm mostly a dragon, remember? I kicked a demon through a window."

"Whoa now," the demon dog said, backing away from where it had been sniffing her knees. "Let's have none of that sort of talk around here."

"It is my job to protect you," Rowan said, self-righteousness all but oozing from him. He waved a hand at the still-growing number of wyverns and their mates gathered at the entrance of the cabin. "I don't know most of these people. Do you? No, I didn't think so. Therefore, I am fully within my rights to protect you from them."

"I don't need protecting," she objected, waving at the mass of wyverns just waiting to pounce on her. Or so it seemed to Rowan. "No one here cares one hoot about me."

"Oh, we care," May said, smiling. "But not the way that Rowan evidently thinks."

"Most certainly not in that manner," Gabriel agreed, his gaze narrowed on Rowan. "Ah, that would explain much."

The other men were examining him in the same manner, which made Rowan feel itchy, annoyed, and oddly antagonistic. He thought seriously of treating each and every one of them to a sound beating.

"Indeed," the wyvern named Drake said, nodding. "A new dragon."

"A new wyvern," the man with the blond woman said. "That makes it even worse."

"Much worse," Gabriel said, with yet another nod, and a somewhat sympathetic smile. "And if Sophea is his mate—"

"We'll be lucky to get out of here without him challenging us all to physical combat," Drake finished.

"Is that a slur?" Rowan asked, his desire to get rid of the wyverns almost overwhelming. "Because if it is, you're on. All of you. At the same time if you like."

"What the hell, dude?" Sophea asked, pulling on his arm until he glanced at her. "What is wrong with you? Why are you acting like the world's biggest ass?"

"Don't blame him. It's not really his fault," May told her. "Wyverns get this way about their mates when they're new—the mates, not the wyvern—and in Rowan's case, he's got both things going against him."

"I don't fight women," Rowan told May, her attention to Sophea generating the direst of suspicions. "But if you have designs on Sophea—"

May laughed at the same time that Sophea whapped him on the arm. "Right, that's it. It's bad enough you acting possessive when you have absolutely no right to do so, but to extend that idiocy to May, of all people, is just beyond enough. Stop it. Stop it right now, and continue to stop it in the future."

"Hiya," the head said in a chipper voice, smiling up at Sophea, and thankfully for Rowan's peace of mind, distracting everyone from staring at her. "I'm Gary. It's Gareth, really, but no one ever calls me that. You're a dragon, too? Everyone is a dragon these days. Or at least a mate of one."

"I have every right," Rowan told Sophea. "It's my job to protect you."

"First of all," Sophea said with an odd expression on her face. It was as if she couldn't make up her mind whether to laugh or to yell. "Your perception of rights is way off base. Just because we've done the sheet tango doesn't mean I'm suddenly helpless."

"Rowan, there you are! Hello, you must be May and Gabriel. We haven't met before, but I've heard about you from Aisling and Ysolde. I'm Bee, Rowan's sister. And I assume you know Constantine?"

Rowan's eyes narrowed on his sister's wyvern. He didn't particularly like the man, especially his habit of calling him the Dragon Breaker. "Bee. What are you doing here? This is Sophea. She's my mate."

"Whoa now! I don't recall agreeing to that," Sophea said, then suddenly turned to face the massive number of dragons who were now filling the cabin. "Your sister? Uh...hi."

"Hello," Bee said politely, gesturing toward the man next to her. "This is Constantine. Have you met everyone? Did you guys see a big splash of light thing, too?"

"Mate?" Constantine asked, squinting at Rowan. Suddenly, he sucked in his breath. "Christos! Am I seeing things?"

"No," Drake said. "Your eyes do not lie. The Dragon Breaker appears to be a dragon."

"A wyvern, in fact." Gabriel frowned slightly. "But what sept?"

Rowan decided to take matters in his own hands. They were capable hands, good hands. Sophea liked his hands—she'd told him so. He straightened his shoulders and said in a loud, authoritative voice, "Everyone out. Go away. All of you. Except Bee. She can stay for a little bit. The rest of you, pack up the head and the talking dog, and leave."

"You're all dragon people?" Sophea asked, ignoring the fact that he, the lord and master of the cabin, had proclaimed an order. "So, we're all like related? I've never had a family before—this is kind of neat. Why doesn't everyone sit down so we can have a chat."

"No one is sitting," Rowan counter-ordered. "There will be no chatting."

"Hi, I'm Aisling. This is Drake. We're green dragons," one of the women said, stepping forward to point at everyone, clearly ignoring what Rowan had just said. "Jim is my demon. I'm a Guardian, which is kind of a demon wrangler. That's May and Gabriel, they're silver dragons."

"We've met," Sophea said with a dark look at them.

"Go away," Rowan said, making shooing gestures. "We are busy coping with things. Important things. We will talk to you later."

"That's Ysolde," Aisling continued. "Her dragon is Baltic. He's the one leaning against the wall looking bored. His father is the First Dragon, by the way."

"Hence the bored expression," Ysolde said wryly. "The First Dragon is the biggest pain in the ass... but I digress. It's a pleasure to meet you both."

"Bee and Constantine you met, and I think... yes, that's Aoife and Kostya just coming in now."

"Are we late? We saw the most amazing light show just as we got to the ship," Aoife said, squeezing through the mass of bodies. Following her was a man who glared at Rowan. Rowan glared right back at him, feeling it was the only right and proper method of greeting another wyvern. "Hiya, Rowan. Bee says you're working with a wyvern's mate? Oh, hello, I didn't see you because of the others in my way. I'm Aoife. I'm Rowan's other sister. This is Kostya. He's the one who's scowling."

Kostya shot Aoife a look. "If I am, it's because you insisted we join the others. I told you that we were not needed here."

"Kostya," Drake said, nodding toward Rowan. "Take another look."

"Why? It's just the Dragon Break..." Kostya stopped, frowned even more, then raised his eyebrows in surprise. "He's a dragon."

"Yes," Rowan said, flexing his fingers. He wasn't the least bit surprised to see that they were now dragon fingers again. "And we are still coping with that fact, and would like to continue doing so in private."

"A red dragon?" Kostya asked, glancing at Rowan's hands.

"The red wyvern," Gabriel said slowly. "Interesting that the First Dragon chose that sept for him."

Rowan sighed and said to Sophea, "They aren't listening to me. Why aren't they listening to me?"

"You're being rude."

He shot her a hurt look, wanting to explain to her that foreign, intense emotions were in possession of him now, and he was doing his best to cope with them. She apparently read his expression accurately, because her gaze softened, and she patted him on the arm. "It's okay, pumpkin. I know this is hard for you. But you might want to give them a little slack. They're just a bit surprised. After all, they thought you were the big bad enemy, and now you're one of them. One of us. Give them a little leeway for having the rug pulled out from under them."

"I don't want to. I don't want them looking at you." He felt a moment of surprise at that. He'd never been an overly possessive man when it came to his romantic partners, and now here he was wanting to throw every single man bodily out of the cabin. And off the ship, for that matter.

"Why?" Sophea asked, looking more curious than annoyed by his statement. "You weren't like that before... oh. It is something dragony?"

"Yes," Baltic answered, pushing himself away from the wall. He gestured to the others. "And the former Dragon Breaker is right—we should not be here while he adapts to being a dragon. A wyvern. Such is not an easy task, and less so when he was not born to it, as we were."

The other wyverns thought about that for a few seconds, then all nodded.

"He has a point," Drake said.

"Not to be rude, but why, exactly, are you all here?" Sophea asked, and Rowan could have kissed her. In fact, he planned on doing that the second the annoying other dragons left.

"The First Dragon," May and Ysolde said together.

"Ysolde said that she and May were told by the First Dragon—somehow, I'm not quite sure on whether it was a psychic thing because they both have a link to him or just an ordinary phone call—he told them that something was up and that it was important to the weyr that there be witnesses. And they told me and Aoife and Bee, and we told our men, and they complained, but because they're smart and know we are wise to the ways of the First Dragon, they agreed we should all pop into the Underworld and see what it is the First Dragon was making such a fuss about."

"The birth of a new sept is an important event," Drake said, looking somewhat skeptical. "But I'm not sure it needed *all* the wyverns present to witness."

"But that's just the point, I think," Gabriel said. "We have witnessed that the Dragon Breaker—Rowan—is now the wyvern of the red dragons, and Sophea, formerly the mate of Jian, is now his mate. We will accept them as such, and the red dragons will be reborn and thus rejoin the weyr."

"You know," Sophea said in a conversational tone of voice, "just once I'd like to understand what's being said without wishing I had a dragon dictionary. What's a weyr?"

"I like you," Jim the demon dog said, snuffling at her sandals. "I like the sword, I like the whole Xena role play thing, and I like that you smell like someone who would give a starving dog some treats. Got any, as we're on the subject?"

"Rawr," Sophea told the demon, sending a little ball of fire to his feet.

"Gotcha," Jim said, nodding and giving her toes one last sniff. "You both need some alone time. Luckily, I'm happy to chill in the buffet line. Ash, babe, lead me to the buffet!"

"We aren't staying, silly," Aisling told her demon. "We're just here for a little bit. Although I do agree that the First Dragon seems kind of high-handed in asking us to come all the way to the Egyptian Underworld just to see a new wyvern made."

Drake shot her a look. "Mate, you should not speak of the First Dragon in that manner. He is a god."

"Demigod," Rowan said without thinking, then made a face. "And if you've looked long enough at my mate—"

"I am so not your mate. Or maybe I am...I'm not exactly sure what's going on here, other than I like you a lot, but I'm really thinking that this is not the time or place to try to work out a blossoming relationship, especially since my first husband—wyvern—whatever—didn't last an hour after we were married."

"You're getting married?" Bee asked. She turned to Constantine. "We should do that."

"We should?" he asked, looking startled.

"Kostya and I are getting married in St. Petersburg," Aoife told Bee. "In September. He says it's really pretty then, and it sounds very romantic."

"Oh my gosh," Gary the head said, bouncing up and down slightly in his jeep. "You three should totally have a group wedding! All the siblings together! Wouldn't that be awesome? I can see it now—all the ladies in white, and the gentlemen in tuxes, and Jim and me leading the way with flowers. And afterward, we could have a ripping party!"

"I wouldn't mind, if Bee didn't," Aoife said slowly.

"Hmm." Bee appeared to think about this. "I suppose we could..."

"No," Rowan said, and made shooing gestures again, this time with broader sweeps of his hands. "We want no part of your plans."

"Well...hold on. Maybe we do. I mean, I'm not big on weddings at all, which is why Jian and I had ours at the courthouse, but I have to admit that a group party with your family sounds kind of fun," Sophea said. "Not that I'm saying I want to marry you, because honestly, I still have a suspicion that there's some sort of kiss of death thing going on with men I marry. I mean, the First Dragon was all set to off you before we winnowed down the number of deaths you owed him, and he decided to take you as one of them."

"Ah, is that how this came about?" Drake nodded. "I wondered why he chose to forgive the debt."

"He didn't forgive it. He simply took our lives for those that were lost," Rowan said stiffly.

"In other words, he saw reason," Sophea said, flashing Rowan a smile that made him want to strip her bare and cover her with kisses. "Which is saying a lot considering that he was ready to smite Rowan where he stood. But back to this group wedding business..." She slid him a considering look. "If we did want to get hitched, then maybe that's something we should consider."

"See? Sophie is on board with it," Gary said, his face scrunched up in thought. "I see it now... an orange blossom arch. The brides in ivory satin with lashings of antique lace trailing after them. Jim with baskets of flowers to be strewn. Me in a top hat, riding him, and cascading petals down the aisle..."

"Dude, I am not a pack mule. Not even for you," Jim told the head. "But I do like the idea of a top hat. Aisling, can I have a top hat for the wedding?"

"Sophea," Rowan told his mate, pausing a moment at that last word. He was a bit surprised at how strongly he felt toward her. Not that he wasn't growing to be very fond of her before... *the event*... but now, no matter what she said, he knew in his heart that she was his mate, the woman placed on the earth to complete him and make him happy to the end of his days. Which had suddenly, thanks to the interference of the First Dragon, grown to an impossible number. "I'm at my limit. Either I'm going to have to fight every man here or I'll kiss the breath out of your lungs in front of everyone."

"Ooh," she said with interest lighting her eyes. "Do I get to pick which you do?"

"Yes. And assuming you're going to go for the kissing, I should warn you that if you don't want witnesses to what I'm about to do to you after that, and believe me, I have a mental list that is growing with each minute you stand there being impossibly deliciously tempting, then you might want to ensure the others leave."

"Now that's what I'm talking about," Jim said with a low whistle. He nudged Gary, and asked *sotto voce*, "You got a camera on you? A dragon claiming his mate for the first time is sure to be Internet gold. Viral video fame, here we come!"

"And I think that's just about enough from you," Aisling said before Sophea could reply to Rowan. She grabbed the demon by his collar, causing Jim to squawk, "Help, help, I'm being repressed!"

"You're going to be a lot more than repressed if you keep that up," Aisling told the demon, and with a backward look at Rowan, said simply, "It was very nice to meet you both. I'm glad you're not a dragon killer any longer, not that I bought that whole story, because I know how stubborn the dragons can be about seeing things their way and only their way. Do let us know if you need any help with demons."

"Don't let us know," Drake corrected her, taking her arm and escorting her from the room. "Mate, I've told you that you are not to undertake dangerous tasks while you are with child. I won't have you risking yourself or the babe..."

"Three down," Rowan muttered under his breath, looking out of the side of his eyes at Sophea.

She had a thoughtful look on her face, and was eyeing him back.

"What?" he couldn't help but ask her.

"Just what's on this list of yours? Is it something... wicked? Something to do with your chest? And me licking it? Is it a nipply list?"

"I like nipples," Gary the head said sadly. "I sure miss mine."

"I believe that is our cue to leave, as well," Ysolde said, sliding her hand in Baltic's. "I'll repeat what Aisling said and welcome you to the weyr. It would be nice to see the red dragons rebound from the terrible tragedy that befell them. If you need Baltic's sword arm, or my magic, do let us know."

Baltic looked interested for the first time as he followed her out of the cabin. "Do you think we should stay? I haven't gotten my hands dirty in a good battle in far too long, not even a heated practice session. Pavel is too busy mooning about his latest *inamorato*, and even Kostya is polite these days. That mate of his has ruined him for sport."

"I heard that!" Kostya yelled, and stormed out of the door after them. "I'll show you who's ruined!"

Aoife gave Rowan and Sophea a wry smile. "So nice to meet you, Sophea. Rowan, welcome to the dragonkin. I'm glad to see you well. Let me know about the group wedding. I think one might be kind of fun. Kostya! Don't you dare get yourself hurt again! If you keep breaking that collarbone, it'll stay broken..." She was gone in a flurry of scattered threats toward her dragon.

"Bee," Rowan said.

She fluttered a hand at him and tucked the other one into the crook of Constantine's arm. "I know, you want some private time with Sophea. And, I assume, to come to grips with what's happened. I have to admit I'm not quite clear on the latter, but since you've evidently not suffered any ill effects—that I can see—I'm going to assume you're hale and hearty and can continue on with the job of getting the ring from that thief."

"*That thief* is a very nice old lady, and he is not going to steal anything from her," Sophea said, bristling.

Bee looked taken aback for a few seconds. "He'd better, or there won't be much of a world left."

"No stealing!" Sophea took a step forward, yanking her sword from her back as she did so.

Rowan caught her arm and pulled it down, pinning her to his side while Bee sputtered indignantly at them. "It's all right, love. You don't have to go Xena all over my sister's ass. I'm not going to steal anything."

"I knew it!" Constantine said, frowning fiercely at Rowan. "The Dragon Breaker has betrayed us. I told you that we couldn't trust him."

"My dear," Rowan said politely to Sophea, "would you mind if I borrowed your sword? I have to beat a man about the head and shoulders with it."

She handed it to him with a smile.

"I'd like to see you try," Constantine said, starting forward.

"For heaven's sake, Rowan!" Bee snapped, pulling her dragon back to the doorway. "Don't you know any better than to antagonize dragons? Especially wyverns. They're very quick to take offense."

"He started it," Sophea said, taking back the sword and sheathing it when Rowan reluctantly handed it back.

Bee rolled her eyes and pushed Constantine out of the room, saying as she left, "I don't care how you get that ring... just get it. The world is lost without it."

"And then there were two," Rowan said, looking at Gabriel and May.

"We have a cabin on the ship," Gabriel reminded him, obviously amused by the proceedings. His expression turned serious when he added, "To be a wyvern is an onerous task on its own. To be created not only a dragon but a wyvern must have consequences. If you have questions or need assistance, know that May and I are at your service. She has unique insight into what it is to become a dragon, and I have been a wyvern for many decades."

"Thank you," Rowan said, deciding that he would tolerate Gabriel and May being on the same ship as Sophea so long as they kept their distance.

"We're on the deck below this one if you need us," May said, then the pair of them left, closing the door quietly behind them.

"At last, we are alone," Rowan said, striking a dramatic pose.

"Mmm." Sophea seemed to be distracted by a thought.

He tipped her chin up. "Penny for your thoughts?"

"I'm wondering why Mrs. P didn't come down to see what was up. That golden light thing was... phew. Intense."

"She's not a dragon. She wouldn't have felt it." He cast a glance toward his bed and wondered if Sophea would object to him simply shredding the clothes off her before working through the many and varied demands that filled his mind. He decided that given the sparse state of her wardrobe she would mind, and simply picked her up and carried her over to the bed, depositing her on it and kneeling to untie her sandals.

"Just what do you think you are doing?" she asked as he freed first one foot, then another.

"I believe the term is 'claiming my mate.' At least that's what the others seemed to feel I need to do."

Sophea sighed, a sound that turned to a moan when he bent down and kissed the inside of her leg. "Oooh! I suppose I could stay for a bit, although I would like to check that Mrs. P and her priestly entourage are okay."

"Why wouldn't they be? There's a vast herd of bodies crammed into her room, so any attacker would stand little chance of getting through to her. And in addition to that, you told me she locked her door, and you locked the cabin door." He rubbed his cheeks on the tender flesh of her inner thighs. He loved the scent of Sophea's skin. It was as if she'd bathed in wildflowers, a slightly spicy, vaguely floral smell that reminded him of sunlit meadows in the flush of summer, flowers moving gently in the breeze.

"Well...I guess that's true. And I'm really not against staying here with you for a bit...although I do think we need to discuss that whole mate thing. If you recall, I was married to another dragon, and that makes me his mate. Maybe I can't be yours because I was Jian's mate. Although that wouldn't be very fair."

Rowan looked down at her where she lay before him, his to claim, the woman who was put on this earth for him, and couldn't help but feel that he was stepping into her late husband's shoes. "Sophea...this is going to sound awkward, but I don't know how else to say it. Are you comfortable with this? With me?"

"Of course I'm comfortable with you," she said, rubbing her leg against him. "You're beefy, but not so beefy that you are unreasonable."

He nipped her calf. "I mean with us. Me being a dragon. More specifically, I now hold the position your late husband held."

She looked thoughtful at that, but smiled after a minute's thought. "You know, I think Jian knew what was coming—although how he could is beyond me, but then again, he was a ghost talking to me at a séance, so who am I to quibble about impossible things. He seemed to be telling me that someone else was coming into my life, and to embrace it. Embrace *you.* So if you're feeling like you're suddenly a Jian substitute, don't. I don't think of you that way at all. Jian was himself, and you are an entirely different man. Both good, just different."

"You are wise beyond your years," he said, feeling a tightness in his chest relax. He'd never had a relationship with a widow before, and wasn't sure how to proceed without feeling like he was stomping over her memories.

"Hardly that. But I have had some time to reflect since we were in Munich." She fluttered her lashes at him. "This feels right."

"We have an obvious connection," he said, sliding his hand up her bare leg. She shivered in response, and he took the moment to reach behind her to unhook the leather bodice. "I am now a wyvern. You are a wyvern's mate. We were meant to be together."

It was amazing just how true that was, and how quickly his mind had adapted to his changed circumstance, and yet already he was having difficulty remembering the time before *the event.*

"Now you're being overly dramatic," she chided, but smiled as she did so. "Why don't we just enjoy the moment, and worry about what sort of a relationship we will want after we've dealt with the whole situation with Mrs. P and the ring?"

He peeled the bodice off her, instantly possessing himself of her breasts, the weight and heat of them in his hands making his blood sing. Desire blazed into being within him, roaring to life with an intensity that threatened to overwhelm. It wasn't until the pressure built up within him that he noticed the floor around them was on fire.

"Is that you or me?" he asked, pausing a moment in the torment of her delightful breasts.

Sophea, who had pulled off his shirt and was nibbling a path along his neck and shoulder, paused to look down, her eyes narrowing. "Yours, I think. Wait." Her forehead wrinkled as she focused, and eventually managed to set her feet afire. "Yes, that's yours. Mine feels a bit different."

"Ah. We should probably stop it, since I doubt if the carpet is fireproof."

"Smart thinking." They both tamped down their respective fires until nothing was left. "Now then," he said, returning his attention to her silken delights. "Where was I?"

"About to give me a chance to play with your nubs," she said, pushing back on his shoulders until he released her.

"No," he said, turning his attention to her skirt. How did it attach? And more important, how did he take it off her?

"Excuse me? Did you just tell me no? I assume your mind is muddled by the trauma of being zapped into dragonness, and that what you really meant to say was 'Yes, Sophea, I will gladly let you reciprocate the wonderful feelings you've been experiencing, for I, too, am looking forward to having my nipples molested.' That is what you meant to say, right?"

"No," he repeated, and having discovered the hooks and eyes that closed the skirt, undid them until the skirt was loose. He stood up, pulling her up with him, causing the skirt to slide down her hips to the floor with a leathery *whoosh*. "Another time you may work your lusts upon my nipple nubs, but right now, I must do this."

"That's just selfish, hogging all the nipple-based pleasure-giving fun—" Sophea started to protest, but he stopped her by kissing her soundly.

"Let me do this," he said softly, giving in to temptation and nibbling on her adorable earlobe. "I can't explain why I have to, but I feel like I must or I'll explode."

Her entire stance softened, her head turning so that her lips brushed his as she melted against him. "I'm sorry. I forgot that you were just bopped on the head with dragon emotions. We are such kick-ass people, of course you feel things stronger than you did before. And I would very much like you to make love to me."

"Another time," he promised as he stripped her of her underwear before hurriedly removing his own clothing, "another time I will allow you to lead. But right now... mmrf." The last word was garbled when he buried his face in her belly.

She giggled and simultaneously sucked in her breath. He looked down at the incredible sight of her lying beneath him, her eyes shining with a light that beckoned to him, her body so perfectly made to fit his, he couldn't imagine ever considering any other woman. But something wasn't quite right, some urge was riding him hard, making him want something... more.

"You are the most beautiful woman I've ever seen, and to the end of my days, I will thank whatever gods were responsible for sending you to me," he said, bending down to press a kiss to her sweet lips.

She sighed. "That is the nicest thing that anyone has—eep!"

Without warning, he flipped her over onto her belly, that delectable, soft, enticing belly, and spread her legs enough to settle between them.

"Don't ask questions," he said, pulling her hips up while sliding a finger into her heated depths. She was, thankfully, ready to receive his attentions, which was good since he didn't think he'd be able to last another second. "I don't know why I have to do this, but I do."

"Well, it's a little different, but I don't suppose it's—goodness gracious, great balls of fire!" She almost sang the last part of that sentence when he slid into her with one powerful thrust of his hips. "That is... wow, that's... oh yes, do that move to the left again."

He moved to the left, and then to the right, and then just because he was a man who believed in covering all the bases, upward and downward as well. As he bent to kiss the back of her neck, intending on trying a few diagonal moves that he hoped would have her squealing with joy, an urge came to him, overpowering him, driving him harder and deeper into her, the pressure building inside until he swirled his tongue on the back of her neck, and breathed fire.

Sophea was already moaning and thrashing around beneath him, but when the fire bathed them both, her muscles tightened around him, and she yelled something incomprehensible into the pillow. He gave in to his own orgasm, his body feeling as if he'd been filled with liquid gold that was lighting him up from within and pouring out into her.

"Okay," she said some minutes later. He was frankly surprised to hear her speak, simply because he was amazed he hadn't succumbed to the perfect ecstasy of the moment. He opened an eye to find himself lying on his back, Sophea's hair brushing his chin, her hand gently caressing his chest. "That was incredibly fabulous. Seriously incredibly fabulous. I wasn't sure when you flipped me over like that, because for a minute, I thought you were heading for the wrong door, but then when you made those little swiveling moves, and then that whole fire thing... wow. Just wow. You can do that any time you like." She tipped her head back to bite his chin, but before she could do so, she winced, and reached a hand to the back of her neck. "What the...?"

"Oh, that." He felt an odd mixture of pride and guilt. "I'm sorry about that. I'm afraid I was so caught up in the moment that I breathed fire on you."

"It hurts a little," she said, rubbing at the spot. "The fire didn't do that before."

"Maybe it's because it was my fire, and I'm not in control of it yet," he said, sitting up to look at her neck, hoping he hadn't seriously injured her. To his amazement when he lifted her hair, he beheld an odd marking.

"Well?" she asked, turning her head when he just stared. "Did it blister? Is it gross? Should I see a doctor? It's not that hurty, just a little stinging, like a sunburn."

"It's... I appear to have... I'm not sure how it happened, but evidently I... for lack of better word, marked you."

"Marked me how?"

He made a vague gesture. "To be honest, it looks like

a henna tattoo. Only this one looks to be crossed swords over a circle."

"Great. Now I have a weird sword thing on my neck." She rubbed at it a little more then lay on her back and stared up at the ceiling. "What are we going to do, Rowan?"

"About your neck? I could ask the captain if there is a doctor on board—"

"No, about this." She waved a hand vaguely. "Us. The dragon people. Mrs. P. The whole world evidently trembling on the verge of destruction if you don't take a ring from an old lady who needs it to get to her long-lost love? What are we going to do?"

He lay back and pulled her into his side, reveling in the sensation of her snuggling into him, her body warm and soft and infinitely comforting. "I don't know, love, I don't know. But we'll figure something out. We have to."

She said nothing to that, but he knew she was worried.

Not as worried as he was, though. Because now there was more at stake than just making his sister happy, and incidentally saving the mortal world from a demon lord.

Now there was Sophea.

Thirteen

"So, let me see if I have this straight in my brain: Duat isn't just the name of the cruise line, it's also a place."

"Yes, that's right." Gilukhipa (who I learned was called Gilly), lay stretched out on a lounge chair next to the small pool on the upper deck of the ship. We were both in the shade, the morning sun being a lot stronger than what I was used to in northern California, and on my other side, Mrs. P lay on an identical lounge, rubbing lotion onto her bare legs. Scattered around and in the pool, the other ladies either sunbathed, swam, or sucked back fruity beverages of an alcoholic nature.

"And it's the Egyptian Underworld, this Duat place?" I asked, wondering why I wasn't surprised to find out that there were such things as cruises to Hell. Then again, in the last few days, I'd discovered I was a kick-ass dragon's mate, had witnessed a perfectly normal man turn into a dragon, and met an actual god. A little cruise into the Underworld was nothing after all that.

"It is. People's Ba and Ka travel through it, you see."

"Ba and Ka? That's... what?"

"The Ka is the soul," Mrs. P answered suddenly, causing me to skew around in my own lounge chair and look at her. I frowned. There was something different about her. Something else different than the night before.

"And the Ba is the physical form that houses the Ka," Gilly said, nodding. "You must have both to travel through Duat and reach paradise. That's why those ancient mortal Egyptians mummified bodies—it was their way of preserving the Ba so it could meet up with the Ka, and be put back together in the divine realm."

"Did you get a wig with your costume?" I asked Mrs. P, still trying to pinpoint what it was that was different. Earlier this morning, we'd dropped our clothing off at the ship's tiny cleaning service, then trooped into the shop and come away with a cowgirl outfit for Mrs. P and a female swashbuckling ensemble for me (which had a gorgeous black frock coat with metal fastenings at the front, red sash, white lace at the wrists, and a short above-knee lace skirt). But it was the tricorne hat and cutlass that sold me on it. The other ladies declined getting costumes, but did give the shop lady a run for her money on sunscreen.

Mrs. P touched her hair, which was gathered into a low bun. Her hair when I first met her was short, white, and floofy... now it was a pale brown with threads of silver, and probably down to her shoulder blades. Her eyes also seemed different. They were still a soft blue, but the outer rings of her irises were darker, the color of which appeared to be leeching inward. And then there was the fact that she seemed to have lost even more wrinkles on her neck and face.

If I didn't know better, I'd say she was growing younger right before my eyes.

"I don't need a wig. My hair is long enough to sit on, although I kept it short for my hoochie-coo dancing. Teddy used to tell me I was his little tomboy." She covered her mouth as she giggled. "He was such a bear of a man. Hahaha."

"Yeah, I get it," I said, nodding but still watching her closely, just in case she was going to change any more. "Teddy Roosevelt. Bear. Ha. Did you get contacts, too?"

She smiled at me, but said nothing, just closed her eyes and settled back for a nap.

Gilly was more than happy to fill the resulting silence. "I like your costume. And how clever of you to wear a different one every day! It makes the cruise so much more fun, don't you think? I just hope you don't get blood on it."

I was still pondering the changes to Mrs. P when Gilly's words sank in. I swiveled around to look at her. "Blood? What blood? I'm not due for that for a few months, when my shot wears off. Sorry, that was TMI, but if you're worried about me messing up this pretty lace skirt—"

"No, no, of course I would never mention something so intimate!" She looked downright shocked at such a thought. "I meant, of course, the first challenge. That's why you're here, right?"

I blinked at her, as if that would make my brain work better. "What challenge? What blood?"

She pursed her lips. "Oh dear, weren't you at the briefing last night?"

"No. I... uh..." My cheeks immediately turned bright pink when I thought of how Rowan and I had spent the night. After dallying in his cabin for a bit, we had moved to mine, since I still felt obligated to keep an eye on Mrs. P despite her clump of priestesses underfoot. Plus, I had a sneaking suspicion that they'd claim my room if I left it vacant for too long. I'd left Rowan sleeping when Mrs. P and I—with the models in tow—had gone off to find clean clothes. "I was busy last night."

"Aset, darling, did you hear?" Gilly tattled. "Your champion did not go to the briefing last night."

I shot her a glare before glancing at Mrs. P and immediately doing a double take. Mrs. P, who waved a languid hand at Gilly, appeared even younger than just a minute before. "Eh. She's a dragon."

"There is that." Gilly made a sad face at me.

"I'm sorry if I missed something important, but no one told me there would be a meeting."

"Her man has sublime buttocks," Mrs. P murmured, and turned over onto her belly. Even her legs looked younger. The varicose veins and pale white-blue skin was gone, replaced with tanned, supple flesh.

"That's understandable, but it's still a shame she missed it."

"Is there a set of notes covering the important points?" I asked, nervous now that I'd screwed up.

Gilly applied a little sunblock on her perfectly toned legs. "No, but I've been on this tour before, so I can tell you what's what. The captain was sure to have gone over the challenges that will be visited upon you as we travel through the Duat. The first are the carnivorous beasts. The second is the lake of fire. And of course, the last is facing Maat and having her weigh your Ka against her measure. If they don't balance, why then you don't get to go to the divine plane, and must remain forever bound to Duat."

"That doesn't sound good," I said, one part of my mind wondering what I would be doing at that exact moment if I hadn't taken Jian's cousin (what *was* his name?) up on the job offer. I certainly wouldn't be floating down a river in the Underworld, facing monsters and lakes of fire and some woman who wanted to weigh my soul. "So . . . when do we get to the Underworld?"

"We're there now. We entered it the minute the ship began its journey," Gilly said.

"Huh. I had no idea. Wait a minute—this cruise is just for the people who are going on to heaven, right? Or rather, whatever their version of heaven is."

"Of course. They can't get to the divine realm without it."

I relaxed back into my chair, wondering what sort of carnivorous animals were going to descend upon us.

"Mind you, no one can leave Duat until Maat weighs your Ka, but if you have a pure soul, that should not be a problem. You'll be allowed to leave and return to the mortal world if you so desire. Which I assume you will, because after all, you are a wyvern's mate, aren't you?"

"How did you know that?" I asked, feeling like I had the words stamped on my forehead.

"Everyone knows that, silly," she said, handing the sunblock to Ipy when the latter emerged from the pool and stood next to us to towel off.

"They do?"

"Were we going to have a margarita party before lunch, or after?" Ipy asked, eyeing Mrs. P's recumbent form.

"Party? Is there a party? I didn't see one on the ship's news this morning. Did you see mention of a party?" Ken bounded over to where we were clustered, clad, as was Barbie, in a shop swimsuit. Each woman had a towel, and Ken carried a flowered straw bag filled with sunblock, paperback books, magazines, and battery-operated personal fans.

"Sorry," Ipy said, glancing at the newcomers and instantly dismissing them. "Private party."

"Hello! Are you Sophea's employer? We've so wanted to meet you ever since we heard about the destruction to all your lovely things. I'm Ken, and this is Barbie, and isn't this a glorious day for a swim? So decadent swimming on a ship, isn't it?"

With a less than tolerant look at Ken and Barbie, Gilly slid off her chair and gathered her things. Mrs. P stretched, jammed a straw hat that she'd filched off another costume onto her head, and, wrapping her towel around herself, padded after Gilly.

Ipy gave the two older women a bright but wholly false smile. "Pleased to meet you. If you'll excuse me, I have much to do. Margaritas don't make themselves." She hurried off before Ken could do more than coo about how she loved a good margarita.

Both women watched the pack of priestesses go before turning back to me. "The first challenge is about due, I understand," Ken said to me. "Are you ready for it?"

"Uh... I guess."

Barbie prodded her companion. "We should find a good place to watch."

"You're right, you're very right," Ken said nodding emphatically. She said in a confidential tone to me, "That's our job, watching over people. And helping them, of course. I didn't catch your employer's name, but if she wants help with the margaritas, why, Barbie here is a dab hand at the blender."

Barbie rolled her eyes and pulled her friend away. "You're boring her with trivialities. Did you remember to pack our rain slickers?"

"Of course I did. We wouldn't want to get gore all over our espadrilles, now would we? Bye bye, Sophea. Good luck with the challenge."

"Gore," I said to myself when they left. "Lovely. And me in white lace."

I returned to the cabin to find the margarita party in full force, with music blaring from someone's phone, a conga line proceeding around the main room's furniture, and much boisterous laughter. I warned them about making nuisances of themselves, then gathered up my hat and cutlass, and went to see if Rowan had returned to his own cabin.

I noticed as I trotted down the stairs to our floor that the ship was docked at another small town. Oh good. Maybe Rowan would want to come with me to find a shop with something to wear that didn't make me look like a reject from a sexy version of *Pirates of the Caribbean*.

Unfortunately, his cabin was empty when I got to it. Rowan's bag was gone, though, showing he'd moved his things to mine, a fact that made me feel warm and squidgy, and all sorts of other emotions that I really didn't want to face at that moment. I peered out of the porthole, noting that a handful of people were streaming down the gangway to the town, clearly fellow passengers doing a little shopping.

"And why shouldn't Hell have shops?" I asked myself, counting the money I'd tucked into an inner pocket. "I'll just go see if they have some skirts or something that I can get for Mrs. P and me." Then I could find Rowan and ask him about those challenges.

Suiting action to word, I made my way to the lower

level of the ship, emerging from its dark depths to the brilliant sunshine of Egypt in late summer.

I felt like I'd been punched with a big fist of pure heat. It was way hotter than on the ship, and I thanked the goddess I was wearing a hat. Maybe I could pick up some fans along with the skirts.

I trotted down the gangway, looking around the town that sat right on the edge of the river. Palm trees dotted the shoreline, along with various shrubs and lots of tall brown grasses that rustled in the breeze. Beyond it sat the village, all the buildings made from the same cream-colored stone (or mud, for all I knew). Most of them were low with flat tops, but there was a central building that had beautiful arches and little domes along the length of its roofline.

From appearances, I could be standing at any small village on the Nile, so much so that I had to remind myself that this was the Underworld, and not reality as I knew it.

Behind the village, the hills rose to their flat-topped plateaus, familiar from many an Egyptian mummy documentary about dig sites. I expected to see dogs and chickens and children running around the village, but as I strolled down the main (and only) avenue, there was no one in sight.

"Hello?" I called out, wondering which building housed the shops. "Anyone here?"

A dog bayed in the distance, and at the same time, a low, deep horn sounded from the ship. I dashed back a dozen steps, prepared to see the ship getting ready to go—leaving me behind—but it was anchored as calmly as ever. The gangway was still in place, held down by ropes and stakes. No one appeared at the entrance of the ship, waving on stragglers.

One of the local dogs must have been wary of strangers,

because I heard a spate of barking coming from the other side of the big building.

"Huh," I said to myself, giving the ship one last look before turning to face the town. Maybe it had been the lunch bell or something. Okay, time to get some shopping done so I could go molest a certain brand-new dragon.

I retraced my steps to the center of the village, hearing more barking. This was louder, and accompanied by some snarling, no doubt the local dogs fighting over a bit of food. I glanced around to see if I could locate them, bracing myself for the sight of feral dogs, but still didn't see any signs of life.

Until I rounded one of the buildings, and then stopped dead in my tracks. Beyond the edges of the village proper, scrubby little shrubs swayed in the wind, petering out to nothing after a few dozen yards. And bounding over the dusty shrubs, heading straight for me, was the most ghastly sight I'd ever seen—a big gray and black dog. No, not dog, a beast! A nightmarish hell beast with slavering jaws, bloodred eyes, and murder in its heart.

My murder!

"Ack!" I turned on my heel and ran like hell down the center of the town, screaming as I did so. "Help! Monster! Carnivorous monster! Someone help!"

The village was dead silent except for my screams and the snarls and slavering panting of the hell beast as it bore down on me, its footfalls dulled thuds on the packed dirt of the village. I rounded the last corner to the ship, and took a chance at glancing behind me. The monster—the approximate size of a pony—was about twenty feet back and closing fast.

There was no way I was going to make the ship in time.

I had a choice: I could either stand and face the horrible beast or I could be torn to shreds trying to reach safety.

I was a dragon, dammit. I was a kick-ass dragon, and kick-ass dragons did not run from monsters, no matter how many nightmares they were made of.

I caught a flash of movement from the depths of the ship as I skidded to a stop and spun around, whipping my cutlass from where it was stuck into my sash. "Right. If I'm going down, I'm going to do it with style."

The dog's eyes lit with an unholy joy when it realized I was standing still, and it gathered itself in a massive leap, obviously about to flatten me before it ripped me into a million bloody bits. I yelled as I lifted my sword, hoping to catch it either in its throat or in its gut, when suddenly I was hit on the side by a blurred shape. I went flying a good fifteen feet, landing in a patch of prickly grasses, cracking my head on a rock. It took me a minute to gather my wits, but when I sat up, rubbing my head, I beheld the most amazing sight.

Rowan was fighting the monstrous beast.

"Rowan?" I asked, getting to my feet, my admiration unbounded as I watched him wield my Xena sword, parrying the monster every time it lunged at him with snapping, razor-sharp teeth. "Great Caesar's goatees, Rowan—watch out!"

Just as I spoke, the monster's body twisted, knocking the sword out of Rowan's hand. I rushed forward with my cutlass raised high, but I underestimated Rowan. He swung around in a roundhouse kick that had connected with the beast's neck with a nauseatingly audible crack, before using both hands to pound on the monster's back, slamming it into the ground with a force that sent dust flying up in a cloud around us.

I choked, coughing like mad, and squinting as I dashed forward, prepared to help Rowan just as soon as the dust settled enough to see.

"Sophea!" Rowan's voice was hoarse and interrupted by a spate of coughing. "Sophea, are you all right?"

"I'm here. I'm okay. Where's the hell beast?"

"Gone. He just disappeared."

I stumbled forward, blind in the cloud of dust until I saw a dark shape loom up in front of me. I hesitated for a minute, then flung myself into Rowan's arms, and kissed every part of him I could reach. "I thought I was a goner for sure. And then there you were, and you were awesome. Goddess above and below, Rowan! Where did you learn to do that?"

"I have no idea," he said, panting and coughing and kissing me all at the same time. "I suspect it was the dragon part of me, because all I could think of was grinding that thing into the dust. You're sure you're all right? I didn't mean to shove you so hard, but that thing was almost to you."

The same low horn noise sounded from the ship as I patted down his arms and chest, just to make sure he wasn't hurt in any way. "I'm glad you did. I mean, I may be a badass almost dragon, but you're a badder-ass full dragon. That was seriously awesome, but don't you ever do it again! You scared at least ten years off my life."

"I scared *you*? I scared the shit out of *myself*," he said with a little laugh, and then kissed me, really kissed me, his body getting into the act to the point where I forgot the near-death experience we'd just shared, and focused on just how hot were the flames he built within me.

People emerged from the big building, trailing out chatting and laughing just as if nothing momentous had occurred. They passed us, calling their congratulations to Rowan for defeating the first challenge, all of which we heard, but really didn't pay attention to, because the kiss had turned into something deeper.

"Our feet are on fire," I said breathlessly a few minutes later, when we managed to pry ourselves apart.

"Up to the knees," he said, then kissed me again. I melted against him, wondering how I had ever existed without him.

A little pang smote me when I remembered thinking the same thing about Jian, but I tucked that memory away gently. Life went on, and although I would never stop loving Jian, it didn't mean I couldn't open my heart to someone else.

"Why are you crying, love?" Rowan brushed a dusty tear from the corner of my eye. "You forget that I'm a dragon now, and pretty much immortal. The monster probably couldn't have killed me."

"It's not that," I said with a little shake of my head. "It's just... I was remembering... oh, hell. Never mind. Let's get back on the ship before something else happens. Besides, I'm starving and it has to be lunchtime. I heard the bell go."

"That wasn't a meal bell," he said, taking my hand as we maneuvered our way up the gangway. "It was the signal announcing the start of the first challenge. At least that's what Gabriel told me, which is why, when I saw you standing outside, I went out to help you."

"Where is he, speaking of immortal beings?" I asked, glancing around as we walked the couple of flights to the top deck. "I'd have thought he would be on hand to help out with that since that's why he said he and May were here."

"I believe they went to protect Mrs. P in case the beast breeched the ship."

"She has her priestesses," I pointed out.

He smiled. "And just like you, he prefers to make sure of her safety without relying on—what did you call them last night? Underwear models?"

"They sure could be," I said dryly, and decided that it behooved me to check on Mrs. P's welfare, too. Just so I could satisfy my conscience that I was earning my way.

We hurried up to the cabin, skidding to a stop at the sight of bodies strewn around the sitting room. Pitchers of icy margaritas melted in puddles that leaked into pools of wet black substances. Stacked tidily along one wall were three bodies of men in various colors, sizes, and shapes. In the middle of the room, Mrs. P sat serene on a chair, while the priestesses puttered around with mops, towels, and trash bags, clearly tidying up the results of what must have been a horrible attack.

May and Gabriel emerged from the bathroom, towels in hand.

I gawked for a minute, then asked, "What the hell happened here?"

"As we suspected, Bael arranged for demons to swarm the ship as soon as the first challenge started," Gabriel said, wiping his hands and looking in distaste at the corpses. As we watched, they started evaporating, leaving behind oily black smears on the flooring.

"How did you—" I looked around for signs of a weapon, but saw none. "How did you kill them? Or rather, destroy their forms?"

May smiled and finished dabbing at a black stain on her shirt. "Dragon form doesn't need weapons. At least, not against some demons. And the priestesses helped, of course."

"We intended to take care of the demons ourselves," Ipy said, picking up a severed hand and tossing it into a bag, along with a knife stuck into half a pineapple. The shaft of the knife was stained black. "But when it became clear that the dragon and his mate would handle destroying the demons, we simply protected our sister while they did the hard work."

"I take it you took care of the first challenge?" Gabriel asked, nodding toward my Xena sword, which Rowan still held.

"Yes." He glanced toward Mrs. P, frowning. "We need to have a talk."

She shrugged. "It won't change anything."

"What won't?" I asked, confused, nodding when May murmured something about them returning to their cabin to change their clothes. They left, and since the models had the cleanup well in hand, Rowan and I sat with Mrs. P.

"I see that your man has been made a dragon." She flashed Rowan a surprisingly flirtatious grin. "I did tell you that the First Dragon would demand payment."

"I had no idea that the payment would consist of my... *self*," Rowan answered somewhat acidly, although that expression faded and he added, "It could have been much worse. I have to say that being a dragon is rather... liberating."

"You may not have my shiny," Mrs. P said, and I let my gaze roam over her. Dammit, she was getting even younger yet, just in the space of an hour. Her hair was entirely brown now, a glossy walnut that made my plain-old-black-hair heart envious. In addition, the wrinkles were gone, all but a few around her neck and eyes, and her arms were toned and smooth. "My beau needs it. Without it, we can't leave."

"Why don't you just stay here with him?" I asked.

"You're both in the Underworld—can't you make your life here?"

"Not so long as Isis is here," she said with a shudder.

I shot Rowan a look. His lips twitched, and I was swamped with the need to kiss him. And lick him. And touch every inch of his wonderful body.

"She would never let us live in peace, and as she's bound to Duat, the only solution is for us to leave," Mrs. P said with a toss of her head. "So all of your entreaties are for naught. I will not give up my shiny."

"Maybe you don't have to," I said slowly, thinking over everything Rowan had mentioned about the ring. I faced him, trying not to notice how bright the gold flecks were in his eyes. Or how the long sweep of heavy muscle in this thighs was outlined in his pants. Or that enticing bit of chest that was exposed by his shirt.

I wondered briefly if I would be able to talk him into a little rendezvous before lunch.

"What are you thinking?" he asked, startling me for a moment with the idea that he could read my smutty thoughts.

A swift glance at Mrs. P—now looking approximately my age—had me biting back a flip answer. The last thing I wanted was a youngish, attractive Mrs. P flirting with Rowan. "I was thinking that if the goal of the dragons is to keep the ring from being used by the demon lord, then the solution is as easy as letting this Osiris fellow have it. If he needs it to get out of Duat, then he's not likely to let a demon get it, and once he's out into the real world, he won't need it. He can simply give it over to the dragons, who can do what they want with it."

Rowan was shaking his head even before I finished.

Mrs. P clicked her tongue and rose from the chair. "I'm

going to have a milk bath. My skin needs hydrating. Khenut, do we have any coconut milk left?" She wandered off into the bathroom.

"Osiris will need to consume the power of the ring in order to leave Duat," Rowan explained to me. "It will in effect be destroyed by that act."

"So then what's the problem?" I asked, confused. "It'll be gone, which is what the dragon people—what *we dragons*—want, right?"

"That's correct, except the essence of the ring will remain behind. And as evidenced by this"—Rowan waved his hand at the black smears on the floor and wall—"Bael does not have any trouble sending demons into the Underworld. They will simply wait for Osiris to use the ring, then collect the essence and take that back to Bael. He will use that to imbue another tool, and we'll be back to the position of Bael having two out of three tools needed."

"Oh. Crap." I thought for a moment, not seeing a clear solution. "This essence... that's what you make?"

He grimaced. "It's what alchemists create when they break magic, yes."

"And what do you do with it?"

He leaned back in his chair, idly watching as one of the priestesses set three bags of trash outside the door. "Generally it's used to create new magical objects. Some essences, especially pure ones, can be used in the formation of a quintessence, which is the most valuable substance in the Otherworld."

"So if we could be on hand when Osiris uses the ring, then you could get the essence stuff, and use it before Bael and his cohorts got to it, yes?"

"I thought about that when Mrs. P told me what her goal

was. It would be possible, but I'd need to have an object ready to receive the essence, and I have no way to prepare one here."

"Then we're just going to have to come up with another plan," I insisted. "Because I'm just not going to steal that ring from her."

"It's pitting one woman's happiness against that of the world," he warned.

"Two people who are in love and simply want to live together in peace," I said, standing, my throat feeling tight. Emotions that I hadn't felt since I met Jian swirled around inside me, leaving me more confused than ever.

Did I want to be Rowan's mate? I knew, despite his posturing before the other dragons, that if I told him we had no future together, he would not force me into one against my will. But the thought of going through life without him was frankly unbearable.

"We can talk about it later. We still have to get through the second challenge before the situation comes to a crisis." Rowan got to his feet as well. "I'll put your sword back. It certainly came in handy."

"Rowan..." I put my hand on his chest, feeling both the smooth cotton of his shirt, and beneath it, the warmth and hardness of his chest. "Do you..." I bit my lip, not able to come right out and ask what I wanted to know. I waited a few seconds until the last priestess had drifted back into Mrs. P's room before asking, "Do you really think I'm your mate? It's not just because I was Jian's mate, and thus am able to fill the position, is it?"

"It has nothing to do with him, and everything to do with us." He tugged me forward, my body pressed against his in a way that highlighted our differences. "It's you I want, Sophea. Not any other woman, just you. We were meant to be together—I see that now that the First Dragon opened my eyes. We were fated to travel to this moment in time."

I tipped my head up to kiss him, saying against his lips, "Then imagine us being separated and doomed never to be together. Because that's what you're damning Mrs. P to if the ring is taken from her."

"Damn it," he said, his eyes bright with passion as he sucked my lower lip into his mouth for a few seconds. "I'd say I hate it when you're right and I'm wrong, but the truth is, I love the way your mind works. You are absolutely right, of course. I can't imagine my life without you, and I swear to you that I'll spend every moment of my life making sure you're as happy as you possibly can be."

And at that moment, I knew with a bright, shining rightness that I would not leave Rowan. "And I promise to make your lips quirk the way they do, and to yell at you when you're unreasonable around the other wyverns, and most of all, to make you happy that the First Dragon turned you into someone who could have a wyvern's mate."

His lips were hot on mine, his tongue doing a little dance around mine that made my toes curl. "You have to keep the costumes, though. I like this one, but the Xena one is very..."

"Kick-ass?" I suggested when he hesitated. "Indicative of a strong woman who doesn't need a man? Representative of the inner strength of women everywhere?"

"Sexy," he said, then gave a mock yelp when I pinched his side. "Very kick-ass," he amended. "Although I'd appreciate it if you took me with you for the next challenge."

"Pfft," I said, brushing that away as we went to find some lunch. "It's just a lake of fire. We dragons are all over fire."

"Famous last words," he intoned as we headed off for the dining salon.

Fourteen

It wasn't until later that evening that I asked Rowan a question that had been niggling at the back of my brain.

"I have something I want to ask you," I said, entering the main part of our cabin where Rowan sat texting someone he said was learned in the ways of magic for ideas on an object he could cobble together before the ring was broken.

He looked up, but before I could say anything more, Mrs. P emerged from her room clad in a Greek goddess outfit, all long, white, floaty dress, gold braided girdle, and dark brown hair curled on top of her head in an elaborate Grecian coiffure. She looked to be in her early thirties now, and I figured at the rate she was growing younger, she'd hit puberty around midnight. The priestess collective trailed after her, each in what I thought of as club dresses—short skirts, tight bodices, and very high heels. Where did they pack all of those clothes?

"Not going to Samba Night?" Mrs. P asked as they all pranced past us, giggling and chatting excitedly. "They have a man giving lessons if you don't know how to dance."

Her eyes were almost entirely sapphire blue now, her face unlined, her flesh plump and smooth and radiating good health. As she glided past Rowan, she reached for the small notebook he had left at the edge of the table, but I *tsk*ed loudly at her. "Ahem. Not yours, Miss Lightfingers."

She clicked her tongue and gave me a wide grin.

"And no, we don't care to go to Samba Night. We have to spend our time trying to figure out how to save the world and still let you and your boyfriend escape his wife so you can live happily ever after."

"Your loss," she said, blithely ignoring the fact that we were sacrificing our time in order to work on the problem. "Perhaps the delicious Gabriel will want to samba with me. Won't that make his mate furious? Too bad you'll miss it. Ah well, happy sexing later, when you are done working."

"He really does have marvelous buttocks," Bunefer said to the others, her gaze on Rowan's backside as they drifted past. "Makes one yearn for a quarter to do a little bouncing-off-of, doesn't it?"

"I once knew a man who had three buttocks," Gilly announced to the others, closing the door behind them before I could hear more.

"In some ways," I said when the door closed behind her, "I'm going to miss Mrs. P and her gaggle of underwear models. And in other ways, I'm going to be incredibly glad to have her off my hands. Especially this younger, nubile version of her. I mean, it was bad enough when she was an old coot, because she was like a wacky grandma and no one took her flirting seriously. But now . . . now she's gorgeous."

"Only if you like that type," Rowan said absently, making some notes in the notebook I had returned to him.

"I'd ask you what type you like, but you'd just be gallant and recite a list of qualities that applied to me. Are you getting any help from your magic dude?"

The corner of his delectable mouth quirked. "I never had a type to begin with, just so you know. And not a lot. Every suggestion he has is beyond what resources we have available in Duat."

"Could you go out and get some stuff and bring it back?"

"No one can leave Duat until his or her soul is judged."

"Oh, that's right. Gilly said something about that. Damn."

Rowan stood up, tucked away his phone, and stretched. "I've had enough of beating my head against that particular wall. What was the question you wanted to ask me?"

"Hmm? Ah." I eyed him. "It might be too invasive a question, but considering parts of you have invaded parts of me, I figure it's within the grounds of reasonable."

"That's right. What's the question?"

"Besides, we're going to be together for the rest of our lives, so if I don't ask, I'll spend countless months wondering. Years, maybe."

"Agreed," he said, putting his hands on my hips and pulling them to his. Instantly my female bits woke up and demanded some hot and heavy Rowan action. "What is it you want to know?"

"And you know, I think communication is a very important part of any relationship. If there's one thing I can fault Jian on, other than not watching for murderous demons in cars, it was the fact that he kept secrets from me. Like the fact that he was a dragon. That's a pretty big secret, don't you think?"

"One of the biggest." He rubbed his hips against mine. "I will not keep secrets from you, but I may well think about tormenting you mercilessly with my tongue and one or two fingers if you don't stop avoiding asking me whatever it is you're curious about."

"That," I said, sliding my hands under his shirt, and stroking both of his adorable little nipple nubs, "is not going to get me to ask the question. Unless you tell me exactly what body parts will be the recipient of the tormenting."

He leaned down and gently bit my lower lip. "Stop it."

I giggled. "All right. I just wanted to make sure you're on board with the whole communication thing. It's important to me." I held up a hand when he growled deep in his chest. "I wanted to know what it feels like to be a dragon."

"I told you—it feels powerful."

"Yes, but there has to be more to it than that. When you were around the other dragons, you were all caveman protective and acting like an adorable but enraging man. With the monster, you were pure heroic, and not that you weren't heroic before, when you helped kick demon butt and all, but that was nothing to what you did with a sword. I didn't even know you could use one!"

"I don't. Or rather, I didn't, but managed to learn fast."

"Right now, for instance," I said, nibbling on his earlobe. "What do you feel?"

He was silent for a moment, his hands tightening on my hips. "Aroused. Powerful. Dominant but protective. Do that last thing again."

I nipped the underside of his chin. He growled again.

"That just makes me…it's difficult to put into words. It's like what I felt before I was changed, only magnified by a power of ten." He closed his eyes for a moment, his chest moving against my fingers as he drew in deep breaths. "I can smell the scent of you, wildflowers in a sunny meadow teasing me and raising my temperature. There's a fire deep inside me and when you are near, when you touch me, it courses through my blood, setting me alight with the need to claim you."

"Wow," I said, marveling at all of that. When he opened his eyes, the gold flecks were glittering brightly. "That's really amazing. I had no idea about any of that. It explains a lot about your behavior with the other dragons, too."

He made a face. "I have a feeling I should apologize for my bad manners, but every time I think about them, I feel exactly the same sense of antagonism."

"That's okay. I think you'll get a handle on your dragonish emotions in time." I slipped out of his embrace and moved over to the end table, opening a little drawer in its side. "Mrs. P gave me something earlier to show you. Before you say anything, I'm perfectly aware that she must have lifted this from someone, and I'm going to give it to the captain so he can return it to its proper owner. But Mrs. P said you would enjoy seeing it."

"It's not an adult toy, is it?" he asked, looking faintly startled.

"No, no, she hasn't stolen one of those since the trip from L.A. to Munich." I pulled out the gold watch from the drawer and went to Rowan with it, holding it up so he could see it. "It's a watch."

The reaction was instantaneous—the red flecks in his eyes glowed scarlet. His whole body stiffened, and red scales rippled up his arms to his elbows. His nostrils flared and a tiny wisp of smoke curled out of his mouth.

"Gold," he said on a breath.

"Mrs. P said gold acts like an aphrodisiac to dragons.

I can see some of that—I mean, I think it's nice and I like to touch it, but..." My words trailed off when Rowan made a noise deep in his chest.

"Run."

"What?" I gazed at him, wondering if I'd heard him correctly.

"Run," he said more loudly, his teeth clenched together.

"Why? Run where? For what purpose?"

He closed his eyes for a second as if he was struggling to maintain control. "It's a sexual thing. I must chase you. Run now."

The light dawned on me. "Ohhh, that sort of run. I thought you meant to go for a jog or something."

Rowan's chest heaved, a pained expression on his face. "For the love of all that's holy, run, woman, run!"

"All right." I trotted to the door, went through it, and got three steps down the hall before a question struck me. I returned to the cabin and asked, "Where am I running to?"

"It doesn't matter," he snapped, his entire body rigid. "Just run!"

"But there isn't really anywhere private to go that others couldn't find," I pointed out. "Assuming, that is, that you'll want to have wild, steamy dragon sex as soon as you catch me. If you tell me where you want to find me, I can go there and wait."

An odd mixture of frustration, anguish, and humor twisted across his face. He closed his eyes and I could see his lips move as he silently counted to twelve. "Run, Sophea. Anywhere. Just run if you want me to survive the next few minutes."

"Gotcha."

I left the room, and this time made it to the upper floor

before I paused, trying to decide if it was worth enraging him to ask if he wanted me to lead him on a chase through the ship before ending up in our shared room.

"The only stupid question is the one not asked," I told myself, and returned to our floor. I had just put my hand on the doorknob when the door was yanked open, Rowan standing in the doorway, his eyes blazing, and half the room alight with dragon fire.

"RUN!" he roared, and I swear to the goddess the glass in the portholes rattled. His image seemed to shimmer and blur, just the way the air did before the First Dragon showed up. And for a fraction of a second, for a fraction of that fraction, Rowan's image shifted to that of a red dragon. It was so quick that I wondered if I had even seen it.

My brain didn't wonder. It registered the fact that there was an impossibly scary thing roaring and smoking and setting fire to everything right there in front of me, and instantly I was running, racing down the hallway, leaping down flights of stairs so fast it was all a blur to me.

All my mind knew was that something big and bad was out there, and I was in its sights.

The very bottom level of the ship was given over to the engines, the electrical works, and things like a minuscule laundry and a kitchen. As I tore down the hallways, careening around corners, I scattered apologies behind me to all the ship's staff whom I crashed into. My ears were deafened to all but one sound: Rowan.

I heard him even as I ran up the employees' staircase at the aft of the ship, a small, narrow, dimly lit metal structure that heightened the sound of a man pounding down the passage behind me.

It was exhilarating, this chase, and yet at the same time

scary as hell. I wanted to tell Rowan to stop it instantly, while begging him to do it every single night. I was just wondering how long it would take me to get back up to our cabin when I rounded a corner and caught sight of a figure just behind me.

I screamed and flung myself at the nearest door, which was, luckily, unlocked. I slammed it behind me, and looked wildly around the room for somewhere to hide. There was only one light on in the adjacent bathroom, leaving the rest of the room dim. It was one of the lower cost cabins, containing two bunks, a tiny little round table, and two suitcases neatly stacked one on top of the other.

That's all I saw before the door was thrown open with enough force that it left a mark on the wall. Rowan stood silhouetted in the doorway for a moment before stalking in. I jumped when he slammed the door shut behind him, and backed up as he approached, alternately watching him and desperately trying to find an avenue of escape.

"There is none," he said, obviously guessing my thoughts. "You're mine now. I claim you."

My inner wyvern's mate squealed with happiness. The primitive part of my brain was telling me to run. I bumped up against the wall, swallowing hard when he took two big steps and then was at me, his body pressing me against the cool, smooth wooden panel.

"Rowan," I said, hiccupping back a laugh. "We can't do this here."

"Why not?" he said in what was more or less a growl. A sexy growl, one I felt to the tips of my toenails.

"Because this isn't our cabin. We can't have sex in someone else's bed. That's just rude. You wouldn't want someone to do that to us."

The light from the bathroom slanted across his face.

He frowned as he thought about that, then grabbed me by the waist, and hoisted me upward, using his body to hold me into place. "Then we'll do it standing up."

A little quiver of excitement ran through me—oh, who was I fooling, by now my entire body was one giant erogenous zone, just waiting for Rowan to touch me. I grabbed his shoulders, and pulled my knees up, hoisting myself a little higher when he placed my legs around his hips.

"This is going to have to be quick," he said in the same low, rough voice that seemed to stroke across my skin like velvet. "I hope you're ready."

"I was ready ten minutes ago. Eons ago. I've been ready for you since the dawn of—Rowan!" He ripped off my underwear, just grabbed it with both hands and snapped the narrow straps, letting the material fall to the floor. "That's my only undies!"

"You can go without," he mumbled, working on his fly.

"Are you crazy? I can't go commando. Not with the short skirts—hooo, Nelly!"

He thrust into me with one smooth, forceful move that left my entire body quivering in pleasure, my intimate muscles doing a little shimmy of welcome and basically singing songs of praise about Rowan.

"I'm sorry. I just can't... you don't know what the chase does... I have to... tell me you don't need more time," he said in a near pleading voice. "I don't think I can stop."

I flexed my hips, the better to accommodate him, and bit the tendon on his neck. "Go, baby, go. Oh yes, just like that. I think... I think..." And that was the point where I stopped thinking and just let my instincts take over. My body moved with his until he tensed up, his face buried in my neck when he yelled his pleasure. That pushed me over the edge as well, and I clung to him, reveling in the exquisite waves of pleasure that rippled outward.

We stayed like that for what seemed like an endless amount of time before Rowan finally lifted his head, his chest still heaving as he panted, "You're going to kill me if you do that again."

"Me?" I asked, unlocking my legs and regaining my feet. I had to cling to him for a few minutes while they turned from jellied blobs to solid form. "All I did was show you a watch. You are the one who turned into a wild man in the bedroom. And it's not even our bedroom. Oh hell, it's on fire, too."

He grinned at me and stooped to pick up my underwear before stamping out the fire that burned in concentric rings around us. "I believe we're going to have to have a ban on gold objects until I can better handle my reaction to it. I'm sorry about your panties. And the wall."

I took my undies from him and stuffed them up my sleeve. "I'll see if I can't repair them. What wall?"

He pointed behind me. I glanced over my shoulder and did a double take at the black shape burned into the wood.

"Oh hell, that's me, isn't it?"

His smile was one of pure satisfaction when he took my hand and led me from the room. "When we do it, we do it properly."

"Uh huh. And how are we going to explain that to the cabin's occupants?"

He gave me a roguish look, kissing my fingers as he said, "If they say anything, I'll offer to pay for a new cabin, all right?"

"All right, but stop swaggering around like having sex so hot you burned my shape right into the wall is a point of pride. We're never going to be able to have nice things if we keep burning them up every time we make love."

Fifteen

I would like to report that the two days following that memorable chase were uneventful, but that wouldn't be even remotely true. The next day started benignly enough, though: Rowan texted everyone he had ever heard of and several to which he'd received referrals.

Mrs. P did much to enrage me by sashaying around in a manner intended to aggravate me. And aggravate she did.

"Why do you look at me that way?" she asked, flipping her waist-length hair back with a practiced move. "It's not like I told your man to leave you."

I pursed my lips. She wore a fairy costume, complete with gossamer wings, nearly see-through low-cut bodice and skirt, and a bag of glitter she called her fairy dust.

"For one, that costume you're almost wearing was supposed to be mine. We agreed that you'd be the cheerleader and I'd get to be the fairy." I gestured down to my cheerleader pleated miniskirt and cotton sweater. "I'm too chubby for this outfit. Your skirt is longer."

"But it suits me much better. See? My bosom is perkier than yours now."

She had a point, damn her. I made a mental note to ask the laundry if they'd managed to clean the Xena outfit yet. Thus far, they'd taken their own sweet time cleaning the items we had daily taken to them. I shook a pom-pom at her. "And for another thing, I saw you trying to score a few points with Rowan earlier. I didn't appreciate it, and if you try it again, you'll find your lovely long hair tied in a knot around your throat."

She laughed, a silvery, tinkly sound that made me very aware that I had what was politely termed a smoky voice, but was really just plain ole rough and unattractive. "I was, I admit. Not that I could bed him here—my beau would know and not be happy with me. But I did want to see what sort of man you had and whether he would remain true to you. I think he will."

"I know he will," I said without as much conviction as I'd have liked.

"Then you have nothing to worry about, do you?" she said, tossing a handful of fairy dust on my head and laughing her way to her bedroom to change for some time at the pool.

I threw a pom-pom at the door and returned to the project of attempting to convert the pair of shorts that came with the cheerleading outfit into suitable underwear.

"I'm feeling distinctly like a third wheel," I commented later that day, when Mrs. P and her coterie of priestesses trooped into the room fresh from the swimming pool.

"We asked you to come swim with us, but you refused," Mrs. P said, tossing off her swimsuit cover-up and heading into the bedroom.

"You didn't miss much, although your friends were up there being nosy again," Bunefer said, plopping down on the window seat.

"May and Gabriel?" I asked, wondering what they were up to.

"No, the two old ladies. Gidget and Moondoggie."

"Ken and Barbie," I corrected. "I think they're just dying to be of help. They are some sort of cherubs or something from a divine place. Kind of a heaven."

"The Court of Divine Blood?" one of the priestesses asked. Ahset, I think, although I got her and her (biological) sister Henit mixed up. She looked thoughtful. "Henny and I spent a summer being apprentices in the Court, and I don't remember seeing them. But then, I didn't meet everyone."

"That's what they said, and I don't see why they'd lie about being cherubs. I mean, that's kind of an odd thing to claim if it's not true."

She shrugged. "After they left, the captain came around and told us to stop being so loud and to stop scaring off other passengers, and all sorts of other mean-spirited things like that, which of course Ipy wasn't going to stand for. She read him the riot act about passengers having the right to play in the pool as they see fit, and if we wanted to have music and drink shooters while we were swimming, then that was no business of his, and oh, all sorts of other things like that. All in all, you probably were better off not being with us."

"Goodness. Sounds like you guys had quite the time of it."

"It would have been far more fun without the captain harshing our mellow, I'll tell you that!" Bunefer said before heading into Mrs. P's room.

Gilly entered the cabin at that point, a large beach bag in her arms. She looked around, a faint frown ruining her normally perky expression. She marched into the Mrs. P's room, then came out to ask me, "Is Ipy in your room, by any chance?"

"Not that I know of. Why?"

"She's not here. Ipy never takes a leave without designating one of us as being in charge of Aset's protection."

I sat up from where I'd been slouched and looked around, just as if I'd discover the missing model hiding behind the love seat. "I haven't seen her since you ladies went off to sunbathe and swim. That was almost two hours ago."

"She said she wanted to get more sunblock because Khenut couldn't find hers and she didn't come back. I thought maybe she had too much sun and came in here to have a little rest. Last night's Beach Blanket Bingo party got kind of intense, and she did, after all, win the tequila shooter contest. I wonder where she could be?"

"I heard she had a little argument with the captain."

She made a face. "That man has the soul of a toad. A crusty, pus-riddled toad. Ipy gave him as good as she got, and he left with his tail between his legs."

"Good for her." I got to my feet. "Let me double check to make sure she's not indulging in a hangover from hell. Literally. Ha!"

But Ipy wasn't in my room, nor was she in any of the public rooms on the ship. Gilly and I searched them all, after she alerted the others and told them to stay with Mrs. P while we looked around.

"Right, this is a wash," I said, emerging from the tiny shop. "The saleswoman said Ipy hasn't been in today."

"Where could she have gotten to?" Gilly asked, wringing her hands.

I patted her arm and started up the stairs. "I don't know, but we're going to get to the bottom of this. We'll tell the captain we're missing a passenger and let him search all the parts of the ship we can't."

"I don't like him," Gilly complained, but followed me upstairs nonetheless.

I kept the thought to myself that the captain scared the bejeepers out of me, feeling that one of us had to put on a brave front. Ten minutes later, we emerged from the room that served as the bridge—the habitual haunt of Captain Kherty—and looked at each other with despair.

"He's not a nice man," Gilly said, casting a dark look at the closed door to the bridge. The sound of it slamming behind us still echoed in my ears.

"No, he's not. That doesn't mean we have to sit around and 'wait for Ipy to come crawling out of wherever she's hidden to sleep off her hangover'—honestly, how that man can live with himself with that sort of attitude toward his passengers is beyond me. No sir. We're going to find her. Come on, let's go rile up a couple of dragons."

"Are you sure that's wise?" Gilly asked, trotting after me when I went to find Rowan.

"What's the use of having tame dragons at your beck and call if you can't get them to overrule a snotty captain?" I asked lightly. "Why don't you go to May and Gabriel's cabin and see if they are there. Ask them to meet me up on the promenade deck. I'll drag Rowan away from whatever bit of research he's doing, and we'll have a confab."

She trotted off to do that, and I proceeded to search for Rowan. We hadn't seen him during our previous search, leading me to believe that he was closeted somewhere working on the problem of the ring. It took a while, but at last I found him on the pool deck, sitting sideways on a lounge facing Gabriel, who was seated likewise. The two men seemed to be in deep conference.

"—do you control it? All I have to do is look at her and I instantly want to take her to bed."

Gabriel smiled, revealing dimples. "Ah, that is the curse of wyverns—our mates are precious to us, so we tend to feel emotions concerning them to a greater degree. Control, as I have said, is the key to all issues—if you can control your fire and your emotions, then you can control your sept. I find it helps to center myself in one place in time, and then use that to ease any rampant emotions that threaten to get the better of me."

"What if I don't have a centering place in time?" Rowan asked.

It warmed my heart that he was seeking advice. I knew that he'd struggled the last few days with all the new and intense emotions he'd been feeling, and I had hoped he'd take advantage of the older and wiser Gabriel. I paused just out of Rowan's sight, although I had a feeling Gabriel knew I was there.

"I'm sure you will find that you do. Just think of a time when you were feeling that all was right with the world and your future was limitless and without clouds. For me, that moment was when May swore fealty to me, and I knew she would be by my side forever."

"Hmm," Rowan said, obviously thinking. "There was the bike my father bought me when I was seven. I loved that thing. Rode it for years, every summer, all day and most of the night, given the midnight sun in Sweden. Rode it to pieces, as a matter of fact."

"An idyllic childhood summer would be a good centering time," Gabriel agreed.

"But I think I'd have to go with the first time I saw Sophea," he said, warming my heart even further.

Gabriel's eyes flickered briefly toward me. "Ah, it was love at first sight, was it?"

"No, far from it," he admitted. "I thought she was a red dragon and was trying to steal the ring from Mrs. P for her own purposes. I thought she was deceptive, and manipulative, and probably quite deadly."

"That doesn't seem like a very grounding moment," Gabriel objected gently.

"Ah, but it was also the first time since the accident with the dragons that I felt fully alive, aware that life spread out before me with endless possibilities, and that Sophea was an opponent worthy of my fullest attention. I had no idea if she was going to beat me or not, but I knew I'd give her my best." He must have felt me approaching because he half turned when I leaned down to kiss his cheek. "And I turned out to be right. She is a worthy of my fullest attention."

"Pretty words, wyvern," I said, moving around to sit beside him, reveling in the feel of his leg against mine. "But let's have a little more of that attention toward not setting everything in the cabin on fire every time we get a little romantic."

Rowan made a face. "I admit I'm not very much in control of fire yet."

"What did you mean when you said that May swore

fealty to you?" I asked Gabriel. "That's like an oath of honor, yes?"

"In a way, yes. All dragons swear fealty to their wyvern, including their mates. It means simply that you as a mate will put Rowan first in your thoughts and will do your best for the sept. In turn, Rowan will swear to protect and honor you. You are not truly considered mated until the oath of fealty is sworn." His eyes held an obvious question.

I ignored it, trying to decide if the promises we had made each other a couple of nights before had been sufficient to be considered an oath of fealty. "Maybe you can tell me what this is. Rowan . . . I don't know what the verb would be—burned? Marked?—anyway, he did this to me, and we are at a loss why he did it. Or even how." I knelt down between the two men, and lifted the hair off the back of my neck to show the odd tattoo.

"Ah, Rowan has placed a sept mark upon you. Interesting choice of images," Gabriel said. "The silver dragons bear the image of a hand with a crescent moon. The sept mark is something all dragons give to their mates and children. If you have given the oath of fealty, then you should be able to reciprocate the mark on Rowan."

"How?" I asked.

"Breathe fire on the same spot on his neck."

I looked at Rowan. He looked back at me. "I don't know how to breathe fire," I told him.

"No, you don't. You can set fire to your feet, though."

"And I did spit out a little ball of fire at that talking dog."

"True. Would that do the trick?" Rowan asked Gabriel.

He shrugged. "It might. Or it might be a matter of Sophea practicing how to harness your fire. No doubt she didn't have time to learn to use Jian's before he was killed, so her abilities might be a bit stunted." Gabriel rose. "If there are no more questions, I must go find May. She wishes to pick out a costume for me for tomorrow's party, and although I can think of few things I'd like to do less than prance around in a costume, I live to make her happy."

"Actually, I do have another question. Ipy is missing. You two haven't seen her, have you?"

Rowan looked thoughtful. "I passed them this morning. They were all wearing swimsuits, so I gathered they were coming here."

"They did, but Ipy left shortly thereafter and hasn't been seen since. And the captain"—I shot a disparaging look toward the bridge—"insists that she's just sleeping off a hangover. But that's not like Ipy. She takes her guard duties very seriously."

"We can have a look around," Rowan said, getting to his feet.

We made it down to the main saloon on the floor below before one of the crewmen staggered into the room, a blanket-covered form in his arms. I didn't have to see under the blanket to recognize what it was—a body.

"Oh, dear goddess, no," I said, my stomach twisting around on itself. "No, not Ipy. Tell me that's not Ipy!"

Another crewman followed with a second blanketed bundle, this one much smaller. Both men looked faintly green. "Get the captain," the first one said to the second, who promptly put down his small bundle, ran to a wastebasket, and threw up violently and noisily.

"I don't want to know what that is, do I?" I asked Rowan, tears making my throat hurt.

He glanced at the small bundle to which I was pointing and shook his head. "Go back to the cabin."

I thought about arguing, but decided this was one time I wasn't going to fight for equality in dealing with difficult situations.

I ran out of the room, almost mowing down May and Gilly as they were coming upstairs.

"Come with me, both of you," I said quietly and, taking Gilly by the arm, steered her down to the cabin.

"What is it? Did you find Ipy? Is she ill?" Gilly asked when we closed the door behind us. My throat was still aching with the need to cry...not cry, scream. Rail. Wail and sob and generally grieve as loudly as I could. But I knew if I gave in, the others would as well. Control, that's what was needed here. Compassion for the feeling of the priestesses, yes, but I had to remain in control to ensure Mrs. P was kept safe.

"Yes, we found her. Come along—I only want to do this once."

May looked concerned, but said nothing as we entered Mrs. P's room. Several of the ladies were lying on makeshift pallets on the floor, one or two reading, one playing on a tablet computer, and a couple with eyeshades on, clearly having a nap. Mrs. P was sitting with Bunefer, having an intricate henna tattoo applied to the back of her hand.

"Ladies—" My voice broke. I cleared it and tried again. "Ladies, I have some very bad news. Tragic news. Ipy has been...she's passed away."

"What?" Gilly screeched and grabbed my arm. "How can she? She's like the rest of us—immortal. She can't just die."

I tried to forget that image of the smaller second bundle. "I think...I think someone did a grievous injury to her."

Silence filled the room for a few seconds, then I was peppered with questions. What had happened? Where was Ipy now? How had she been killed?

Although I expected the questions, what I didn't expect were the dry eyes and relative sense of calm.

"I…" I stopped and shook my head. "I don't want to sound callous, or like I'm judging how you're grieving, because I know from my husband's death that everyone grieves differently, but aren't you guys… upset?"

"Why should we be?" Mrs. P asked as Bunefer continued inking a fanciful pattern.

"Because one of your dear sisters just died," I said, my hands on my hips. "Great Caesar's balls, woman—one of your fellow priestesses is no more!"

"She'll be back," Mrs. P said, giving me pause.

"She will?"

May's gaze was on nothing as she clearly thought through the situation. At last, her eyebrows rose, and she gave a little nod. "I see. She died in the Underworld."

"Ahh," I said, enlightenment dawning. "You mean she's in the prefect place to be… reborn?"

"Most likely in spirit form, I'd imagine," May said, glancing at Mrs. P, who nodded.

"She should be along shortly, full of fire for what happened," Gilly said. "I can't imagine who would be idiot enough to kill someone in the one place where death has no meaning. Not in that way."

"Well, at least we'll find out who did it to her," I said, my mind thinking of that smaller bundle. I shuddered despite the relatively happy ending to the tragedy.

"Most likely so."

May and I left shortly thereafter. May's demeanor

was slightly ruffled, and she murmured something about finding Gabriel and talking to him about the possibility of it being a demon attack. I decided to find Rowan and demand some solace when Mrs. P poked her head out of the bedroom and gestured toward me.

"Did you need something?" I asked, approaching her.

She caught my wrist and pinned me back to the wall with her sapphire gaze. "You are my champion in all things, Sophea, and I appreciate that fact. I didn't understand until now why he brought us together, but it has been made clear to me. Do not fail me. All will be lost if you do."

"Who brought us together?" I asked, but she simply closed the door in my face. I stared at the wood for a few seconds, then sighed, carefully locked the cabin door behind me, and went out to find Rowan.

I badly wanted some answers and just hoped he'd be able to provide them.

Sixteen

"I like Gabriel's attitude," I told Rowan when I finally found him.

He looked first surprised, then angry. "You're my mate! You're supposed to favor me over all others!"

I laughed and licked the tip of his nose. "You're adorable when you're enraged about something so silly. Calm down, I didn't say I liked Gabriel—I said I liked his attitude. And by that I was referring to the fact that he was so willing to do something that would please May. Do you live to make me happy?"

"Of course," he said, relaxing enough to give me a look that damn near steamed my cheerleader socks.

"Well then, since Ipy's death isn't the tragedy that I thought it would be—and really, can we have a moment to process the fact that everyone is just fine with her being killed and turned into a ghost?—what say we go back to my room and I can harness your fire?" I gave him a come-hither look. "Mrs. P said Ipy won't return in spirit form for a few hours, so we might as well put them to good use and let me try to put this mark on you, so we can match."

"Only if you promise to do a couple of cheers for me afterward," he said, goosing me as I sashayed past him.

I had to admit, the fire thing sounded a lot easier than it was. Rowan, lying facedown on my bed, said patiently, "How long is this going to take?"

"I don't know," I said, looking down at his bare neck. "I've never done this."

"Just spit a bit of fire at me, so we can get down to business."

"What business?" I asked, thinking he wanted to discuss the magic ring issue again.

"I'm going to sex you up until you can't think straight."

"Oooh. I like the sound of that. All right, brace yourself, one sept mark coming up."

He tensed as I leaned over him, gathered my thoughts, and imagined the ring of fire that frequently appeared at my feet when I was kissing Rowan, translated into a ball. A bright glow the approximate size of a quarter danced before my eyes. I mentally threw it at the back of his neck.

One of his shoulders twitched. "Was that it?"

I peered down at him. "Well... not really. I mean, I see a bit of a mark there. I think it's a sword, and a C shape behind it. Is your mark supposed to be different from mine?"

"I don't believe so. Maybe it's not complete?"

"Oh, good point." I summoned up more fire. This time, it formed a ball the size of a small lemon. I reached out to hold it, feeling that a little more control was in order, and tossed it up in the air a couple of times before splashing it onto the back of Rowan's neck.

"I felt that," he said, arching his neck for me to see.

"Did it hurt?" I asked, worried that I'd messed up.

"No."

"Good. I see more of a circle shape, but it's still not like the one you say is on the back of my neck. It's more a K with a C behind it."

"Try again."

In all, it took three more balls of fire (the largest of which reached the size of an orange) before I managed to get the whole image imprinted on his neck. Two more balls of fire set fire to a nearby book and the pillowcase, but at long last I traced the image of a pair of crossed swords over the outline of a circle. "Okay, this is pretty cool, I have to admit, although it did ding my pride a bit that it took you only one try to do it, and I had to have several goes at it."

Rowan rubbed his neck as he sat up. "That's because I'm a wyvern."

I smiled at him. "You sound so comfortable saying that, like it's a perfectly natural thing."

"It is natural, now," he said, eyeing my sweater. "You look hot in that."

I tugged the miniskirt down. "You don't think it's a bit too short? I don't have long svelte legs like Mrs. P has now, and having a bunch of underwear models running around is making me paranoid that my legs are pudgy and stocky."

"Your legs," he said, rubbing a hand up the back of one of my legs, "are beyond delightful. They are in no way pudgy or stocky, but are instead delightfully satiny, well formed, and arousing beyond human belief."

"Dragon belief," I corrected him breathlessly as he pulled me toward him. He was still sitting, so his face was at the level of my belly, a fact he put to use when he slid his hands upward toward my recently repaired underwear.

"That, too." He pushed my sweater up and kissed my belly. "I actually meant that you looked warm in the sweater, but you are also hot in the arousing sense. Very arousing. So much so that... oh no."

He sighed.

"Oh no what?" I asked, suddenly worried that my stomach had offended him.

He held up an arm. The hand was covered in red scales. As I watched, the scales rippled up his arm to his bicep. "It's you. Every time I think about making love to you, this happens. And that." He slapped out the fire that was burning merrily next to him on the bed.

"Actually, I think that was my doing," I said. "I really liked the way you slid your hands under my undies. Oh, goddess, yes, right there!"

His fingers dipped into my hidden parts, a fact I enjoyed greatly until I looked down and saw his expression. "Rowan? Is everything okay down there?"

"Hush," he said, his face screwed up in concentration. "I'm finding my happy place."

I wiggled my hips. His fingers were still inside me. "You sure as shootin' found *my* happy place."

He opened one eye to glare at me. "I am attempting to find my inner calm, woman. Stop distracting me with your breasts and belly and all the warm, soft, wet parts of you that are even now beckoning me to explore their depths. With my mouth. And dick. Oh, lord, this isn't helping. All I can think about is burying myself in you."

"Focus," I told him, wanting to help him gain control. "Keep breathing. Think about the summers riding your bike."

"No, I'll think about you on the plane," he said, his eyes closed. He wiggled his fingers inside me. I did a little Kegel to show support. After about a minute, he opened his eyes. "There. Now I have it."

"You do indeed," I said, nodding to where his hand disappeared under my skirt.

He smiled, a wicked, wicked smile, and withdrew his hand to slide my skirt off. In one move too fast for me to follow, he had my sweater and bra off, as well, and had tossed me down onto the bed. "And now I have you exactly where I want you."

"Oooh, are we role playing?" I asked, pleased to note that he had, indeed, regained control, leaving his arm entirely human again.

"Oh, you're going to be ravished," he said, and peeled off his shirt.

I squealed softly and reached for his wonderful chest.

And at that moment, a deep gong sounded from somewhere in the bowels of the ship.

Rowan froze.

I stopped trying to wrap my legs around him and frowned. "Was that—"

"Yes." He swore under his breath and rolled off the bed, jamming his feet in his shoes at the same time he grabbed my Xena sword. "Dammit, what a time for the second challenge."

He was gone out of the room before I could even ask what he was going to do.

"Fire," I said to myself as I snatched up the first garment I could find, which turned out to be his shirt. I slipped it over my head, grabbed the cutlass from my pirate outfit, and ran after Rowan, going down, not up, to where I knew the gangplank would be.

As I suspected, the ship had docked at some point, and Rowan was already standing on shore. I ran down after him, his shirt falling to midway down my thighs. "What's going on? Where's the fire challenge?" I asked, panting a little when I reached him.

The second I stepped off the ship, it disappeared, just blinked out of existence, leaving Rowan and me standing on a yard-wide bit of dirt surrounded by a lake of fire.

"Ask and ye shall receive," Rowan said, surveying the situation. I looked behind us, but evidently, we had been stranded in the middle of a fire lake, with no obvious way to shore.

I squinted into the distance, trying to calculate how far it was. "Can we swim that, do you think?"

"I'm not sure how deep it is. Perhaps we can just walk through it. I see now why Mrs. P insisted that a dragon be the one to deal with the challenges—anyone else would have issues with fire."

I smiled, confidence filling me with a positive outlook despite the situation. "And we are masters of handling it."

Rowan bent to use the sword as a measuring stick, but yelped and jerked his arm out of the fire almost instantly. We both stared in horror at the red welts and blisters that formed on the flesh of his hand and forearm.

"Great Caesar's gob!" I exclaimed, wanting to do something to help him, but unable to think of anything. "That fire burned you."

"I noticed." His voice was gravelly as he took a couple of deep breaths.

"But...but...how? You touched my hand with fire in that restaurant in Germany and it didn't burn me. It just felt warm. Why is this different?"

"I don't know." His face reflected the pain of the burn. I turned around, desperately seeking something or someone to help him. "Perhaps because it's Duat fire and not fire from our reality. It's not deep, probably about waist high, but we definitely won't be able to swim through it."

"What about your arm?" I said, doing a little dance of frustration when a spasm caused his lips to tighten.

"Gabriel said all dragons can heal themselves," he said slowly, taking another couple of deep breaths. "Although the silver dragons are evidently the best at it. He said it's just a matter of focusing on the hurt part."

"Do it," I said, putting my hands on his non-injured arm as if that would help him heal. "Just go to your calm place, and then focus on your arm."

He stared sightlessly into the distance, his breath evening out, and after a few minutes of silence, the blisters began to sink back into his flesh and disappear. I watched in amazement as the redness and welts also faded away. Five minutes after he started, he waggled his fingers and sighed in relief. "Well, that's a handy skill to have. I wish I'd known how to do that before. I once had an insect bite on my calf turn septic, and I spent a week in a Sao Paulo hospital before I could walk again."

I gently took his injured hand, turning it over to make sure there wasn't any residual burning or scarring, but it was just as hale and hearty as before he stuck his hand in the fire. "I'm going to be sure to send a thank-you note to the First Dragon just as soon as we get back to the normal world. But the question remains—how are we going to get back there? And just where is everyone else? Why aren't they stuck out here with us?"

"Only one person on the boat has to successfully complete the challenges," he said, eyeing the shore on the opposite side. "I suspect the rest of the passengers are quite content to let us do all the work."

"That's well and fine, but unless you've got a couple of asbestos blankets hidden on your person, I don't see how we're going to beat this one."

He looked thoughtful. "Why would Mrs. P want a dragon for this job if the fire was going to be harmful to us?"

"I don't know." I was silent for a moment as I mulled that over. "It must be because we can do something no one else can do. Change into a scaly beast?"

"Possibly. What are dragons known for?"

"Love of gold," I said, ticking the items off on my fingers. "Breathing fire. An interest in virgins."

One side of Rowan's mouth quirked upward. "Give me a lusty brunette widow any day."

"You get an extra fondle on your noogies for that. Later, that is." I bit my lower lip as I continued to dredge through my memory. "You can heal yourself, but there's no way you can walk through that fire, let alone me do the same."

"Fire," he said thoughtfully, and with a face filled with concentration, set his hand on fire.

"That's your fire," I said, clicking my tongue at my inanity. "Sorry for being Captain Obvious, but that's not the same fire as what's all around us."

"No, but this fire doesn't hurt us. And it's what dragonkin are known for, right? So perhaps this is the answer."

"You're going to try burning the fire in the lake with dragon fire?" I asked, confused.

"No. I'm going to use my fire as an asbestos blanket." He took a deep breath and flashed me a smile. "Ready?"

"For what—Rowan!" I screeched, and tried to grab his arm when he plunged it back into the fire. This time he didn't yelp and he didn't pull his arm out instantly. He swished it around a few times, then stood up straight and held the arm out for me to examine.

It was uninjured.

I stared at it for a few minutes, then looked into his eyes. Quiet triumph was there, tinged with some well-deserved pride. "You're a genius. Except... can you cover your lower half with fire?"

His brows pulled together in concentration. Fire sprang up at his feet, spreading upward over his knees, and continuing to spiral up to his waist. He let it get as high as his stomach, then looked at me speculatively. "Can you do this?"

"I don't know. I've never tried. The best I've done is the ball I had to splash repeatedly on your neck." I closed my eyes and tried to find a place in my head that would allow me to access Rowan's fire.

Three tiny little lemon-sized balls formed in my hands. I tried to smear them on my bare legs, but they just went out.

"That answers that question." Rowan looked out at the shore. "We're just going to have to risk it."

"Risk what? You carrying me?"

He nodded. "Actually, I'm going to put you up on my shoulders. Just pretend you're a small child trying to see over the heads of others."

"You're kidding," I said, looking from his shoulders to the fiery inferno all around us. "I'll crush you into the fire and then we'll both burn to death. And I won't be able to heal up. Not that, obviously, you can heal yourself from death. At least I don't think you can. Can you?"

He laughed, and kissed me so swiftly I wasn't able to respond before it was over. "I appreciate you thinking I can conquer death, but no, I'm certain that even wyverns can't do that. We are both immortal now; according to Gabriel, you became so the second you accepted either your husband as your mate—assuming you had time enough to do that—or accepted me. And since I know you did the latter, you, my adorable half-naked nymph, are practically immortal."

"But we can both still be killed, right?"

"Yes. It just takes a lot more to accomplish that."

I gestured to the fire. "Seems to me that would do it."

His smile faded. "It would if we didn't have my fire. Ready?"

"Not even remotely," I said, shaking my head and backing up the one step that was all the available landscape.

"I won't let you get hurt," he promised. I smiled a little to myself—that was most definitely the wyvern talking. The question was, did I trust his newfound wyvern abilities to handle this seemingly impossible position?

"All right, but if you drop me and I die horribly in the fire, I'm going to haunt you 'til the end of your days."

"I should hope so. Up you go."

It took a bit of time to get me hoisted up onto his shoulders, and then my balance was so wobbly I had to clutch his head.

"Sophea, I can't see if you're going to cover my eyes like that," he pointed out.

"Oh. Sorry." I adjusted my grip, my legs tucked back underneath his arms as if we were in a pool playing chicken fight.

"Here we go. Flame on!"

"Ha ha ha, very funny. I just hope—aiee!"

Rowan stepped down into the fire, his body up to his adorable belly covered in dragon fire. I curled my toes into his sides and clutched his hair as he walked toward the far shore, praying to any and all gods I could think of (including the First Dragon, should he be listening) that the lake got no deeper.

It didn't.

"Well now," Rowan said twenty-three minutes later when he deposited me on the bank at the other side of the lake. He leaped up to join me, the sweat beading on his brow the only sign that he was as nervous as I was. "That wasn't so bad, was it?"

I stared at him. "It's as if you are a normal person, and yet you're speaking utter and complete tripe. Not so bad, Rowan? *Not so bad?* We could have died out there! Immortally died!" I clutched the dried grasses of the bank and contemplated just what we'd been through. "I almost fell off you seven times."

"Six. I wouldn't count the time I stumbled as being your fault."

I held up my foot, which was now sans one tennis shoe. "I'm lucky that it was only my shoe that got it when you almost fell and I slid around the front of you."

He had the nerve to smile when he pulled me to my feet, wrapping an arm around my waist and turning me so the fire lake was to our backs. "Ah, but I greatly enjoyed you twisting around my body to get back into place. I would have liked it more if you'd done as I suggested and gone commando."

I glared at him and limped forward. "It's bad enough

I'm just wearing your shirt, and don't you think I'm not going to have a lot more to say to you about your fantasy about me going commando, but right now, I just want to get back to the ship, take a very cool shower, put on my Xena outfit—assuming the laundry people finally got to it—and make sure that hussy Mrs. P and her gaggle of sexy girls haven't had some horrible accident while we were stranded. Following which I may lie down and refuse to deal with any more shenanigans of this type."

Rowan took my hand, whistling softly to himself. Part of me was annoyed that he wasn't as traumatized by our near miss as I had been, while the other part was filled with admiration. I hadn't been sure when we started across the lake, but now I had every confidence that Rowan would make an admirable wyvern. If the man could handle walking through a fiery hell with a panicky woman clinging to his head and still make it out alive, then he could handle anything other dragons threw at him.

The bank rose in a gentle slope, and as we crested it, we could see the ship sitting placidly on the river some two hundred feet away.

Cheering broke out on board the ship as we approached, all the passengers lining the upper deck waving and calling congratulations at yet another challenge bested. I glared at them all, making a mental note to speak to them about someone else taking a turn, but realized as we entered the relative coolness of the lowest level of the ship that the final challenge was personal to each individual.

And as soon as it was over, Mrs. P would present the ring to her boyfriend.

As we stepped on board, the captain greeted us, saying, "You completed the challenge."

"We did," Rowan said, and I felt a little flame of ire within him.

I couldn't blame him. The way the captain stated the obvious made my hackles go up a bit. If I didn't know better, I'd have sworn he would have liked us to fail.

Captain Kherty watched us for a moment, his expression completely unreadable, before giving a brief nod, and gesturing us toward the stairs. "You will no doubt wish to celebrate your accomplishment at the party later this evening. You will be my guests of honor."

It was a statement, not a question, and although I wanted to tell him that we might have other plans, I reminded myself that antagonizing a man who could quite probably toss us off his ship wasn't the best policy.

Besides, I had a couple of questions for him.

"One moment, please," I said, pausing at the bottom of the stairs. "Have you found out who killed Ipy?"

"No." His black eyes were as unreadable as his face. "We have not discovered a weapon or motive for the assault. The lady's spirit has returned to the ship, and she herself does not know who her attacker is."

"Doesn't that concern you?" Rowan asked. "Were I in your shoes, I'd be more than a little worried about a murderer running rampant on my ship."

"But you are not in my shoes," the captain replied. "And this is Duat. All who travel here—all who are *rightfully* here—are not among the living. What is another death when you are already in spirit form?"

"Ipy wasn't dead," I argued. "Neither are any of the other priestesses, or Mrs. P, or May and Gabriel, and of course Rowan and me. There's lots of non-dead people here, and as one of them, I'd sure as shooting appreciate it if you could get off your ass and find the mad decapitator, so he can't go around lopping off anyone else's head."

"Get off my ass?" the captain asked, his voice filled with menace. "You dare speak to me thusly? I will not have it!"

Instantly, Rowan kicked into high dragon gear. He moved in front of me, his body language reading irritated aggression. "Do you threaten my mate?"

"I will not be addressed in that manner. *I* am captain of this ship."

"Then do your job and keep your passengers safe," Rowan snapped.

The captain growled and took a step forward.

Rowan's body tensed, as if he was getting ready to spring.

"Whoa now," I said, realizing that my ill-advised comments had pushed things too far. I insinuated myself between the two men, using my body to force Rowan back a few steps. "I may have been a little rude with the 'get off your ass' comment. If so, I apologize. Tempers are a bit frayed what with the whole escaping near-death in a lake of fire situation, so why don't we all just agree to move past this, hmm?"

The captain glowered at Rowan, but after a moment in which I thought the two men were going to get into a physical altercation, the captain gave a sharp nod. "Your apology is accepted. The party starts at eight p.m. I will expect you there."

I tugged Rowan up the stairs, ignoring his rude comments toward the captain. "Sorry to get you riled up. I was just so angry about the way no one sees Ipy's death as being a big deal."

He took a deep breath. "We have to remember that these aren't mortal people, and we are not in the mortal world. Death here has a different meaning."

"Gotcha."

Ahead of us, Mrs. P and her team passed by an intersection of the hallway, singing a song in a language I didn't understand. I was heartened to see Ipy in their group. Gilly spied us and ran down the hall to give Rowan and me big hugs.

"I'm so happy to see you both safe again! I bet the challenge was awful. The captain said you likely wouldn't make it and someone else would have to go out to do the job."

Ken and Barbie rounded a corner at the same time that the captain, behind us, emerged from the stairs, and with a smoldering look our way, proceeded up the next flight.

"I'd like to say it wasn't that bad, but it was hideous," I told Gilly, suffering her to give me another bear hug. "But honestly, all the credit goes to Rowan. He was downright magnificent in the way he problem-solved."

Rowan looked modest. "I was inspired to beat the situation."

Gilly eyed my unconventional garb and burst into laughter. "I can see that you were. I'll let you go. I'm sure you want to... debrief."

"Cute," I said when she snickered. "I see Ipy is back."

"Yes, her spirit is." She glanced over her shoulder when Ken yoo-hooed us midway down the hall. "She says she didn't see who lopped off her head, but she's sworn vengeance on him or her. Luckily, her Ka is still intact, so she'll be able to leave Duat, although she'll always be a spirit."

"Kinda puts a crimp on your day, I would imagine."

"She doesn't seem to mind," she said, giving my arm a squeeze before she dashed up the stairs.

"Hello again!" Ken called, bustling up to us before we

could follow Gilly. "Hail the conquering heroes. I would ask you how the challenge went, but the very fact that you are here tells me what I want to know."

"It was pretty frightening," I told them, a little irritated at having to stay and make small talk when I wanted to think over the afternoon's events.

"I imagine so, oh, I can imagine it was very frightening. And your employer there, she looked so very happy to see you unharmed."

"If you'll excuse us," Rowan said before I could straighten out Ken's misimpression, "we are a bit tired, and I know Sophea would like to get cleaned up and changed into something a little less revealing."

"Of course you would. Oh, you poor thing, having to traipse around in your . . . er . . . shirt."

"Lucky you weren't fried to a crisp," Barbie said with her usual gruff manner.

I forced a smile to my lips, then allowed Rowan to pull me up the stairs to our cabin.

"Not that I don't like them, but thank you. Standing there dissecting the challenge is the last thing I want to do right now."

"Good," he said with a lascivious waggle of his eyebrows. "I have other plans for you, anyway."

We entered the cabin, but all the ladies were in Mrs. P's room, evidently toasting our success (or the return of Ipy in ghost form) if the cries of happiness audible through the closed door were accurate.

Oddly, melancholy gripped me as we entered my room. "The cruise is due to end tomorrow."

Rowan unloaded his pockets, dumping his small notebook, a couple of pens, the three bits of broken pinkish glass, and his cell phone onto the nightstand. The face he turned to me was as grim as my heart. "That's right."

I swallowed back a lump in my throat. "I don't suppose you've had any insight as to what we can do to stop the ring's doohickey from falling into demon hands?"

He shook his head. "There's one last person I can contact in the morning. He's an archimage, and has more than a little passing interest in alchemy. He's also in charge of the group that polices the Otherworld, so he's difficult to get hold of. I've been told he might answer a call from me in the morning."

I sighed and plopped down on the bed. "That seems very last chance, but I don't suppose we have an alternative."

"None," he said, sitting next to me. His shoulders slumped just a little, making me scoot over until I was pressed against him. He put his arm around me, and we sat like that for a long time, looking out of the porthole as the ship got underway again.

There just didn't seem to be much more to say.

Seventeen

"Goddess above, below, and behind!"

Rowan looked up from his notebook when Sophea stormed into their cabin, slamming the door behind her. In her hand she held two bags. "Problems, my sweet?"

"Great galloping... gah!" Sophea struck a dramatic pose and waved a hand around. "Now Gilly's disappeared."

A little chill caressed Rowan's spine. "Are you sure? No, that's a stupid question. Of course you're sure. Has the captain been notified?"

"Ha. Big fat lot of good that would do." Sophea set down one of the bags, using the other to gesture. "I told one of the officers that Gilly never came back after we had seen her, and he just said that if passengers wished some privacy, then it was nothing to do with them."

Rowan raised his eyebrows and pondered whether it was worthwhile to demand the captain search the ship. "We were the last ones to see her?"

"Yes. She ran upstairs right after the captain passed us."

"Hmm." His mind turned over memory of their return to the ship. "Tell me again how you found out that the first priestess was missing."

Sophea gave him a long look. "Why? Do you see a connection other than they're both underwear priestesses, and no one is overly alarmed if they disappear or have their respective heads lopped off? It *was* a head that was under that blanket, wasn't it?"

"It was. But I'd like you to tell me about the situation with Ipy."

"All right, but I demand you tell me what you are thinking, because I'm totally clueless." Sophea spent the next ten minutes telling and retelling the conversation with Bunefer and Gilly.

"Hmm," he said again, thinking about it.

"Okay, your turn to dish. Hmm what?"

"Hmm, does it strike you that each time a woman has disappeared, the captain has been present or just left the scene?"

Sophea opened her eyes wide, goggling at him in a manner he found especially adorable. "You can't... the captain? I mean, I don't like the man, but... really? You think he's the madman?"

"He's certainly got a temper on him and a bit of a dictator attitude."

"Yeah, but lots of people are bossy like that, and it doesn't make them a murderer."

"True, and I'm not ready to accuse the man. I just think it's interesting that one of the last people to see the two women is him. And evidently he had an argument with Ipy before she was killed."

Sophea obviously mulled that fact over. "Does that help us find Gilly?"

"Not really, no. If you would like, we can search the ship."

"It would make me feel better knowing we at least took the time to hunt for her in case she's in trouble." Sophea set down the other bag.

On the way out of the room Rowan asked, "What is in that bag?"

"Your costume."

"I don't want to wear a costume. Come to it, I don't want to go to the costume party. I just waded through a lake of fire. I want to make love to you, try to contact the archimage, and then go to sleep. I'm willing to forgo the last two so long as I get the first one. You'll notice that nowhere on that list is spending time with the others on this cruise while wearing fancy dress."

"Gabriel is doing it," she told him as they headed for the lowest deck. "You can just suck it up, buttercup, and do it as well. It's our last night on the ship, and Captain Bossy Pants AKA the Possible Executioner has requested our presence." Sophea's face looked unusually drawn, and instantly Rowan wanted to sweep her up into his arms and kiss her to the point where she forgot her troubles. "Besides, this isn't a horrible costume. I had the shop lady set it aside the second day, so no one else would grab it. Do we split up or search together?"

They had reached the lowest level of the ship. Rowan hesitated a moment, then said, "We search together."

She smiled and took his hand, a gesture that kicked his dragon fire into high. "I like it when we think alike."

"Oh, you're thinking about making love to you, too?" he asked with an innocent expression.

She laughed and pinched his arm. Rowan enjoyed the warm glow her presence brought him as they searched all levels of the ship.

Almost an hour later, they emerged from the dining room, hot, tired, and without any success. "Shall we beard the lion in his den?" Rowan asked, gesturing toward the bridge.

"Do you think it will do any good?" she asked.

"We won't know until we try." Rowan didn't wait for her to answer and pounded on the door to the bridge.

It was opened by the captain, whose eyes narrowed when he saw who it was. "What do you want, *dragon*?"

"A few answers, *ferryman*." Rowan wrestled for a moment with his dragon fire, but managed to keep it from flaring out around him. "Are you aware that another passenger has disappeared?"

"*Another* passenger?"

"The first one was decapitated, if you recall," Rowan said, wondering if the man was just pretending to be dense or if he really cared so little about his passengers.

"She did not disappear. She was found," Kherty said dismissively.

"Only after she'd been killed. Now a second one is gone."

"I know."

"And are you doing anything about it?"

The captain shrugged. "I am informed that you just searched my ship—did you find anything?"

"No." Rowan felt an irrational anger build toward the man. Dammit, it wasn't *his* job to be searching the ship. Why wasn't the captain taking more of an interest?

"Then there is nothing more for me to do. Sending men

from their duties to search the ship after you just did so—yes, my crew reported your actions—would be a waste. I prefer to wait patiently for the woman to return."

"With or without her head?" Sophea asked sweetly.

The captain shot her a dark look, then started to close the door.

"I think everyone would be happier if a more formal search were instigated," Rowan said firmly. "One conducted by individuals who know all of the secret places on the ship."

"My ship has no secret places," the captain said firmly, and closed the door in Rowan's face.

Sophea turned to him, her expression of frustration no doubt mirroring his. "Am I crazy, Rowan, or does no one here think it's a big deal for someone to disappear and possibly be killed?"

He took her arm and led her downstairs. "We aren't crazy, love. It's just a different world, one where death is not a permanent end. Most of the passengers consider it an intermediate phase before they go to a new existence."

"Yeah, well, I'd like to talk to Ipy to see how blasé she feels about having had her head lopped off. I just hope Gilly is okay."

"I hesitate to say this because it can only sound callous, but I suppose in the end, we'll find out from her."

"You mean because..." Sophea didn't finish the sentence.

"Yes. If she has met with a fatal accident—or deliberate attack—then she, too, will reappear in time. And perhaps she will have seen who her attacker was."

Sophea rubbed her arms as they entered the cabin. "I don't know about you, but I don't want to be a ghost. So if there's a deadly madman running around, I want him caught."

He gave her a look that let her see the true extent of his emotions. "I will not allow any harm to come to you."

She gave him a blinding smile in return, and after inquiring of the priestesses if Gilly had reappeared (she hadn't), they reentered the bedroom, where Sophea handed him one of the two bags.

He sent her a pleading look. "Do I have to?"

"Yes. Look, it's not as bad as all that." She pulled items out of the bag and laid them out on the bed.

He eyed them. One of the objects was a brown fedora. "What am I supposed to be?"

"Indiana Jones." A fleeting smile graced her lips before she returned to looking worried. "I figured it wasn't so far off from what you really are. Were. Before the First Dragon bopped you on the head, that is."

He took the costume, eyed the accompanying bullwhip, gun with holster, and canvas bag, and decided that the situation could be worse. "I am a sociologist, not an archaeologist, but I agree the costume is not obnoxious. Although I refuse to carry around the rubber snake."

"I think that's meant to be more of a prop than anything." She gathered up the second bag and headed for the door. "Since Mrs. P and her pride of models were heading upstairs to the party, I'll change in her bathroom so you can have ours to have a shower and stuff."

"You don't wish to shower together?" he asked with a waggle of his eyebrows.

"In a heartbeat, but not in that shower. I can barely fit into it as it is."

He had to allow that the shower was very small.

"It might take me a little longer to get ready, so I'll meet you upstairs, okay?"

"Very well." He glanced at his cell phone, willing the mage to call him early. He'd never felt so much like he had his back firmly against a wall, and he didn't like the sensation one little bit.

Twenty minutes later, he scooped his phone and other items off the table and into the canvas bag slung across his chest, and made his way to the upper deck, there finding the party fully underway. Music played—lively, danceable tunes—at the fore of the ship, the area around it having been cleared to serve as a makeshift dance floor. Beyond that were scattered round tables, two banks of buffet food laid out in the form of a smiling crocodile, and a giant punch bowl. Balloons waved gently overhead, tied to the strings of festival lights that festooned the length of the ship. Standing separated from the others were the captain and two of his officers.

Rowan pushed his hat to the back of his head, feeling rakish despite the silliness of being forced into a costume. Perhaps it was the bullwhip coiled at his belt, or some new dragon emotion running rampant through him, but there was more than a little hint of a swagger when he strolled over to where May and Gabriel stood sipping glasses of what looked to be champagne. "Good evening."

"It is, thanks to you," May said, lifting her glass to him.

Gabriel's lips twisted. "I apologize for not being on hand to help with the challenge. We...erm...we..."

"We were otherwise occupied," May said smoothly, a smile hovering around her mouth. "Although Gabriel did wrap things up quickly so he could go help you, but the challenge had already started. Was it awful?"

"Moderately so," he answered, remembering the pain of his burned arm. Absently, he rubbed it.

"There's only one more to go, and that should not be too onerous." Gabriel shot him a piercing look that grated on Rowan's already frayed nerves. "That is, if your soul is not found wanting."

"I did *not* kill those dragons," he ground out through his teeth, and would have given Gabriel a piece of his mind if not for two things: the first was Mrs. P, who was now wearing a *Black Swan* ballet costume, complete with tiara and theatrical makeup. Behind her a woman followed, a woman who made his heart beat faster just watching her. It was at that moment that Rowan realized that what he was feeling wasn't just attraction held by a wyvern for his mate but love. Actual love. The kind that hit him hard in the gut and stripped all the breath from his lungs. It pierced his heart, making him simultaneously giddy and a bit frightened. He'd never felt such depth of emotion for anyone, let alone a romantic partner, and here he was completely and utterly besotted with Sophea.

"Hello, everyone." Sophea smiled at them all, then said with a little nod toward Rowan's gun belt, "I decided that if you were going to have a gun, then I got one, too. And a knife, and a bow and arrows." She pulled a gun from the holster strapped to her thigh. He had a hard time taking his eyes from the form-fitting black sleeveless shirt she wore, until he noticed the equally tight black shorts.

"Hmm?" he said, wondering if people would think it was rude if he picked her up and carried her downstairs.

"Gun. One. We both have. And now I'm evidently doing a Yoda impression. Oh, you look nice, May. Is that a flapper outfit?"

May smiled and did a little twirl. "It is. Isn't the beaded dress exquisite?"

"It's really very pretty. I'm amazed at the quality of these costumes, to be honest."

"And you're Lara Croft?" May guessed.

"Yup. Game version, not Angelina movie version. Game version has lots more weapons." Sophea did a twirl of her own, one that Rowan much appreciated since it allowed him to admire her ass in the tight shorts without having to stand behind her and blatantly ogle. "I feel armed to the teeth. Doesn't Rowan look dashing?"

"Very Indiana," May agreed. "Rowan says you had a hard time with the challenge?"

"Oh, it was awful!" Sophea took a deep breath, then launched into a retelling of what they had gone through, finishing up with, "I can't tell you how thankful I am that Rowan was there, because if it had been up to me to finish the challenge, I'd still be standing on that little plot of land."

"I've never heard of fire we could not harness," Gabriel said with a frown. "It burned your flesh? Actually burned it?"

"Definitely," Rowan answered, rubbing his arm again. "But the healing technique you mentioned helped ease it."

"Hmm." Gabriel looked thoughtful. "I must mention this to the others. I don't like to know there's something out there that is unique to the dragonkin over which we have no power."

"I think there's probably a lot of that," Sophea said. "We still have this third challenge tomorrow, and that's not going to be open to persuasion by dragons. I'm still a little unclear as to what's going to happen."

"As I understand it," May said, "we present ourselves to a goddess named Maat, and she decides if we've lived a good life or not. If not, we have to stay here. If we have, we get to leave."

"That's simplifying it greatly," Gabriel said, nodding. "But that's the basics of it."

Everyone looked at Rowan. "I have lived a good life!" he protested, reading the unspoken comment in May and Gabriel's eyes. At least Sophea wasn't looking upon him with suspicion—she had nothing but warmth and admiration in her expression, a fact that made him feel several feet taller.

"I'm sure you have," May said soothingly, then obviously changed the subject. "Gabriel refuses to put his costume on."

"It's not a matter of putting it on. It's what has to come off," he said, giving Rowan a look that pled for sympathy.

Rowan was having none of it, not because he was being harsh, but because it suddenly occurred to him that if he could admire Sophea's delightful ass in her Lara Croft shorts, then so could other men. He wondered whether if he tied his shirt around her waist, she'd protest much.

"What is the costume?" Sophea asked.

With a martyred sigh, Gabriel pulled an object from his pocket. It was a black shirt collar with attached tie.

"Magic Mike," May said with a little giggle. "But he refuses to take off his shirt."

"I have no need to do so," Gabriel protested, and snapped the collar around his neck. "There. I'm wearing the costume. Are you happy?"

"Very," May said, leaning into him and giving him a look that didn't need any explanation. Rowan eyed

Sophea, who was watching the other two dragons with a tolerant smile. That is, she was until she noticed him staring at her.

"What?" she asked.

He nodded toward May and Gabriel, who were now speaking together at a volume meant only for their ears. "Why don't you look at me the way May looks at Gabriel?"

Startled, she shot May a quick glance before turning back to him. A slow smile took hold of her lips. "You wouldn't by any chance be jealous, would you?"

"Intensely so," he said, much to his amazement. Quickly he attempted to make the admission more reasonable. "It's the dragon emotions."

"Uh huh." Her smile grew until she leaned into him and, nipping the end of his nose, gave him a fleeting kiss. "I promise to look at you exactly the same way later tonight, all right?"

"Very well, but I will hold you to that." He caught a movement from the corner of his eye, and asked her softly, "What is Mrs. P doing?"

Sophea glanced over to where Mrs. P was dancing with the captain. "I believe what we're seeing there is an example of the hoochie-coo done while wearing a tutu. Kind of boggles the brain, huh?"

"It does indeed. I suspect it's also illegal in many countries, Egypt probably being one of them."

"Hopefully not so in the Underworld part of it."

"There you are!" a cheerful voice called out. Rowan turned to find the two cherubs approaching, Ken clad in a costume that had both Sophea and him staring.

Ken stopped in front of them and did a twirl. She wore what Rowan could only think of as Marie Antoinette's idea of shepherdess's outfit, complete with beribboned staff, giant hoop skirt at least two yards wide, a fake lamb on wheels, and towering wig with a hat perched on top. "You like? I saw it and I just knew I had to have it. Isn't the lamb the cutest thing ever? I call her Mary. Get it? Mary!"

"Wow, that's...that's really impressive," Sophea said politely, her eyes huge as she took in the ensemble. "I've never seen a powdered wig so tall. However do you keep it from toppling over?"

"It's all balance, my dear," Ken said archly, and gave the ribbon tied to the sheep a twitch. "Good comportment can never go wrong, I always say."

"And Barbie is..." Sophea paused for a moment. "A gladiator?"

Barbie smiled.

Rowan felt like he had been kicked in the gut. He narrowed his eyes on the woman standing before them in gladiator armor, and thought a great many thoughts in quick succession. Before he could pursue those thoughts, Sophea frowned and crossed over the deck to the railing on the other side. "Hey. We've docked again," she said when he followed her, Ken and Barbie close on his heels.

He looked down to where she pointed, noting a small group of people approaching from a bright red roadster typical of 1930s movies.

"That's interesting." He watched the new passengers with vague suspicion.

"Oooh, new people?" Ken asked, peering down. "Oh, they're not in costume. I hope the captain doesn't let them join us. It'll ruin the whole ambiance."

A woman led the way to the gangplank, followed by three men, two of whom held armloads of books, while the third staggered along with a wooden table that all but obscured his vision.

Rowan considered them. "That's curious. I wonder who they are."

"I have no idea. More people to go to the promised land, do you think?" Sophea asked.

"We wouldn't have picked them up midway through Duat if that was the case," he told her.

"Let us go greet the new arrivals," Barbie said, nodding toward the door into the ship.

"And leave the party?" Ken said, looking horrified. "But we just got here! And I haven't gotten to show everyone my darling costume, let alone join the costume contest, which you just know I'm going to win because honestly, no one else's costume comes even close to the quality of mine. No one else has a familiar…er…sheep with them." Ken gave them a bright, and very brittle, smile. "Present company excluded from that comment about other costumes, of course. Yours are excellent, truly excellent."

"Come," Barbie said, jerking Ken forward so that her wig wobbled precariously.

They moved toward the doorway leading to the inner rooms of the ship at the same moment that a second car pulled up, and two more people emerged, but this time, Rowan was familiar with them.

"That Barbie is kind of rude…whoa. More people? Oh, it's them," Sophea said, noting the newest arrivals. "Your sister and that guy with the long name."

"Constantine." Rowan fought with a spurt of irritation that threatened to blow up into full-fledged anger. "Why are they here interfering? Are they checking up on us? They've already seen that we are now dragons—I don't see why they have to come around bothering us again. Not that I mind seeing my sister, but that dragon she's mated to is another matter."

Sophea slid him a little smile and took his hand, her fingers tight around his giving him a surprising sense of comfort. "Now, now, they haven't done anything to be so testy about. Although I admit I feel a bit like the dragons are keeping tabs on us, which is annoying at best. But I suppose Gabriel and May have helped a bit with watching Mrs. P."

"Let us see if they have any insight as to why those dragons are here." He turned to call Gabriel over, but froze, staring in mingled surprise and anger at the sight of several men climbing over the railing, water pouring off them. Each was armed with at least two swords, and a couple had knives strapped to their legs.

Rowan roared a Portuguese oath and leaped forward, pulling out his gun before he realized that it would do not good—even if it was a real gun, bullets did nothing but enrage demons.

And demons these were. He didn't have to catch the stink of their origins to know—the way they poured over the rail of the ship and pinpointed Mrs. P and her ladies told him everything he needed to know. He threw away the gun and jerked his whip out of the holder just as the passengers realized that they were under attack.

Screams filled the night air, drowning out the music until someone, in their desperation to get away, knocked the CD player over the edge into the water.

The captain took one look at the invasion and shoved Mrs. P at the nearest crew member, pulling from the belt of his Captain Nemo outfit a very real looking scimitar.

"Get her to safety," Rowan yelled at the crewman as he hustled Mrs. P past him. "Sophea! Guard her!"

The whip cracked without him even realizing he'd swung it, and the first of the demons rushing toward him slammed into the railing with a sick snapping sound. He shook the whip free, not in the least surprised to see Gabriel leap past him in a flying tackle, taking down the next demon, wrapping his costume's tie around the demon's neck and tightening it mercilessly.

People stampeded past Rowan to get to safety, but he didn't risk a glance behind him to see if Sophea was taking Mrs. P away to their cabin. He yelled a native insult he'd learned from a shaman and swung the whip at two demons who rushed toward the entrance to the lower levels of the ship. One of them he caught by the leg and pulled back to where the captain was, his scimitar stained black. But the second one was too fast, and just as Rowan started after him, something whistled past his ear. He paused, staring in surprise at the arrow that projected from the back of the demon's neck as it fell to the floor.

He turned to look behind him. Sophea had already nocked another arrow and adopted an archer's stance, her eyes narrowed as she sighted another demon who was about to run him through.

The bow sang, and the demon went down with a squawk. Rowan stormed over to her, not seeing Mrs. P with her. "What the hell do you think you're doing?" he demanded.

"Shooting demons." She quickly pulled out another arrow and fired it off. Behind him, Rowan heard a demon scream. "I have to say, this is the best outfit ever. I mean, I thought the Xena one was good, and it did a whole lot for my boobs, but this bow and arrow is just pure awesome. Duck!"

He opened his mouth to protest, but instead moved to the side just as she shot down another demon. This one did a perfect swan dive over the deck into the water, the arrow projecting from the side of its head.

"Where did you learn to shoot like that?" he asked, shoving her to the side and snapping the whip at the demon who was charging them with a sword held high. He caught the man around the neck, and with a jerk, slammed him into the navigation room wall. The demon fell back and feebly staggered toward them.

"College. Had to take athletics to graduate. I hate sports, so picked archery as the least obnoxious."

"Where's Mrs. P?" He leaped on the back of a demon that had the poor judgment to run too close, sending them both crashing to the ground, whereupon he pounded the man's head into the floor until he went limp.

The bow sang twice in quick succession. "May is protecting her. Damn. I'm out of arrows."

Rowan picked up a chair and walloped a demon with it, sending him tumbling over the rail. "Go help her. This is no place for you."

"Ha! I've killed more demons that you. I just need more arrows…"

"Go away," Rowan roared, hefting the table, and using it to bash two more demons against the wall.

"Why? I'm holding my own." She pulled out a tactical combat knife, and with a yell, stabbed it into the ankles of the two demons he'd just downed, severing their Achilles tendons. One of the demons slashed out with a sword, just catching the outer edge of her arm.

Blood rolled down her arm, causing her to gasp in pain. Rowan screamed an oath and lunged at the demon, twisting its head until the neck snapped. "Get below!" he ordered, his voice an unrecognizable snarl. "You're not safe here."

"I'm fine. I just didn't realize he wasn't as hurt as I thought he was." She glanced behind him, looked around, and plucked her bow from her back, swinging it like a club. It connected with the head of a demon with an ugly noise. The demon dropped.

"Just do what I say!"

"Look, I'm helping," she argued. "Give me one good reason why I should leave when I'm taking down demons."

"Because I love you, damn you!" he bellowed, slamming together two demons with a force he had no idea he possessed. Both fell to the floor with a *whump*, black demon blood making the deck slippery. "I couldn't live if you were killed, all right? Take yourself off now so that later I can peel those shorts off you and caress the glorious globes of your ass, and your breasts, and lick every inch of—"

A demon threw itself on his back, sending him careening forward. He twisted in an attempt to get the demon off, feeling the sting of metal against his flesh as the demon tried to cut his throat, but before he could break the man's arm, Sophea stabbed her blade into the man's wrist, causing the demon to howl and drop his sword.

Rowan flipped him to the deck, stood with his foot on the demon's hand, and said, "Tell your master that his tricks are useless," before snatching the knife from the wrist and jamming it into the demon's heart.

Sophea stood next to him, panting. Rowan turned

to locate the next demon, and beheld a deck scattered with black blood and bodies. At the far end, the captain was wiping his scimitar on the shirt of one of the dead demons. Two more, their bodies broken, tried to crawl to their weapons, but Gabriel kicked them overboard, and then tossed the demons after them.

Rowan caught sight of the blood on Sophea's arm and was instantly filled with rage anew. How dare someone harm his mate? He snatched up a napkin from one of the destroyed tables and tied it around her wound. "We will find the ship's doctor. He must see to your hurt."

"My what? The scratch?" She shook her head and pulled the napkin from her arm in order to use it to press to his neck. "That's nothing compared to you. Sit down. You're losing a lot of blood, and I don't want you to get excited or you'll just bleed more heavily. Can you do that healing thing? Gabriel?"

Sophea strong-armed him into a chair that was still standing. "I'm fine," he protested. "Stop fussing over me and let me attend to your injury."

"Someone's hurt?" Gabriel asked, his eyes widening a little when he saw the front of Rowan's shirt. Rowan glanced down. It was soaked red, from his collar to his belt. "Ah. Just so. If you will let me examine it, Sophea—I am a healer."

"Are you? Like a doctor?"

"Like a doctor," Gabriel agreed, taking the napkin from her. He examined Rowan's neck. "This isn't too bad, although you got off lucky there. He missed your jugular. You should be able to close the wound yourself, but if it gives you trouble, let me know and I can put a little healing salve on it."

"I'll be fine," Rowan protested again. Sophea was

making little worried noises when Gabriel stood up. “Check her arm. She was cut.”

“Scratched,” Sophea corrected him, but she suffered Gabriel to look at the wound. Amusement filled his eyes as he gravely pronounced that Sophea would suffer no ill effect from the injury.

“See? Now you sit right there and concentrate on that wound,” Sophea said, and gave a little shout of annoyance when he started to get up. She plopped herself down on his lap. “You annoying dragon man! Sit here and heal!”

He looked at where her breasts swelled enticingly beneath her tight shirt, and felt an answering swelling in his trousers. “There's no way I can possibly concentrate on my neck with you sitting there tempting me into doing things that I doubt you want me doing in public.”

“Oh. Good point. Sitting on you makes me want to kiss you and touch you and nibble on your ears, and... and... yeah. Point taken.”

She got up just as the captain strolled past them, pausing to raise an eyebrow at Rowan. “Do you need assistance?”

“No. It's not a deep wound, and it should heal,” he answered.

The captain nodded and continued past, giving orders to his crew to clean up the mess once the demon bodies disappeared.

He turned back to them, adding with a wave toward the shore, “We are ahead of schedule. Maat has come on board and will proceed with the third challenge shortly. The journey is now at an end, and your trials will soon be over.” His black eyes moved from Rowan to Sophea and back. “Let us hope the ending is one you seek... and not a punishment.”

Eighteen

"Boy, he really is a little ball of sunshine, isn't he?" I commented as the captain hurried off to greet the goddess Maat and her entourage. "Wait, don't answer that. You probably shouldn't talk or move until your neck is healed."

Rowan came perilously close to rolling his eyes, but instead clearly decided to heed my advice and closed his eyes, his face filled with concentration.

"That really is amazing to watch," I said, marveling at the way the cut flesh stopped bleeding, then began to seal itself up into a raw, red scar. Judging by his hand, I figured even that scar would fade away. "I wonder if you can teach me to do it."

"I will try," he said, his eyes still closed.

I looked down at him, this man who had come into my life and shaken me to my core. "Are you—did you mean what you said?"

His eyes opened at that, confusion fading into

understanding, which melted away under the onslaught of little sparks of golden fire in his eyes. "Yes."

"Oh," I said, my breath catching a little.

"Oh?" His lips thinned. "Is that all you have to say? 'Oh'? Not even a 'how nice,' or 'golly, that's great,' but 'oh'?"

"I'm sorry," I apologized with a giggle. "I don't really say golly. I'm more a 'great Caesar's ghost' sort of girl."

He rose and took my arms in his hands, giving me a gentle shake. "Woman, now is the time for you to tell me just how madly in love with me that you are, and how you cannot conceive of living your life without me, and how you want to spend all of your days with me, and more, all of your nights. Not this 'oh' business that leaves me feeling vulnerable and angsty."

I laughed out loud at that. "I never thought I'd hear you admit you were angsty over anything." I tipped my head back, and said against his lips, "I do love you, you know. It scares me to admit that because I loved Jian, too, and he was taken away from me before I really got to know him, and I don't want to lose you. Promise me you won't leave me, Rowan. I really don't think I could go through losing a second husband."

His breath was hot in my mouth, his tongue hotter, and his fire hottest of all. It wrapped around us like a blanket of desire, causing the heat building in me to burst into an inferno of need and wanting... and love.

"We're on fire again," Rowan said, nibbling on my lower lip, his hands drawing intricate patterns on my behind. I had slipped my own hands under his shirt, and was stroking the muscles of his back.

"You got that right," I answered, doing a little nibbling of my own.

"The captain will not be happy if we scorch the deck."

"Screw the captain," I said heedlessly.

Rowan swung me up in his arms, obviously ready to carry me down to our room where I very much hoped we'd engage in wild, steamy sex. "I'd much rather screw—"

"Ah, these must be the dragons you spoke of." A woman's voice interrupted Rowan's statement and my smutty thoughts.

Rowan turned to face the newcomers, setting me down in the process. "Er... hello."

The woman was dark-skinned, petite, and had wild, curly shoulder-length hair and a wide, genuine smile firmly affixed as she bustled forward. Behind her came the three men, followed by the captain and a couple of his officers. After that, the deck filled up with returning passengers, all of whom chatted excitedly.

"The captain told us you two championed both challenges," the woman said. I figured she had to be Maat, especially since there was a feather tucked into her springy curls. "Well done. Duat needs champions like you. If you choose to remain here, we will be most happy to find you a position in our court."

I wasn't sure if she was speaking for her three lackeys, who were even now setting up a table with the stacks of books, or if she was using the royal we.

"Thank you," Rowan said, making her a bow that made my stomach go tight with pleasure. "We will take your offer under consideration."

My shiny pink behind we will, I thought to myself, but didn't contradict Rowan in front of the others.

"Now then, shall we form an orderly line?" Maat said, turning to face the rest of the passengers. She clapped her hands for silence and repeated her request. "You will approach me one at a time, making sure your Ka is in your possession, and then I will weigh it against my feather. If it is lighter than my feather, you may pass on to the divine realm or your choice of destinations. If your Ka fails or you do not have possession of your Ka, then you must remain in Duat. In that case, we will send you to Osiris, who will find employment for you. Is everyone ready?"

Enthusiastic cheers answered her and people jostled and jockeyed to get to the front of a straggly line.

Mrs. P, I noticed, scanned the three men, disappointment sharpening her expression. Her shoulders sagged a little as she took up a place at the railing.

"Hello, hello. I'm sorry I'm late. I was dead, you see, and I had to travel back to the ship, and my, that was a journey, let me tell you." Gilly materialized out of nothing, her face expressing happiness. The other priestesses greeted her with calls of welcome. "Oh, is it the third challenge already? I'm so glad I didn't miss it."

"Where on earth have you been? Wait, you were dead?" I asked, staring at her. She looked perfectly normal.

"Yes! Hullo, Aset. You look pretty in that outfit. Yes, Sophea, I was dead. Someone pushed me over the edge of the railing, and I hit my head underwater, and the next thing I knew, Osiris was greeting me and telling me to get back to the ship. It was all very exciting, although I do wish I'd been asked if I wanted to be a spirit."

Rowan's body tensed as she spoke. I glanced around to see if there was a threat that he perceived, but I saw nothing other than Ken and Barbie moving over to the other side of the deck, standing together and speaking quietly.

Gilly drifted off to join her priestly sisters in line.

"Is anything wrong?" I whispered to Rowan.

"I think very much so, yes," he answered, and he glanced across to where May and Gabriel were greeting Constantine and Bee.

"About...?"

"Everything," he said, annoyingly mysterious.

"Where can he be?" Mrs. P sighed, gripping the railing and staring out onto the shore. "He knew I would be here. He knew I had the shiny for him."

"Your boyfriend?" I asked her, and without thinking, said, "Where exactly is the ring? You're not wearing it that I can see."

Her brow was lined with worry. "I hope Isis has not tried to stop him...hmm? Oh, it is here." She gestured toward her stomach.

"You swallowed it?" I asked, startled.

"No, I had my belly button pierced using it. That way I knew it would always be safe."

"Clever," I admitted, giving her arm a little pat. "Don't worry about Osiris. The captain said that Maat was here early, so maybe Osiris didn't get the word that you'd be ready to release him just yet."

She sighed again, and I left her to her melancholy thoughts, moving over to stand next to Rowan.

"I am a bad person," I announced softly to him.

He was watching the other dragons, now in conference, his gaze moving from them to the captain to Ken and Barbie. "No you're not. Is this the point where I should ask you why you think you are?"

"Of course you should." I waved my hands around. "You don't let your mate make statements like 'I am a bad person' without both disputing that fact and then asking her to explain, thereby allowing her to bare her soul to you."

"Fine. Why do you think you're a bad person?"

"Because I am judging Mrs. P. She's running away with a married man, Rowan. I know that isn't a big deal these days, but when I think of some hussy running off with you, I see red. And knives. Gelding knives, and lots of them."

"Ah, but you are not considering two points," he said, turning to face me. "First and most important, I would never run away with a hussy. You are my mate, and you are going to stay my mate. I have informed you that I love you, a statement I don't make lightly. And second, you forget that Osiris and Isis were wed thousands of years ago. They were actually brother and sister, and there were a limited number of gods to go around, so they had to wed."

"That's just seriously ew," I said, trying not to grimace.

"You might ask Osiris what sort of a marriage he had before you make a final judgment on Mrs. P for wishing to be with him."

"Oh yes, that's going to be an easy conversation to have. 'Pardon me, god of the Underworld, did you enjoy your incestuous relationship with your sister, or are you just tired of her and want fresh meat?' Yeah, I think I'll pass on that little chat."

"Why are they excluding us from their conversation?" Rowan asked, looking back at the dragons. "They are planning something. They wish us to be out of their precious weyr."

"I think you're being a little paranoid. Why don't we go ask them what's going...hey!"

Rowan's eyebrows rose when I grabbed his arm. "Hey?"

I nodded toward Bee and Constantine. "It just struck me—they were here before, along with the others, and they got to leave. They didn't have to wait around for Maat."

"They were visitors, not travelers on the ship," he said just as if that explained everything. I looked at him until he unbent. "It is the act of traveling through the Duat that signifies the deceased going to his or her destination. People can and do visit the Underworld without being stuck here. But if you are a passenger on the ship through it, you are considered a pilgrim, if you will."

"Oh. I wish someone had told me that before—I would have rented one of those fancy cars and just driven through it."

"Then we would not have been able to face the challenges, and that is what was required of us. Come. I grow tired of them deliberately slighting us. We shall go demand to be included in whatever plans they are making."

I didn't let him see me giggle at his offended tone, just allowed him to steer me over to where the four dragons were deep in confab.

"Here you are. We wondered if you were coming to join us," Bee said, smiling warmly at us. "May says you had all sorts of trouble right as we arrived, but I see you took care of it."

Rowan inclined his head at Constantine, who returned the gesture.

"Rowan was seriously awesome, although I won't be so modest that I won't mention the fact that I kicked some booty with a few well-placed arrows. Would you take offense if I asked you why you're here?" I asked Bee.

She looked mildly annoyed.

Constantine's jaw tightened, but he managed to get out, "We were summoned here. *Again.* Despite the fact that we have important things to do, the First Dragon insisted that we return here. I informed him that we are not at his beck and call, but he just said something about me needing to be here, and thus we had to dash off to Egypt."

"Wow, this place seriously needs an elevator," said the head named Gary as he rolled up on his RC jeep. "I got stuck on the second flight of stairs, and had to beg a lift from a passing steward."

Constantine frowned at the head. "I told you to stay below, where you won't get into trouble if there is fighting."

"Connie, Connie, Connie, you know me better than that!" Gary said, zipping over to us. "Hi, Rowan! Hi, Sophea. That's a super outfit, Sophea. Is it *Tomb Raider*?"

"Yes," I said, trying not to stare. I still hadn't really come to grips with the idea of a bodyless head riding around.

"He really is the biggest pain in the butt," Bee said. "The First Dragon that is, not Constantine. I mean, we were just here, and then he sends word to Constantine that we have to come back, all the way from London."

"Was he planning on being here?" May asked, looking a little worried. "I had no idea the First Dragon was coming back."

"I gathered that was the point, but I don't see him."

Constantine, who had his back to the group of passengers, now turned to scan them. About half of them were gone, having passed Maat's test while we were talking, the successful applicants joyously trotting down the gangplank to a waiting bus.

"I don't know why he called us... Oh."

We turned to see what he was looking at. Two of the

men were working the line of remaining passengers. To our left, Ken and Barbie stood with the captain. To the right, Mrs. P stared out at the shore. Four of the six priestesses had been cleared to move on, and evidently, that meant they couldn't linger, for they bade us all farewell before proceeding off the ship.

"Oh? What oh?" Bee asked, craning her neck. As she did so, one of Maat's men broke off and came over to us, a faint smile on his lips.

"Just why have you called us here?" Constantine asked the man. "*Again.* We only just got back home when you summoned us once more."

I gawked at the man who stopped in front of us. He was about my height, had light brown hair, and a mild expression that quickly registered chagrin. And then before our eyes, his figure shimmered and became that of the enigmatic First Dragon. "You have seen through my glamour. Alas, I was never very good at them. Certainly not as good as you, Bael."

To my absolute surprise, he didn't speak that last sentence of any of us. He had turned to face Ken and Barbie.

"That's it," I heard Rowan say softly. "*That's* what's wrong with them. It's a glamour."

"What on earth is a glamour?" I asked, but Rowan had no time to answer before Barbie stepped forward.

"It is rare to hear the First Sire admit a failing in any area—except that concerning me, of course." Barbie's voice was as sharp as a razor. "And yes, my abilities with glamours have served me well. No one has ever seen through them . . . until now."

"Great Caesar's gallbladder! That's . . . that's the demon lord guy? Barbie?" I gasped when it was Barbie's turn to change form: that from a stocky woman into a man, his long face and aquiline nose giving him a snooty appearance that went right along with his sarcastic voice.

"His name is Bael," Constantine said, his voice choked.

Rowan, however, gave a little nod as if it all made sense to him.

I stared at the demon lord who was such a threat, trying to resolve the image of the middle-aged woman to that of a man who held so much power, he could destroy the mortal world. The glamour must have allowed him to fool us all. I made a mental note to ask Rowan for more information later.

Ken likewise transformed into another man, this one small and pinched-looking. He glanced quickly between the First Dragon and Barbie...no, Bael...his expression unhappy. "My lord, I wish you had not dismissed the glamour altering my appearance. I told you that I greatly enjoyed my new body, and wished to retain it."

"Silence," Bael ordered, strolling toward us. His eyes flitted past me to where Mrs. P still stood mooning over her lost boyfriend. "Your opinion is not needed nor desired."

"But I went to all the trouble of altering this costume so it would fit my female form," Ken protested. He pulled off the wig and set it down with reverence. "And the sheep! It wasn't easy manufacturing that out of nothing, you know! Plus, everyone liked me as Ken. I don't want to go back to being just another demon. I want to be Ken again, and wear cute swimsuits, and sunbathe, and dance the limbo with the captain, and flirt with that handsome steward, and—"

"SILENCE!" Bael bellowed, and I swore I saw little black tendrils of power reach out and bite at Ken.

The latter yelped and jumped back a few paces.

To a man (and woman), everyone in the line waiting turned to look at us. Maat looked as well. The captain sidled away from Bael, his officers following.

Even Mrs. P turned around to see what the commotion was.

Mrs. P! I knew at that moment that Bael realized who she was. "So that's why you've been offering to help us so much and trying so hard to meet Mrs. P," I said, moving toward the woman in question.

Mrs. P just looked confused.

"Well, you're not getting her or the ring!" I declared, taking up a stand in front of her. I'd gathered up my arrows and wiped them off as best I could. Now I pulled my bow from my back, and nocked an arrow.

Bael smiled. If his smile as Barbie wasn't the prettiest thing in the world, the smile as his real self took at least five years off my life.

Behind me, Mrs. P gasped.

Rowan quickly moved in front of me, the dragons all taking their places around him, effectively providing a barrier between Bael and Mrs. P. May handed out the demons' swords, which had been left behind when their bodies disappeared, to all the dragons, the women included. "My mate speaks the truth. You should leave now, Bael. You will not get what you came for. The ring will be broken and its essence locked away where you can't get it."

Bael's upper lip curled. "You think to challenge me, dragon? I have more power than you can conceive of in your tiny mind."

"Really?" Constantine drawled, facing him with an intractable expression. "Then why have you waited so long to reveal yourself? Why have you not taken the ring before this?"

"Because he didn't know which of the priestesses held the ring," Rowan said slowly, his voice gaining confidence as he spoke. Clearly, he'd figured out all the bits about which I was still fuzzy. "That's why you killed the two who you saw speaking with us."

"Oh," I said, enlightenment dawning. "I thought it was the captain who killed them and tried to cover it up by making it look like it was someone else—"

Captain Kherty was close enough to hear our conversation. He turned a scowl on me that had me mouthing an apology at him.

"And if he couldn't tell just by looking at the women which was the one he sought," Rowan continued, warming to his exposition, "then I'd guess that meant that these great powers he holds aren't quite so potent in the Underworld."

"Powers based in another world never are as effective in other domains," the First Dragon said, waving his hand toward the stairs.

"Hullo, what do we have here? Maat doing her thing already? I was told that you wouldn't need me to run the others to the next world until tomorrow." A man emerged from the stairs, a good-looking man of Egyptian heritage, his glossy black hair swept back from a high forehead. He was dressed casually in jeans and a blue silk shirt, and was accompanied by two men who clearly held the post of guards of some sort. They were dressed in what I thought of as ancient Egyptian outfits—the white linen kilted skirts, metal bracelets, and a wide gold necklet. Each had swords crossed on their respective backs, and they were bare-chested.

"Is that who I think that is?" I asked Rowan in a whisper.

"Osiris himself, I believe," he answered.

"My beau!" Mrs. P squealed, and dashed toward Osiris.

He looked started for a moment, then his eyebrows rose. "By the gods, is it the chief priestess? Aset! I have not seen you in many centuries."

I realized too late that she had run in front of me, and I lunged after her to stop her from getting near Bael, but I was too late. He moved more swiftly than I could follow, one moment standing next to Ken, the next across the deck with a knife held to Mrs. P's neck. "I do not need magic to take what I want in this domain," he snarled. "Stand back, or I will slay the woman. And unlike the others, she shall not rise again."

"Can he do that?" I asked Rowan. "Kill her for good, I mean?"

He glanced toward Osiris. "I don't know, but I'd guess he could."

"Who is that man?" Osiris asked, squinting a little as he peered at Bael. He clucked his tongue and pulled a pair of glasses from his shirt pocket. "Eyesight isn't what it used to be. The wife keeps telling me I should get myself that laser surgery... oh, he's not a mortal, he's a demon lord. Why is there a demon lord in my Underworld?"

"Hiya." Gary rolled over to Osiris, beaming up at him. "I'm Gary. Well, Gareth really, but no one calls me that. I don't know why there's a demon lord here, but I did want to say that I really like your Underworld. It's super interesting. I used to be with Asmodeus—did you know him? But then Bael over there killed him, and Connie and Bee took me in, and now we're just one happy family. So, you're Osiris himself! That has to be cool."

Osiris considered Gary with pursed lips, and then said, "Ah. Just so. A head. Interesting choice of pets, dragon."

Constantine looked martyred for a moment. "He has his moments."

"I just wish I knew why demon lords and dragons and loose heads are running around and causing fights." Osiris looked around as if someone would provide him the answer.

The First Dragon shook his head. "You really are out of touch, brother."

"Brother?" I said, just as Bee said the exact same thing.

She turned to Constantine. "Osiris is your uncle? Is *everyone* in the Otherworld related to you?"

Constantine looked even more put upon. "Not everyone. And there's a reason I keep my family tales from you. Now you see proof of why I do so."

Osiris lifted his glasses and squinted at the First Dragon. "You're here, too?"

"I started it," the First Dragon said, spreading his hands. "I felt I should be at the end, as well."

"Ah. Yes." Osiris glanced at Bael. "I see your point. You, demon lord—"

"My name is Bael," the man in question snarled. "I am the premier prince of Abaddon. I rule the Otherworld and am soon to rule the mortal world. You would do well to temper your tone, lord of the Underworld, lest I turn my sights to you, too."

"I tremble with fear," Osiris said, clearly not in the least bit worried. He gestured for Maat to come forward.

I looked over at her, surprised to see that all the other passengers had gone. She was sitting on the edge of the table, watching the goings-on with interest.

Osiris walked toward Bael, the dragons falling into the place behind him. Mrs. P squealed when the tip of the blade dug into her flesh, a line of blood dripping down her neck, disappearing into the bodice of her costume.

"Stop there, or I will kill her," Bael warned. "And then I will damn her soul to eternal torment. I might not have my full powers here, but I have enough remaining to see to it that your beloved suffers for eternity."

"What an asshat," I said softly to Rowan, my eyes on the knife. "What are we going to do?"

He looked at me out of the corner of his eye. "With gods and demigods scattered all around, you expect *me* to take charge of the situation?"

"Yes," I said firmly, taking his hand. "Because you truly are a champion, as well as a butt-kicking dragon. And you're not the sort of man to let others fight your battle."

"I wasn't aware it *was* my battle." One of his eyebrows rose as he spoke.

"Well, okay, it's probably more my battle, but we're a couple now, and that means we share things like that. Right?"

His mouth quirked. Dear god, how I loved his mouth. And his chest. And his legs. Oh, who was I fooling, I was wildly, insanely, madly in love with him. I couldn't imagine life without the man, and that thought suddenly stopped scaring me, and made me feel like the happiest woman alive. "You are correct. Very well. If you insist I take action..."

He strode forward, handing his sword to Constantine as he passed by, no doubt to show Bael that he was no threat. I had no idea what he was going to do, because at that moment, someone grabbed my Lara Croft braid and brutally yanked me backward, knocking my bow and arrow from my hand.

"Argh!" I screamed, and out of the corner of my eye I saw two men climb over the rail. Evidently a few more demons had been held in reserve, and one of them now held an arrow to my throat, the tip of it piercing my flesh.

Rowan spun around and roared his anger. He leaped toward us, his body changing in midstep into that of a red-scaled dragon, his eyes all but spitting fury.

Bael slammed Mrs. P to the ground, pinning her to it with the knife, while he chanted something that sounded extremely bad, his hands waving over her chest in a strange pattern.

What I can only describe as a tear in the middle of nothing opened up, and a two small men emerged, both of them drawing symbols around us.

Pain wracked me as the two newcomers spoke. Rowan reached the man holding me just as Baltic and Gabriel shifted into dragon form, the two of them leaping on the chanting men.

For a moment I was terrified by the dragon bearing down on me, but then I saw his eyes and realized I could never be afraid of Rowan. Not my Rowan of the gentle heart, odd sense of humor, and passion that made me melt into a puddle of goo. Suddenly, the arrow was gone, and I was falling forward.

Rowan caught me with one scaled arm, while his tail lashed out and knocked the second demon across the deck, where he slammed into the bridge.

I turned to see the first demon bent over the railing... backward, in a position that told me the man's back was broken.

Rowan said gruffly, "Don't look, love," before turning to help the others. He ran toward Bael, and just as Bael lifted the knife high, about to plunge it into Mrs. P's heart, there was a flash of white, and one of Osiris's guards was there, dragging Mrs. P to safety at the same moment that Rowan threw himself on the demon lord.

They went down in a tangle of arms and legs, some human and some scaly. The knife flashed, and blood spurted in a wide arc. Someone screamed, and it wasn't until I had picked up the punchbowl and was bashing Bael on the head with it did I realize it was me.

Things calmed down a bit after that.

"Wow," Bee told me when Constantine plucked me off of Bael. "I didn't know you had that in you. You were positively scary. And you look so nice, too."

"I *am* nice," I said, panting, adrenaline making me want to go bash Bael in the head a few more times. I caught sight of a gash on Rowan's chest and pulled away from Constantine, running to the love of my life. "Not again! You're all bloody. Medic!"

Gabriel and Osiris had hold of Bael, whose hands were quickly tied behind his back. "So he can't cast any more spells," Osiris said to no one in particular.

Bael spat invectives and was roughly shoved down onto a chair for his troubles.

"It's not bad," Gabriel said, examining Rowan. Gabriel had switched back into human form, but Rowan was still a red dragon.

And he suddenly must have realized that, because when he looked down at his chest to assess the wound, his eyes widened and his arms flailed wildly. "What the hell? WHAT THE EVER-LIVING HELL?"

"It's okay, pumpkin. You're just a dragon, that's all," I said, feeling like an idiot, but doing my best to calm him down.

His eyes were huge with emotion, his nostrils flaring, little puffs of smoke and fire coming with every breath. "How do I make it stop? I don't want to be like this!"

"Breathe, Rowan, breathe," I said, stroking the non-hurty side of his chest. He was dangerously close to a panic attack, and I was clueless as to how to calm him down.

"Like everything else, it's a matter of control," Gabriel said. "Take charge of your fire—you're scorching the deck—and harness it to focus your mind. Once you have achieved that control, you will be able to shift at will."

"Breathe," I repeated, stroking the long, curved dragon neck. I kept my eyes firmly on his, because that provided a connection that we both needed—him to keep from freaking out, and me to keep from realizing that the man I loved had a form that was frighteningly different from what I was used to. "Just keep breathing deep breaths, and make your fire do what you want."

Slowly, second by painful second, his eyes calmed and his breathing slowed. The fire he was puffing disappeared, and his body began to shimmer and wobble in and out of focus. It took a couple of tries, but at last he was back to human form.

There was a smattering of polite applause, which I ignored, as I leaned my forehead against his. "You did it! You conquered your dragon self. I'm so proud of you, I could ride you like a rented mule."

He laughed and pulled me to him for a very quick, very fiery kiss.

"Sorry," he said into my mouth before releasing me. "I guess I don't have as much control over my fire as you thought."

"Well done, champion," Osiris said, then gestured

toward Maat again. "Now that the dragon shape crisis is over, I believe you have a few more people to process."

"Hello," Maat said, greeting us. "Would you like to start things off?"

I realized with a start she was looking at me. "Um... all right." I tucked my bow into the quiver on my back, and couldn't help but muse that my life hadn't been as blameless as I'd hoped.

Maat stopped in front of me, pulling the feather from her riot of curls.

"I should warn you that there are a few things I've done that perhaps don't look too good on my record," I said nervously. "But I had good reasons to do them—"

She smiled and held out the feather. "Palm up, please."

I glanced at Rowan. He nodded, giving me a little smile that warmed me to the tips of my toes. If nothing else, I knew that my love for him was honest and true. I held out my hand.

She dropped the feather onto it. I waited, braced for something profound to happen.

Nothing did. It just sat there, being a feather. "You may move on as you like," she told me, picking up the feather.

"I can?" I blinked a couple of times. "I passed?"

"You passed." She nodded to May, who handed her sword to Gabriel, and came forward with her hand outstretched. "You may move on as you like," Maat repeated. May gave her a tight smile, murmured her thanks, and retrieved her sword.

In quick succession, Maat went through Gabriel, Ken (who was sulking in the background), and Constantine, who insisted on having a try even though he hadn't been on the cruise.

"I just want to see if I'd pass muster if the First Dragon insists on repeatedly summoning us here," he told Bee as Maat laid the feather on his hand, and told him that he would pass the challenge.

Bee gave him a tolerant, but fond, look in return.

I swear the First Dragon gave a little snort of amusement, but when I looked at him, his expression was as placid—and otherworldly—as ever.

At last the only three people to remain were Rowan, Bael, and Mrs. P. Maat approached Rowan, and I felt the dragons hold their collective breaths.

It was time for the Dragon Breaker to have his soul judged.

Nineteen

"Hand," Maat said, holding her feather.

Rowan hesitated a second, then, with an unreadable look at me, held out his hand for her.

She placed the feather on it. It seemed to ruffle in the wind, bouncing ever so slightly on his hand.

My stomach dropped with fear. Dear goddess, what would I do if he couldn't leave Duat?

Stay with him, of course, my inner voice answered. *As if there were a choice.*

My panic quelled a bit at that. Although I would prefer not to live in the Underworld, so long as I had Rowan in my life, then we'd make it work.

Maat tipped her head to the side as she watched the feather. She picked it up off his hand, examined it, and then put it back on his palm.

It repeated the little fluttering motion.

Her eyebrows rose as she reclaimed the feather. The

silence was so thick you could have heard a molecule hit the deck. "You may move on as you like."

I released a breath I didn't know I was holding. Rowan's shoulders sagged for a few seconds before he straightened them and tried to look as if he wasn't worried to death.

Gary cheered. "Wooties! Now we can have that wedding in the fall. I've always wanted to plan a wedding, and I just know this one is going to be fabulous. I'll have to call Jim. He wants to help plan."

"Now then," Osiris said, gesturing at his guards, who had been flanking Bael. They promptly returned to their master's side. "Since Aset is recovering from her mistreatment, I believe you should attend to this demon lord first."

"Oh, he can't possibly pass her test," I said aloud, alternating between batting my eyelashes at Rowan in an attempt to tell him how much I loved and admired and was proud of him and keeping an eye on Bael. "The man is pure evil. His soul has to be one giant mass of sins."

Bael snarled something at me that had Rowan taking a step forward. Constantine caught his arm and kept him from proceeding.

"Do not pay his words any heed. He speaks lies."

"I have no need for lies," Bael said, the black aura of power around him snapping and crackling, but despite that effect, he looked remarkably calm. In fact, he appeared calmer and more placid as each second slipped past us.

"I must have his hand," Maat told Osiris. He nodded, and one of the guards moved behind Bael.

"Something's up," I said softly to Rowan, watching the guard free Bael's hand.

Rowan had his gaze firmly affixed on the demon lord,

his eyes glittering with little bits of gold set against the dark peaty brown. "He's done something."

"What?"

"I have no idea, but whatever it is, he believes it will allow him to pass the challenge. Hold up!" he said that louder, stopping Maat as she was about to place the feather on Bael's hand. "Something is not right here. I suggest you examine Bael to ascertain whether he has his Ka or not."

"Can you see a Ka?" I asked aloud.

"Oh yes, if you like. It resembles a little spark of light," Maat said, tipping her head as she considered Bael.

I swear the man smiled.

"Would you mind showing us your Ka?" Maat asked.

Bael shrugged, and with his free hand, reached into his jacket. When he opened his hand, a little spot of purplish pink light pulsated, like a bizarre firefly on a late July night. "As per the requirements, you can see that I have my Ka with me. Conduct the challenge."

"Wait!" I said, hurrying forward. Mrs. P was sitting with May, who had dabbed up the blood that dripped down her front. "His soul couldn't possibly pass muster."

"That is for the feather to decide," Maat said primly.

"Yes, but that's not what I mean." I glanced at Rowan, who looked a bit confused. Evidently he hadn't seen what I had. "I meant that for him to be *wanting* to have the challenge conducted, for him to be clearly anticipating it is a sign that the Ka he's holding isn't his. It's just that simple."

Silence filled the night air. Everyone looked from me to Bael.

"If it's not his, then whose is it?" May asked.

The pieces clicked together in my head. "It's Mrs. P's," I said, going over to where she was taking a sip of water. "I saw him doing something to her with the knife. When the demons jumped me, that is. He was making some motion over her heart, and I just bet you he's taken her Ka."

Mrs. P lifted her head, but said nothing, her eyes on Osiris.

"Priestess, are you up to the challenge now?" Maat asked her.

"If you like." Rowan helped her to her feet. She held out her hand, saying tiredly, "I just want this day to be over so that my beau and I might start our life together."

I bit my lip as Maat approached her, the feather in her hand. My stomach roiled, and I tried desperately to think of a way to stop her, but my mind was a mass of worry and fear and dread, and offered no helpful suggestions on a way I could change what was about to happen.

The feather floated down to her hand. Maat smiled, and gently plucked the feather from Mrs. P's palm. "You may move on as you like."

"*What?*" roared Bael.

"Oh, did you not notice?" Mrs. P smiled sweetly. "I was told to switch my Ka with yours when I took the ring. You've had mine all along, and a few minutes ago when you took what you thought was mine, you simply exchanged it for yours."

He lunged forward, his face a terrible sight to behold. He took the chair with him, and with his free hand, slammed it into one of Osiris's guards. Rowan leaped forward at the same time Constantine and Gabriel did the same, but Bael wasn't lying when he said he had enough power to do as he wanted in the Underworld—with a shouted word, there was a loud percussive noise, and all three men flew backward a few yards.

Bael headed straight for Mrs. P and me. I snatched my bow from my back and hurriedly fit an arrow to it, but before I could let it fly, he was on us. I stabbed the arrow into his hand when he reached for Mrs. P, kicking out at the same time and hearing the satisfying crunch of his knee taking the brunt of my attack. Rowan reached us first, with Gabriel and Constantine immediately behind him, and all three men, with the aid of Osiris's two guards, pulled Bael off and rebound him to the chair. This time they tied one of his hands to his leg, palm upward.

He started chanting in a singsong voice, causing a horrible pressure to build up inside me (and I gathered everyone else, since Mrs. P and May both clutched their heads), but Osiris stopped that by simply marching over to Bael and whacking him upside the head with the same punchbowl I had used on him earlier.

"None of that, now!" Osiris said. "I will not have you casting curses in the Duat. If I want people cursed here, then I shall do it." He turned to Maat. "Finish the challenge."

Bael spat at her, literally spat at her, which just caused Osiris to snap his fingers. One of the guards brought a napkin from the overturned banquet table, which he used to gag Bael.

Maat approached Bael, who struggled against his bonds, but it was no good. She dropped the feather into his hand. It curled up onto itself, rolling up tight, then fell off his hand to the ground with a *thunk*.

Bael's eyes locked on first Mrs. P, then on me, and finally, Rowan. The sight of them was so horrible, I had to look away. Even Rowan looked pale after receiving Bael's full attention.

"You may not go as you please," Maat said quietly. "You are henceforth bound to Duat."

I thought Bael's head might explode, so furious was he, but he had to content himself with trying to take more years off our lives with his deadly glare.

Mrs. P shook off my supportive hand and turned to where Osiris was standing. Her face lit with an inner joy that was wonderful to see. "At last, my beau, I am here before you. And I have brought you an offering to our love, that which will allow us to live together in peace."

"Eh?" Osiris said, looking somewhat startled. "What's that about living together? My wife wouldn't like—"

"My beau, oh my beau," Mrs. P said, pulling the ring out from her belly button. She ran with it to Osiris... and then passed him by and threw herself into the arms of the taller of the two guards. She kissed his face and his neck and his ears, and he picked her up and spun her around, kissing her in return.

"What the..." I stared at them, shaking my head before turning to Rowan. "Do you see that?"

"Interesting," he said slowly, watching Mrs. P and the guard murmur sweet nothings to each other. "I believe we have been mistaken in our assumptions."

"Well, you can say that again. Mrs. P!" I marched over to her and tapped her on the shoulder, feeling that the situation allowed for me to do a little interrupting. "What the hell?"

"What is your problem?" she asked, glancing quickly at me before returning to coo at her boyfriend.

"My problem is that all along you've been talking about being with Osiris. You know, your beau."

"Silly gel," she said with a tinkly little laugh, clinging to her guard. "His name is Bo. And he's mine, all mine, and now that he has the offering, he shall use it to leave Duat, and we shall be together forever."

"That was a close thing," Osiris told the First Dragon. "I thought she was going to demand I leave with her. My wife would never condone such a thing. Just the other day she was ranting about one of her priestesses who had given me a deep tissue massage some seven hundred years before. The woman has the memory of an elephant, I tell you. And the temper of a devil. She's always claiming my guards are lusting after her."

"I told you not to wed our sister," the First Dragon said mildly. "Such things can never end well."

"Come, dragon," Mrs. P said as she gave the ring to the guard named Bo. "You wish to preserve the essence of the ring? Be ready to catch it."

The guard released Mrs. P long enough to bow to Osiris. "My lord, have I your permission to make a life elsewhere?"

Osiris sighed. "It's always the way—I train up a guard just the way I like it and he finds a way to leave. Yes, yes, be gone with you. There's nothing I dislike more than a moping guard."

Rowan's face clouded. He moved forward hesitantly. "I want the essence, but I don't know what I can use to bestow it upon."

The First Dragon drifted over to us, shaking his head sadly. "I had such high hopes for you, too."

Rowan frowned. "You made me a dragon, and I have embraced it. In what way have I disappointed you?"

"I gave you the means to make whole the sept, to provide for my children, and yet when faced with the opportunity to do both, you refuse."

"I'm not refusing to do anyth—oh." Rowan thought for a few seconds, then hurriedly searched his canvas bag until he pulled out the three pieces of the broken glass. "This has importance to you? To... dragons?"

"It is a shard of the dragon heart," the First Dragon said in a carefully neutral voice. I heard the intake of breath from May when Rowan held up the broken pieces. "Guard it well, wyvern."

"There you go, then," Mrs. P said, and gestured for Rowan. He stood next to them as Bo the guard took the ring, and with an arm around her, held the ring aloft. There was a flash of blue-white light that made my eyes water, and then they were gone.

As was the First Dragon.

"She didn't even say good-bye." I blinked and wiped my eyes, moving to Rowan's side to add, "Did it work? Did you get it?"

Rowan had his back to me, his shoulders slumped in a way that made my stomach tighten painfully. Then he turned around and held up the shard for me to see—made whole and glowing with a deep ruby light.

"Welcome to the weyr, Rowan," Gabriel said with a genuine smile. "You bear a shard of the dragon heart. There can be no more valuable artifact for your sept."

"Wrong," Rowan said, smiling at me. "It's the second most valuable item. The first is standing before me, looking like she has a hundred questions that need answering."

"Just two, actually," I said, blushing at the compliment, and thinking to myself of the many and varied ways I was going to thank him that night.

"What's the first?" he asked.

"It concerns them," I said, nodding toward where Bael was sitting still bound and gagged. Next to him, Osiris,

Maat, and two of her men were listening while Ken pled for sanctuary. "What will happen to them?"

"That is up to Osiris, I believe," Rowan said.

Maat must have heard him, for she glanced over and said with a little smile, "Do not fear that this one will escape," she said, gesturing with the feather toward Bael. "Once bound to Duat, he cannot leave without extraordinary circumstances happening."

"And I shall make sure that such a circumstance does not occur," Osiris said.

Ken plucked at his sleeve and made murmuring noises.

"Ah, yes, a demon, are you?"

"Please, my lord, do not force me to leave. As an unbound demon, I will be preyed upon by any other demon lord who is of that mind, and I will be forced into another life of slavery and torment, and not be allowed to wear the pretty clothes that I did as Ken. If I were to stay here, I could make myself of great service to you. I am very good with decorations and have a keen eye for colors, and I can whip up the most astounding costumes out of nothing."

"He can," I agreed, feeling badly for the poor little guy. He truly did seem happier as Ken.

"Very well," Osiris said magnanimously after a moment's thought. "My wife did mention wishing to redecorate. You may stay in Duat."

"Thank you, oh, thank you," Ken said, on his knees in gratitude. "I bind myself to you most willingly."

"None of that, now, none of that," Osiris said, looking embarrassed. "Glad to have you."

"One last boon, my lord," Ken said, his lower lip wobbling. "Could you order me to take the form that lord Bael cast on me via the glamour? It was much comelier, and I feel it better suits me than this one."

"Certainly," Osiris said, waving a hand. "Be in whatever form you like."

Ken's body shimmered and morphed back into that of a plump middle-aged woman. He beamed at us all and ran after Osiris as he and Maat, with the captive Bael before them, left the ship.

"What a very odd demon," Bee said, watching them leave.

"I like her. She was a little chatty, but seemed nice enough," May said. "I'm glad she got away from Bael."

"I do so like a happy ending," I said, sniffling slightly at the sight of Ken happy again.

Bee leaned into Constantine, who had an odd expression on his face. "And what about you? Are you going to be happy knowing Bael is stuck here?"

"Yes." He was silent for a moment, at last giving her a smile. "He will hate every second of it to the utmost of his being. I call that penance for all the suffering he's brought the world."

"Indeed it is," Rowan said, then tipped his head a little and nudged me. "And what is your second question?"

I leaned close and said softly, "When you were in dragon form, what did it feel like?"

He took a long, deep breath, his eyes closing for a moment. I felt his fire stirring deep within him, and an answering burn inside of me coming to instant life. "Run," he said.

Chills ran down my spine despite the heat of his fire. "Really?" I asked, glancing at the other dragons. "Right now?"

"Run," he repeated, opening his eyes. They glittered brightly with passion and desire... and yes, love.

I felt as if I were drenched in fire. "Okay, but this time, let's have a game plan. Where exactly do you want me to—"

"RUN!" he yelled, and I didn't wait; I took off.

But as I skidded through the door, I heard Gabriel say, "A chase! What an excellent idea. We haven't had one of those in far too long, little bird. Rowan, what say you take the lowest level of the ship. I'll take the middle for our chase, and Constantine can have the upper..."

Twenty

Fall in St. Petersburg may have been Kostya's idea of lovely, but it certainly wasn't balmy by any stretch of the imagination. I shivered in the small anteroom that had been assigned as my dressing room. Aisling (heavily pregnant, but downright glowing with happiness), Ysolde, and May bustled between the three rooms given over to us brides, each updating the other.

"All the grooms are present and accounted for," Aisling announced, her demon dog padding after her.

"As are their assorted hangovers," Jim said with a snicker.

I glanced at them in the mirror, which I sat in front of while a stylist fussed with my hair. "Oh, dear. Even Rowan? He's not really a drinker, although I know he would have had a few drinks last night during their joint stag party."

"He looks like he was dead, got run over with a heavy

cart loaded with oxen, was resurrected, and then the oxen trampled him to death again," Jim said, sniffing at the table that held a plate of snacks, evidently provided by the caterers to keep the brides from fainting away with hunger. "You gonna eat that cheese and bread?"

"Oh, he does not look anything like that," Aisling scolded her demon, then gave me a brilliant smile. "Rowan looks dashing, absolutely dashing, and I know he'll be just fine as soon as the headache meds kick in. Jim, leave the food alone! You've already eaten both Bee's and Aoife's 'don't faint while you walk down the aisle' snackies, and you don't need Sophea's as well. Honest to Pete, I can't take you anywhere..."

They drifted out the door just as May leaned her head in. "How are you holding up? Oh, your hair looks nice. I like the little leaves twined through it."

"They're not leaves, actually," I said, wincing when the stylist, with a mutter to herself, adjusted one of the metal decorations that curled through my hair. "They're tiny little dragons."

"Very nice," May said. "Almost makes me wish we'd done a proper wedding, not just the civil ceremony that Gabriel's mom demanded we have. Almost."

She grinned when I made a face at her. "This isn't my idea of bliss, but it's kind of nice having a group celebration with Rowan's sisters."

"Gotcha. Oh, you have a visitor." She pulled back a moment, then poked her head back in. "You up for it?"

"I don't know," I said, slightly startled. "Who's the visitor?"

"It's me!" Mrs. P pushed past May, rushing to me to give me a hug. "Or should I say, it's us. The other priestesses are in the hall, getting good seats. What a lovely idea you had to get married in a Russian palace. It's very grand."

"It is, but it wasn't my idea at all. For that we can thank the head wedding planner, and by head I mean just that—Gary might not have much to him, but I'll admit he whipped together a hell of a wedding. How are you? Where's your Bo?"

"I'm blissfully happy, and my Bo has just run to town to fetch a tuxedo."

I thanked the stylist when she murmured the hair was as good as it was going to get, and she toddled off to help the next bride. Carefully, so as not to wrinkle my flowered 1950s style dress with sleeveless bodice, bell-shaped skirt, and crinoline underpinnings, I turned to face Mrs. P. "I'm sure he doesn't need a tux for the wedding. We're not really being that formal. Aoife's dress is more of a short dinner dress than a wedding dress. Bee's the only one who went in for the full princess-style wedding dress and veil. From what Rowan said, not even the men are wearing tuxes. They have some sort of dragon outfit planned, although he wouldn't tell me just what."

"The tuxedo is for your man, actually, in case they can't get the stain out of his tunic," she said blithely, wandering over to fuss with the small bouquet of flowers I would be carrying.

"Stain?" I asked, aghast. "What sort of stain? Alcohol? Dirt?"

"It's nothing, really. I gather dragonweave, that material the men's tunics are made of, is just a bit hard to clean when it comes to blood, that's all. The tux is really just a worst-case scenario, so don't worry at all. I'm sure they'll get the tunic cleaned in time. And that handsome Gabriel had already fixed the broken noses."

I closed my eyes for a moment or two, wondering if I should throw tradition to the wind and go check on Rowan. I hadn't seen him since the night before, when he had kissed me and taken himself off to the stag party. "I knew they shouldn't have let those other wyverns plan it. Clearly it got out of hand."

"I gather," Mrs. P said, pulling one of the carnations out of my bouquet and tucking it into her chignon, "that there were some words about the past, and the relative merits of a larger sept versus one of the newer, smaller ones, and things got a bit heated. But I'm sure it's all better now, and you can hardly see Rowan's black eyes. And that Constantine fellow's sling is actually made of the same material as his tunic, so you barely notice it." She paused in thought. "Although Kostya's missing front tooth is a bit noticeable. Still, if you don't look right at his mouth, it's fine."

"Oh goddess," I said, dropping my forehead to my hands. "What an auspicious start."

"Don't worry," she said, moving over to pat me on the shoulder. "It'll all be lovely. The priestesses are thrilled to death to be here—that was very nice of you to invite us all."

"Well, I'm very glad you're here. I haven't had a chance to talk to you at all since you and your Bo left Duat. You look radiant."

"I am," she said simply, and helped herself to the bottle of champagne that sat untouched before me.

"Would you mind answering a question?" I asked, relieved that I finally had a chance to learn the answer to a question that no one seemed to be able to answer.

"Not if it has anything to do with my time as hoochie-coo dancer. I'm saving all that for my memoirs, which Bo is going to help me write. He's literary, you know."

"No, I didn't know, but I don't see any reason why a guard to the lord of the Underworld shouldn't be literary. My question goes back to that last day of the cruise."

"Mmm, I do love champagne," she said, sipping a second glass. "What about that day?"

"You said something about you were told to swap your Ka with Bael's when you took the ring. Rowan and I tried to figure out what you meant by that, but we could never find a satisfactory answer."

She gave a delicate shrug. "It means just what it says—I was told to swap my Ka."

"Yes, but by whom? And how did you know where the Ka would be? I mean, most of us take it with us, or so I gather."

"You are not allowing for the fact that Bael is a demon lord—he would not keep anything of value or power upon him lest his enemies gain hold of it and use it against him. His Ka, as was the ring, was kept in a strongbox."

"Right," I said slowly, giving her a long, hard look. "And how did you know that?"

"I was told, as I said." She helped herself to a petit four, a silver pen that was intended to be used to sign the register, and my lipstick, tucking the last two items away into her small clutch. "Mmm, lemon."

"Who told you?" I repeated, ignoring the petty theft.

She sighed and gave me a long-suffering look that she had no right to use upon me, not after all I had to put up with. "The First Dragon, of course. I've known him for, oh, ever such a long time, and when I told him that I was tired of the mortal world without Bo, he said he would help me since it would aid his descendants as well. So he sent me to Bael's stronghold to fetch the Ka and the ring, and then he approached you, since he knew I'd need a dragon, and you were just drifting, and the rest you know."

My jaw sagged a bit. "He approached me? Jian's cousin! The one whose name I can't remember! That was the First Dragon?"

"So I gather." She rose and leaned in to check herself in the mirror.

"I can't wait to tell Rowan. That and the reason he summoned Constantine to be there at the last challenge were driving us nuts. Until Rowan finally broke down and asked Constantine, but he, being a typical dragon, wouldn't give us a straight answer."

"Oh?" Mrs. P frowned. "Why was he there?"

"According to Gary—you know, the head that drives around on the little radio-controlled car—it's because Constantine needed closure with Bael. Gary said that Bael killed Constantine's mother, and Constantine had been angsting over it for centuries, and that his psyche was all tormented about it, and so on. Which is totally understandable—I mean, who'd want a demon lord for a parent? I'd much rather be an orphan than have that blighting my life."

"Your parents were very nice people," Mrs. P said, taking another petit four. This one she wrapped in a napkin and stuck in her purse. "I met them once, oh, around the turn of the nineteenth century. Your father was very dashing and had a fine eye for a hoochie-coo. Your mother disliked me, I think, but then she was mortal, and she feared I was trying to steal your father away from her."

I looked suspiciously at the gorgeous woman standing next to me. "And were you?"

"Maybe just a little," she said with a little smile. "But not seriously, because that's when I was involved with my president. Oh, dear, does that music mean what I think it means?"

"Five minutes!" The door opened and Gary rolled in, did a turn, and immediately zoomed outward. "This is your five-minute call. You have five minutes." He stopped at the door and said in a soothing tone, "And I don't want you worrying about a thing, Sophea. They got the blood out and set Rowan's hand. He's been focusing on healing it for the last half hour, so I'm sure it'll be just fine when it comes time to exchange rings. Gabriel's head wound closed nicely, and Baltic insists he doesn't need the crutches at all, so there won't be any unwelcome thumping when the wyverns escort the grooms in. One of Gabriel's men, who is also a healer, took care of Drake's dislocation, so all is well there, although really, you'd think that beings who could heal themselves would do so rather than drinking themselves into insensibility, not to mention the fact that they were engaging in fisticuffs to begin with. But you know how it is with gentlemen and their stag parties. Still, all's well that doesn't end in death and dismemberment, and all that, so don't worry, Sophea, everything is just fi—what? No, you can't come in! Don't you know it's bad luck—"

Gary was unceremoniously pushed aside as Rowan entered the room. He was indeed wearing a tunic, a gorgeous deep red embroidered with golden dragons on the front. It wasn't at all traditional bridegroom wear, but then, we weren't very traditional people. To my amusement, he held a hand over his eyes. "I won't look at you if you don't want me to, but I wanted to make sure you were all right."

"You can look," I said with a little laugh, then choked on it when I saw the two black eyes that darkened his face. "Oh, Rowan!"

"It looks worse than it—hoo." He lowered his hand and blinked at me, a slow smile curling his delectable lips. "You look gorgeous."

"Thank you. I'd like to say the same, and I would except for your eyes. What happened?"

He glanced at Mrs. P.

"Am I *de trop*?" she said brightly, then got to her feet and patted my shoulder, saying, "You see? I told you they wouldn't need the tux."

Rowan waited until she left before closing the door and leaning against it. He looked tired, but happy, beat up, but there was heat in his eyes, and a fire simmering inside him that warmed me to my toenails. "The bachelor party got a bit... contentious."

"So I gather. Too many wyverns in too small a place?"

He made a wry face. "That, and too much alcohol flowing. My eyes are much better than they were when I woke up this morning. Gabriel says they'll heal if I have some quiet time when I can focus on them."

"Well, it'll make the wedding photos something to remember," I said, wanting to laugh but not wishing to hurt his feelings. "I'm glad you found me, although from the sounds coming through the door, Gary is having a hissy fit about you seeing me early."

"He can have any sort of fit he wants. I needed to make sure you were okay with this. With me."

I looked at him in confusion, unsure why he'd suddenly

think I'd changed my mind, then realized what he was asking. I got to my feet, pulling him forward a step as I took his hands in mine and kissed the tip of his nose. "You're not replacing Jian, Rowan. You're the new wyvern of the red sept, yes, and you're the love of my life, but you're not ousting him from my heart. I'll always love him, just as I'll always love you. What we have is a new start, both for the red dragons and for us."

His jaw worked. "I want desperately to kiss you. I want to nibble on your delicious earlobes. I want to suck on that spot on your neck that makes you moan with pleasure. I want to lift up that skirt and bury myself in you. But I suspect Gary would have my balls on a platter if I mussed you up, so I'm just going to tell you that you have my heart. And soul. And every other part of me, from now until the end of our days."

"If you make me cry and ruin the makeup that Ysolde was so careful to apply," I murmured, tracing one of the gold embroidered dragons on his chest, "I'm the one who will have your balls. Although not on a platter."

He fought for a good twenty seconds, then swore. "To hell with Gary—" His lips were hot on mine, but not as hot as the fire that swept through him, and into me, binding us together.

"I really must insist—" The door opened behind Rowan, banging him on the back. "Aha! I knew it! Just look at the wrinkles you've put into the bodice by grabbing her on the waist like that. Rowan! Let her go!"

Reluctantly, Rowan released me, his eyes lit with love and laughter, and everything I had ever hoped for. "It's not my fault. She was standing there looking impossibly lovely, and I couldn't resist her..."

Gary herded him out of the door, returning almost immediately to say to me, "Oh, mercy, look at the time. Three minutes! Everyone, we are at T minus three minutes! Where's Jim? Is he harnessed to the carriage? For the love of all that's holy, people, it's show time! Let's get this done right!"

The door closed behind Gary as he scattered orders left and right.

Fifteen minutes later (there was a slight issue with the little carriage that Gary rode in, drawn by Jim, and which had an automatic petal-scattering device), Aoife, Bee, and I gathered outside the closed doors of the palace's ballroom.

"Well?" I asked the ladies, waiting for the music cue Gary had insisted on before the doors were thrown open and we would march down the aisle. "Are we ready for this?"

"We are, but it sounds like the men are in pretty poor shape," Aoife said with a little laugh. "Honestly, if Kostya wasn't so adorable, I'd brush these dragons off and never look back. Imagine fighting on the night before your wedding."

"Constantine says it was your adorable Kostya who started the whole thing," Bee told her sister.

Aoife immediately took issue with that. "Kostya is the mildest of men! Okay, he likes to frown a lot and make dramatic statements, but that's just part of his charm. It's Constantine who's always picking on him. And then Baltic has to come nosing his way in, and now Rowan, who we all know is still trying to get a grip on his dragonness, and... and..."

She stopped and bit her lip.

Bee's mouth quivered.

I sighed. "I think, ladies, we're going to spend the rest of our lives keeping our respective menfolk from beating the ever-living tar out of each other."

"I think you're right," Bee said when Aoife laughed aloud. She gave me a smile that may not have been the warmest on earth, but which at least recognized that we were all in the same boat. "Welcome to the family, Sophea."

"The dragon family or the Dakar family?" I asked as the doors opened, and the music swelled.

"Both," Aoife answered, and as the youngest member of the bridal trio, started her walk down the aisle, preceded by Jim drawing Gary's carriage. Black, white, and red petals scattered ahead of Aoife. Bee lowered her veil and swept forward next, her long dress scattering the petals. I paused at the door, looking past where the ladies were proceeding, my gaze finding that of Rowan.

One corner of his mouth quirked, and I was filled with an immense sensation of joy.

This dragon I would keep.

Nothing could prepare Aoife Dakar
for a gorgeous man shifting form before
her eyes. Thrust into a fantastical world
that's both exhilarating and terrifying,
she's about to learn just how hot a
dragon's fire burns…

Please see the next page for
an excerpt from

Dragon Fall.

Three

"I don't see how this can possibly be a good idea, Bee."

My sister looked up from where she was throwing some clothing into a suitcase. "Leaving you by yourself? Dr. Barlind says you're perfectly fine to be on your own—"

"Of course I'm fine to be on my own. Two years of intensive therapy have done wonders," I said with a bright, "I'm not insane anymore" smile.

"Me going to Africa, then?"

"No, of course I think *that's* a good idea. You're going to be helping all those people get fresh water."

She dumped her drawer full of undies into the suitcase, glancing around the room. "I don't know why you want to stay here by yourself, I really don't. Rowan won't be back for a couple of months, so you'll be alone here in the house." She shot a look out the window. Beyond a scraggy hedge, the dull gray and brown sand could be seen stretching out to pale bluish gray water. Overhead, a couple of gulls rode the currents, searching for signs of food, and even through the insulated glass I could hear their high, piercing cries. "I wouldn't wish that on my worst enemy."

"That's because you're a city girl now, Miss Lives in Venice." I rubbed my arms and leaned against the wall, looking out at the endlessly moving water. "I like the isolation of the Swedish coast. Especially after spending two years in a house with forty other people. You can hear yourself think here."

"You're lucky if you can hear anything over the constant sound of the gulls. Never mind, you don't have to tell me that you love it here. I know that you do. You take after Dad that way." She paused and glanced at the family picture that sat on her dresser before turning back to the suitcase. "You promise to call me if you have another… incident?"

"I'm not going to have an incident," I said, standing up straight and giving her another brilliant smile. I tried to remind myself to tone down that smile just a bit, since Bee was much more perceptive than Dr. Barlind had been. Bee always was able to tell when I was bluffing her, and the last thing I wanted right now was for her to cancel her trip in order to babysit me.

"Of course you aren't. Still, I don't understand why Dr. Barlind insists that you confront your inner demons by returning to that weird fair that started everything. Oh." She cast a perceptive glance at me, which made me swear under my breath. "*That* is what you were talking about not being a good idea, wasn't it? Well, I agree. It's just bound to lead to all sorts of grief for you."

I rubbed my arms again and turned my back to the beach. Unlike my metropolitan-loving brother and sister, I could happily spend hours wandering up and down our little stretch of the coast. "I don't know about grief... It's not like just seeing GothFaire again is going to make me snap, and I see Dr. Barlind's point about confronting my personal bogeys. She's very big on cathartic experiences and thinks that until you directly confront what is giving you issues, you can never really be cured. To be honest, though, I don't have any desire to see GothFaire again. What if the people remember me as the woman who wigged out? I would die of embarrassment."

Bee lifted her shoulders in a half-shrug. "What if they do? They don't mean anything to us." She paused in the act of gathering up toiletries. "Would you like me to cancel my trip and stay here with you for the next month? Maybe it's too much asking you to stay on your own right after your release—"

"No," I interrupted firmly. "I'm fine, I really am. Dr. Barlind wouldn't have let me go unless I was, right?"

"Mmm," she said doubtfully. She placed the items in her bag and zipped it up, turning to face me. "Aoife, you're a smart girl. If you don't think you need to go to that fair, then don't go. Why stir up all those unpleasant memories? With all due respect to your precious Dr. Barlind, you're out of danger now, and that's all that matters."

"I never *was* in danger," I started to argue, then stopped myself. I took a deep breath, remembering Dr. Barlind's favorite saying: *think twice before you speak once.* If I made too much of a fuss, Bee would cancel her trip, and I very much wanted time to myself where I could sort out the shattered remains of my life. I didn't want to go back to the GothFaire, didn't want to see the face of the blond man who had lied, and certainly didn't want to see the same field where I'd seen... but, no, it was better not to think of that.

"Aoife?" Bee prompted.

"You're right," I said, deciding that it was worth a little white lie if I could get her off on her trip. The thought of two lovely months of solitude was damn near priceless in my eyes. "I'm sure it would be better for my mental peace to avoid GothFaire."

She smiled, clearly relieved, and patted my cheek in that annoying way older sisters have. "Good girl. Ack! Look at the time! I'll be late for my flight if I don't leave now." She set down her luggage to give me a hug and a kiss on both cheeks. "Call me if you need me. Or Rowan. You know we both love you."

"Love you, too," I said, walking with her to her car. "Take care of yourself. Don't get yourself kidnapped, because you favor Mom's side of the family more than Dad's."

"Ha. As if. Smooches!"

She drove off with a wave, and I reentered the house, leaning against the door and sighing at the blissful silence. Really, there wasn't a more ideal place than the house that my father built when he moved us to Sweden.

"I miss you," I told the last family portrait we had taken, about seven years ago. My mother's face beamed out of it, her red hair and freckles making her look like a stereotypical Irish girl, whereas my father's gentle brown eyes and dark chocolate skin radiated quiet warmth and love. Tears pricked painfully behind my eyeballs, but I blinked them away. "Dr. Barlind says that while it's fine to regret loss, there is no sense in holding on to grief and that one way to let go is to state your feelings. So that's what I'm going to do. I feel sad. I miss you both. And I'm angry that you went to Senegal even though you knew it was risky. I'm furious at the men who killed you and even more furious at the politics that caused the situation. But most of all, I love you, and I wish you were here so I had someone to talk to."

The picture didn't answer me—of course it didn't! That would be crazy, and I was as sane as they came. I laughed out loud at that thought and pushed down the nagging little voice in my head that pointed out that no matter what I told Dr. Barlind, no matter how many times I repeated that I had been mistaken and confused and not quite with it mentally speaking two years ago, no matter how often I told everyone that I had learned much during my stay at the Arvidsjaur Center and had come out a better person for it, the truth remained buried deep in my psyche.

"I'm not listening to you," I told that voice. One of the side effects of the therapy was that I now spoke aloud to myself. Dr. Barlind said it was a perfectly normal habit and that to stifle it would be to cease communication with the emotional self, and *that* was the cause of half the world's problems. "I'm quite normal and not at all weird, and I will not think about things that are impossible, so there's no sense in trying to stir up trouble."

The voice didn't like that, but if I had learned anything during the last two years, it was not to let the voice in my head push me around. Accordingly, I padded barefoot into my room and considered the small suitcase that sat on the chair. In it were the things that I'd brought with me from the

Arvidsjaur Center but that I hadn't yet unpacked. There the suitcase sat, almost taunting me, implying that although I could ignore the little voice in my head, I couldn't pretend reality didn't exist.

"Right. You can shut up, too," I told it, and with my chin held high, I opened the case and took out the bag full of paperbacks that Bee had brought me over the duration of my stay. Clothing was the next to be removed in the form of the pajamas and utilitarian bathrobe that had been given to me, followed by the pants and shirt that I'd been wearing two years ago when I was carted off to the loony bin.

A small vanilla envelope lay underneath the last items, my name and admission date neatly printed in block letters. Inside were the contents of my pockets when I'd been hauled to the hospital—driver's license, a little money, keys, and the jewelry I'd been wearing. I tossed the necklace and earrings into my jewelry box but stood frowning down at the remaining object.

It was a ring.

"Terrin's ring," I said, prodding it with my finger. I'd forgotten all about it, but there it was, sitting there looking like a perfectly normal ring.

It's magic, he had said. I closed my eyes, for a moment swamped by the memories of that terrible night, but I hadn't been ignoring the voice in my head for two years without learning some tricks.

"Fine, you want to be magic?" I shoved the ring on the fourth finger of my right hand. "You just go ahead and try."

I held out my hand, but of course nothing happened.

"You're no more magic than I am," I said with a snort of derision, and proceeded to put the rest of my things away in their proper place.

Swayed by Bee's comments, I almost didn't go to the GothFaire, but the memory of Dr. Barlind lecturing me on the subject of confronting issues rather than avoiding them resulted in me driving to the next town where the Faire was being held. "Fine, I'll do it, but I refuse to have a cathartic experience," I grumbled to myself as I parked in a familiar field. The GothFaire had returned to the same spot it had been in two years before, and just as it had been on that fateful night, people were streaming into the big tent, no doubt waiting for the band to start that night's concert.

I sat in my car for a few minutes, my hands gripping the steering wheel in a way that had my knuckles turning white. My breath came in short little gasps.

"I can do this," I told the silence around me. "It's just a traveling circus. It's not like Terrin is even here."

Who's to say he isn't? the annoying voice in my head asked.

I got out of the car slowly, trying hard to hang on to the sense of calm that Dr. Barlind said would get me through the worst experiences.

Anxiety is your mind being a bully, she had said during a very bad week when she had ordered electroshock therapy. *Don't let it make you a victim. If you can master your fear, you can master anything.*

"Easier said than done," I muttered, shoving away the memories of that horrible week and locking the car before I followed a group of three girls heading straight for the big tent.

As I passed by the first row of cars, I couldn't help glancing down the line, just in case a body was lying there. "Ha, smarty-pants brain. There's nothing there, so you can just stop trying to freak me out and get on board with the 'a whole mind is a healthy mind' program that Dr. Barlind says is the key to happiness."

The Faire was much as I remembered it—weird booths, loud music, and people indulging in the sort of excited laughter and high-volume chatter that went along with a day's adventures. I strolled up and down the center aisle, not entering any of the booths but watching people with an eye that was soon much less vigilant.

"No Terrin," I breathed with a sigh of relief. I hadn't really expected him to show up, but as my brain had pointed out, who was to say he wouldn't have? "See, inner self? Nothing here but a circus full of pierced people and demonologists." I passed by a booth with a sign that read SPIRIT PET PSYCHIC. "And ghosts who talk to animals. Nothing at all out of the ordinary."

I swear I could feel my brain pursing its lips in disbelief.

Ten minutes later I started up the car and bumped along the field toward the exit.

"Leaving so soon?" asked the young man who collected the money for parking. He had been sitting on a folding chair, a camping lantern next to him and a book in his hand. "You didn't stay long. Do you want your money refunded? I'm afraid we don't normally do that, but since you weren't here long enough to partake in any of the delights to be found at the GothFaire—"

"That's not necessary. I was just here...er...to check on something."

"Oh? Did you find it?"

"No. As a matter of fact, it was anticlimactic in the extreme," I answered with a friendly smile. "But no worries—now I can tell my therapist to relax. There's no chance of me having another mental breakdown."

"Er..." The man backed away from my car. "That's good."

"It is indeed!" I gave him a cheery wave, and the car lurched off the grass and onto the tarmac. I hummed to myself as I zipped along, enjoying the feeling of freedom after two years of incarceration.

"I have a bright new life ahead of me," I told no one in particular. "Dr. Barlind said she was certain I have great potential in something. I just have to figure out what. Maybe I should try painting again. Or writing. Oh, poetry! Poets are always tortured and angsty, and after what I went through, I bet the dark, tormented poems would just ooze out of— Son of a fruit bat!"

The car fishtailed wildly when I slammed on the brakes, the horrible thumping sound of a large object being struck by the bumper echoing in my brain, but not even coming close to touching the sheer, utter horror I felt at the thought of hitting something. Ever since I had been a child and my father had hit a deer in a remote section in northern Sweden, I feared running down a living thing. And here I was, happily yacking away to myself and not paying attention to the road...

With a sick heart and even sicker stomach, I got out of the car, peering through the darkness at the road behind me.

"Please let it be something old and ready to die... please let it be something old and ready to die," I repeated as I stumbled forward a few steps.

Just a sliver of the moon was out, but we were far enough north that we got the midnight sun effect—since the sun didn't fully set at night, the sky wasn't as pitch-black as it was elsewhere. Instead, we suffered through what I thought of as deep twilight—too dark to read but with enough residual light to see the silhouettes of large objects.

My heart sank at the sight of the big black mound in the middle of the road.

"Please be an elderly deer that was ready to die, please oh please oh please." My voice was thick with the tears that were splashing down my face. I felt perilously close to vomiting, but I could no more leave whatever it was I hit lying on the road than I could have sprouted a second head.

The black mound resolved itself into the shape of a large black dog. "Oh my God," I moaned, guilt stabbing at me with hot, sharp edges. "I've killed someone's beloved pet!"

I knelt next to the dog, the tears now falling on my hands as I ran them over the animal, my heart aching with regret. If only I had been paying attention. If only I hadn't been so caught up in myself. Right at that moment, I would have given anything to take back the last five minutes and live them over again.

Heat blossomed under my hands where I touched the dog. There was no visible blood, no horribly mangled limbs, but the animal wasn't moving. "Noo!" I wailed, wanting to hug the poor thing and make it all better. "No, this can't—Sweet suffering succotash!"

To my astonishment, the dog jerked beneath my fingers, then leaped to its feet and shook. We're talking a full-body shake, the kind where not only the head and ears get into the action, but also the sides, tail, and evidently, copious amounts of slobber. He was big, with thick black fur and droopy lips from which stretched tendrils of slobber that lazily reached for the earth.

"You're not dead. You're okay?" Hope rose inside of me

at the sight of the dog. "Did I just stun you? Man, you're big. You're the size of a small pony, aren't you? Let me just look you over and see if there are any serious injuries..." I patted him up and down his body, but he didn't seem to react as if he was in pain. In truth, he looked more dazed than anything. He kept shaking his head, which sent long streamers of drool flying out in an arterial pattern. My left arm took the brunt of much of that slobber.

"But I don't mind," I told the dog, getting to my feet. "So long as you're all right."

He sat down and promptly howled, causing me to wince in sympathy.

"All right, you're not quite unharmed, but at least you're not dead, and that's the important thing. Here... um..." I looked around but didn't see signs of any nearby houses. "Damn. Houses here can be a mile or more apart. Looks like you're my responsibility now. Great. Ack, don't howl again! I'll take care of you, I promise. What we need is a vet. Can you walk? This way, boy. Or girl. Whatever you are, here, doggy. Car ride!"

I opened the door to the backseat. The dog looked at the car, then looked at me. I patted my leg. "C'mon, doggy. Let's go for a ride in the car!"

He cocked his head for a moment, then got to his feet and limped over to the car, hopping nimbly onto the backseat. "Well, thank heavens I don't have to haul you into the car. I'm not sure I could do it if I had to. You look like you weigh about as much as me. Right, let's go find you an emergency vet hospital."

Two and a half hours later, I emerged from a twenty-four-hour animal hospital, the Swedish equivalent of $180 poorer. "I don't quite see why I should be the one to take him home."

"You ran over him," the vet, an older woman with a no-nonsense haircut that perfectly matched her abrupt manner, told me. "He's your responsibility."

"Yeah, but you have a kennel where you could keep him until his people come to get him."

"He has no collar, no identification of any form, including a microchip, and you said you ran him down on a rural stretch well outside of any town."

I flinched at the "ran him down" mention.

"Therefore," she continued, opening up the rear door of the car. The dog hopped in and plopped himself down, taking up the entire backseat. "He's your problem. We don't have the space or the resources to take care of him."

"Yes, but—"

She pinned me back with a look that had me fidgeting. "If you insist on leaving him here, he'll be collected by the animal welfare people in the morning. A dog of his size is virtually unadoptable. He might be a purebred Newfoundland, or he might not. Either way, he would be put down in less than thirty-six hours. Do you want that on your conscience?"

"No," I said miserably, and got into the car. The rest of the trip home was accomplished in silence... if you didn't count the snores of a 150-pound dog.

Four

"You can stay here for the night," I told the dog when we got home. "But my sister is allergic to your kind, so it's just a short visit for you, and then we'll find somewhere else for you to go."

The dog wandered off as soon as I let him out of the car.

"Hey!" I shouted after him when he ran across the dirt drive and the scrubby grass that was the only thing that would grow so close to the water, and bounded over a large piece of driftwood and onto the rocky beach. "Dammit, dog, don't make me chase after you. Wait, are you going home? Do you know your way home from here? Home, doggy, home!"

I followed after him, half hoping he'd head back to the road and to wherever it was he belonged, but instead, he turned down the beach and loped along the edge of the water until he disappeared into the semidarkness.

"Great. Now he's gone. Oh well, at least the vet gave him a clean bill of health."

I walked back to the house, trying to convince myself to forget the dog, but I couldn't even get across the threshold.

The vet was right—the dog *was* my responsibility. He might not be hurt, but I had hit the poor thing, and since I had opposable thumbs and he didn't, I had to see to it that he was either returned to his people or handed over to folks who would find him a new home.

"Yo, dog," I called, doing an about-face and heading down the beach after him. The weak light from the horizon seemed to glow across the now-inky water, making it possible to see the large rocks and tree trunks that dotted the shore. A familiar scent of seaweed, damp sand, and salty air filled my lungs. "Here, boy! Treaties! Or there will be once I get you into the house."

Ahead of me, over the soft sound of the water lapping at shore, I heard a muffled *woof.*

"Doggy?" I yelled. My nearest neighbor was a good three miles down the beach, so I didn't worry about waking anyone up. "Hey, dog, if you found something dead and stinky and are planning on rolling in it, I'd like to encourage you to change your mind. For one, it's not nearly as attractive a smell as you think it is, and for another, I don't think you'd fit in my bathtub— Oh no, not again!"

By now I'd come upon the dog, who was standing with his nose pressed against a black shape that was slumped on the ground.

"If that's a dead seal or something equally nasty..." I started to warn him, but stopped when I got a better look at the shape.

It was a man.

A dead man lay at my feet.

Right there on the beach. The tide was going out, leaving the ground sodden with seaweed, the tang of the night air stinging my eyes. I stared at the black shape, wondering who was screaming.

It was me.

"No!" I said in protest, wanting to turn on my heels and run away from the horrible sight. "No, no, no. I can't have this. I can't have men lying dead at my feet. The last time that happened, I ended up hooked to a machine that zapped me full of a kajillion volts. I refuse to be crazy anymore. Therefore, you, sir, cannot be dead. I forbid it."

I reached down to turn the man onto his back, jerking my hand away when a static shock to end all static shocks snapped out between my fingers and his arm.

"What the hell?" I rubbed my fingers, wondering if the man had some sort of electronics on him that had gotten wet. But before I could ponder that, he moaned and moved his legs, his head lifting off the rocks for a few seconds before he slumped down again.

"What is this, my day for seeing dead things that aren't really dead?" My mind shied painfully away from that thought. "Hey, mister, are you okay?"

It was a stupid question to be sure—he was facedown, obviously having been deposited on the shore by the tide, and clearly unconscious. But at least he was alive.

Tentatively, I reached out a finger and touched the wet cloth of his sleeve. "Mister?"

There was no static shock this time, so I tugged him until he rolled over onto his back. His hair, shiny with water and black as midnight, was plastered to his skull, while bits of seaweed and sand clung to the side of his cheek and jaw. His chin was square and his face angular, with high cheekbones that gave him a Slavic look and made my fingers itch to brush off the sand. There was a bit of reddish black stubble on his jaw that I really wanted to touch. I was willing to bet that it was soft and enticing...

Fall in Love with Forever Romance

A BILLIONAIRE AFTER DARK
by Katie Lane

Nash Beaumont is the hottest of the billionaire Beaumont brothers. But beneath his raw charisma is a dark side that he struggles to control, until he falls in love with Eden—the reporter determined to expose his secret. Fans of Jessica Clare will love the newest novel from *USA Today* bestselling author Katie Lane.

Fall in Love with Forever Romance

DRAGON SOUL
by Katie MacAlister

In *New York Times* bestselling author Katie MacAlister's DRAGON SOUL, Rowan Dakar can't afford to be distracted by the funniest, most desirable woman he's ever set eyes on. But no prophecy in the world can ever stop true love…